LOVE, LIES
and Lunch

AN ANTHOLOGY OF SHORT STORIES BY

DIANA KAY

LOVE, LIES
and Lunch

AN ANTHOLOGY OF SHORT STORIES BY

DIANA KAY

MEREO
CIRENCESTER

Mereo Books

1A The Wool Market Dyer Street Cirencester Gloucestershire GL7 2PR
An imprint of Memoirs Publishing www.mereobooks.com

Love, Lies and Lunch: 978-1-86151-898-9

First published in Great Britain in 2014
by Mereo Books, an imprint of Memoirs Publishing

Copyright ©2018

Diana Kay has asserted her right under the Copyright Designs and Patents
Act 1988 to be identified as the author of this work.

This book is a work of fiction and except in the case of historical fact any resemblance to actual
persons living or dead is purely coincidental

The address for Memoirs Publishing Group Limited can be found at
www.memoirspublishing.com

The Memoirs Publishing Group Ltd Reg. No. 7834348

Typeset in 9/12pt Bembo
by Wiltshire Associates Publisher Services Ltd.
Printed and bound in Great Britain by Biddles Books

To Belinda, my most avid and appreciative reader.

These stories, written over many years, are often dated, yet
I feel they are of their time.

I would like to thank my editor Chris Newton for his helpful
advice and his enthusiasm, for believing in me and for
'getting' my sense of humour.

Contents

Blind Date	1	Goodbye to Love	184
Strawberry Fields	14	Suspicion	194
The Test Pilot	24	Talking to John (1)	207
Beware of Telling Lies	31	Talking to John (2)	211
Girl With A Secret	37	The Babysitter	215
Blue-Eyed Boy	46	The Cherry Stone	225
Champagne	52	Goodbye My Darling Daughter	232
Matchmaking	57	Never, Ever Tell	236
Love for Raoul	67	Matron Knows Best	244
Plain Jane and the Great Author	74	Sarah's Awakening	252
Lunch at Pepe's	82	The Wicked Stepmother	258
Rendezvous with Rory	91	Beth	269
The Lonely Rose	97	The Winning Streak	276
The Plastic Slipper	106	Crossed Lines	287
Scatterbrain	115	Fateful Turning	293
The Big Dipper	123	The Cabin Boy	299
The Girl Who Liked Cream Cakes	129	Cousin Tessa	305
Who is Sylvia?	138	The Do-Gooder	310
The Summer Girl	143	The Girls in the Office	320
A Second Chance	149	The New Girl	326
Don't Tell the Neighbours	161	The Lift	333
After the Honeymoon	172	The Fir Tree	341
Dear Aunt Gwyneth	179	The Laughter of Agnes Mallory	351

Blind Date

It was all Jemima's fault. She had arranged it, made the appointment and everything.

"You simply can't go on like this any more, darling," she told me. "It isn't natural."

"What isn't?"

"Your nun-like existence. One must have a man."

"Must one?"

"Absolutely, darling." Absent-mindedly she plucked a piece of apple out of the bowl of salad I was making for our lunch.

"Actually I'm quite enjoying my nun-like existence," I said. "I can do what I like and when, eat or not eat, no need to bother about James and his voracious appetite. For all I care he can get stuffed."

Jemima looked shocked. "But that's so selfish, Estelle," she said. "You will become crabbed and sour. In fact," she began tactlessly, "Already I have noticed…"

1

That was enough. I had no wish to become crabbed. I had no idea what it meant, but it sounded revolting.

"OK, you win," I said.

"All you have to do," said Jemima, "is feed your particulars into this computer."

"Feed my particulars? What do you mean?"

"Oh you know. All about yourself. Measurements, size of boobs – that sort of thing."

I shuddered. "It sounds very vulgar."

"The trouble with you," said Jemima, "Is that you're not with it. You must move with the times."

"Oh dear – that I of all people should stoop to going to a…"

I couldn't say it, even quietly.

"A marriage bureau," said Jemima. "Look, I'll do it for you. I'll get all the details and feed them into the computer myself. Then you won't have to go near the place. I've got the form in my bag, we may as well start straight away. Here we are: Colour of eyes?"

"Green."

"Oh, would you have said *green*, darling?"

"Certainly. What would you call them?"

"A sort of pale… khaki, I should think."

"I see," I said stiffly.

"Now – colour of hair."

"Honey blonde," I said.

"Beige," she corrected. "One has to be scrupulously honest."

"But it said honey blonde on the packet."

"You have to go by what it turns out on you and it certainly turned out beige. Now – figure?"

"Willowy?" I suggested.

"Pear-shaped," she wrote down.

We went through the lot. It was quite depressing that she, my best friend, should see me so entirely differently from the way I saw myself.

It was a bit easier when it came to Likes and Dislikes. For Likes I wrote Wimbledon, Lunching at the Ritz, Picking Flowers, Travelling and The Theatre.

"What a thoroughly off-putting list," said Jemima. "It has a very false ring about it. I mean, when did you last lunch at the Ritz?"

"When I was eighteen, with Hugh Rees-Whitaker."

"But that's years ago. You can hardly count it as one of your Likes."

"Why not? It was an emphatic Like."

"As for Picking Flowers, that sounds so fey. If you insist on sticking to this list you will get someone you don't really fancy at all, someone pillow-shaped with specs, who likes to go searching for beetles in the Lake District in a fawn mackintosh."

"That would be no use at all – and if your computer hasn't enough sense to know that, then I can't see why we're bothering."

"Come on," said Jemima, "You mustn't be so defeatist. It will be a giggle if nothing else."

"For you, perhaps. For me, a yawn."

"Let's do your Dislikes."

"Spiders, housework, pompous people who say 'good Morning *to you*' instead of 'good morning,' not having enough money, and parties where you don't know anyone."

"Oh dear," said Jemima. "I'm not sure you're presenting the right image at all. I would really think twice about putting not having enough money as a Dislike. People will think you're a gold digger."

"And they'll be right," I said. "Love may not be lovelier the second time around, but it's going to be a damn sight more expensive. I'm not looking for romance in a garret, I'm looking for comfort and hard cash. It's the least I should expect in exchange for my independence and having to wash the Y-fronts. And think what they're getting!"

"I'm thinking," said Jemima. Now she was the one to be lacking in confidence, whereas I was bubbling with it.

"A mature, lovely woman with intelligence," I said.

She looked more doubtful than ever. "I wouldn't have said lovely," she said, "I'd have said wholesome."

Really, I think that of all my friends Jemima is the one I find the most irritating.

Well anyhow she got on with the technical side and in due course the computer coughed up the ideal partner for me, at least the most suitable of the ones they'd got on their books.

"How many have they got – two?" I asked.

"Don't be silly, Estelle. His name is Desmond – Desmond Green. He's an orthodontist, a widower – I think – aged forty-five, wears gold-rimmed specs, tall and thin with wavy brown hair."

"I hope that doesn't mean crimped," I said. "I can't stand men with crimped hair."

"I expect it means wavy, like it says. You ought to give the computer a chance. Your chap likes pressing wild flowers into albums – and the opera."

"The opera? How depressing!"

"Couldn't you try and like it a tiny bit between now and your first meeting?" said Jemima. "I'll lend you a book I've got called *A Hundred Favourite Operas.*"

"How can you possibly have a *hundred* favourite operas? I shouldn't have thought there were a Hundred Heartily Disliked Operas, let alone a Hundred Favourite ones. Anyhow it would bore me to read it. I am as I am. It would be hypocritical to pretend otherwise."

But Jemima took no notice. She arranged for our first meeting to be held the following Saturday, booking us in for lunch at a small, private seaside hotel.

"Very suitable," she said. "Very genteel. Afterwards you can stroll along the sea-front. Just picture it – walking by the sea. It will be a perfect setting for a romance."

"What about ten-pound notes – will they spring up?" I asked. "Well-heeled, is he, Desmond Green?"

"Don't be so mercenary," said Jemima. "That can come later."

"But not much later, I hope. I don't want to waste my time."

"As a matter of fact," she said, "he happens to be very well off indeed, so you're in luck. And if you find you're getting on well you can stay for dinner and the night…"

"I'm certainly not doing that!" I interrupted. "So soon? It would be most unsuitable. He would think I was a push-over. If I've got to do that I might just as well hang about outside the hotel and be done with it. Really Jemima, I'm surprised at you for suggesting such a thing."

"I didn't mean it like that," she said. "You can have your own room, for goodness sake! What you do or don't do in it is your business. I simply meant that if you find you're getting on well you may as well extend your meeting and have Sunday as well."

"I'm not sure…"

"Well keep Sunday free anyway. And have an open mind. And don't forget darling, he's *very* well off."

So there I was on Saturday, sitting in the dining room at the Sea View private hotel, waiting for Mr Desmond Green to turn up and feeling slightly silly and also irritated. It was surely not in his character, I felt, to be late.

A waitress entered. She was elderly, with tight grey curls and a florid complexion.

"Would you like to order?" she asked.

"No thank you. I'm meeting someone, so I'll wait until he arrives."

"Very good, madam."

"Is there a bar here?"

"No, but we are licensed."

To kill, I wondered?

"I'll have a large gin and tonic, please."

Suddenly the door opened and who should come through it but not Desmond Green – James, my ex-husband. His fury on seeing me was something to behold. Yes I would say that, even allowing for the fact that he was an ex-husband.

"What the hell are you doing here?" he said.

"That's none of your business," I replied.

"I'm not so sure about that. It's too much of a coincidence you should turn up in a dump like this."

"I have my reasons," I said stalling for time. (I would die rather than let him think I had gone to a marriage bureau.) I thought, Jemima is at the bottom of this. Now what is she up to? Perhaps Desmond Green did not exist. Perhaps it was all a plot to get James and me together again, in which case, how wrong-headed, how inane!

"I suppose you've come to spy on Marjorie and me," said James.

"Marjorie?" I said in astonishment.

"Oh don't give me that for God's sake. You know perfectly well who Marjorie is, don't act the little innocent."

"I imagine she must be your latest love," I said, "Merely a conclusion to which I have jumped. Don't flatter yourself I am interested enough to keep tabs on you or your sex life."

"There is no sex life about it," said James, "yet." He permitted himself a wry smile. "Marjorie is not that sort of woman."

"Poor you, you must be slipping to have landed yourself with the other sort," I observed. "She is like her name then? Marjorie – like a loaf of wholemeal bread, worthy but dull."

"I see you are still as bitchy as ever," said James.

At this point the door opened timorously and a tall, thin bespectacled man ventured through it. He reminded me of a stick insect. I was immediately thrown into a state of confusion. The room was too small and too empty for every word of our conversation not to be overheard by James.

"Good morning to you," said the stick insect. "You are Estelle, I take it?"

"Of course!" I said lightly, "Really, you are so vague, Desmond – you always forget my name!"

But my attempt to make James think we already knew one another clearly made Desmond Green think I must be mad. He recoiled slightly and started to say something, but I quickly interrupted him.

"Have you been to the opera again lately?"

"Again?" he asked, puzzled.

"Since the last time, I mean."

"Oh I see. No, as a matter of fact, not."

"I thought wild horses wouldn't keep you away from *Aida*," I said. Out of the corner of my eye I could see James looking at me in amazement. "How is your flower pressing getting on?"

Desmond's face lit up. "Oh, very well," he said. "I am on the Stachys genus at present," he said. "The *Stachys recta* to be precise, or the Yellow Woundwort, as you would say."

"Oh I wouldn't," I said. "Absolutely not!"

"Have you been picking many flowers lately?" he asked.

"Yes indeed," I said with a rapt expression. "I have bluebells in jam jars all over the house."

"Have you?" said James, surprised.

"I haven't ordered yet," I said to Desmond. "I thought you would probably want a drink first."

"Oh," said Desmond. "Well, perhaps a small sherry."

"There doesn't seem to be a bar here," I said.

"Not like the Ritz, eh?" said Desmond. "Ha ha."

"Ha ha," I echoed. I tried not to notice James's expression.

The waitress came back. I hoped Desmond would take the initiative, but he didn't, so I had to do so instead. "Could we have the menu, please?"

"Certainly, Madam. Would you like another aperitif?"

"I would like a large gin and my friend will have a sherry. Tio Pepe?" I asked him.

"I'd prefer a small Bristol Cream."

I couldn't help despising him a little for that.

The door was pushed open and in came a small solid woman, not unattractive, looking as if she had just got off a horse, with a bun done up in one of those funny strong nets. I did hope it wasn't Marjorie.

"Marjorie," said James, adding rather heavily, "My dear." He stood up and, I was riveted to see, embraced her. Their noses clashed, which was not difficult as hers was of the large, beaky variety.

"Would you like the soup?" said the waitress.

"Is there an alternative?" I asked.

"Pardon?"

"I said, is there anything else?"

"No. Just the soup. Brown Windsor."

7

"That sounds good," said Desmond, smacking his lips as if he meant it. Perhaps he was the sort of person who liked Brown Windsor soup; I had always wanted to meet one. It was perhaps significant that there was no one else in the dining room but we four people and a little old lady sitting silently in a corner.

Out of the corner of my ear I could hear Marjorie coyly asking, "well, what have you been up to Jamie, since I saw you last?"

I knew James hated being called Jamie, and he didn't look as if he'd been up to anything for ages. He had put on quite a lot of weight and looked rather bloated. I strained desperately to hear his answer.

"Not a lot," he said with a self-conscious giggle.

Really Jamie, I thought, not a very sparkling reply.

"How are the Bs?" he enquired.

Bs? Perhaps she had a lot of very naughty children, but still it was impolite of James to describe them thus.

"Very well," she replied. "They made me five pounds last week."

Could she mean £s or lbs? Either way it didn't seem a lot. Nothing to crow about. I for instance make 20lbs of marmalade every year and I once made £200 from selling Tupperware door to door.

"Oh well done!" said James. "Jolly good!"

I regarded him sourly. He had never said that to me! I don't think he had ever said that to me in his whole life. It just shows how a man can be ensnared by a pretty face, or even a not-so-hot one.

Their 'aperitifs' arrived. Hers was a pink gin, for which I gave her bonus marks. Quite a devil on the quiet was Marjorie. At the same time Desmond Green and I received The Soup followed by The Beef, very thin slivers embroidered with lacy yellow fat and covered with see-thru gravy. With it we had 'horseradish', roast pots and very dark green cabbage.

"Not bad, is it Jamie?" said Marjorie, tucking in when they received theirs. "Quite a find really, if you like good plain English fare."

Plain was putting it a bit mildly, I thought, and I have always been suspicious of people who talk of food as 'fare'. The most charitable way in which I could describe them is pseudo. There was sponge pudding with custard to follow, which was so plain it was hard to decipher any flavour whatsoever, yet Marjorie, James and Desmond loved it to distraction. They praised the heaviness of the sponge and the thickness of the custard.

"Pleasant to have something filling for a change," said James. Looking at his stomach I thought it would be quite difficult, let alone pleasant. Jemima was right – I had become crabbed and sour. I would try hard to be nice from now on.

After milky-pale coffee in thick white cups, Desmond said:

"Would you fancy a breather on the prom?"

"A what on the prom?"

"A breather? You know – a breath of fresh air."

"Oh how delightful!" I said. "Just what I would fancy."

"What would *you* like to do, Jamie?" said Marjorie.

I knew damn well what Jamie would like to do. The trouble was, Marjorie wasn't that sort of woman.

"How about a spin in the country?" she suggested.

I could see them spinning round and round in a wooded glade perhaps carpeted with wood anemones, earwigs, ants and long-legged spiders. The ground might be uneven and boggy and Marjorie might twist her ankle if they spun too furiously. (I was ever an optimist.)

Out on the prom, the fresh air was raucously fresh. It got everywhere: in one's eyes, up one's nose, down one's neck and up one's skirt – if one was wearing a skirt, that is. I had no wish to envisage which part of Desmond Green's anatomy it was penetrating.

"Isn't this tremendous?" he said to me, excitedly breathing it in.

"Tremendous," I gasped. Tears spilled from one of my eyes.

"Wonderfully exhilarating, what?"

"You can say that again!"

"I said, wonderfully exhilarating!"

"Indeed."

"Would you like to sit down somewhere?"

We came to an empty seat in one of those shelters to be found at intervals along the front, and sat down on it. "Whew!" he said, "That's better. Now we can look at the sea in comfort."

We looked. I wouldn't have described this as comfort myself. But the next moment I felt my hand being seized. Desmond Green uncurled my fingers with his clammy ones and studied my long red fingernails. I wondered if he disapproved.

"Lovely, slender white hands," he said. "Soft. Gentle."

"And all because the lady uses Fairy Liquid," I said, wondering if I could extract my hand and put it back in my lap without giving offence. But when I tried he held on tightly. He looked into my eye, the one nearest him, which was no longer watering.

"Estelle," he said. "I've thought so much about this meeting, wondered so much about what you would be like."

"Oh, really?"

"I imagined someone simple."

"You mean, a bit simple?" (One would have to be, I thought, to go to a marriage bureau.)

"I mean, childlike, gentle, dreamily picking flowers all the day long. But you're not like that at all, are you? You are so sharp and sophisticated and not…"

"Your type?" I interposed.

"Oh, but on the contrary, you are exactly my type, Estelle — more than I could have ever hoped. Tell me — how do I strike you?"

"My God!" I said. How could I tell him dismally, drearily, with depression?

"Just the answer I should have expected," he said. "I shan't press you. We have all the time in the world. You don't have to rush back to London tonight, do you? We could check in for dinner and book…"

"Now look," I said, "Just how sophisticated do you think I am?"

"Oh my dear, I respect you enormously."

"Well" I said. For I did rather want to see what had become of James and Marjorie.

Funnily enough it transpired that they too had booked two single rooms for the night. Ho ho, I thought. One up for James?

Back at the Sea View Hotel we had tea in the afternoon, better known as Afternoon Tea. There were scones and an undefined sort of red jam. "Will you have a scone?" said Desmond, rhyming it with 'stone'.

There was no sign of James or Marjorie. I thought they must have collapsed giddily onto the wood anemones. Also, I hoped, the ants, the earwigs and the long-legged spiders.

After tea we sat in the Lounge and Desmond told me all about himself. He was an only son who had got married at twenty, against his mother's wishes, to a lady called Linda. It appeared Linda had gone.

"You mean over?" I said. (Or under, or on, or wherever people go when they expire – I wasn't going to be caught by that one!) But no, actually it seemed she had gone off and left him.

"For another?" I said sympathetically.

"Yes indeed."

Not surprising, really. There could be no flies, I thought, on Linda.

At seven o'clock the wanderers returned, flushed pink from their exertions. I looked for straw in their hair, but in vain. We had some good plain English fare for dinner at eight.

"I do dislike this snobbery about Continental food, don't you Jamie?" said Marjorie. "I mean, take French food – just because they smother everything in sauces reeking with wine and herbs they think they can get away with murder. And English people – some English people – think it's fantastic. It's all so pseudo."

There was a pause, then she went on, "That was a lovely drive Jamie, thank you. And that little place we found, it was so peaceful and unspoilt. Our little piece of Heaven, Far from the Madding Crowd." James would miss that one, I thought. "I shall always think of it as Our Spot."

I smiled at her sweetly over the top of Desmond's frizzy brown hair.

After dinner we had more of the milky-pale coffee and then Desmond suggested a game of two-handed whist before 'retiring.' I did hope James hadn't heard, but I rather suspected he had, from the pinkness of his ears and the sudden coughing fit which overwhelmed him.

"Well, perhaps not," I said, "Cards aren't quite in my line."

"I should have guessed," said Desmond admiringly, "but roulette is, I imagine. I see you at the Casino in Monte Carlo, sitting at a roulette table in a low-cut gown with diamonds."

His diamonds, I wondered? Or did he imagine I had my own? Well, he could imagine what he liked, I couldn't really be bothered. Marjorie was telling James about Foreign Parts with which she was familiar. I thought it might have been Bodies, but it was definitely Parts.

"Florence – such a disappointment," she said. "What is your favourite haunt, Jamie?"

"I've always had a soft spot for Poros," he said. (How dare he mention Our Spot!) "It's one of the Greek islands – do you know it?"

"No. Perhaps you'll show it to me one day," she oozed.

"I think perhaps I'll retire early," I said. "Today has been quite a day, one way and another."

"It certainly has. My horoscope said a fortuitous meeting would lead to romance," said Desmond, "and it has proved entirely right." He gave me a knowing look.

So it was that I found myself in a dreary, sparsely-furnished little room overlooking a lot of grey roofs at the back of the hotel. I felt deeply depressed. It was crystal clear to me that Desmond Green was not my type. No matter how many thousands he had or how many diamonds he bestowed upon me, I could never be His.

I was just wondering what on earth I was doing there when there was a knock at the door. Well really – if Desmond thought his fortuitous meeting was about to lead to romance, he had another think coming. I was about to tell him so when the door was flung open and there was James.

"Come along, pack your things and get your coat," he said, "We're leaving."

"What do you mean?"

"This farce has gone on long enough. This farce cooked up by your friend Puddleduck."

"Oh you mean Jemima fed your details into her computer?"

"And came up with Marjorie, yes."

"But I thought you liked her?"

"I thought I did too till today, but now she's driving me mad."

"As Desmond Green is driving me."

"Any fool can see that he's not for you." He pulled my coat out of the wardrobe. "Here, put it on."

"But surely we can't just leave – what will they think?"

"That we're both mad and that they're well out of it."

"Perhaps they will find solace in one another."

"Let us hope so."

"Do you think," I whispered as we crept down the stairs and climbed stealthily into James's car, "that we might go somewhere to eat first? I should so very much like something smothered in sauce and reeking with herbs."

Strawberry Fields

She would always think of that visit afterwards as like looking at snapshots in an album. The first picture was of Joanna flanked by two rosy-cheeked, flaxen-haired boys, standing on the small wooden platform and waiting to meet her in a check shirt and dungarees (getting a bit broad in the beam now Jo, Isabel thought but didn't say) with no make-up and her hair a mess, just as it always used to be when they were at school together.

"Izzy! I'm so glad to see you!" cried Jo, giving her a bear hug and a great smacking kiss on the cheek.

"Is it really twelve years ago?" said Izzy. "Where did the years go?"

"I don't know. This is Bobby and this is Tim. Patrick's still at school. You look wonderful, Izzy. Slim as ever. How's Brian? How are the girls?"

"Fine – fine."

"I hope you brought lots of photographs."

Soon they were jogging along in the old Land Rover, passing through deserted country roads lined with meadows filled with yellow buttercups. Up and up and up they climbed till they reached the farm where Jo and Angus lived.

"It's beautiful!" said Izzy, drinking it all in. "After London it looks so green and fresh."

"We take it very much for granted," said Jo. "Mind you, I couldn't live in a town."

"Some of us have to," said Izzy.

Then there was Jo's kitchen with its thick white walls, Aga cooker, tiled floor and red check curtains blowing gently through the casement window. On the wide sill was a jam jar filled with over-blown roses and the table was set for tea on a clean checked cloth.

"Everything you see on that table is either home-made or home-produced," said Jo proudly. There were veal and ham pies, wholemeal bread, creamy butter and cheese and shiny red strawberries and cream in cut glass dishes.

"My goodness Jo – really?"

"Not the sugar," said Angus drily in one of his rare speeches. Angus was the epitome of the strong silent man, and he didn't often smile either. Perhaps he had nothing much to smile about, thought Izzy. He got up at 6 am and went to bed at nine and in between there was a lot of hard work. Jo worked hard too; she had the poultry to look after, hens, ducks and geese, not to mention a goat to milk and the sale of vegetables, eggs and dairy produce. These she had to deliver every day to the farm shop in the village. And then Jo – well you might have guessed, thought Izzy – she was the main prop of the local Women's Institute, bottling or freezing quantities of fruit and vegetables, making pickles, jams and jellies and storing them on shelves in her cool cellar from whence they were brought out, to be given away for stalls at village fetes if not eaten by the family.

"You're wonderful, Jo!" said Izzy, meaning it, as she stood on one leg watching Jo churning cream into butter. She felt helpless and inadequate, as town people so often do in the country. She didn't think

Angus was over-keen on having her there at all, his wife's old school-friend — for a whole week too. She saw herself through his eyes, wearing silly frivolous clothes, chattering and giggling when they were used to silent meals. Even the boys were silent, as if anything they had to say could just as well be kept to themselves. Not like Izzy — she'd started at tea time and gone on through breakfast all next day.

"D'you remember that time when there was a heatwave and we skipped afternoon school and bathed in the river instead? And we got our knickers wet."

"Oh yes, I remember. I got into awful trouble when my mother found out. I think there's going to be another heatwave now."

"And d'you remember Mademoiselle? How we locked her in the loo?"

"Yes?"

"She took an overdose a year ago."

"She didn't, did she? I knew we shouldn't have locked her in the loo."

"She probably would have done it in any case. And d'you remember Gillian Stokes?"

"The red-haired girl in the form below us?"

"That's the one. She went to Tibet and married a Lama."

"I don't believe that!"

"I swear it's true. She certainly ran off with him, even if they didn't get married."

"Oh Izzy, I'm so glad you came. It's such fun having you."

But Angus pushed back his chair, picked up his plate and carried it to the sink.

"Are you off now, Angus?" said Jo.

"Yes."

"To Four Acre Field?"

"Uh huh."

"I'll leave your lunch for you. We're going to have coffee with Mother because she wants to see Izzy and then we're off for a pub lunch at the Fox and Goose and then on to the vicarage fete in the afternoon."

Angus nodded and put on his boots.

"Goodbye Angus," said Izzy.

Did he answer? Probably not.

The three of them sat in the garden hammock at Jo's mother's cottage and breathed in the scent of honeysuckle coming from the wall behind them.

"How lovely to see you, Isabel!" said Jo's mother.

"And you, Aunt Carrie."

"You're looking radiant my dear, and slim as a reed. Marriage suits you. How long is it now? Remind me!"

"Since Brian and I got married? Seven years."

"And Joanna's been married twelve. But of course you were at their wedding. How time passes. What do you think of my three grandsons?"

"They're gorgeous, Aunt Carrie. And did you know I'd got two little girls? Ruth and Becky, look, let me show you."

For the umpteenth time she produced the photographs.

"They're sweet! Where are they now, Isabel?"

"Staying with my sister."

"How nice that you could come."

"It's better than nice. It's heaven!"

"That's the good thing about Izzy," said Jo. "She appreciates everything. She doesn't need to be entertained. She just likes walking along the road and seeing cows in the meadows and sheep in the hills." She laughed as though it were a little mad.

"The perfect guest," said Aunt Carrie.

The next day Angus came into the kitchen while Jo was making tea. "Come," he said to Izzy, "I've something to show you."

"The calf?" said Jo.

"Yes. Are you coming?"

"No, there are scones in the oven. Tea'll be ready in ten minutes."

Izzy went into the farmyard with Angus.

"Get in the Land Rover," he said. "It'll be quicker."

He drove down the lane till they reached the cowshed. She followed

17

him out of the bright sunshine into the dark shed and when her eyes became accustomed to the darkness she saw a little brown and white calf lying in the straw with its mother.

"Oh!" she said, "It's lovely."

Angus turned and gave her a slow, sweet smile. How happy and at home he seemed here with his animals, she thought, away from the world. They stood leaning over the wooden rail looking down at the calf with its liquid brown eyes.

"When was it born?"

"This morning."

"What sort is it?"

"Ayrshire."

"Oh." She *had* meant, was it a boy or a girl. "You must think me very ignorant."

He didn't answer. His bare arm brushed hers for a moment as they stood there and he drew it quickly away. Presently they drove back to the farmyard, and soon after that the three boys arrived back from school and they all had tea.

It was getting hotter. Every morning Izzy was woken by the farmyard cockerel and she'd stretch in bed and lazily watch the martins dive back and forth above her window where their nest was. They'd all have breakfast, Angus having been up for hours already and Jo as well, but they always had it together, and then the boys would cycle off to school. Every day Izzy went with Jo round the hen houses, sprinkling corn for the hens and collecting eggs. She wore a sleeveless shirt and shorts and her long legs were turning brown. She loved to put her hand inside the nesting boxes and find the eggs lying there, so smooth and round. Later they'd cut broad beans and marrows and cucumbers and dig for little new potatoes that were fun to find because sometimes the earth would be bare and other times when you turned it over you'd find a whole cluster of them, white and round like the eggs. They'd carry them to the kitchen and wash them and put them in boxes, and wash the eggs and stack them in corrugated trays and drive them to the village shop.

"I love your life," said Izzy.

"Do you?" said Jo.

Now that was a funny thing: once, she might have said, "Oh Izzy, wouldn't it be marvellous if you and Brian could come and live in the country and Brian could get a job and we could find you a house and we could see you every week!" Yes once, yesterday or perhaps the day before she might have said that; now she just said, "Do you?" and carried on driving.

That afternoon they picked strawberries in a neighbouring farmer's field, and there was Jo and Jo's mother and the three boys and a girl called May and Izzy all picking strawberries under the hot sun. They had to squat right down to pick, and put their hands under the leaves; and some of the fruit was so heavy it even touched the ground and some seemed to ripen even as they picked it. Their hands became red and sticky with juice and Izzy would occasionally pop one into her mouth, but she felt guilty doing this because they were not for eating. No, they were for jam – all for jam! They filled more than seventy punnets, and it did seem an awful lot. And when they got back Jo started straight away getting out the large copper preserving pan and the clean jars that she had left to warm in the Aga and weighing out sugar. Izzy washed and hulled the berries as quickly as she could, but she felt she wasn't doing it as fast as she might have done. She sensed Jo's impatience. It seemed a shame to have to stand in a hot kitchen making jam over a hot Aga on such a hot evening, but it had to be done. Well of course, that went without saying, otherwise the fruit would go to waste.

"What about a cup of tea?" said Angus, coming into the kitchen.

"There's the kettle, help yourself," said Jo, busy with her stirring.

"Can I make it?" said Izzy.

"I don't know – can you?" said Jo a little rudely – but she was tired and hot.

Izzy found a big brown teapot and Angus showed her where the tea canister was and how many teaspoons to put in.

"I'm sorry to be so helpless," she said, aware of Jo's irritation, and

Angus gave her his slow, sweet smile in a look that did not escape Jo's notice as she turned to say, "You can give me a cup too while you're at it."

It was the fourth day of Izzy's visit and it was hotter than ever. Angus took off his shirt and walked around with his trousers rolled up.

"I think there's going to be a storm," he said, "looks like it's brewing up for one."

Suddenly there wasn't as much to talk about – they had gone through all the schoolgirl reminiscences and for the first time since they'd known each other Izzy and Jo had nothing to say. There was the faintest feeling of constraint between them – but perhaps it was just the weather.

"Would you mind very much if I wrote a short letter to the girls sometime?" Izzy asked timidly.

"Why should I? You can do it this afternoon if you like. The boys go swimming after school today and I'll have to meet them and take them to the baths and bring them back afterwards. You can do it then – unless you want to come with me, of course."

"No, I'll stay here and write."

"You can use Angus's study," said Jo. "I'll leave you to it, then."

It was cool in the study. Izzy sat on the wide blue cotton-covered window seat and spread a sheet of Jo's writing paper on the back of a magazine.

'My dear Ruth,' she wrote, 'I'm having such a lovely time with Auntie Jo. There are lots of animals here, you would love them, a pet lamb from last year that has now grown into a sheep but still comes over to say hello, it's so funny, and the day before yesterday I saw the sweetest little calf…"

The door opened suddenly and Angus came in. "Hello Izzy," he said.

"Angus!" she was surprised. "I didn't expect you at this time of day."

"No. I've got some paperwork I may as well do while it's so hot."

"It's cool in here."

"Yes."

"Would you like me to leave?"

"No."

"You're sure I won't disturb you?"

He didn't answer that, sitting down at his paper-strewn desk, his back towards her. She hesitated, shy with him, unsure whether he really wanted her there but reluctant to go. She listened to his pen scratching over the paper and outside the humming of bees and the thrush in the elm tree. A white butterfly zigzagged across the width of the window.

'…and yesterday we picked strawberries all afternoon and in the evening we made lots and lots of lovely jam and Auntie Jo is going to give me a jar to bring home to you,' she wrote. 'I hope Becky is being a good little girl…'

She couldn't concentrate. There was only a short space between her and Angus sitting there with his back to her, his muscles tensed, his pen poised as it had been for the last ten minutes. There was a silence as if they could hardly dare to breathe.

"I think perhaps," she said slowly. "I might go home tomorrow after all."

"Will you?" He turned to look at her and she noticed that his eyes were green with little brown flecks in them. He gave no indication of whether he was glad or sorry.

"I won't write any more now," she said. "If you don't mind I'll go down to the stream at the bottom of the garden and dip my feet in the water."

"That's a good idea," he said. He didn't offer to accompany her, nor did she want him to.

When Jo came back and she told her she had changed her mind about staying on, Jo accepted it with something like relief.

"Afraid of what Brian might be up to while you're away?" she said.

"Well…" said Izzy. She let it go. Why argue?

The next day before school Tim, the middle boy, suddenly ran into the kitchen and deposited a punnet of strawberries beside Izzy's plate.

"They're to remind you of your visit," he said.

"But they won't last more than a couple of days!" objected Bobby.

"That doesn't matter. I'll always remember, whenever I see strawberries," said Izzy. She was deeply touched. She thanked him and turned away to hide her emotion. She wished now she had seen more of the boys while she had been staying with Jo, but they had been at home so seldom and had been so little in evidence when they were there. It's a sad thing, she thought, that you pay less attention to children when they don't demand it – not like her own little girls.

Presently they said goodbye to her and set off to school.

Her train was at 11.38. She packed her case after breakfast and left it in the hall. The oak boards were polished and shiny in the sunlight.

"We'd better not leave here later than eleven," said Jo, but at ten to she was putting Izzy's case into her shooting brake. "Now have you got everything?"

"Yes." But where was Angus? She must say goodbye to Angus!

"For goodness sake don't leave anything behind. I hate having to pack up parcels."

Oh come on Angus, I'll never see you again!

"Are we all set then?"

"Yes but – what about saying goodbye to Angus?"

"I expect he's forgotten you're going," said Jo calmly.

But then they heard the slam of the Land Rover door and saw his tall figure striding across the yard. He did not kiss her goodbye as he had done in welcome. This time he shook her gravely by the hand.

"Goodbye, Izzy," was all he said.

There was nothing between them but the knowledge of what might have been, told in a look that lingered a little longer than it need have.

"You'd better get your mac out," said Jo. "Looks like you're going to need it."

She didn't though. The storm passed overhead, leaving heavy grey clouds in its wake.

"You don't have to wait," said Izzy when they got to the station.

"Oh I'll stay and see you off," said Jo.

"I've had such a lovely time."

"I'm glad."

"It's a funny thing," said Izzy as she climbed into the train, "To me it's been an event I'll always remember, but for you country people it's nothing. Your lives will go on just as they did before I came, as if I'd never been here at all."

But Jo, as she later hung out the washing, and Angus, as he forked hay out in the fields, both thought that things would never be quite the same, ever again.

This story won First Prize, Writers' Billboard, 2008

The Test Pilot

I'm not in the habit of falling in love. I don't have crushes on film stars or television news-readers, like some girls I could mention. I'm not a giggling girl, nor sentimental nor silly, and I don't go in for romantic day-dreams, not as a rule – but he was a rather special man, the handsomest man I had ever seen, in a manly, rugged sort of way, deeply tanned with dark brown hair and decisive grey eyes.

He strode along the platform, peering into the railway carriage windows, hesitating slightly before mine. On he passed, then came back; flinging open the door he threw his two suitcases into the rack and sat down in the seat opposite mine. He produced a newspaper and began to read.

I pretended to read too and suppressed a feeling of excitement. We had the long journey to Edinburgh before us. It must be fate, I thought. After all, if fate had meant him for somebody else it could have put him in somebody else's compartment don't you think? I mean why choose mine out of all the rest of the train? Well anyway that's the conclusion I came to.

Ten minutes passed and then, just as the train was about to start, the door opened again and a fat bald man climbed in and sat down panting in the far corner of the carriage. I was annoyed because I felt possessive about the carriage. Besides I couldn't see where this bald man would fit into the cosy tête-a-tête that was about to begin between my dream man and myself.

The train sped away through the grimy city suburbs. Gradually the houses thinned out, giving way to patchy pieces of countryside, flat unenterprising fields with posters advertising seeds and paint stuck up upon them. More towns passed by and suddenly the sun came out and shone thinly upon a countryside which was now rich, green and fertile.

Still the handsome man continued to read his newspaper. I dared to steal a glance at him from behind my book, and began a slightly fantastic but very satisfactory day-dream.

"Would you mind," he would say in my dream, *"If I open the window?"*

"Not at all," I would answer with a bewitching smile.

He would stand up and pull the window effortlessly with great, manly strength. He would look at me with his cool grey eyes, a long quizzical look.

"You're going to Edinburgh too, I suppose?" he would ask.

"Yes. I'm spending the holidays with my uncle and aunt, who live about fifteen miles from Edinburgh."

He would, of course, be deeply interested. He'd want to hear all about Aunt Helen and Uncle Jack and their weedy son George with his freckled face and his red, carroty hair. But naturally it was I who really interested him.

"Where have you been all my life?" he would say. (No, it was a little soon for that. That would have to come later.) First he would ask me all about myself, what I had done in my life, what I wanted to do. And I would tell him I was fifteen and wanted to be a vet, that I had two

young brothers and a cat called Gladys and we lived in London with my parents in one of those tall old-fashioned houses near the river. He would be fascinated by me. (I might tell him I had an unhappy home life to make myself a tragic and therefore more interesting figure.) And of course in between telling him all this I would learn about him too. He was a… what could he be? A captain in the US Navy? A mountaineer? No, he could be a test pilot. He liked to be by himself. He was a lone wolf. He had no family and, naturally, no wife. In fact he had had no particular interest in women at all until now. He was a man's man – or had been until he saw me in that moment when he hesitated outside the door of my compartment. Something about my face intrigued him. He passed on unwillingly, but was unable to resist coming back to sit in the same compartment, opposite me. He cursed himself for his weakness and stopped himself from speaking to me, although he had wanted to – God he had wanted to!

Now (still in my dream) the dining steward would come into the carriage. "*Second sitting for lunch now, please,*" he would say as he popped his head round the door.

"*Perhaps you would like to join me for lunch?*" my companion would say.

"*Oh, thank you!*" I would be cool and gracious and I'd devastate him with my green eyes and bewitching smile.

At lunch he would say, "*Where have you been all my life?*"

Of course it would be terribly corny if he used those exact words, but you see what I'm getting at.

Now we are out of the train and walking across the hills. (Quite what we have done with Uncle Jack, Aunt Helen and Cousin George, who are supposed to be meeting me on the platform at Edinburgh, I do not know, but that is the satisfactory thing about day-dreams. I can say the magic word, fix them with a stern look and they will shrivel up and disappear, conveniently leaving me with my dream man shrouded in mist on some romantic Scottish hill.) It is rocky and dangerous and he is ahead, guiding me, showing me the way. At one place there is a big steep rock and we have to jump, first him and then me. *"Look out!"* he cries, anxiety sharpening his voice – but my heel has caught between two rocks and I am falling dizzily… with a quick movement he is there before me. He catches me in his arms in the best old movie trek-through-the-jungle tradition. For a moment I'm stunned. Then slowly I raise my eyes to his and they meet. (Our eyes, I mean.) He holds me closely in his strong arms as though he will never let me go. His hot breath sears my neck and suddenly he rips the thin red silk of my gown (not that I go in for gowns much, T-shirts are more in my line, but they are a bit tough for easy ripping). He'd have quite a job to rip the thick tweed coat I'm wearing now, I thought and even if he managed it that there would still be my blue woollen jersey between us. I couldn't help smiling to myself at the thought…

And then I came down to earth, and realised I was back in the frowsty compartment and alas, this tough handsome man had still not even looked at me. It was a bit of an anti-climax. Surely he must be wanting the window open by now? He had laid his paper down and was staring out at the passing countryside.

"Excuse me," said the bald man in the other corner of the compartment, whom I had quite forgotten. "Have you finished with your newspaper?"

"Why yes," said the Test Pilot, giving him a pleasant smile. "Would you like to see it?"

"Thanks very much. Didn't have time to buy one before the train started."

He got up and took the newspaper and there was silence again while some uninteresting countryside jogged by. Then the Test Pilot spoke again.

"D'you mind if we have the window open?" he asked.

Ah, at last it had begun. I said, giving him my bewitching smile, "Not in the…"

But he was looking at the bald man.

"No, go ahead and open it," replied that miserable creature. I was not consulted by either of them!

"Are you going far?" asked the Pilot.

27

(Not far enough, I thought.)

"To Edinburgh. Is that where you are going?"

"Yes – at least that's as far as I'm going on this train. I've been out in Bahrein and boy, will I be glad to get home again. It's been eight weeks since..."

I heard no more. Something had gone very wrong. It was altogether quite unbelievable.

The door slid open and the dining car attendant stuck his head round.

"Take your seats for lunch now, please," he said.

"Come and join me for some lunch, will you?" said the bald man to the Test Pilot. I noticed with distaste that the bald man had a wart on his cheek from which hairs sprouted.

"Thanks, I'd be glad to," said the Test Pilot, and together they got up and went out into the corridor. After a while I too got up and walked along to the dining car. I was the forsaken damsel, but I didn't care. I tossed my mane of nut-brown hair and passed through the tables with my head held back defensively, aloof, looking neither to left nor right. (Not that it mattered much anyway, for I noticed out of the corner of my eye that all the rather dull-looking businessmen were far too occupied with their roast lamb and two veg to even glance up as I passed.) I sat down, my lunch was brought to me and I ate it in sulky silence.

I was back in our compartment before the other two. They had probably had soup ordinaire, vin ordinaire and conversation très, très ordinaire - those corny little jokes men always find so amusing. At any rate, when they eventually came back from lunch you would have thought they had known one another all their lives.

"Well now John, what about that game of chess, eh?" said the bald man, producing a tiny chess-board from his brief case.

"Oh yes rather, Roger!" said the Test Pilot.

Roger and out - out, preferably of the window, I thought waspishly. So my Pilot's name was common-or-garden John. And he played chess. And what he could see in that dull little man with a wart on his cheek was quite beyond my comprehension. It was all very disillusioning. I had been so certain that Fate had brought him into the compartment because of me. By rights that unpleasant fat creature who had not had time to buy a newspaper should have missed the train altogether. Fate had made a tragic mistake.

And so the hours passed and the train jogged and jolted its way northward and the game of chess and the friendship between the two men developed rapidly. It was really, I thought sourly, rather sweet. Rather touching, I thought, and I leaned back resigned and watched them with a smile intended to be condescending and a little sardonic.

It was dark now and a bit chilly.

"Would you mind," I enquired pleasantly, "If we had the window closed now?"

"Oh, not in the least!" cried the Test Pilot with a smile and "Not at all," said the bald man and they both leapt to their feet. With a great, huge effort the Test Pilot managed to pull the window up. (Most of his manly strength seemed to have been used up in the game of chess.)

At last the train pulled into Edinburgh and we three passengers started to put our things together and pull our various pieces of luggage down from the rack. The bald man was the first out. "Well goodbye John, and all the best. Mind you take her with you next time," he said.

"You bet," said the Test Pilot. "You have our address now, haven't you? Don't forget to come and look us up."

"Hello John," said another voice, enthralling and low.

"Why Charlotte darling!" he said, and leapt out of the carriage.

Charlotte darling was tall and slender and she wore a beautiful camel coat slung across her shoulders. Her hair was swept back into a chignon and she had long, lustrous eyelashes surrounding wide, violet eyes. She was a bit ancient, I thought, at least thirty, but she was exotic and beautiful like a model. Oh well, no wonder, I thought and felt better. I saw them embrace and turned hurriedly away to pick up my suitcase and leave the carriage.

I searched up and down the platform for Aunt Helen and Uncle

Jack, but I couldn't see them. There was just a very tall sturdy young lad wearing a kilt and a tweed jacket with leather-bound cuffs. He had brown eyes and flaming red hair like a fox and – oh it was Cousin George!

"Is it really you, Jilly?" he asked unbelievingly as he approached me.

"Jill," I corrected him. "Yes, it's me."

Suddenly I was so very pleased to see him. The next moment we were laughing and hugging each other.

"I can't get over it," he said, "Let me look at you again. Whatever happened to the podgy, spotty-faced cousin with straggly pig-tails that I remember?"

I was indignant for a moment, but then I saw the funny side and laughed. "Nothing," I said, "Except that like Cousin George, she grew up."

"My word, he said, "She certainly did."

I was warmed by the admiration in his brown eyes. It did such a lot for a girl's morale.

"Oh Jilly, do you remember that picnic we had by the loch last time you came, when you fell in?"

"You pushed me!" I said.

"I never did!"

"But I didn't mind. Then you jumped in after me and we had a swim, and then we lay in the sun to dry our clothes"

I stood there, remembering what marvellous holidays we'd had when we were children, the long walks over the heather-covered hills and tea and girdle scones when we returned, in Aunt Helen's kitchen.

"You always were a dreamer," said Cousin George softly into my ear. He picked up my luggage. "Come on, Jilly. We've got all the holidays before us. Don't let's waste a minute!"

Sold to Fab, *1976*

Beware of Telling Lies

I first met Julian at Mrs Raymond's tea-party in aid of the Red Cross. Mrs Raymond is a pillar of society in our town and her tea-parties are *always* a crashing bore. I *always* try to get out of them and it is *always* in vain. This one promised to be as bad as the others, with its herd of middle-aged ladies in jersey suits and 30-denier tights, sprinklings of old retired men who have forgotten what they did before they retired, the odd poodle or two and, of course, me. My mother should have been there too, but she'd cried off, saying it was her day for the Citizen's Advice Bureau.

"But you will let me have Kate, won't you?" shrilled Mrs Raymond. "You know I'm counting on her."

"Oh yes, you can count on Kate," said my mother.

It's a good slogan that, I thought, YOU CAN COUNT ON KATE! And of course they can. They all think I'm awfully nice. I'm so demure and quiet, never speak unless spoken to, never say boo to a goose. I've quite restored their faith in modern youth. You should see the way I leap about at these dos, passing plates of sandwiches round – a full-time job in itself. You start with Mrs Adams near the door, and before you get all the way round she has finished and wants another. And they all have ten cups of tea at least. I am fearfully polite. I stand up when they come into the room and I open the door for them when they go out. I ask them how their rheumatism is and how their sciatica is and how their dahlias are. I'm a well brought-up girl and if I'm also dreadfully dull, well – it's what they expect of me.

When I first saw Julian, I got a bit of a shock. I mean, I wasn't expecting to see this tremendously tall, dark young man amongst the assortment of pebble tweeds. He was, I learned, Mrs Raymond's nephew, just home on leave from the Far East or somewhere. He was a Naval Officer, they said.

"Kate," said Mrs Raymond, "Come over here, dear. There's someone I want you to meet."

All the ladies stopped talking and watched as I walked shyly and demurely across the room. I think they expected to see a romance spring up as fast as a flower in a Disney cartoon. Well, that's all right by me, I thought, looking up at Julian's bronzed face and romantic, brooding eyes. But he hardly gave me a second glance!

I was mortified. After all, I'm not bad looking. No, really I'm not, so why beat about the bush? I mean I have a figure that goes in all the right directions in the right places, and nice grey eyes with long lashes and well-brushed gleaming hair that swings about like those telly ads for shampoo, yet this obstinate nephew of Mrs Raymond's just refused to succumb to my charms. Didn't even flicker an eyelid.

I thought, it's this awful act I put on here, this Tea Party at the Vicarage act, which is OK for the tweedy ladies but a total turn-off for any young man with an ounce of character.

So – how to attract his attention?

I considered several things, like bursting into song, or doing a tap dance on top of the piano or a strip-tease in the middle of the floor, but rejected them all immediately. I'm just not that type somehow.

Meanwhile Julian was deep in conversation with one of the tweedy ladies while the others looked on enviously. How she revelled in his attention: her cheeks were faintly flushed pink under the powder and she had to crane her neck to look up at him, he was so very tall.

After a while the tea party came to an end and Mrs Raymond turned to her nephew and rather obviously, I thought, suggested he should take me home. "Kate has a long and rather lonely walk and it'll be dark soon and we don't want anything to happen to her, do we?"

I could have hugged her. I've done that walk hundreds of times and no one's ever cared if I got home or not before - well I expect they have, but they've certainly never thought I wouldn't. But today I was a precious piece of china to be cherished particularly, since she was in one of her match-making moods, by Mrs Raymond's nephew.

So there we were walking along the road and me searching for that fascinating witty thing to say that would render me instantly desirable and coming up with – nothing! Not a thing, apart from "The evenings are closing in again," ("I guess so,") and "How long are you staying?" ("About a month.") I'm so unoriginal, I thought sadly.

"How about you, what do you do?" he said, but not as if it mattered a row of beans. It was now or never, so I said, "I'm an actress."

Ah – *now* the light of interest was kindled in his eyes. And not just interest, respect. And admiration. It was wondrous to behold, that three little words could wreak such a change in a man.

"*Are* you now?" he said, looking at me as if seeing me for the first time. "And what have you done up to now?"

"Oh, Juliet," I said airily. "*St Joan* – Cecily in *The Importance of Being Ernest* – *Candida*."

"Television?" he said.

"I've had offers," I said. "But I prefer live theatre. It's a purer form."

"And what are you doing now?"

"Rehearsals for *My Fair Lady*."

"And when's your next production?"

I was beginning to feel worried. "Oh, er… in about five weeks."

"Maybe I'll see you, I might get another week's leave."

"Or perhaps six or seven weeks, I'm not sure."

"Well if I can't see you myself I'll ask Aunt Rosamund to go and give me a full report."

I smiled at him modestly, but inside I was starting to panic.

"Prior to London production, is it?" he enquired.

"Yes – yes, actually."

He could stop talking about acting now and concentrate on me, I thought.

"Did you train at RADA?"

"Well, yes, actually."

"Oh, I wonder if you ever came across a friend of mine – Patrick Doran, his name is."

"Well as a matter of fact I wasn't there all that long really, just a – few weeks, you know. I learnt acting the hard way."

"In rep, you mean?"

"Yes, rep. That's it, rep."

"That must have been tough," said Julian.

"Oh it was. It was."

"Didn't you ever mix up the play you were doing in the evening with the one for the following week?"

"Well I – tried not to," I said bravely. *Oh help*, I thought, *why ever did I start this and how can I keep it up and – thank goodness, we're nearly at my house, and then that will be that.*

"I must see you again," said Julian.

"Oh must you?" I said.

He looked at me with his lovely dark eyes. "But I suppose you're tied up in the evenings?"

"Tied up?"

"With rehearsals."

"Oh yes I see what you mean. Rehearsals. That's right."

We'd come to my gate. "Well thank you, Julian," I said, "This is where I live."

But he followed me through the gate.

"It was nice of you to bring me home," I said.

Did he expect to come in and, oh horrors, meet my parents? Well Dad wouldn't be home yet and Mum might still be at the CAB – no she wouldn't, it was half-past six, she'd be at home. I looked for my latch key but couldn't find it.

"Aren't you going to ring the bell?" he asked.

"Yes," I said meekly, and rang it.

In a moment my mother appeared. I introduced her to Julian.

"He just brought me home," I said, "Thank you Julian, good night."

"What a pity you have to rush away," said my mother.

"I don't," he replied.

"Then come in and have a drink. It's quite chilly now the evenings are drawing in."

Oh Mum, I thought. You see – that's where I get my conversational brilliance from.

"What will you have?" she asked.

"Beer would be fine."

"Kate, run and fetch a beer for your friend."

Run, indeed! I thought. I went and fetched a tray with a badly-poured beer for Julian, a sherry for my mother and a gin for myself. Actresses drink gin, don't they?

My mother's eyebrows went up. "Darling, you hate gin, you know you do!"

"Not any more," I said swallowing bravely.

"I've been hearing all about your daughter's career," said Julian..

Here goes, I thought.

"Oh her cookery course?" said my mother.

"I meant, her acting career," said Julian.

"Oh you mean the local dramatic society," said my mother.

He didn't bat an eyelid.

"*Candida*?" he said, "Juliet? *St Joan*?"

"Well she was only prompting them, of course" said my mother modestly. "but she is under-studying Liza in *My Fair Lady*, aren't you darling?"

I wanted the carpet to swallow me up, but Julian didn't miss a beat.

"She's clearly a most brilliant actress," he said, "with a great future. You have only to hear her speak to know that."

And he turned to me and gave me a most enormous wink.

"Can you really tell that from the way she speaks?" said my mother much surprised. "Well, fancy that!"

He turned to me. "I wonder if you would like to come out with me tomorrow night?" he asked. "It sounds as if you might have a little free time for a chap like me after all."

This story was sold to OK *in 1978 and* Just 17 *in 1984.*

Girl With A Secret

How am I going to tell them? That's what I ask myself.

I am sitting up in bed at Thornleigh Grange, sipping early morning tea from a fine porcelain cup, and I should be happy, with my wedding just a week away, but instead I'm afraid.

As usual I am in the Lake Room with its beautiful view, its spaciousness and luxury. I have a big wide bed with pink linen sheets and a rose silk quilt. We haven't even a spare room at home. Mum and Dad have the front, me and my two sisters share the larger back room and my brother Nick has the Box. I've never known a morning when there haven't been squabbles and shrieks and outside you can always hear the heavies pounding up the main road past our house. But here deep in the country at Thornleigh Grange it's so peaceful, only the whirring of martins in the eaves above my window. The sun pours in through the open casement, making patterns on the carpet.

There's a sudden gentle tap at the door.

"Ginny! Are you awake?"

"Yes, come in."

The door opens and in comes Simon Allenby, tall like his father, in pyjamas and a red silk dressing-gown.

"Hello, darling!" He sits on the edge of my bed without touching me, but with such a look of warmth and love in his eyes that my heart lurches.

"You got tea!" he says accusingly, "more than I did!"

"Your sister brought it in. She spoils me dreadfully. Would you like some?"

"Yes." He drinks from my cup and I watch the strong lines of his face, loving him so much that it hurts. He sets the cup down and turns to me.

"This time next week, Ginny!"

"Yes I know, Simon, I haven't forgotten."

How could I forget? It will be a large country wedding in the same Anglo-Saxon church where Simon was christened and afterwards a reception here in the grounds of Thornleigh Grange with a marquee on the lawn and champagne and speeches by affectionate Allenby uncles with fat stomachs and kindly red faces.

The Allenbys, you should know, are the backbone of the county, good, solid and oh so respectable!

"You are happy, aren't you darling?"

"Yes, Simon, I'm happy."

"Completely?"

"Yes," I lie.

"If only I could think of a new and original way to say it."

"Say what?"

"That I love, love you Ginny!"

He is so sincere and I want to believe him – I do believe him. And I want to tell him that I love him too – but first I must tell him this other thing that I only learnt myself on Friday. Will he still want to marry me when he knows the truth? Will he stop loving me? Do people stop loving people for such things? And what of his parents whom I have deceived? What will they think? I can't bear to think of it!

"Well I'd better go, I suppose," says Simon reluctantly. "I promised my father I'd help him this morning. He's got a load of work to do. And I gather Mother wants to show you some linen and silver she thinks we might like."

It is not the first time I have been to stay here. I can remember how overawed I was when I came here first. It was all so much grander than I had expected, so entirely different from where I live. Not that I want to disparage my home – it may be shabby with threadbare patches in the carpets, chair covers worn on the arms and furniture scratched with much use, but it's home to me and I love it. Still, it's a far cry from Thornleigh Grange with its spacious rooms, its luxury, its elegant good taste. From my bedroom window I have a view of vast rolling lawns edged with rhododendron bushes and beyond them, the lake. I can see a small white dinghy moored to the landing stage and a pair of graceful swans browsing by the water's edge.

That first morning I had a bath in my own lilac pink bathroom and as I leaned back in the hot scented water I marvelled at it all, how just through a chance meeting in a train I should come to be here, living this charmed life. He picked me up, you might say. Oh that doesn't sound very elegant, but that's the way it happened just the same. From where I lay in the bath I could look through an arched Gothic window straight across fields to the country church on the brow of the hill. It was like looking at a picture framed in an arch. Everything in the bathroom was beautiful, the colours, the lights, the rose-patterned china fittings. The towels in shades of pink and lilac, so different from the skimpy, threadbare ones we have at home. Mum bound them at the edges last year, now they are puckered, beginning to break away from the binding, but they'll not be thrown out till they fall apart. That's the way Mum is – she never throws anything away and even when she buys something new it's put in a cupboard and stored there until some mythical time that will never come. Dear Mum, I think, in a rush of affection.

That first weekend I spent at Thornleigh I was actually homesick! It was all too much somehow; Simon's parents were very kind of course, but they were overpowering. Colonel Allenby was so immensely tall and when he looked at me it was as if his deep-set eyes were boring right through me. Nothing, no detail could escape that look.

"My dear Ginette, we've heard so much about you," he said. "May I call you Ginny? But you are even prettier than we were led to believe!"

He was charming, but he unnerved me. I didn't know how to respond. I was awkward and gauche. Simon's mother was charming and smart. Her hair was grey but so pretty. She wore those very simple, well-cut clothes that make everyone else feel overdressed, and she had green stockings and green leather shoes with silver buckles. I thought she was gorgeous and I longed for her to like me too.

Time passed, and my visits to Thornleigh became more frequent. The Allenbys welcomed me and I was happy there with them. Simon asked me to marry him. It was as if all my wishes were coming true.

And then on Friday I heard the news about my father.

We are sitting round the table now, having lunch. Everything is comfortable, pleasant, safe. What will they think when they hear my sordid piece of news – that my father, who I told them was dead, is not only alive but in prison, and due for release this very week? There – sounds nice, doesn't it? Nice and cosy. He got ten years for robbery with violence, but with remission and parole it was reduced, so he will have been inside for just six years.

Rachel, Simon's young sister, hands round silver dishes of peas and broad beans while Colonel Allenby carves the roast lamb, brown and crisp with pale pink juicy meat and the faintest hint of rosemary, beautiful like a picture in a cookery book. Mum just carves it in the kitchen and shovels it onto plates out there because it saves washing up. Shall I tell them now, or shall I wait till the dessert? A shame to spoil a lovely roast...... the minutes pass. The plates are stacked and placed in the hatch. Simon's fingers brush mine as he passes the fruit bowl and his eyes have that heart-melting look when he turns to me. Presently we are peeling yellow-skinned pears with slim silver knives.

I'll tell them at tea-time.

Oh Dad, why did you have to do it? If you only knew what we've been through these last six years you wouldn't have. I remember how Mum told me when I was twelve that you'd got to go to prison and I sat on the stairs all evening till the sun went down and it was quite dark and still I couldn't believe it, because grown-ups you *know* don't do things like that. Even children know that stealing is wrong and robbers are bad men, so how could you, my own father, be a robber and be going to prison? Mum never let us see she minded but she did, of course. It broke her heart because the neighbours looked down on us and Mrs Warren wouldn't let her kids come and play. Even Aunt Mildred when Nick pinched one of next door's apples sniffed and said, "Blood will out, my dear, blood will out!" I didn't know what she meant then, but I know now.

Mother went every week to visit you in prison. Girls at school made cracks saying did she bake cakes with files in them to take you? She never let us go. To us you might have been dead. If only you were! It was bad when you went away but so much worse now you're coming back. And I hate you for making me hate myself for thinking it.

We are having tea on the lawn, near the lake. It's very quiet, you can hear nothing but the lazy buzzing of bees, the sudden "quark" of a moorhen, the gentle plop of the water. It's like a scene from another century. The clothes are wrong of course, but the feeling, the peace, the gentleness must surely be the same.

Now I'll do it. Now I'll say what I have to say.

"Mrs Allenby – "

"Would you like some more tea, Ginny dear?"

"No thank you… I've got something to tell you – "

"Simon?"

"Yes please, Mother."

"Pass your cup, then. What was that you were saying, Ginny?"

"Well, it's…"

"Don't move, Rachel! There's a wasp crawling up your arm!"

Moments of panic till the wasp is safely despatched. I start again.

"Mrs Allenby, I was just saying…"

"Oh yes, Ginny, I'm sorry, what *were* you saying?"

"It's about my father."

Now they're listening. Now they're looking at me watchfully somehow, waiting.

"I told you he was dead – but he wasn't really. He was in prison. Six years for robbery with violence. He comes out next week."

There. I've said it. I wait for the explosion.

Nothing. Just silence. I look round at them, at Simon staring at me, stunned; Rachel pink in the face – excited, I think. Simon's parents, quiet, grave.

"Yes Ginny," says Mrs Allenby, "We know."

"You *know?*" I am incredulous.

"Your mother told us."

"My *mother?* But why? When did she tell you? I don't understand."

"We've known a long time," says Colonel Allenby. "As soon as you and Simon became engaged. Your mother came over to see us one afternoon and she told us then."

"Don't blame her for it," says Simon's mother quickly. "She knew how very unhappy and ashamed you were about your father. She wanted everything to be out in the open and she didn't know how much you would have told us."

"I hadn't told you anything!"

"You would have, in your own good time. We know that." Colonel Allenby looks grave, but there's such kindness and understanding in his face I want to weep.

"And – Simon?"

I look at him briefly, his face is blank, inscrutable.

"No, Simon did not know," says his mother. "It was not really our place to tell him."

"Oh Simon." I turn to him for reassurance. "Tell me you don't mind? That it doesn't matter?"

But he doesn't answer. He cannot tell me what I want to hear and there is misery in his eyes.

"I – *love* my father," I tell him, stung. "I love him very much and I won't brush this under the carpet. I want him to come to our wedding, you know!"

"Of course you do," says Mrs Allenby gently, humouring me as if I were an invalid. "There's no question of his not coming. It will be an ordeal for you at first but you must be brave my dear. Act as if nothing were wrong and people will believe that nothing is. Hold your head high. We'll be behind you."

I'm suddenly, unbelievably angry.

"Oh of course, that's how you do it, isn't it? The stiff upper lip bit, I'd forgotten. Stand together, say nothing, whatever you do don't let the side down! It's quite easy really. Like when Cousin Harry went off his rocker and stabbed the butler in 1832…"

"Shut up, Ginny!" cried Simon fiercely. "Don't try to be so damn smart. What do you expect my mother to say? She's taken it damn well I think, so's my father. Did you think they'd throw their arms around your neck and say how proud they are your father's not dead but just a vicious little crook? Is that what you expected? Well I can tell you this. They may not care, but I do. I'm shocked, appalled, sickened. The thought of this man being your father, of his coming to our wedding revolts me. But that's honesty for you. You sneer at kindness and good sense, perhaps you'll like that better. You can't be patronising about honesty!"

"I thought it might come to this," I fling back at him. "We'll call the whole thing off, of course. I can't marry a man who can't accept my father too."

"That's for you to decide," says Simon coldly. "You're a liar, Ginny, and besides that, you're a cheat."

"What do you mean by that?"

"You lied to me about your father. You told me he was dead. And why have you told the truth now? Because he's coming out of prison and we would have found out anyway. What if he hadn't been, would you have told us then? I don't believe you would!"

"Oh Simon," objects his mother, "You're being very unfair. Of course Ginny would have told us."

"No, no!" I cry in sudden despair. "He's right – I *wouldn't* have told you, not if I thought you wouldn't find out. I'd never have told you, never! Now you know the truth about me. But don't worry, I won't bring disgrace on you. Nothing would induce me to marry you now, Simon. There won't be a wedding, I won't blacken the family name!"

"Don't be melodramatic," says Simon sternly. "It cheapens you."

I laugh bitterly. "I'm already a liar, a cheat and I don't know what else – isn't there something about me you've forgotten to mention?"

He looks at me, the coldness has gone but oh, the anguish, the sadness in that look!

"Yes. That I love you Ginny, that I'll always love you, whatever you do, whatever you are. I love you for yourself. If you want to wriggle out of our marriage go ahead, but remember this: it'll be your choice, not mine."

Then he pushes his chair aside and gets to his feet.

"Oh yes…"

And I think, sitting here on the lawn, you have no idea really what it was like: That first bitter knowledge, the long hopeless evening on the stairs, goose pimples on my arms, darkness stealing over the landing – the wretched end to the myth about my father. I cannot pretend not to know what Simon feels.

"This news of your father is a shock to him, but that's natural," says Mrs Allenby. "He'll get over it. Don't imagine it will affect his feelings for you. If you don't mind my saying it Ginny, *you're* the one who can't accept this, not us. You told us your father was dead rather than the truth. You're the one who's been in turn angry and bitter and miserable. You're torn in two – part of you loves your father and wants to stand by him while the other part is resentful and ashamed. Well, whatever he's done, he's paid for it now. You must forget it and let him take up his life afresh, knowing that you are with him."

Yes, she's right. That's what I must do. I know that Simon loves me.

That in a little while he'll accept this, just as his parents do. That it's really me that can't accept it.

The Allenbys are big enough, solid enough, broad enough to take this, but next week – when I become one of them – I shall be too. It just needs time.

Now I'll go and look for Simon.

Sold to *Romance*, 1977

Blue-Eyed Boy

Everyone thinks I'm mad because I don't like Geoffrey. Well, I do of course, I mean everyone does – but not in *that* way. It's a shame really because he's so potty about me and I can see that it's a waste, but I just can't help it. I mean, I only wish I *did* like him, it would make life a lot easier, but the trouble is I think he's just too good to be true.

He is very tall indeed, about 6'4" I should think, because my father's 6'3" and he's taller than *him,* and he's got glossy blond hair and what are generally called classical good looks. He has very blue eyes and when he looks at me in *that* sort of way my heart doesn't skip a beat in the least, in fact if anything he makes me yawn!

My mother goes into raptures over his manners. She can't get over them. He says Good Evening to her and asks her how she is and she's so amazed, because grunts are all she's ever had from my other boyfriends, that she can't remember *how* she is except in a tiz because of Geoffrey). He leaps to his feet when she enters a room and holds open doors for her and lifts back her chair when she sits down until she's practically swooning.

He's got a marvellous steady job with a firm of accountants and although he's only a trainee he'll be amongst the 25% or so who'll pass his exams, because he's not the type who fails. He's the good boy, you see, the Blue-Eyed Boy. Everything's always gone right for him, all along the line.

Yesterday my mother came in all smiles and starry-eyed and said, "Guess who came round today looking for you, Stephanie?" and I said, "Oh God, not again?" and she said, "Now be sensible, dear. Who do you think it was?"

"I can't imagine. Uncle Tom Cobley? Jack the Ripper?"

"No, dear. It was Geoffrey."

"Oh, him." As if I couldn't guess. "What did *he* want?"

"To see you, of course. I asked him to come back later."

"Well, I wish you hadn't. I don't *want* to see him later."

"I can't imagine why not, Stephanie. He's such a nice young man, good-looking – and so sensible with it."

"That's just it," I wailed. "He's a bore!"

I turned and went upstairs to my room.

The fact is I like a different type altogether. The type I like – at least I think I do but I've never actually met him yet – is dark and lean and handsome, the prototype hero of the romantic novels, Mr Darcy in the flesh, sarcastic with a raspingly attractive voice. He is aloof, but I see his dark eyes watching me…

"Stephanie! That was the door bell." (…and suddenly I find out…)

"Stephanie!" (…that he's loved me passionately…)

"It'll be Geoffrey, dear." (…all the time.) "Could you let him in?"

Damn and blast Geoffrey.

He stood on the doorstep, neat and tidy in a dark blue suit – a suit! with a clean shirt and a glistening white collar and his cheeks had a healthy scrubbed look.

"Hello, Stephanie."

"Hello, Geoffrey."

"I was wondering... if you'd like to go out tonight?"

(I was *wondering*... Good GRIEF! Where's the forceful, dominating male there, then?

"Well actually, Geoffrey, I would and I already am – going out tonight I mean." (LIAR!)

He looked awfully surprised. Awfully.

"Really? Your mother never mentioned..."

"No, well my mother doesn't know everything."

"Where are you – I mean..."

"Going? You wonder where I'm going?" I said, playing for time, for I was wondering too. "I'm going," I said slowly, "to the cinema with Sharon. We're going to see that horror movie they've been advertising such a lot lately."

But he wasn't satisfied with that. "How are you getting there?" he asked.

"On ye olde two legges I suppose," I replied lightly, "unless a bus comes."

"I'll run you there."

That was pretty forceful for him, I thought. Just when I didn't want him to be.

"It's all right, really!" I began.

"No – I'll run you," he said decisively. "When are you meeting Sharon?"

"In about an hour," I lied.

"That's fine. We'll go now, then we can have a cup of coffee before you meet her."

Oh Lord, that meant I couldn't phone her first. I went slowly upstairs to get my coat. I couldn't see any way out.

Geoffrey parked his Mini in the cinema car park, then we went into a nice little coffee house nearby. All the girls looked at him when we walked in, then looked enviously at me. There was always this reaction wherever I went with him. It would get very boring, I thought, though I suppose I – *quite* liked it.

At half-past seven we went and stood on the cinema steps waiting for Sharon not to appear.

"Well. thanks very much Geoffrey," I said dismissively.

"That's OK," he said, not going.

"Well, goodbye then."

"I'll wait with you till Sharon comes."

"Oh you don't have to," I said, horrified.

"I know I don't have to, but I'm going to, just the same."

We didn't talk much in the next half hour, I was too embarrassed and he didn't seem over pleased I thought, when I looked at him once or twice out of the corner of my eye. In fact, rather annoyed.

At eight o'clock he said abruptly, "Well she's obviously not coming, so we'll go in without her."

"Oh! Are *you* coming then Geoffrey?" I asked in a small voice. He didn't reply, just produced his wallet and paid for our tickets. Then he took me by the elbow and pulled me – rather roughly – up the stairs and to our seats in the circle.

Why ever did I suggest that film? I hate horror films and this was far worse than the ones you see late at night on the box. This was *terrifying*. But then I never expected I'd have to actually see it. We were immersed in an atmosphere of pure evil. I was so frightened I hoped Geoffrey might realise and put his arm round me or at least hold my hand, but he didn't, and I certainly wasn't going to let him think I wanted him to, so we sat next to each other but as far apart as if we'd been strangers. You'd have thought he'd have realized when I started to shake – actually shake – with fear, but he appeared not to even notice. I might as well have been the cat, except if I had been I might have got patted. As it was, nothing. And I thought he was supposed to be interested in me – huh!

When we came out I realized he really was angry. I could tell by the tight line of his jaw. He fairly hustled me along to where we'd left his car. "Get in," he said.

Heavens! What had become of those beautiful manners? How disappointed my mother would have been.

"I wonder what could have happened to Sharon," I said chattily, just for something to say.

"I wonder!" he replied. Did I imagine it or was there a trace of sarcasm?"

Neither of us said a word on the way home and I was feeling slightly uneasy, wondering what he was thinking about, when suddenly there was our road and he'd driven straight past.

"Hey! That was my road!"

"I know."

"But why? Where are we going?"

"You'll see."

He sounded very grim. The next minute he'd pulled into a lay-by, not the sort that's right on the road but the sort with a hedge in between, and further up a large heavy goods lorry had parked so the driver could have a sleep. It wasn't a very nice lay-by, the hedge was dotted with old fish and chip papers, and there was a pile of rubbish further along, a margarine carton, some tins and an old mattress.

"Now I'd like an explanation," said Geoffrey quietly.

My heart missed a beat. "What – what do you mean?" I mumbled.

"You tell me."

It was stupid of me to try and brazen it out, but I was suddenly scared.

"I don't understand what you're getting at," I said.

"You little liar," said Geoffrey. He spoke with icy cold contempt, and when I dared to look at him I saw his face was pale in the harsh sodium lights. "You've been lying to me all evening, haven't you?" he said. "You were never going to meet Sharon at all, you just made it up, but *why*, that's what I'd like to know? If you didn't want to go out with me, why on earth couldn't you have the guts to say so instead of inventing this stupid load of garbage?"

"I don't know," I said, and I really didn't. I felt like bursting into tears.

Still he looked at me as if he hated me, with that awful cold contempt.

"I ought to beat you," he said. Then he seized me roughly in his arms and kissed me.

"Why Geoffrey," I said after a few surprised but pleasurable moments, "does that mean you still like me, a little?"

"I suppose it must mean that," he said, "but don't you ever lie to me again, EVER."

"No, I won't," I said.

And presently I said, "You really ought to be dark, you know. They're always dark, not fair. Still – I expect I'll soon get used to it."

Sold to *Blue Jeans*, 1977

Champagne

I felt a right twit in my smart wedding outfit, and there wasn't anyone to talk to either. You never feel so lonely or stupid as when you're in a crowd of strangers who've known each other all their lives, all chattering away with effortless abandon.

I stood awkwardly and studied the cake standing on a table at the side of the room. It had three tiers, with pillars above and below each tier. I had endless time to study the cake. I could have written a thesis on Wedding Cakes, Construction Of.

Suddenly this guy got wafted over on a tide of champagne and sort of landed in my lap. He would have been *in* my lap if I'd been sitting down.

"Sorry," he said. "Oh God – sorry!" and he picked up my hat, which had sailed to the floor, and replaced it carefully on my head. "Frightfully becoming," he said, staring at me intently. He had beautiful deep green eyes with the sort of long lashes a girl would give her back teeth for. "You ought to wear hats more often."

"How do you know I don't?" I said, "Seeing as you've never seen me before in your life."

"Well," he said, "I shouldn't imagine that you do. I mean, girls don't, do they? Much."

"No," I conceded, "They don't, much."

"You a friend of the bride?" he asked.

It's nice the way you can just start talking like that at weddings.

"No – of the groom."

"Oh, you're a has-been?"

Not so nice after all!

"No. A might have been if I'd wanted, which I didn't."

"I know what you mean. He's my brother. I don't know what the bride saw in him either."

"Oh dear – I'm sorry!"

"It's OK. I like people who put their foot in it. It's refreshing. Have some more champagne – but don't put your foot in that!"

"Thank you," I said stiffly.

"Don't just sip it. Take a good swig."

I took a good swig and then another. The fizziness of it made me burp, and I hoped he hadn't noticed. I was beginning to enjoy myself. I saw a waitress pass by with some delicious looking things on a plate, but before I could take any of them she whisked it away in someone else's direction.

"Do you think you might be able to grab some of that?" I asked.

"No, I don't think I could," he said. "Why don't *you* try?"

"I just did, but she didn't take any notice of me. Anyway guys are better at getting what they want."

"Well I don't want anything just now. I had a large pub lunch. As long as they keep topping up the champagne I'm happy to wait for the cake."

"You're not very gallant, are you? I mean, don't you think *I* might like something to eat?"

"You shouldn't, though." He studied me. "You are just right as you are – but just one vol-au-vent too many and you'd be undone. You would bulge."

"Oh, thanks a lot," I said. "You do know how to make a girl feel good, don't you?"

Yet I wasn't really annoyed. As a matter of fact, he did make me feel good.

He told me he was an actor. Not an ac*ter* as most people say, but an ac*tor*. Rather affected, I thought, to pronounce it like that.

"I suppose you're resting," I said.

"Now why should you suppose that?"

"Because I don't recognise you. What are you doing at the moment, then?"

"Telly ads," he said.

"Oh!" I was disappointed. "I don't call that real acting."

"There you go. Putting your foot in it again."

"No, but let's face it, Laurence Olivier didn't go on about Persil washing whiter than white, did he?"

"No – still everyone has to start somewhere. Actually, I'm not really the brother of the groom. I was just joking."

"So I've been covered in confusion all for nothing!"

"But I could have been," he pointed out.

"And I could have been the Queen of Sheba."

"I'm not sure you could. I'm not sure she's in the land of the living. I'm not sure there's any such place as Sheba now. Nowadays it's just a name for a dog. Have some more champagne."

"Yes please."

"Don't sip it. Knock it back – like this."

I knocked it back and burped again, only this time I didn't care if he saw or not.

"Waitress!" he said, indicating our empty glasses. She refilled them to the brim.

"I suppose you know lots of people here," I said.

"No," he said, "Only you."

I thought that was kind of endearing.

"I only know you too," I said.

"Are you attached to anyone?" he asked. "Boyfriend, or anything?"

"I've a long-standing boyfriend to whom I'm deeply attached," I said lightly.

"Oh dear. I'm sorry to hear that."

"What about you?"

"I'm in love with a girl called Judith."

"Oh. Does she love you too?"

"Of course. Passionately."

"What is she like – this Judith?"

"She's blonde, intelligent and beautiful."

"I have quite gone off Judith," I said.

"What's the name of your boyfriend?"

"Nigel."

"You should never trust a bloke called Nigel. You can take it from me, blokes called Nigel are not to be trusted."

"At least he'd have got me something to eat."

"Then why isn't he here, getting you something to eat now?"

"He wasn't invited. Anyway, where's Judith?"

"She wasn't invited either."

"I suppose that's why you're talking to me, otherwise you'd be with Judith, whispering sweet nothings into her ear."

"I don't know," he said. "We've passed that stage now."

"Oh – how sad!" Suddenly I wanted to cry – or was it the champagne? For Nigel and I had passed that stage too. And it's such a lovely stage. Exciting, romantic, full of promise. It should last for ever. Does it ever do that, I wondered. Does it ever last?

Then someone clutched my sleeve and said, "Emily, I didn't know you were here! How are you? I haven't seen you for ages."

I turned and there was this girl I'd been at school with. I talked to her, and when I turned back the actor had disappeared.

"Hello little girl, you look lost," said an elderly man with pale leering eyes and a paunch. "Here, let me give you some champagne."

"No more," I began.

"Come on," he wheedled.

I looked round desperately. *Come back. Please, please come back!*

And suddenly there he was, the actor, at my elbow. He bent and whispered in my ear, "Shall we escape?"

"From this?"

"This – everything. I'll buy you a take-away curry and we'll eat it by the river."

"But what about Judith?" I said.

"Oh – Judith will think I'm still here. Look," he said, "I'm not married to Judith. I'm not even engaged to her. Anyway, what about Nigel? Will he be waiting for you?"

"I hope not. I told him I didn't know what time it would end."

"That's all right then, he's probably gone on the razzle with a blonde."

"Nigel's not like that."

"No, blokes called Nigel never are, worse luck. Come on," he said. "I want to see if you look as sweet without your hat as you do with it."

"I expect my hair will be all squashy."

"That's all right. I have a weakness for girls with squashy hair."

And so we escaped. Hand in hand we crept down the stairs and out into the open air. At least, we didn't so much creep as sail along on a great bubble of champagne.

I know it will burst in the end, but up till now it's done quite well. Perhaps it was a special kind of champagne – a super brew.

Matchmaking

I thought Edward was the most irritating man I had ever known. Goodness knows why I should have thought of him as a suitable candidate for matchmaking. Perhaps it was his mother – my godmother – who first gave me the idea. I grew rather tired of hearing her say to my mama, "Oh dear, I wish Edward would get married! I'd so love to have a nice daughter-in-law. I'm always introducing him to girls and sometimes he takes them out, but it never comes to anything. He's not shy, he likes girls I know – but why doesn't he get married? He'll be thirty next birthday you know. It's not much to ask, is it?"

Poor old Aunt Julia! I didn't think anything more about this until one day last May, when Edward approached me full of enthusiasm for a new idea.

"Listen Angie," he said – he always calls me Angie, although everyone else calls me Angela – "How would you like to go to Portugal for your summer holiday this year with Robert and me? We're going to fly to Lisbon and then hire a car and drive it all the way down to the Algarve coast."

I was flattered, until he added, "You see we need two more people to help share the petrol and other expenses."

I might have known! Edward is so honest it never occurs to him to try to flatter a girl. He says whatever he thinks and sometimes he comes out with the most tactless things.

"We couldn't think of anyone to begin with because it's such short notice," he continued, "But I knew we could count on old Angie."

Old Angie indeed!

"Temps can always take weeks off whenever they want, can't they? And I'm sure you must have some nice girlfriend you could bring along – preferably small, blonde, fresh, unspoilt and intelligent."

"You don't want much, do you Edward? Well, all right, I'll try to rack my brains and think of somebody."

The holiday, I learned, was to be taken the following month during the last week of June and the first week of July. That very evening I set about thinking of a girl I could bring for Edward, and it wasn't long before I thought of Lily. Lily is light mouse, which is as near blonde as I could get, and she is quite small, certainly not tall and fresh, like in the telly ads, and she cleans her teeth regularly. She is as intelligent as any of my friends might be expected to be and I should think 'unspoilt', but I would never dream of asking, and I really don't know what Edward was meaning when he said that anyway. I knew she had just suffered a "disappointment in love" so she was between boyfriends.

I phoned her up from the office and it was while I was speaking to her on the phone that I suddenly thought of Aunt Julia and how, if I played my cards right, Lily might be the very one we were all looking for, and we might even arrange the wedding by Christmas.

After I had explained to her about the holiday and she had squeaked with excitement at the prospect, she asked me what Edward was like.

This has got to be good, I thought. "Well he's 29 years old and tall," I said, "ish. Rather broadly built – manly, you know. He has fair hair and freckles on his nose. He's got the most attractive smile, and what a sense of humour!" Then I stopped, because I didn't want to overdo it and I felt a bit mean with Lily probably imagining she was going to Portugal with some Adonis. I didn't tell her anything about Robert, because between you and me and the gatepost I rather fancied him for myself. Now there really was a good-looking man for you. I thought Lily could jolly well keep her pink, pudgy little paws off him.

Edward arranged everything to the last detail and one June day four weeks later we arrived at our hotel in a small resort on the southern coast of Portugal. It was a quiet little place, almost uninhabited and peaceful like a garden, full of orchards and groves of almond trees and flowers. I shared a bedroom with Lily and we had a balcony overlooking the sea, deep deep blue, shimmering like silk and transparent turquoise in shallow patches where you could see the shapes of white rocks beneath.

We unpacked and bathed and changed prior to joining the men for dinner. When she was ready Lily looked really pretty and I was proud of her. Just what Edward was looking for, I thought, small and blonde and fresh, etc. etc.

We had a table on the terrace overlooking the sea. It was very romantic in the darkness with the lights from the fishing boats bobbing about under the slim, silver moon and the stars as if hanging from threads against the black, velvet night sky. We had a handsome Spanish waiter to serve us, dark and smooth and glossy with brown eyes that looked at you as if you had no clothes on. At least that's the way he looked at Lily, and she seemed to like it! I thought it was disgusting – but I suppose it was just sour grapes really. I mean, I'd have been delighted if Robert had looked at me like that, but then Englishmen never show their feelings much, do they? Not like the Continentals.

After dinner we left the hotel and wandered along the promenade until we reached the casino. It wasn't really a casino, just a little place where you could go and drink wine, and there was a small three-piece band. Robert asked me to dance and I got up casually, not wanting him to see how much I had been hoping he would ask. He was a rhythmic dancer and I found him easy to follow. He was witty and amusing, but I didn't feel I was getting to know him any better and I couldn't gauge what sort of impression I was making on him. The only indication that he liked me at all was that he danced with me continually – and this of course had the added advantage of leaving Lily with Edward. They seemed to be getting along fine, I thought. They seemed to sit out quite a bit and as we passed their table I could hear them chattering away about some mutual acquaintance who had emigrated to Canada. I thought it was not a bad thing to sit out, you can often get to know a person much better that way than when you are jigging about on a dance floor. Besides, Edward, unlike Robert, was not what I'd call a natural dancer. I felt really hopeful about them.

And so the holiday began.

The next morning we joined the men for breakfast at nine o'clock. We sat at a table on the terrace under a striped umbrella, and a little waitress called Anita brought us hot rolls and blackberry jam and thick white cups of coffee. I thought it was all delicious, for I was determined to find no fault with anything, but Edward said he wanted a boiled egg. He spoke to Anita in painful pidgin French of which she couldn't understand a word, and said he wanted a boiled egg for breakfast because he always had a boiled egg for breakfast. He flapped his arms like a hen and made clucking noises, but she looked quite blank, until at last Carlos, our handsome waiter of the night before, appeared, yawning and stretching his lithe frame, and explained to Anita what Edward wanted. I couldn't help feeling irritated with Edward and more so when, after breakfast, he went up the road to the local shop to buy an English newspaper. He was English and proud of it, and he wasn't going to forget it, not even for one little fortnight in the year.

Later on we went down to the beach and lay in the sun and by lunchtime Edward's fair skin was burned to a violent salmon pink and we all had to take turns in rubbing cream onto his back and shoulders. It took ages with his saying all the while, "Ah-hh! and "O-ow!" and "Careful!" Poor Edward. I couldn't help feeling sorry for him, because while Robert was turning a deep olive hue and Lily a nice shade of gold I wasn't making much headway myself.

Robert and I went for a swim, but the others wouldn't come. Edward said he was feeling too sore and Lily had never been much of a one for swimming, preferring to sunbathe. Besides she had brought a delicious assortment of bikinis with her. I thought it was a chance for them to be alone together, but I was disappointed on coming out of the sea to find them lying yards apart, Lily on the rug turning over at punctual 15-minute intervals and Edward on his little beach towel reading his English newspaper. He could be very irritating, I thought. If he didn't hurry up and improve his technique Lily was going to get fed up and I was going to have nothing to tell Aunt Julia at the end of the holiday.

After lunch we took the car and drove up into the mountains, where there were palm trees and sub-tropical plants. Robert talked nostalgically about the Phoenicians who were in the Algarve 3,000 years ago and how they colonized it before the Romans came, or something. I tried to look intelligent although I hadn't a clue really, for I loved to hear him talk; but Edward had no interest in the past, being essentially a man of today, practical and down to earth. Whilst we stood looking down at the remains of a great Phoenician civilization Edward was thinking about the Common Market and the plight of the farmers and worrying about his stocks and shares.

Lily took one look at Robert and me, and then went up to him and took his arm and said, "Come on Edward, let's go for a little walk and leave these two here to dwell in the past."

Edward sprang away, crying, "Mind my arm! It's very tender you know!" but he did allow himself to be led away. You wouldn't call him a dashing suitor but nevertheless he was rather endearing, I thought indulgently. Very English and very predictable perhaps, but also kind and dependable. I felt sure Lily would be won over by him in the end.

I wished he would be a bit more romantic towards her, though. I wondered what I could do to get things going and when I got the chance to speak to him alone I asked him to be especially nice to Lily because she had just had an unhappy love affair and her morale was low. In response he gave me a quizzical smile and said nothing, but I really think it had the desired effect, for he was much kinder and gentler with her after that.

Our holiday fell into a kind of routine. We would breakfast at nine and then go down onto the beach. After lunch we would get the car and go off into the mountains; but Edward and Lily got fed up with the Phoenicians and more often than not he would stay behind in the village going for walks. Later on we'd bath and change and have dinner and then wander down to the Casino.

The days passed all too quickly.

On the last night of our holiday Lily and I were changing for dinner in our room and she put on a pink dress I had not seen before. With her golden tan she looked all pink and gold and there was a sort of radiance about her. I couldn't help exclaiming how stunning she looked.

"What's come over you?" I asked.

She blushed to the roots of her hair. There could only be one explanation for that look.

"You two – you're in love, aren't you?"

She grinned like a schoolgirl.

"Oh Lily!" I cried, "I'm so glad!"

Her face lit up. "Really? But he's never said anything."

"Well, I expect he finds it difficult. I mean, he doesn't know how you feel yet, does he? I think you should give him some encouragement."

"Do you really? But I don't want to make myself cheap."

"He's probably just shy. It's really up to you to make the first move."

"I suppose it is. Perhaps I should." She looked thoughtful.

Presently we went down to dinner, and Edward and Robert joined us.

We had a different waiter to serve our meal. He was small and skinny and his face was pock-marked.

"Look at Mr Universe here!" said Robert. So much of Robert's wit was at the expense of others, I was beginning to notice.

"Where is Carlos?" I asked the waiter.

"Tonight Carlos go dancing," grinned Mr Universe.

After dinner we went to the Casino as usual. There was to be a cabaret at eleven o'clock and we managed to get a table quite near the centre of the dance floor. We ordered our drinks and watched the dancing for a while. Suddenly I spotted someone I recognised.

"Look," I said, "There's our waiter dancing with one of the chambermaids."

"They certainly seem to be enjoying themselves," said Robert. "One thing about these people – they know how to live. Plenty of energy and joie de vivre."

It was true. Carlos looked happy and full of zest as he danced with the little chambermaid.

"That girl's really rather a stunner when she's dressed up," commented Edward. Lily looked quite hurt. Edward can be so tactless.

"Will you... dance with me, Edward?" she asked him suddenly in a funny, tight little voice. Oh dear, I thought. When I had suggested she make the first move I hadn't really meant her to ask him to dance. I couldn't help noticing that they were scarcely talking at all and that she looked strained and miserable. What had gone wrong, I wondered? Perhaps I should intervene again. Drop him a hint, maybe.

Later on he asked me to dance and I came straight out with it.

"You do like Lily, don't you Edward?"

"Why yes," he said surprised. "She's a very sweet girl."

"You really are fond of her, then?"

"Well I wouldn't say that!"

"You do know she's in love with you, don't you?"

"Good God, whatever makes you think so?"

How strange he could not see it for himself. If someone were in love with me I should know it instantly.

"She told me so tonight in our room. Now Edward, if you hurt her I'll never forgive you. I told you she was getting over an unhappy love affair. Whatever happens she mustn't be let down a second time."

"What am I expected to do about it?"

"Just use your head. For a start you can dance with her for the rest of the evening."

He stared at me for a long, long time.

"Is this really what you want, Angie?" he asked.

"Yes, yes!" I cried impatiently, "Go on, this dance is over now, leave me to dance with Robert."

"By God, I will!" he exclaimed, and turning he strode off, leaving me standing there in the middle of the floor.

I must admit I was a little taken aback at his abruptness. Before I could think about it a stranger had grabbed hold of me for the next dance. When it was over I went back to our table and found Robert sitting there alone.

"The others have gone," he told me. "Lily felt like some air and Edward has taken her for a walk. Care to dance, Angie?"

"Thank you," I said a trifle absently. I found I was not concentrating very hard and twice I tripped over his feet. He looked annoyed. He could be very intolerant, I thought. And his conversation was sophisticated and glib, but there wasn't really much behind that surface gloss. I was never altogether at ease with him. His wit was unkind and he didn't seem to care at all about his fellow human beings, not like Edward. Dear Edward!

Then suddenly something struck me with such force that I stopped dead in the middle of the floor.

"For God's sake!" said Robert, "You're letting the side down."

I looked at him blankly and stepped on his toe.

We left the floor in silence, me thinking – astonishingly – of Edward and of the way he had looked at me just now, and of how kind he was, and how steady and how predictable and how endearingly English and dear he was. So that was how it happened: I realised I was in love with him myself. And now it was too late. Lily was in love with him and he was as good as in love with her and I had thrown them together and I had lost him.

"I'd like to go now," I said. "Will you take me back to the hotel?"

"Certainly, Madame!" said Robert mockingly. "We're not exactly scintillating tonight, are we?"

But I didn't really care what he thought of me.

Lily wasn't in our room when I got into the hotel. I pictured her walking along the beach with Edward, in the moonlight. I lay in my bed hearing the clock in the square strike every quarter until just after 3 am, she crept into our room.

"Are you awake, Angie?" she whispered.

"Yes."

"What do you think? He has asked me to marry him!"

It was like a knife going into me.

"Do you think I should, Angie?"

What could I say? "Yes, if you love him and you think you can make him happy."

"Oh, I do and I will! I'm glad you're on my side – but Mother will be furious!"

I couldn't see why. Edward had a very good job with excellent prospects. Most mothers would have been delighted to have him as a son-in-law. Of course she was very young.

"You'll promise you won't tell a soul, won't you. We're keeping it a secret. And I hope one day you and Robert will be as happy as we are," she said, snuggling down into bed.

I let that go. No use explaining. Anyway, better she should think that than anything else.

Next morning while the others were packing I escaped and went to the beach for the last time. There was a steep flight of steps hewn out of the rock leading down to the sea. I took off my beach robe and ran in. The water was wonderful – cool and fresh and invigorating. I swam out a long way, round the edge of the cove where I found a large rock slipping into the sea, and I put my feet down and hauled myself onto it. I sat on it with my legs dangling in the sea and my hair hanging over my shoulders and felt forsaken. The lonely mermaid, I thought sadly. Even in my unhappiness I could appreciate this thought. It was peaceful sitting on the rock and the sea looked quite green beneath me. Here I could forget about the others, about Lily and Edward.

Then I heard splashing sounds, and out of the corner of my eye I saw Edward swimming round the point towards me. I didn't want to see him. I pretended I hadn't, until finally he swam right up to my rock and said, "Make room for me on that rock, Angie, I'm coming up."

"Couldn't you find a rock of your own?" I said.

He ignored that. "I saw you from my bedroom window," he said. "Listen, Angie – this may come as a shock to you. Lily has run away with the Spanish waiter."

I gasped. It couldn't be true!

"But I thought…"

"I know what you thought. Or rather, what you wanted to think. After all, it was you who kept throwing Lily and me together. We only fell for it because we thought you and Robert wanted to be on your own."

I knew he was speaking the truth. I had been blind.

"All the time it was you I loved, Angie," he said and he looked at me again, that same lingering look that he had given me last night that had done such strange fluttery things to my heart.

He told me how when they had left the Casino the previous night Carlos had been outside waiting for Lily and he had gone back to the hotel alone. And they must have been meeting every afternoon when I had thought Lily was with Edward.

"But then what were *you* doing in the afternoons, Edward?" I asked suddenly.

"Well," he admitted, "As a matter of fact…" and he looked a little shame-faced, "I was having a siesta."

"Oh Edward, you are hopeless!" I laughed, hugging him; and presently he pushed me into the green, green sea and together, slowly, we swam back to the shore.

Sold to *Red Letter*, 1975

Love for Raoul

Every day I see him, the man of my dreams. He is amazing and wonderful. The problem is that he doesn't see me, which is sad. Worse than sad, it's tragic. It's desperate.

He's very tall, this man – well so you would expect, and he has fair hair and deep blue eyes – well those you might expect too, I suppose, since men of women's dreams nearly always have. His name is Raoul. Funny name, Raoul, sounds like growl, and that's what he's apt to do to me as a rule. He's very serious, he hardly ever smiles, but when he does it's a thing of beauty, something to remember for the rest of your life, and maybe I'll have to – but don't say that!

Every day at the same time he comes through our office on the way to his and I sit at my desk and wait for the swing doors to swing open and for him to swing through – well no, that's not quite right, he's not the swinging type really, not even jaunty – but he comes in firmly, with rugged – well maybe not quite rugged – determination.

Yes, that's it, determination. He wears…

"Caroline Brown! Stop staring into the middle distance and get on with your work."

"Yes, Miss Frobisher."

I'm not staring into the middle distance, actually. I'm staring at the round porthole windows in the swing doors. Silly old faggot. Miss Frobisher's our supervisor. Through the porthole I see – Andrew Fullerton. Randy Andy, we call him. Or Sexy Rexy.

"And how's the luscious Caroline today?" he says, giving my shoulder a squeeze as he goes by.

"Oh go away Andy, can't you see I'm busy?" I retort.

"Not with the naked eye," he quips.

That's all he ever thinks about. Nakedness. Nudity. Not like Raoul. That's the trouble. Oh well. As I was saying, he wears a dark suit as a rule – Raoul, that is. Or sometimes a light raincoat if it's raining, and if it isn't he carries it over his arm in case it does later – and sometimes, just sometimes, the raincoat brushes against my desk – seeing as I sit on the aisle – as he goes past, but not often, because he's usually very careful to steer a middle course and not touch anyone or anything.

Then at around 10 I go into Eleanor's office – she's his secretary – with the coffee tray and give one cup to Eleanor and then into his office with his. It's only instant, instant coffee, instant milk and instant boiling water from the Ascot, but I make sure his cup is extra clean and his spoon polished and what else can you expect in an office? We're not Caffè Nero, there's no Caffè Nero or Starbucks round here.

"There you are, Mr Hampson."

"Thank you."

"Would you like some sugar?

"No thanks, I don't take it."

"Oh, I keep forgetting." (I don't really, but it prolongs the conversation.)

"Would you like a doughnut from the corner shop?"

"No, thanks."

"Or a sticky bun?"

"No, thanks."

(I always ask him this and he always says no but I keep hoping anyway.)

"It's no trouble."

"No!" He glares, and I leave the office backwards, so's not to miss a precious second, and bump into Eleanor's filing cabinet.

"Ouch!"

"Serves you right."

"It shouldn't have such sharp corners. I've a good mind to invent a filing cabinet with sleek rounded corners. It would sell like a bomb."

"Don't count on it."

"Well – maybe you're right. I say Eleanor, are you thinking of leaving here?"

"Why should I?"

"So's I could be promoted to your job."

"*You*, Caroline? You must be joking."

People always say that to me, as if I was inefficient or something. It's just as well I'm not over-sensitive.

"I mean it, Eleanor. Why shouldn't I be promoted to your job?"

"You couldn't do it in a hundred years."

"Well thank you very much. Thank you very much for those few heart-warming words of confidence."

"I don't mean to hurt your feelings, Caroline, but honestly you couldn't cope with the pace of this job. Mr Hampson keeps one constantly at it."

"At what?"

"Not *that!*"

"Pity."

"Anyway, I'm not thinking of leaving."

I never really thought she would be.

"You know I'm mad about him, Eleanor."

"I could hardly fail to notice that. No one could fail to notice that."

"Do I have a chance with him, d'you think?"

"I wouldn't know."

"Well, for a kick-off, has he got a wife? Or a fiancée?"

"No, but just as bad, he's got a mother."

"Oh!"

"She's apt to ring up and ask if he got the fish. You know."

That was a bit of a blow, I'll admit. I had to revise my picture of Mr Hampson, Away From The Office, to take in The Mother. I visualised him arriving home to be met by a grey-haired paragon, bearing a pile of freshly-ironed shirts in one hand and a plate of steak and kidney pudding in the other. She could, I thought, be quite a stumbling block.

"Look Eleanor," I said, "I'll have to enlist your aid. I'm desperate. *You'll* have to tell me what makes him tick."

"OK," she said. "But then what will you do?"

"When I've built up a picture of the inner man I'll know what kind of girl I'll have to be for him to fall madly in love – and then can't you just see the picture? Wedding bells and orange blossom."

"And Mother…"

"Yes – but I'm sure we'll get round that," I said.

Just then Mr Hampson appeared at the door.

"What, still here?" he said to me. (Not *too* well pleased, I thought, and it was not the most encouraging of remarks, either.)

"Eleanor, could you come in and bring that letter from Webbs?"

Just the same, I mused, he might have meant it differently. I tried out various permutations: WHAT, still here? What, STILL here? What, still HERE? Wacko and three cheers didn't seem to go with any of them.

A week later Eleanor had some news for me.

"He likes Shakespeare," she said.

I can't say I rejoiced to hear that. Still, I thought, if he likes Shakespeare I'll just have to learn to like him too, won't I? I mean, it's not as if Raoul's the first person to like Shakespeare, is it? There's lots of others – quite normal people, I expect. (Not that I can think of anyone off-hand, except our old English teacher, and she was a right twit, but still.)

"I had to ring up for tickets," continued Eleanor.

"Oh really? How many? And when for?"

"Two, for Friday the 21st July."

"Two? Friday the 21st July – yes, I would be available then. D'you have any idea who the other ticket's for?"

"None whatever. Mother, maybe."

"Oh blast, Mother! Why can't she stop interfering? What's the play?"

"Romeo and Juliet."

Romeo and Juliet! My mind raced ahead. What a bit of luck. The very thing to put a man, even Raoul, in the mood for love. I wondered if I should tint my hair red.

"D'you see me with red hair, Eleanor?"

"Not especially," she said tactfully.

Well I tried to read Romeo and Juliet, I really did, and it's damn boring if you want to know. The bit about him and her, it seems to get lost in so much other completely irrelevant stuff.

"Isn't there anything else," I asked Eleanor eventually, "that Raoul likes?"

"Mozart."

I groaned. "Apart from Mozart. Something normal, like – *East Enders* or *The X Factor.*"

Eleanor said gravely, "I think, you know, you're going to have to raise your sights a little. Develop a slightly more discerning taste."

"You might be right. I know, I'll take a cultural course at night school. What d'you think I should do first? Philosophy? Archaeology? French Literature?" The prospect of all three filled me with gloom.

Then Mr Hampson appeared round the door, all six foot four of him, with tousled fair hair and startling blue eyes. "I want you in my office, Eleanor," he said.

Why, the luck of some people! I want you, I need you, I must have you.

"What, all in the office, Mr Hampson?"

"Yes, shut the door, get on the floor and shut up..."

I became aware that Mr Hampson was staring at me with unmitigated annoyance.

"You here again?" he said, and this time there was no mistaking his meaning.

"I came to see if you'd like a doughnut... or a sticky bun," I faltered.

"Neither," he said coldly and dismissively, and withdrew into his office.

I must say I'm not doing too well, am I? You couldn't, with any stretch of the imagination, say I was making progress, could you? Oh Raoul – growl....

But hope springs eternal in every damsel's breast. Or something. I read that somewhere lately. Probably Juliet said it to Romeo.

The next week Eleanor told me that Raoul liked tennis.

"Now that has possibilities," I said. I could see myself coming into the office in a crisply pleated white skirt and saying "Anyone for tennis?" Or he could say it himself, all dressed up in his white flannels and vee-necked cable-stitched sweater. He'd look fantastic. He'd say, "Anyone for tennis?" and I'd answer in a sultry undertone, "Just try me," and we'd stare at one another and then everything would go blurred and we'd disappear down the central aisle, through the swing doors and out into the sunset.

"Caroline Brown, *will* you get on with your work?"

"Yes, Miss Frobisher."

Randy Andy caught hold of my hand as I passed his desk. "How's my favourite girl?"

"I am not your girl, favourite or otherwise."

"How do you know?" he said, and looked at me the way I wish Raoul would.

A month has passed, and Eleanor has come up with something not even I could have guessed.

"I don't quite know how to tell you this," she said.

"Start at the beginning, go on to the end and then stop."

"All right, I will. You know those two theatre tickets for *Romeo and Juliet*?"

"Friday the 21st July. Yes?"

"I know who he's going to take."

"You do?"

"I do."

"Who?"

She hesitated.

"Go on then," I said, "Don't keep me in suspense."

"Me."

"You?"

"Yes. I know, I can't believe it either."

I noticed her eyes were all starry.

"He took me to dinner last week and told me he loved me!"

"Oh Eleanor! It must have been you all the time. Now that's what I call a real romance. I see it all – wedding bells..."

"And orange blossom," said Eleanor dreamily.

"And Mother!" I said, suddenly appalled.

"Never mind," she said, "We'll get round that. Mother's emigrating to join her daughter in Australia."

"Some people have all the luck! I'm awfully glad it's you," I said.

"I must say, you've taken it very well," she said.

"Yes, well I'm a good loser," I said generously.

And besides, Raoul's not for me, I see that now. All that Shakespeare and Mozart and who's for tennis, it's not my scene.

So you see, I'm left with Randy Andy. Well, maybe he's not so randy really. I mean, if your name's Andy you're bound to get nicknames like that, aren't you?

And it is nice to be somebody's favourite girl!

Plain Jane and the
Great Author

I was pretty fed up, not to say livid, when my mother broke the news to me. "Philip," she began in her tentative way, "Next week, when your aunt and uncle go to Spain…"

"Oh no," I groaned, "Don't tell me. You've invited Cousin Jane to stay. Oh my God, what have you let us in for?"

"I'm sorry," she said, "What else could I do but ask her? She was supposed to be going to Scotland to stay with a school friend, but apparently the friend's brother's gone down with measles so it's off, and there was nowhere else for Jane to go. You couldn't let the poor girl stay in that house all on her own now, could you?"

"I could," I said.

"Anyhow I had to offer and of course your Aunt Vi jumped at it."

"Well," I said glumly. "Don't expect me to do anything about her, will you?"

But even as I spoke I knew I'd have to. My mother would count on me to help entertain my dear cousin. Sure enough…

"Look, I know it's asking an awful lot," said my mother, "But could you possibly postpone your Welsh camping holiday? You'll still have a month after Jane goes and I'm counting on you to help entertain her."

There – what did I tell you?

I said resignedly, "Oh, all right. Though whether I'll be able to rearrange it at this stage I rather doubt, but all right, I'll try. Damn and blast Jane!"

Next day I went to meet her at the station. Perhaps she's changed, I thought in a wild moment. Perhaps she's blossomed into the most beautiful and charming and talented girl I've ever seen in my life.

No such luck. She was worse if anything, lumpy with mud-coloured hair scraped back behind her ears, and just to top it, glasses. I wondered if she had any idea at all how my spirits fell when I saw her and how distastefully I viewed the prospect of her visit. But I doubt it, not Jane. She has the hide of a rhinoceros. Besides, I didn't let on. Well I mean, you can't really, can you? You've got to be polite. And she was so obviously glad to see me – that was the pathetic part.

"Now let me see, Jane," I said in my best older cousin manner. "You're fourteen now, aren't you?"

"No, fifteen," she corrected me. "And let me see, you must be all of seventeen – am I right?"

"Nineteen," I said briefly. I felt irritated. For two pins I'd have said she was sending me up.

"And have you written your learned novel yet? I've always heard about your wanting to be a Norther," she said wickedly.

"Actually no," I admitted. But she had touched my weak spot. I didn't normally let it get around about my ambitions to be a Great Writer, but of course you can't trust mothers. I could just see Mum and Aunt Vi yackety-yacking about it, blast them. I'd got as far as Chapter One and I'd hoped to add to it quite substantially this holiday. The trouble was, I kept putting it off. To get these marvellously inspired wise and noble thoughts was easy, but when I came to put them down on paper they seemed to undergo a subtle change from wise to prudish, original to commonplace. Why that was, I couldn't make out. Anyway it was easy to say I was *going* to do it and put it off into the vague future, and so much less tedious than actually doing it.

"We're going to have a marvellous two weeks while I'm here, you'll see," Jane said confidently.

"D'you think so?" I said.

She sure was sure of herself, I thought. By the way, did I tell you her teeth stuck out? Well they do. (As well as everything else.)

"We'll swim in the river and go for walks up that hill behind your house and have picnics. And we'll play tennis. You do still play tennis, don't you? And perhaps we'll have a barbecue one day. That would be fun, wouldn't it?"

"Yes," I said. I felt deeply depressed. I looked at my calendar. It was now August. In eight weeks I would be going up to Oxford. How could I wait that long? How would the time ever pass? I tried to rearrange my Welsh camping holiday, and for a time I thought I had succeeded. After I'd cancelled my side of it and Trevor and Matt had agreed to postpone it for three weeks, Trevor found he couldn't go then after all, so they were going to take it as originally planned but WITHOUT ME. I was hurt and put out, betrayed by my best friends. I mean, Matt didn't have to go with Trevor, did he? "Et tu, Brute?" I said sadly to Matt and he nodded and said yes, or si, or whatever it was. Well thank you Jane, I said to the banana I was at the time eating. Thank you very very much, I must say. The banana looked back at me. It was a better shape than Jane anyway.

We did everything just as Jane had said. We bathed in the river, and it was surprisingly refreshing. Jane wore a black woollen costume that might have been her grandmother's. It certainly showed up her lumpy figure to distraction.

"D'you think I've filled out since you saw me last?" she asked.

"I would say so," I replied with caution.

"I'm not too fat, am I?" she asked anxiously.

What could one say?

"I mean, d'you like your girls on the ripe side?"

I shuddered. "Jane, really......."

"I'm sorry, I shouldn't have asked you that. I'm irrepressible, everyone says so."

We played tennis. Jane was a rabbit at tennis. I've seen some rabbits, but this was the rabbityest rabbit of them all and the curious thing was, she had no idea of it. She either missed the ball altogether or hit it wildly, miles into the air. It was embarrassing. We played on some public courts that were overlooked by a main road and I was on tenterhooks in case someone who knew me saw us from the top of a bus, but Jane played on blithely, getting steadily pinker and punctuating her shots with monotonous cries of "Sorry!"

She was a pain, a pest. I could do nothing I wanted with her around. She reminded me of a little puppy, grimly determined to go everywhere I went, dejected if spurned but joyously forgiving. Nothing seemed to upset her for long. How could I get rid of her?

One day I felt a sudden inspiration to write Chapter Two of the Great Novel. I felt so inspired I could have burst. If it's inside it's got to come out, my mother always says – so wisely – and my goodness, this would come out, if I could only have the chance to be alone. I must just get away from Jane!

But after breakfast she bounced up to me in her usual cheerful way. "I see you're ready," she said. "I don't think it'll rain but I've put plastic macs in to be on the safe side."

I looked gloomily at the basket she carried. "Look Jane, I don't know what you intended, but..."

"A picnic on top of Lodge Hill, don't you remember? We discussed it yesterday. Aunt Gwen and I have made us a smashing lunch. Aunt Gwen says we can get a bus as far as Arundel Wood and walk up from there."

"I'm sorry, but you'll have to count me out."

She looked as if she'd been kicked. "How d'you mean, Philip?"

"I mean that I'm not coming. I'm going for a walk."

"I'll come with you," she said immediately.

"By myself, if you don't mind. I want to think."

"I promise I won't say a word."

"No, but you see I want to write."

"Oh, I thought you wanted to walk?"

"Well I do but I want to think as well."

"*And* write?"

"Right."

"Well, I shan't disturb you if I just come too."

"But you will, don't you see? You'll be there," I said irritably, "and that's enough to put me off."

My mother came into the room then. "Are you ready?" she asked.

"We're not going. Philip *varnts to be alon*!" said Jane.

"Oh Philip!" said my mother reproachfully (suddenly the house seemed full of kicked-looking females). "Don't disappoint poor Jane."

"But what about my novel?" I demanded.

"Philip dear," said my mother, "The novel's waited seven years. I really don't think two weeks will make any difference."

"Oh don't you?" I said, "Well I bet Sebastian Faulks doesn't keep having to be interrupted when he gets an idea. Or D.H. Lawrence."

"D.H. Lawrence is dead," said Jane.

"Well I bet he didn't get interrupted when he was alive."

"I didn't know you were writing that sort of book," she added significantly.

"Lawrence didn't just write that sort of book," I said.

"Oh you do know the one I mean, then!"

Funny the way I kept feeling she was laughing at me.

So we went on the picnic to Lodge Hill. Well, of course. All that inspiration gone for a burton, I thought sadly. All those sentences sizzling out of the top of my head doomed to evaporate in the desert air. We sat on top of Lodge Hill and Jane dispensed ham rolls and cider and as she bent over the picnic basket I looked at her dispassionately and imagined wringing her podgy neck like a chicken's (not that I have ever wrung a chicken's) and hanging her from a hook in a fishmonger's shop. It cheered me up quite a lot. I thought it might be more fulfilling to abandon the Great Writer idea and become the Boston Strangler instead. I thought the Boston Strangler might well have started like this if he'd had someone like my cousin Jane to practise on.

A couple of days later Tim, a friend of mine, phoned up. There was a motor bike rally on in a neighbouring town and he wanted me to go with him.

"Oh yippee!" said Jane when I told her. "I love motor bike rallies. We can easily put off our barbecue till tomorrow."

"Look Jane," I said, "I'm going on my own with a pal. I'm sorry but – well it's just the two of us this time."

Again that kicked look.

"You mean, you're not going to take me with you?"

"Look, there won't be any other girls with us."

"I don't mind."

"You wouldn't enjoy it."

"I would, I would!"

"It's just the two of us, you weren't invited."

"Oh please Philip, I won't get in your way."

"For crying out loud," I said exasperated. "Will you stop getting in my hair? You've already ruined my holiday, can't you be content with that? You messed up my Welsh camping holiday and you've stopped me getting on with my novel. I've done enough things with you haven't I? Haven't I gone on walks and swims and picnics with you? I mean OK, but enough's enough. Doesn't it ever occur to you that I might want to get away on my own sometimes, without having to have an ugly, buck-teethed cousin trailing after me all the time?"

She had gone quite white. "I had no idea you felt like that, Philip," she said.

"No – well maybe I was too polite to tell you."

"I thought you'd enjoyed our walks and picnics."

"Well now you know, don't you?"

I knew I was being brutal, but she didn't seem to understand anything else.

I went on the motor bike rally with Tim and it was a good day out. I enjoyed it. I thought about Jane once – no more. I would make it up to her in the last two days of her visit, I thought lightly. But when I got home at the end of the day she wasn't there.

"Where is she? Not gone out on her own, surely!"

"She went home," said my mother. "It seems a little odd to me, but she insisted on going. Said she wanted to open up the house ready for her parents' return."

"And you mean – you *let* her go?"

"Well I had no choice, she was quite determined. She'd only got two more days here anyway."

"Did she seem upset or anything?"

"No. Well why should she be upset? Oh Philip – don't tell me you quarrelled?"

"No," I answered. I wouldn't tell her anything she didn't want to hear. Besides, we hadn't actually quarrelled, had we? I'd just driven her away, that was all. She shouldn't be so touchy, I thought. I didn't feel remorse, just relief that she had gone. At last I was free again. Now I had all the time I could want in which to write my novel.

Next day I took my notebook and climbed the hill behind our house. I sat down on a clump of heather which turned out to be a disguised ant-hill, and presently ants began to infiltrate under my shirt and up my trousers. How Jane would have laughed if she had been there. I didn't seem to feel much like writing after all, so after a while I put the book away and climbed back down the hill again.

Next day I walked up a different hill and the next to a valley, but it might as well have been the Slough of Despond.

"What's the matter?" said my mother.

"Nothing."

"You seem to be mooning about a bit. You don't seem to have anything to do."

She was right. I felt strangely flat and at a loss. I had wanted Jane to go, but now that she had I wasn't glad after all. There's only one word to describe how I felt, and that's homesick. It may seem strange but I felt homesick for Jane and lonely without her. And I felt sorry too — really sorry that I hadn't been nicer to her.

As for the novel, many times I sat and stared at the blank pages of my notebook, but when I came to write I couldn't do it. What was there to write about?

You see — I had nothing to say.

This story was sold to Just 17

Lunch at Pepe's

"If only I was sophisticated!" sighed Patsy Ann. "Then I wouldn't mind eating lunch by myself."

"I'm afraid it's the rule," said Maureen. "One of us has to be here in the lunch-hour, otherwise I'd come with you. Come on, Patsy," she added. "You'll have to grow up a bit now you're a working girl. Stop being so timid. There's absolutely nothing wrong with you – you've just as much right to go into a restaurant as anybody else. Just have a bit of confidence."

"But the agony of it!" said Patsy Ann, "All eyes on you, some pitying and the rest eyeing you up with idle curiosity. You read the label on the sauce bottle over and over or stare out of the window as if you've just caught sight of something absolutely riveting outside. Anything for somewhere to feast your eyes."

"Why don't you take a good book?"

"I can't seem to concentrate on reading somehow. I've hardly read a book since leaving school and as for good books they're the worst. I can barely manage the first page."

"You could bring sandwiches, like I do."

"My sandwiches are so disgusting I never feel like eating them when the time comes."

"Yes, I see what you mean." (Maureen had sampled one of Patsy's the previous day.) "Perhaps if you tried slicing the tomatoes instead of just squashing them between two bits of bread they wouldn't be so squelchy," she said. "But maybe you're just not the sandwich type."

"I guess not."

"Why don't you try Pepe's, that new place in East Street? I haven't been myself but I've heard it's nice, all scrubbed pine and red checked tablecloths. Cheap, cheerful and homely. You won't feel conspicuous there."

"All right, I will," said Patsy. "East Street, you said? Cheerio, I'll see you later."

It was pouring with rain, absolutely tippling down. Patsy put up her umbrella, but it was a silly paltry thing that kept blowing inside out and one of the spokes was bent and poked inelegantly through to the other side, so she was thankful to get to East Street and the shelter of the restaurant with its warm pink lights setting the windows aglow. She went down a step and had to duck slightly because the entrance door was so low. Inside it was even nicer than it looked from the street, simple and homely and cheap, with pine tables and red checked tablecloths, just as Maureen had said. There were candles and little posies of flowers on each table.

But it *was* rather crowded. She stood for a panicky moment inside the door wondering where to sit and her plastic see-through mac steamed and the water from her umbrella made a little puddle on the floor. Everyone stared, as they always do, and paused with their forks half-way to their mouths, and rather than plunge through them all she planted herself quickly at the first empty seat she could see at a table next to a window and with three other people at it already.

Oh dear – *three other people!* They looked at her with surprise, especially as there were other empty tables she could have picked on instead of theirs, but somehow it was too late to move. To make matters worse or at least more complicated, the three appeared to be easily the most interesting and/or beautiful in the room. Had they worn hand-knitted woollies with brown and white dogs across their fronts and push-on felt hats it mightn't have been so bad, but these three looked as if they had descended from another planet, like Hollywood for instance. There was a tall, dark, handsome man on her left with a sardonic sneer on his face, and a beautiful aloof girl opposite with pale, gleaming hair piled elegantly on her head, and on her right a blond bearded giant of a man with deep blue eyes, like some intellectual Viking.

"Well, well!" said the dark man with the sardonic look, "What have we here? A young, wet female, if I'm not much mistaken."

"I'm s-sorry," she said in a flurry, half rising. "Isn't this seat free?"

"I'm not sure," said the man, "Are you free, Seat? 'I'm free – it's free, sit down."

"Ivan, really!" said the aloof girl aloofly.

Patsy sat gingerly and slid the umbrella under the table, where it hooked itself round the Viking's ankle. "There's an umbrella and coat stand over there," he said gently, unhooking himself.

"Oh thank you." She got up and promptly tripped over the umbrella and sprawled headlong in the aisle between the tables. And everyone stared, as they always do, their forks half-way to their mouths.

"Are you all right?" said the bearded Viking, helping her to her feet.

"Y-yes thank you," she stammered, scarlet faced. She practically ran the full length of the red-checked tables to the coat stand. It *would* have to be as far away as possible. She put the umbrella in the stand where it rested aloft on its broken spoke, hung her plastic mac on an overburdened hook and had just turned away to go back to the table when she heard a terrible rushing crash, and turned to watch one plastic lady's mac and fifteen heavy gents' overcoats bite the dust.

"Oh dear, I'm *terribly* sorry!" gasped Patsy. Puce in the face, she bent to pick them up, but there was now no possibility of their going back on the hooks and nowhere else they could go instead except across a chair at a table where the occupants stared coldly at having their view suddenly obscured. Once more she ran the gauntlet of the room, manoeuvring her way back through the crowded tables, still as crimson in the face as if she'd been naked, in her boring blue skirt and yellow jumper, and sat down quickly.

A waiter came across and handed her an enormous menu and oh - it was VERY EXPENSIVE! To think she had been deceived (and Maureen had been deceived) by the simple cottagey atmosphere and the simple checked tablecloths into thinking it would be a simple cheap meal – no siree! But to walk out now meant traversing the whole of the room to retrieve her despised and steaming plastic mac and umbrella with its broken spoke, and that she could not do. It was too late. She stared at the enormous menu and saw none of it. All the items merged together in a terrifying great blur, while the waiter hovered over her, his notebook in his hand.

At last the Viking, who must have been aware of this traumatic silence on his left, said "Why not try the Pâté Maison? I can recommend it."

"Can you?" she said gratefully. It was amongst the starters, yet it cost little short of the five pound note she had in her purse.

"I'll have the Pâté Maison," she said to the waiter, "if that's all right."

"That *ees* all right, ees very goot, oll things here vary goot," said the waiter, offended.

"I'm sure they are," she said hastily.

"And – to follow?"

"Oh – nothing to follow."

"Nussing?"

"Nussing."

"It is unheard of to have nussing to follow," said the man called Ivan with the sarcastic voice.

"I'm not hungry," she explained, "I'm - slimming."

"You've no need to slim," said the Viking. "You're already as slim as a reed."

"Come now, Jago, have you ever actually seen a reed?" said Ivan. "They're a bit straight and narrow, reeds are. With a nasty cutting edge as a rule."

"True – not a very good simile," said the Viking.

Then they seemed to lose interest and turned away to continue their interrupted conversation about books and writers – way above her head. She gathered they were something in the theatre world, the stage or TV perhaps. They were not, at any rate, in the office of a small company that made the springs for ballpoint pens, that was quite clear.

"Now Waugh," said Ivan, the one with the sarcastic voice, "has a different 'genre' don't you think, Jago?"

"Oh I disagree entirely," said the Viking.

Some waiters arrived with three luscious-looking steaks, garnished with mushrooms and tomato. "Mm, they look good," said Patsy Ann.

The next moment she could have bitten her tongue out.

"Did I hear a voice?" said Ivan the Terrible. "Yes, I *did* hear a voice. It must have come from here, I think. This decidedly pink, still damp young female spoke. Did you speak, Young Female?"

"No – no, I only – "

"It spoke again! Tell me, Young Female, what are *your* views on Waugh?"

"War," she said resigned to her fate, "is unnecessary, an immature way to settle an argument."

There was a stunned silence. Then the Viking laughed. "My sentiments entirely," he said. He turned to Patsy Ann, "What's your name by the way? I think we ought to know that, since we're sharing a table."

"Patsy Ann."

"And what do you do?"

"I'm a typist. I work in an office."

"Oh really?" They looked at her as if she were an insect under the microscope. She hesitated. "We – make springs for ballpoint pens. At least we don't make them ourselves, we just work for a company that does."

Ivan was helping himself to French fries. He turned and inspected her quizzically. "I suppose somebody has to," he remarked.

"Ivan, really!" said the girl. "That's rather rude, you know."

"My speciality," said Ivan. "Rudeness."

"Take no notice," said Jago. "How long have you worked there?"

"It's my fourth day."

"You're quite a new girl, then."

"Yes."

"Are you a reader, my dear?" said Ivan. "What do you read? Let me guess. What would a young, pink, slightly damp English female read – Rupert Brooke, I should think. Right?"

"Wrong," said Patsy, stung by his sarcasm. "Cornflakes packets, or Rice Krispies. There's quite a lot of reading on them you know. History and geography and so forth, recipes too sometimes, and you get something different every six weeks or so."

"I do believe she means it," said Ivan.

The aloof girl gave an aloof laugh, "*Une ingénue*," she said.

The waiter arrived and set before Patsy a plate with a piece of pâté like a small ice cube on a lettuce leaf with a sliver of tomato. She nibbled at it, unsure whether to use her knife and fork – weren't you supposed to spread it on mouthfuls of toast or something? Or should it be a fork on its own?

Seeing her hesitate, Jago the Viking said, "Here's your toast."

"Oh thank you."

"I'm Jago, and this is Anita – she's an actress. Anita Lane – I expect you've seen her on the small screen."

"Yes," she lied. "That's wonderful!"

Anita Lane half smiled and inclined her head.

"And what do you do?" Patsy asked, turning to Jago.

"I write scripts, for TV. I co-write on various series."

"You must all lead such interesting lives. I suppose other people must seem quite ordinary to you."

"Extraordinarily ordinary," said Ivan, helping himself to courgettes, but Jago smiled at her. "Not so ordinary – it's refreshing to meet someone unspoilt and genuine for a change. Most of the girls I meet seem to be born cynical and blasé."

"Well, thanks Jago," said Anita, "It's been nice knowing you."

"I don't mean you, Anita."

"Don't you?" she said coolly.

"Cut!" said Ivan. He helped himself to more French fries.

"What does *he* do?" asked Patsy Ann.

"He's a producer."

"I bet he gets the best out of people," she said, "Shock treatment."

Ivan turned to her with raised eyebrows. "You were right about her the first time, Jago," he said. "She *is* like a reed with a cutting edge!"

Jago laughed. "Good for you," he said to her. "but you mustn't mind him – he doesn't know how to behave." He looked at her empty plate. "You've hardly had anything to eat. Why don't you have a steak?"

"No, thank you," she said.

"It's good, I can recommend it. Waiter!"

"No, please Jago, you don't understand, I –"

"Waiter!" he said, ignoring her. "We'll have a T-bone steak with mushrooms for the young lady. And bring another wine glass."

It was no use arguing. The steak arrived, succulent and delicious. The waiter put it before her with a flourish. She felt terrible, like a thief. There could be no more awful feeling than eating a meal in an expensive restaurant and not having enough money to pay for it.

"I'll do the washing up," she said to the waiter in a low voice.

"Si?" he said.

"But not this afternoon, if you don't mind. I have to go back to the office. I'll come this evening instead. I suppose you are open in the evenings?"

"Si?"

"Or have you got a dish washer? Never mind, I'll explain to the Manager later."

She ate the steak and drank the wine poured out for her by Jago with the utmost enjoyment. After all, she reasoned, if you're going to sink anyway you might as well go down with all flags flying. And she probably wouldn't be charged for the wine, seeing as it came out of their bottle.

Meanwhile the other three were having coffee, and presently Ivan summoned the waiter, who brought them their bill. Ivan settled it with an American Express card. How easy and what a marvellous way to pay for a meal, thought Patsy Ann, who did not possess a credit card.

They began to gather their things together prior to leaving, and she felt sad as if she were being abandoned. She wanted to say, 'Please don't go!', but of course that was absurd.

They stood up. Ivan the Terrible gave a deep exaggerated bow. "Goodbye, Young Female. A little drier now, I think," he commented. Anita bestowed a faint smile upon her.

"Goodbye," said Jago. And then they were gone.

She felt lonely without them. She had rubbed shoulders with the gods and now that they had vanished, life was a little bleaker than before. She finished her steak and laid her knife and fork carefully together. There was no sauce bottle to look at and she felt people were staring, but she didn't care. *Go ahead and stare*, she thought, *you'll stare a whole lot more when the bill comes and I'm arrested*.

The waiter came back with a cup of coffee.

"I didn't order this," she said.

"Si?" said the waiter.

"This — I did not — order!"

"Si?"

"Oh do stop saying si, you quite obviously don't. I think you'd better bring me my bill."

But he only shrugged, not seeming to understand.

It was time to go. Maureen would be wondering where she was. She got up, picked up her bag and made her way to the entrance. The Manager was standing near the door, smiling — not at her, surely? It must be the Manager, he was wearing a black coat instead of a white one. "About my bill," she said approaching him.

He waved it aside. "That is taken care of, Madame," he said. "The gentleman with the beard, he stayed behind and settled it."

"Oh!" she said faintly.

"There was a message." The Manager gave her a note scrawled on the back of an envelope. It was from Jago.

"I did enjoy meeting you," it said, "Perhaps we could have lunch next week too?"

The words spun in front of her eyes like whirling stars.

"Let me help Madame on with Madame's coat," said the Manager. He took the plastic mac and held it out for her at arm's length.

"Thank you," she said.

"We will see you next week at the same time, Madame?"

"Yes," she said happily, "you certainly will. It was the loveliest lunch I've ever had in the whole of my life"

The little waiter to whom she had been less than gracious, stood nearby smiling. She smiled back and pressed some coins into his hand.

"Next time," he said, "I find small table for two in dark corner, very romantic, si?"

"Si," she said, "Si."

He held open the door and she bent her head and went out to find the rain had finally stopped and the thin wintry sun had emerged to colour the pavements with gold.

Rendezvous with Rory

On Thursday Rory rang and asked me to meet him.

"It's a little difficult," I said. "I don't want to upset Brian."

"Please try," said Rory. Try to upset Brian, he meant.

"All right. It'll have to be the lunch hour, then. Where did you have in mind?"

"Harrods."

"It'll be packed with Christmas shoppers."

"Never mind, everywhere's packed at this time of year. Come to the usual place, and try to make it twelve-thirty. If you're late I'll go on through to Books."

"All right then."

But I was early, as it happened. I managed to squeeze myself through the crush of people on the ground floor choosing expensive gifts of silver and leatherware and jewellery, hampers of pâté de foie gras and smoked salmon, crystallized fruits, oranges in brandy, chocolate truffles and marrons glacés. The main display hall was beautiful, all silver and white and frosted glass, but I paused only for a passing glimpse as I sped through to join the crowds jostling for the lifts. Olive-skinned aquiline-nosed Arabs rubbed shoulders with pink-cheeked loud-voiced English women in tweeds, up from the country for the day.

It was quieter upstairs and I made my way easily to our old meeting place in the Pets Department. I gazed into the cages one by one. A fluffy grey Persian kitten gazed back at me, and past him three appealing long-haired dachshunds and next to them, a Cavalier King Charles spaniel with soulful eyes and glossy black and white markings.

"Which one are you having, Maggie?" said Rory into my ear.

"I don't know. I'm terribly torn, but I suppose in the end I'll plump for the Persian."

"I knew you would," said Rory, "You were always a catty girl."

"Darling!" I said with irony.

He laughed. "You know I don't mean it. Are you hungry?"

"Not so much."

"What about the Health Bar? Are you feeling in a raw carrot juice mood?"

"No – just raw."

"Ah. A good stiff gin is what you need."

We took the lift to the ground floor and went out. It was not an inspiring day for our clandestine meeting. I wish I could say the air was sparkling or the snow was falling in great white flakes, casting its silent mantle over all, but it was damp with beads of smutty moisture in the air.

We went to the bar of a nearby hotel and Rory ordered the drinks.

"Did I tell you," he said, "how good it is to see you again?"

"No you didn't."

"But I don't need to tell you, do I? You can read it in my eyes."

"My God," I said, "That sounds like a bad line from an old and rotten film."

"Thanks," he said, "for dampening the ardour."

"Well, what's the point? You know we agreed not to go on meeting."

I stared at a large lighted Christmas tree that almost smelt of damp pine in the corner of the bar-lounge. A pretend tree, its branches hung with pretend presents, large regularly-shaped packages wrapped in gold and silver paper.

"Are you ready for Christmas, Rory? Will it be just you and Lynne? How is Lynne, anyway?"

"As well as can be expected."

"Well, I don't know what can be expected."

"Headaches and things. You know."

"I see."

"She's a headachy sort of person."

"I hadn't realised."

"How's Brian?" he asked stiffly, not really wanting to know.

"Fine," I said, not really wanting to tell him.

We were silent, sipping our drinks, me twiddling the stem of my glass, him gazing at some spot left a bit, down a bit from my left ear.

"Just how involved with Brian are you?" he asked abruptly.

"Heavily," I said.

"Oh." He looked depressed.

"I owe him five hundred quid."

"That's sheer carelessness, Maggie," he said.

"I know."

"Well, what else?"

"He depends on me for everything."

"Like waking him in the morning, d'you mean? And making him cups of coffee?"

"That sort of thing, yes."

"Couldn't he get someone else to do that?"

"He wouldn't dream of looking for anyone else."

"Not even if he found out that you were unfaithful?"

"But I'm not, technically, am I?"

"You could be, technically."

"I could be," I agreed.

"I mean," said Rory, "It does strike me as funny – peculiar – that you've never mentioned love. Not once have you used the word."

"Oh well," I said, "That's because I find it embarrassing. After all we're not teenagers any more. It's not a word one bandies around."

"Or even affection," he continued. "Can't you even say you're fond of one another without squirming?"

"I suppose I could say that," I said.

"I mean, that's what strikes me," said Rory, "The total lack of enthusiasm."

"But why should I tell you how I feel about Brian?" I said. "You of all people. It's not your business."

"Every word you *don't* say tells me more," he said. "There's nothing, is there? That's why you're embarrassed. That's why you can't say anything, because there isn't anything to say. It's stone dead. If there ever *was* anything."

"Oh there was, to begin with."

"I suppose so," said Rory. "There always is, to begin with."

"Will you get me another gin?" I said. "I find this a very self-defeating conversation. I don't know why I agreed to meet you. We said we wouldn't see one another. We should have stuck to it. I don't know what you want from me, or what you expect me to say. That I don't love Brian? That he doesn't love me? That we're unhappy together?"

"That would be a start," said Rory. He stood up. He took my glass and went over to the bar.

"Don't get another tonic," I said. "I've got enough here."

I waited for him to come back. I took a nut that I didn't want. My mind was in a turmoil.

"You're looking thinner, and quite pale," he said when he returned with the glasses. "You're not still dieting, are you?"

"No."

"I expect it's missing me that's doing it. You're pining for me. Wasting away."

"I wish you'd shut up," I said.

"I think you ought to have something to eat."

"I couldn't eat a thing. I even choked on a nut."

"You *are* a nut, Maggie," he said tenderly. I blushed. It was the way he looked at me that did it.

"I'll tell you what I want," he said, continuing to look at me. "I want to take you away for Christmas. To that nice old hotel on the river where we stayed before. D'you remember?"

"Yes. Christmas at Windsor," I said nostalgically. "How could I forget? That was romantic, if you like! The roaring log fire in the great hall, the delicious hot punch. They welcomed us as if they really meant it."

"On Christmas morning we went to the service in the Chapel," he reminisced. "We walked up the hill with the church bells pealing. We thought we'd drop in at the castle for a drink afterwards."

I laughed. "Yes, but we went for a long walk instead, didn't we?" I said. "We went across the bridge over the river, and when we got half way we stopped and watched the water flow under the bridge. I threw a twig and we waited for it to come through the other side, but it never came."

"It must have got caught up somewhere," said Rory.

"I suppose so."

"D'you remember what we talked about?"

"Yes, I remember. What a lot of water must have passed under the bridge since then. Perhaps some of it is the same water, come round again."

"No, that's not possible. It has to be fresh water. It only goes under once. Just that one time."

We were silent, remembering.

"You'd never get into that hotel now anyway," I said. "It'll be booked to the hilt. It always is."

"I'm already in," said Rory. "I made the reservation in July."

"That was presumptuous."

"Not at all. If you hadn't agreed to come I'd have gone with Lynne."

"But I haven't agreed to come," I said.

"Well – will you?"

"How could I? Besides, it's too late now."

"No it isn't. It's just in time."

"But what would I say to Brian?"

"This is what you'll say," said Rory. "You'll say, 'Brian, we've made a mistake. We thought we loved one another but it was just an illusion. We should part before we make each other really unhappy, as we've made Rory. He hates living with his sister and he'll never love anyone but me. It was only meant to be a trial separation, we're still married and now I want to go back to my husband.'" He paused and looked at me. "I think that just about covers it, doesn't it?" he said.

I smiled and pushed away my glass. "Yes," I said, "That just about covers it."

This story won First Prize, Southport Seminar

The Lonely Rose

Once upon a time there was a queen whose garden was the most beautiful in the world. There grew flowers and shrubs of every scent and hue, and trees which had endured the seasons for centuries; there flew brilliantly-coloured butterflies, and birds of bright foliage whose songs would delight the most insensitive ear but to which it was the privilege of very few to listen. There was an orchard where the trees came out in pink and white blossom every year and bore fruit which was firm and plump, and in the long grass around grew daffodils and narcissi in wild abundance. There were gravel walks bordered with purple and crimson rhododendron bushes, and in their season flowered beds of tulips and forget-me-nots, sweet peas, carnations and freesias. Brightly-coloured fish swam in ornamental pools and waxen waterlilies floated on the surface of the water. There was an old wooden seat in a quiet corner surrounded by mauve and white lilac bushes whose fragrance was famed throughout the kingdom. There were plants of every shade, every scent, to every taste. But there was not one rose tree in the garden.

One day the Queen and her son the Prince Nicholas were walking over the lawns near the Palace. "Look," said the Queen, "Are not the tulips lovely? They have just come out this last week."

The Prince said nothing.

"And look at the gladioli!" she cried, "And the orchids – I do not remember ever seeing orchids so beautiful."

Still the Prince was silent.

"Why I declare," said his mother, "The smell of the jasmine almost overpowers me. But Nicholas," she turned to her son, "have you lost your tongue?"

"Mother," he said, "More than anything else I love roses. Yet you have no roses in the garden. Will you not plant some roses for me?"

"Why of course," answered the Queen, and smiled graciously.

So she sent for the Head Gardener and asked him to bring a small rose tree. When he had brought it, she told him to plant it in the centre of a tiny lawn in a hidden, faraway corner of the garden. And he did as she asked him.

At Christmas time the gardener came to the Queen and said, "Your Royal Highness, the little rose tree you planted is doing well. There should be some fine red roses on it in June."

In January came the cold weather. Heavy white snow fell upon the grass and thickly coated the branches of the trees. Icicles hung from the fountain in the middle of the ornamental pool. The frost was cruel to the buds of the flowers and nipped them off, but to the little rose tree it was merciful, and the tree continued to flourish. Months passed: April came, then May, then June. Suddenly twelve little hard green buds appeared and grew bigger day by day. At last the protective outer green coverings parted to show twelve shy little roses. Eleven of them were crimson red, but the twelfth rosebud was the purest white.

It was the height of summer and the garden was looking more beautiful than ever. The warm sun shone and the hours passed happily for the little rosebuds. They shook themselves, glanced round in wonder and stared with curiosity at everything that came in sight.

"Do you know," said one, "That we live in a Royal Garden?"

"Oh!" cried the other buds, "Isn't that wonderful! Isn't it fun to be alive and growing all the while and seeing all the many birds and bees and butterflies flitting past in this beautiful garden!"

Soon some bees came for their first visit to the rose-tree.

"Hello, little girls," they buzzed. "When are you coming out?"

"Soon, soon," murmured the buds, but they spoke so softly that the bees did not understand them.

Two yellow butterflies hovered near. "How strange," said one. "Do you see that white bud there? Whatever is a white rosebud doing growing on a red rose-tree?" And the other butterfly smiled and shrugged its wings and fluttered on.

But the little white bud was sad. "Is it true?" it asked of the other buds. "Am I really different from all of you?"

"Yes you are, it is true," they answered. "But after all, what does it matter?" So the little white bud was happy again.

"Tell me," she said to the little red bud on the branch below, "What is your dearest wish?"

"I never thought about it," said the red bud, "but perhaps most of all I should like to see the inside of the Royal Palace. What about you, little white sister?"

"Most in all the world," said the little white bud dreamily, "I should like to be of real importance to someone. What is life for if one is only to live and to die and to pass away without being remembered? I want to do some good while I am here, so that someone will say, 'I could not be happy were it not for the white rose.'

"My! What a strange thing to wish for!" giggled the little red bud.

Then the sun went down, and the twilight came, and the moon with all her stars, and the garden was bathed in magical white light. The little rosebuds quivered silently on their tree and watched the bats swoop low beneath the trees, and listened to a million crickets singing.

The next morning the buds were further out. An exotic scent pervaded each one of them and they cast shy, wondering glances at one another. Soon the bees came and loudly buzzed their approval.

"How beautiful you will be when you are full-blown," they buzzed and pressed closer to whisper the secrets of the garden into the inmost petals of each credulous rosebud. Once more the hours passed happily for the young buds and there was a feeling of exultation amongst them, because soon they would be in their prime.

The night came and went and when the sun rose early the next day, there quite suddenly were eleven perfect red roses on the little tree. But the twelfth remained a white bud, unchanged from yesterday.

"What is the matter with me?" wept the poor thing, and large dewy tears slipped from her petals to the earth.

"Do not weep," answered the red roses. "You are delicate; that is why your complexion is so pale. But never fear, your turn will come." And they turned airily away to flirt with their admirers and revel in their new-found beauty.

Later on the Queen took a walk in her garden, and passing down the path came to the lawn where the rose tree grew.

"Ah," she said to herself, "At last, and on the eve of my son's wedding day, the roses are out. "How beautiful they look!" And she went to fetch a pair of white gloves and a basket and some scissors.

"What an incredible scent!" she said bending over one. "Certainly Nicholas was right. I must plant some more roses in the garden. Then she took her scissors and cut the first rose and laid it in the basket.

"Why, how very strange! A white rosebud growing on a red rose tree – whoever heard of such a thing! Nature has indeed erred there. Well, I will cut the red roses and put them on the dinner table tonight. They will be a perfect centrepiece and how glad Nicholas will be to see them on his last evening." And she began to cut the roses one by one and place them in her basket.

"Alas! Do not go! Do not leave me!" cried the poor white rosebud.

"Do not worry, little sister," said the red roses. "Your turn will come. Farewell – be happy without us!"

"I am to be left! What is the matter with me?" moaned the white rosebud in despair. But the red roses were excited at the thought of seeing the palace and did not heed her.

At last there remained only the red rose on the branch beneath.

"Do not leave me here alone! Won't you hide?" begged the white bud.

"I cannot, it is too late," sighed the other, and she too was cut and carried off. "Farewell!" she cried.

How silent the garden had become! The white rose was far more unhappy and lonely than she had imagined without her sisters, and for her all the joy of the beautiful garden had vanished. The chances of her wish coming true seemed remote indeed. Far from being of importance to someone, she was not even important enough to adorn the Queen's table with the others.

But during the night she too was changed. The next day all the bees and all the butterflies came to visit her and they flitted back and forth.

"What is the matter now?" asked the rose wearily.

"You must be bewitched," they cried admiringly. "You are more luscious than any of your sisters and your scent is lovelier than all of theirs. You are the most perfect of flowers!" It was true: not only had the white rosebud bloomed into a rose, she was a queen of roses. But she was a lonely rose, and sad; she had become a rose too late.

Up at the palace there were great celebrations, for it was the wedding day of the young Prince Nicholas and, so it was rumoured, he was marrying the fairest lady in the land, as custom demanded. The excitement in the royal garden was intense. News travelled fast; there were red geraniums in boxes at every window in the palace eavesdropping on every royal conversation. They whispered their gleanings to the busy bees who spread the news to every growing flower and shrub in the garden. The birds and butterflies passed from the flowers to the great trees waiting patiently; they were always the last to hear anything, but they could keep and remember the secrets of the garden for more than a thousand years.

Prince Nicholas was being married in great ceremony at the vast cathedral in the centre of the town, and in the afternoon there would be a reception in the Royal State Palace. From there the young couple would drive to their new and lovely home, for the King was giving them half his kingdom as a wedding present.

The trees in the garden were sad at the thought of their prince leaving them. They had watched him grow up from a tiny infant and toddle on the lawns at the base of their trunks, and later on play hide-and-seek in the bushes with his nurse. As a serious student he had taken his books and studied them, lying on his back in the grass. He had gazed for hours at the blue chinks of sky showing between the leafy branches. He had always taken an interest in every growing thing, season by season. But now he would not come again to the garden.

It was therefore greatly to their surprise and delight when, late in the afternoon, a sparrow arrived with an important message. It flew swiftly around and informed everyone that the Prince and Princess were on their way to the Palace to say a last farewell before they set off on their journey. It was not long afterwards that they arrived, and because all the guests, not having seen them slip away, had remained at the reception, the Palace and the Royal Garden were deserted. The Prince took his bride from room to room, and finally he brought her through the French windows and led her across the lawn and down through the orchard. Soon they came to the patch leading to the hidden faraway corner of the garden; it was quiet and warm there, though the sun was sinking. In the middle of the lawn the lonely white rose, fresh and pure, glowed on the tree.

"Why, isn't that a beautiful rose!" cried the Princess. She bent forward to sniff its scent. "I do not think I have ever seen one so exquisite."

The Prince stared at the rose closely.

"This must be from the rose tree I asked my mother to plant a year ago," he murmured. Seeing its grace and perfection, he wondered again why there should be no other roses in the royal garden. He stretched out his hand, and the rose, remembering her wish, quivered with an uncertain joy. He plucked it at the base of its narrow stem and gave it to the Princess.

"For you," he said. "This rose has blossomed on our wedding day. Its beauty is only matched by your own, and you must have it as a token of my love for you. Its beauty cannot last, alas, yet though it must die I swear to you that I shall love you everlastingly."

She thanked him, and held the rose like a priceless treasure in her hands.

Soon afterwards they left the garden of his childhood behind them and set off on the journey to their new kingdom. For seven days they travelled, stopping only at night when they slept at modest wayside inns and leaving the next morning with the dawn. The journey was long and arduous but being young and in love, they were unaware of any discomfort or fatigue, and knew only a deep, dreamlike happiness.

The white rose too was happy. It was greatly cherished by the Princess, and to her surprise and delight, it lost none of its beauty but remained as pure and graceful as ever.

They expected to reach their destination on the night of the seventh day. The Princess watched the passing countryside and wondered with growing excitement what it would be like. But she was destined never to know.

Before the night came an accident befell the carriage. They had come to a fork in the road, and the Prince alighted to study the signs as to the direction they should take. As he stood on the grass bank by the side of the road he noticed how black the sky had become. Then a few drops of rain began to fall; there was a tremendous clap of thunder, followed by a flash of lightning which hit up the whole sky from horizon to horizon. At once the four jet-black horses, startled, leapt forward, and before the Prince could stop them they gathered up speed and tore away with the carriage behind them. The wheels spun round and round, the carriage rattled from side to side and the horses galloped faster and faster. Suddenly they came to a curve in the road and being unable to stop, they plunged over the brink, down a steep bank and into the river below. It all happened so quickly that nothing could have been done to save them.

When the Prince came dashing up, he found the carriage on its side with two of the horses sprawling nearby on the ground. One had escaped and was galloping in terror along the edge of the river, while the fourth was struggling in the water. The Prince wrenched open the carriage door and gathered up the limp, warm body of the Princess.

He laid her gently on the grass and knelt beside her with fear darkening his eyes.

"Alas," she whispered, "death has come to part us so soon. Do not let me die, Nicholas, I am afraid!"

"You shan't, you shan't!" he cried in frenzy.

"But it is too late," she said faintly. "Treasure my rose for me, Nicholas."

Then death passed over her, silently and slowly, as though with reluctance, and he was left alone.

He picked up the rose and held it in his hands. He had never known a rose to live so long; for seven days it had remained fresh and exquisite, and it was unbelievably beautiful still, while the body of his lovely Princess lay crushed and lifeless in the dust.

He caressed the petals of the beautiful rose with his fingers. "Oh, that you could bring my Princess back to life for me!" he cried. Then he sat down by the side of the road and wept.

The funeral of the Princess took place the next day and she was buried in a little churchyard not far from the place where she had died. After a short service the Prince knelt and placed the rose at the head of her grave, and he went into the church with his heart breaking, and prayed.

That night a white dove came down to the churchyard and settled on the Princess's tombstone.

"Fair rose," said the dove, "I have a choice to put before you. Here lies the Princess who can never breathe the air on earth again, while you breathe still, and though you will soon fade now, every summer you will bloom again. But if you could give up those precious days of life each year and lend your spirit to her, she could be reunited with her Prince."

The little rose lay on the grave and her petals fluttered.

"I cannot ask you to sacrifice yourself, white rose," said the dove. "You must make the choice yourself. Which will you do? Will you live to bloom each year, or will you give your life to the Princess who loved you?"

"If indeed the Princess could live again in my place, then I should have done some good in the world, and to her I shall have been important," said the rose. And wistfully she thought, "So my wish is coming true after all."

"This will mean everlasting death," warned the dove.

"I will accept it gladly," answered the rose.

Then the dove flew away, and presently the petals of the rose began to fade. Gradually they shrivelled and withered and died, and it was not long before the spirit of the rose went up to join that of the Princess in Paradise.

And every year afterwards, for a few precious days in the month of June, the Princess breathed once more, and for the brief space of a rose's lifetime she was reunited with her Prince.

But the white rose never bloomed again.

This story was broadcast on radio in 1956.

The Plastic Slipper

Once upon a time there was a beautiful young girl called Golda. The trouble was, she wasn't really that beautiful. Her skin wasn't as taut as it ought to have been in the places where it ought to have been, there were positive rally tracks above her nose, and the pouches beneath her eyes were so deep you could have stowed a baby kangaroo in each of them. And she wasn't all that young, either. She was actually forty-two years and seven months old, so you couldn't really call her a girl, in the strictest sense of the word. But what the hell, who wants to be strict? And at least her hair really was golden - a lot more golden than it had been when she was eighteen.

Golda's life had been sadly unsatisfactory so far; her marriage to a trendy go-getter had broken up, because he had gone and got more than he was entitled to and had ended up in Wormwood Scrubs. Her children had grown up and emigrated to Australia, which was just as well as she had not liked admitting to their ages. That left her at the age of forty-whatsit living in a dismal little house in the Liverpool suburb of Maghull with nothing but a budgie named Charlie – a right dead loss, he was – nursing an unrequited passion for a pop star called Frank Incense and doing a dreary job cleaning the large house of a dreadful woman and her daughters Silver and Myrrh in Dreadnaught Park. All day long – well at any rate from ten till twelve – she was kept at the grindstone, hoovering around and polishing away till the sweat drove grimy tracks through the orange pancake make-up on either side of her nose, and that all for a paltry five quid an hour.

"If only…" she sighed to herself, breaking off at half ten for her elevenses and sinking her teeth into a dreary old cream cracker. "Now what was I going to moan about today? If only I had me time over again? No, that wasn't it – if only I had some of her stinking dough? No. If only she'd get some Custard Creams occasionally? No… oh yes, I remember. If only I could spend an hour, just a single hour with Frank Incense, I'd be made up. I wouldn't ask for another thing on this earth, so help me God."

Frank Incense was gorgeous. He had an Afro haircut, wore spangled trousers and danced and sang sexy songs that sent women everywhere, Golda included, into transports of delight. She had written off to his British publicity agent for a lot of glossy pix, a tin badge and a tee-shirt with I LOVE FRANK INCENSE inscribed across the bosom. She had travelled to Newcastle-under-Tyne four years before to see him in one of his British concerts, but there'd been that much screaming she hadn't heard any of the songs. Still it had made a nice outing with people who shared a common (a very common) interest. She had all his discs and played them over and over on her iPod, but somehow it wasn't enough. She hankered to see him in the flesh.

And then one day the Dreadful Woman came in from her golf, singing, which was unusual for her, took off her fly-away specs with the diamond trimmed rims and said gloatingly, "Guess what? We're going to a ball, the girls and I – well a dinner-dance you know, at the Queen's Hotel in Southport – and who do you think is doing the cabaret? Frank Incense. It's being sponsored by Granada Television and it'll be on the telly – we'll be on the telly! During the evening Frank

Incense is going to mingle with the guests and whoever wins him in the raffle will dance with him and spend the rest of the night with him. Well – maybe not night," she corrected herself. "Evening. I'm sure it must be evening."

"Oh," sighed Golda wistfully. "How I should love to go! Do you suppose you could get me a ticket too?"

But the Dreadful Woman said, "Certainly not! The tickets are forty pounds apiece, you could not afford to pay for one."

Then Golda said, "Yes I could, what with the dole I'm claiming on the side and the alimony and all."

And the Dreadful Woman said, "I suppose you could – but you shan't, because you are just my cleaning lady and it wouldn't be fitting."

So back she went to her golf, leaving Golda sitting by the radiator in her Primark seconds, snuffling away and weeping tears into the instant coffee, bemoaning her lot.

But then, even as she wept, she heard, without the word of a lie, the two-tone chimes of the doorbell, and opened the door to find a beautiful lady standing on the doorstep.

"Why do you weep, my poor dear?" said the lady kindly, seeing Golda's tear-stained face.

"Because I am forced to clean the house every day from dawn till dusk (well, ten till twelve) for a Dreadful Woman who is always out playing golf and who is very cruel to me. She makes me wear her tattered cast-off clothing and forces me to eat cream crackers for me elevenses."

"Well I declare!" said the beautiful lady sympathetically. "That is a poor do."

"And now," wept Golda, "There is to be a ball – well, a dinner dance – at the Queen's Hotel in Southport, but I am not to go, although Frank Incense will be there, because it would not be fitting."

"Nonsense!" said the beautiful lady. "You *shall* go to the dinner dance, my dear."

"How come?" said Golda, "I've nothing to wear and besides, look at me ravaged face."

"I'd rather not," said the lady. "But your worries are over, my dear, for I am your Avon – I mean Mersey – Representative. I have in here," and she tapped her attaché case with her nylon tipped pen, "the answer to your problems. It is Youth Drops. One smear of the liquid across your skin and all the wrinkles will melt away. There is just one thing I must warn you about. The magic Youth Drops only last a few hours, so beware! Whatever happens you must leave before midnight or the effects will wear off and then you'll have more wrinkles than ever."

"Oh thank you, thank you, I won't forget," cried Golda, "You are me fairy godmother!"

"Well I wouldn't go so far as to say that," said the beautiful lady hastily. "It'll cost you eleven pound ninety-five with a pound off if you buy a lipstick as well."

"Can I pay it on the never never?" said Golda.

"Of course, my dear. I've got my machine here."

In no time at all the sale was done.

"And now I must be gone," said the Mersey Lady.

"Yes indeed," said Golda fearfully, "for I hear the squeaky tyres denoting the return of me mistress – vanish, vanish!" And with that she disappeared as quickly she had arrived.

"What is that ghastly smell?" said the Dreadful Woman, stopping short in the hall to sniff the scented air.

"It's a new brand of Instant spray-on polish I've been trying," said Golda.

"You are very trying," said the Dreadful Woman. "Kindly take it away and do not use it again my house. It smells like a brothel!"

(And who should know better than she? There's more to this golf lark than meets the eye, you know.)

So Golda hobbled off home, seeing it was five to twelve and her feet were drawing something wicked.

Well you should have seen the preparations that went on in Dreadnaught Park as the night of the ball drew near. The Dreadful Woman and her daughters got themselves all tarted up with new dresses and they got their hair all tinted and primped and frizzed and tonged and sprayed till they were a mass of rigid curls.

Now unknown to them, Golda too had acquired tickets for herself and her friend Dawn, but she didn't let on she was going, seeing as they wouldn't have thought it was fitting.

When the night arrived she and Dawn took a taxi to the Queen's Hotel, as Dawn said no way was she going on the bus in her evening get-up. They left their fake furs in the Ladies' Cloaks and made their way to the ballroom. It was very grand, the ballroom, all white and gold paint and chandeliers. There were tables set round the dance floor and little red plush chairs with spindly legs. Golda and Dawn straight away grabbed one of these tables and sat down and ordered two double gins. Across the other side of the room sat the Dreadful Woman of Dreadnaught Park with her two daughters.

In the centre of the stage in front of the mike stood a famous television personality who was acting as compere. The television cameras zoomed down on him.

"Good evening, ladies and gentlemen," he said presently, to a round of applause, "and good evening to our audience out there! I'd like to introduce the man you've all been waiting to see, the man who's flown all the way from America in the USA to be with us tonight, ladies and gentlemen, it's the one and only – FRANK INCENSE!"

There was a burst of clapping as the star-spangled figure of Frank Incense mounted the steps to the stage. His lovely hair was as stiff and frizzy as a Brillo pad. His skin was as smooth as a baby's bottom. His silver suit was as tight as a tick. There was a gasp of approval from the audience as their idol spoke his first immortal words.

"Hi ya, everybody!" he said.

"And now," said the compere (who, let it not be forgotten was also a famous television personality), "we have the results of the raffle. In this barrel here are the other halves of your entrance tickets. Frank Incense is now going to put his hand into the barrel and draw out the lucky winning number. And the number which the lucky winner will have on their ticket is – three – five – oh- nine!"

"Well for crying out loud," said Golda, "If that's not the number on me ticket!"

"It's not?" said Dawn.

"It is," said Golda.

(And if you, dear reader, think that's too much of a coincidence, let me remind you that this is a fairy story.)

So Golda, with her heart bursting for joy and pride, rose to her feet, weaved her way across the empty dance floor and mounted the steps to the stage, quite a feat since the skirt of her dress was very tight and her platform shoes were very high and the two gins she'd drunk had been very large. Still as Frank Incense was high on barbiturates, he didn't notice. All he could see was a beautiful twenty-five-year-old blonde drifting towards him. Of all the luck! He might instead have got that woman with the Dreadful Frown darkening her already dark red features, or one of the ugly ones sitting either side of her with their inane moon faces and thick glasses.

"And here comes the lucky lady now who has won the fabulous Frank Incense in the raffle!" said the compere, beaming benevolently into the mike. "What's your name, love?" he whispered in an undertone.

"Golda as in Golda Meir, Mahoney."

"Golda Meir?"

"No, Golda Mahoney."

"Miss?"

"No, Mrs."

"And is hubby with you, dear?"

"Not flippin' likely. He's inside."

"OK, well we won't go into that dear," he whispered. Then he straightened up and addressed the audience.

"Miss Golda Mahoney, this is your... lucky... NIGHT!"

Frank Incense then put his arm round Golda and kissed her on the cheek, and everyone clapped and roared and whistled and cheered, with the exception of the Dreadful Woman, who was gnashing her teeth in rage.

"And our lucky winner is a very lovely young lady," said the compere with practised gallantry. "She is wearing a low-cut gown, as you can see – " (and see they could) " – in gold, and it is covered, ladies and gentlemen, literally covered in sequins! There must be thousands of sequins on this gown…"

"And I sewed them all on meself," said the winner proudly.

"And our lovely winner sewed them all on herself…"

"By hand."

"…by hand. And now, ladies and gents…"

"What about me shoes?"

"Oh yes, the shoes – well…"

"They're *my* shoes!" squeaked an indignant voice from the crowd, but nobody took any notice. "Of all the nerve. Mother, why don't you *do* something!"

"Well these shoes," said the compere, "Have got very high heels, and they're made of glass, it looks like. Is that glass, love?"

"No luv, see-through plastic."

"And we can all see through them, can't we?" he quipped. "Well now, ladies and gents, can we have a few words from our lucky winning contestant? Go on," he said to Golda, shoving the mike in front of her nose.

"I'd just like to say," she said and paused. "I'd just like to say," she hiccupped, "I'm in me seventh heaven. I never thought I should live to see this night. I am truly, word of honour, made up. I am, without the word of a lie – over the moon."

"Thank you Golda Mahoney!" said the compere.

"And I'd just like to add," she added, "This night must rank as the happiest, the truly happiest night of me life, and ladies and gentlemen, I just want to say a big thank you to you. I owe it all to you, me public. I couldn't have done it without you. I think you're wonderful…"

"Yes, all right, all right. Who does she think she is, Shirley Bassey?" he said with a grin to the audience. "Well thank you, thank you very much Miss – Golda Mahoney. Give her a great big hand, folks!"

And they did. Indeed they did.

Then the music struck up and she and Frank Incense stumbled down the steps onto the floor for some unrecognisable dance or other.

They made a remarkable pair, he nearly spilling out of his silver suit and she actually spilling out of her gold one.

"Oh Frank," she said huskily, "If you only knew what this means to me."

"But I do know, doll," he drawled. "This is the happiest night of your life. You are truly (hiccup) word of honour, made up. You are, without the word of a lie, over the…"

"Now watch it Frank, you can go off people, you know."

But she was only joking. She really was in her seventh heaven. The next two hours went by in a flash and were quite taken up with dancing, and with not being talked to by Frank Incense; but then not being talked to by Frank Incense was so much better than being talked to by anyone else. Besides Frank never said much at the best of times, seeing he never had much to say.

At half past nine they all filed into the dining room for a delectable supper. On a long table spread with a whitish cloth was a lovely, if predictable, buffet, and behind the table a row of waitresses in black dresses and whitish aprons with hair in assorted tints did a quick hand-out of the usual tired slices of ham, flabby-skinned chicken legs, bits of lettuce in which could be seen, if you looked hard enough, the occasional fly, Russian salad that should have defected back to Russia and stale sausage rolls, and afterwards there was sherry trifle, alas inaptly named, being made of jelly and cake crumbs and lots of mock cream. Then, when they had eaten and drunk their fill, there was a rush by the ladies to the Ladies to spend pennies and check on their mascara.

"Nice is this place," said Golda, "I've always wanted to come here, have you Dawn? Lovely thick carpets you sink right into. Wasn't it a beautiful meal?"

"Beautiful," agreed Dawn.

"How're you doing, Dawn? You OK?"

"Fantastic. I've met this terrific fella."

"Great! How are me Youth Drops bearing up?"

"Fantastic! You look great! Not a day over twenty-nine."

"Go on!"

"No truly, without the word of a lie."

"I'm just a teeny bit worried if me face'll last out, and me feet."

When Golda returned to the ballroom, Frank Incense greeted her with surprising enthusiasm. "Here's my gorgeous golden girl," he said, "C'mon, let's dance."

Her cup of happiness was almost full, but Golda was reluctant to dance.

"Me feet are killing me," she explained, "It's me bunions you see."

"Take your shoes off," said Frank. "Here, I'll put them in my pocket."

So they continued to dance and were admired by all who saw them. Except for the Dreadful Woman of course. But alas, as the evening wore on, Golda's face wore off. Finally, as the clock struck twelve, she gave a cry of anguish and ran from the room.

"Come back! Where is she? I must find her!" said Frank Incense. He dashed after her in hot pursuit, but she appeared to have disappeared from the hotel. Then through the revolving doors he saw a shoeless blonde in a tight gold dress hobbling into a taxi.

"Stop!" he cried. "Is it? Can it be?"

She turned, revealing the face of an ancient crone.

"My God!" he cried in horror, "My God!"

"Why did you have to follow me?" she said sadly. "Why couldn't you just have let me go?"

"You left your shoes in my pocket."

"They're not my shoes. They wouldn't fit me now anyway, me feet are that swollen. They belong to Myrrh. Take them to her. Frank Incense and Myrrh go well together."

"Gold and Frank Incense go better," he said. "Come on, I'll see you home."

He stepped into the taxi and sat beside her and in the ghastly neon light she saw that his face had undergone a change as well. It no longer looked like a baby's bottom. It resembled a ploughed field.

"Not you too?" she said.

"Yeah, me too," he answered. "Goddamn Youth Drops!"

Scatterbrain

The trouble with me is that I'm always late for everything. I suppose it's laziness really – at least that's what my mother thinks; she's really worried about it. My headmistress thought the same. "Daisy Merryweather!" she used to say in exasperation, "You'll be late for your own funeral!"

I could never see why that should matter anyway, but it's mattered a lot in my life so far. It's meant that all sorts of nice things haven't happened to me and all sorts of unpleasant things have. And now I've lost the only man I've ever really fallen for.

I didn't know him well, but there was definitely something between us – if only anger. Of course, you could argue that if I hadn't been late that Wednesday morning three weeks ago I would never have met him at all, but meet him I did and I felt sure he was the man for me. The only man, I think now tragically, sipping sherry. (Sherry is such a comfort when you're down in the dumps.)

To go back to that Wednesday. I don't know what it is about Wednesdays, but I find them most unlucky. Terrible things seem to happen, like chemistry exams and early closing and being sacked. The previous Wednesday I had been sacked from my secretarial job just because I had been late a couple of times and so there I was, a lady of leisure but no means.

Now this particular Wednesday I was going to the dentist, and as usual I was late. "You don't suppose Pa will mind if I borrow the car, do you?" I asked my mother as I gulped down eggs and bacon. (My mother is one of those people who thinks you'll fold up and die by the side of the road if you go out in the morning without breakfast.)

"Oh dear," she said, looking troubled. "You will be careful, won't you Daisy?" she begged me.

"Of course," I said. Well honestly! I mean, as though anyone goes out and has an accident on purpose! So I grabbed my coat and the car keys and rushed off.

I was doing quite well till I got to Kings Road. That's the big main road that runs through our town, and it's always busy. That morning was no exception and I had to wait hours for a pause in the traffic. You know what it's like, as soon as there's a gap in one line the other line closes up and you're stuck again. At length I saw my chance and was just swinging round the corner when I saw this bright red shiny Mini Cooper speeding towards me at a rate of knots. Oh God, I thought, where did he come from? I slammed on my brakes but it was too late and the next minute – wham! My front had bumped his side with a crunch.

I jumped out and ran round to the front to survey the damage. It looked nasty, very nasty, with the grid, or whatever you call that bit on the front of a car, all buckled and one of the headlamps broken. I had visions of my father's furious face.

From the irritable hooting, I was made aware that we were blocking the traffic stream and that my assailant in the red Mini was backing into a side road. I got back into the car, and shocked and shaken though I was, I contrived to move it approximately to the kerb. (I use the word 'approximately' in the loosest possible sense.)

Then I saw a tall, thin young man approaching. The owner of the other car. He was most attractive, with a sun-tanned face and wavy brown hair and deep-set blue eyes but right now he looked very angry. He stuck his head through my window and said, "You nincompoop! What the blazes do you think you were doing?"

"I might ask you that question," I said with dignity.

"I might give you an answer which you might not like," he said through clenched teeth. (Nice teeth too, I thought.)

"Well?" he demanded.

"I was turning right onto the main road," I said. "What difference does it make? The point is, we collided."

"The point is, you never saw me, did you?" said the angry young man.

"Of course I saw you," I said indignantly. (I wasn't going to admit I hadn't for anything.) "You were going too fast," I accused him. "It's your fault. You were speeding!"

"Rubbish! It was my right of way, girl! Have the decency to admit you were in the wrong!"

"I most certainly do not admit it," I said with spirit.

"Women drivers!" he snorted. "Heaven preserve us men from women drivers!"

That was a bit much, but I forgave him. I liked the cleft in his chin, it made him look rugged but endearing. I thought it such a pity that this dishy young man whom I had by chance encountered should have to be so angry with me. Not an auspicious start to a romance, I thought.

"We'd better exchange names and addresses," he said. "What's yours?"

I told him my name was Daisy Merryweather and he wrote it down on the back of an envelope together with my address. His name, he told me, was Adam Irving and his address was c/o a firm of stockbrokers in Bridge Street called Adams and Budsworth.

"And may I suggest," he said with sarcasm, "that you stick to your sewing machine in future, Miss Merryweather. At least you can't do any damage to anyone else with that – at any rate I shouldn't have thought so."

I think that's the stupidest thing I ever heard. I do not own a sewing machine, for the very good reason that I cannot operate one. That he should assume I did was irritating in the extreme. He was obviously of the "woman's place is in the home" school. I shall make jolly certain I am never in the home when it comes to my turn, except for fleeting visits. I am not handy with a needle or with a scrubbing brush and although I am not entirely proud of this I don't see why I should be ashamed of it. And I've always thought I was a good driver and I still think so, whatever he said.

Thus, coldly, we parted.

I decided to give the dentist a miss for the day and drove straight home and my mother looked at the car and wrung her hands and said she had known it would happen. She can be amazingly clairvoyant at times. And my father was furious as expected, and though I stuck to my story like glue he smelt a rat and banned me from driving for six months.

Meanwhile I continued to be unemployed, and this was a matter of anxiety to my parents, who feared I was going to sponge on them for evermore. Talking of sponge, I was making gingerbread one day when my mother came in with the local paper folded back and a thick blue line drawn round the Sits Vac column. (Incidentally, I may not be able to do much else but I'm jolly good at making gingerbread – everyone thinks so, all my family and all our friends think my gingerbread is quite unlike any other gingerbread they have ever tasted. And friends of my mother's who can only do it the right way say they could try for fifty years and never get it so deliciously squidgy and gooey and wrong. But that's just by the way.)

My mother said that she really thought, and my father really thought, I ought to start writing off for another job, and just to placate her I gave the paper a cursory glance. Although I'm not quite sure what a cursory glance is I'm sure I gave one to the paper, and lo and behold, there was a vacancy for a shorthand typist at a certain firm of stockbrokers by the name of Adams and Budsworth. My eyes were immediately riveted and that night I sat down and wrote my letter of application. A few days later I got a reply, offering me an interview.

Oh, I could see it all – I would walk in, and there would be Adam Irving and we would start all over again and he wouldn't be angry a bit. I would do his letters and I would do them so beautifully and he would be so grateful and he would say, "What would I do without you, Miss Merryweather?" and he would take me to lunch – for a start.

Of course I had to get the job first, but that would be a cinch. There was only one snag. The interview was on a Wednesday.

If I tell you I was late for the interview I know what you'll think. You'll think how *stupid* I was and how *careless,* but honestly it wasn't my fault. I mean how was I supposed to know there was a bus strike on that day? Nobody told me, it wasn't on the news. I did think it a little odd there was no one else at the bus stop for such a long time but I am used to standing alone at bus stops. When the penny dropped, I found a phone box and called a taxi and I was only ten minutes late, which was quite good considering. And one usually has to wait at interviews anyway.

One didn't have to wait at that one, though. Oh no. One was shown in, panting and all, into the Managing Director's room where the Managing Director sat wide-shouldered in his wide chair flanked on one side by a fearsome female in pink angora and on the other side by Adam Irving himself. He looked very surprised to see me. I wish I could say pleasantly surprised, but I couldn't.

I sat down in a chair in the middle of the room and faced them, still panting, and uneasily aware that an unpleasant smell was emanating from some dog dirt on the underside of my left shoe. "I'm sorry I'm late," I began, "but you see what happened was…"

"Quite," said the Managing Director.

Funny thing to say, I thought. Quite what?

"So we meet again, Miss Merryweather," said Adam Irving drily.

"You know her, then Irving?" said the Managing Director.

"We have bumped into each other," replied Irving with a deadpan expression and I thought, you lovely man, I adore you! But then he asked, rather nastily I thought:

"Why did you leave your last job?"

"I was sac – I mean, stuck," I said.

"Stuck?"

"In a… rut, you know."

"I see. How long had you been there?"

"Five and a half – um weeks," I said.

There was a pause.

"Quite a rut!" commented Adam Irving.

After that the interview didn't seem to go my way at all. He had put me at a definite disadvantage with his sarcastic remarks. It wasn't fair. Why I should have so much wanted the job and to type his beastly letters for him I don't know, but I did. Life with him in it seemed suddenly interesting and full of promise.

"Well now, Miss Merryweather," said the Managing Director, "If you will go with Mr. Irving he will give you some dictation and then you can transcribe it."

So I went willingly with Mr. Irving to his untidy office and I sat down with pad and pencil poised and looked at him over his paper-littered desk.

Well I could do the first bit all right. "Dear Sir, Thank you for your letter of the 6th instant." That was easy. Then he began to speed it up a bit and there came a 'precipitate' and an 'incommensurability' and a couple of 'uncircumstantiated's' and I was lost.

"Could you repeat that last bit, I didn't quite get it?" I asked.

"Certainly not, this is a test, Miss Merryweather," he said, shocked.

"But you're going awfully fast."

"My normal speed."

"But you must be doing 140 at least and I never got further than 110 and that only on my best days."

"That isn't my concern. You always think I'm going too fast, don't you Miss Merryweather? Our last confrontation, I'll have you know, cost me a hundred quid."

"I'm frightfully sorry, I promise I'll make it up to you."

"I doubt if you'll have the opportunity," he replied, scathingly.

I know you'll think I'm mad, but I still wanted that job even then. I mean, how else was I going to go on seeing him?

Presently the fearsome female entered and took me away into another room where there was a desk with a typewriter. "There's some paper," she said. "Just two copies please, and your machine is the usual type."

Not to me, it wasn't. The very least usual.

"Can I have a practice first?"

"That is not usual here."

Well, needless to say it was a colossal failure. One chunk I put in twice and another not at all and none of it made sense. I tore the paper into little tiny pieces and put them in my handbag and started again. An hour later I was told not to bother going on any further. The Managing Director popped his head round the door and said he was going to lunch and he was sorry I had not been successful in obtaining the post. I mean, I knew I hadn't, but I could still feel tears pricking my eyelids as I scrambled into my coat.

Then Adam Irving reappeared.

"Well," he said cheerfully, "You can't drive and you can't do shorthand. As I told you before, you really ought to stick to your sewing machine in future!"

"I'm beginning to go off you," I said coldly, wiping a tear away on my sleeve.

"Whereas," he said, "I feel the opposite about you. But I can't think why. What can it be, I wonder?"

"And you can spare me your sarcastic remarks too," I cried and swept out, tripping over the mat on the way.

And that's where we came in. With me sitting sipping sherry and sobbing. Well, perhaps not quite sobbing but certainly sipping. Presently the phone rang and I thought let it ring and I let it.

But presently it rang again and this time I answered.

You'll never guess who. It was – Adam Irving.

"The suspense is killing me," he said. "I'm going to have to find out if there's anything you *can* do."

"Well," I said, "I can make gingerbread for a start. And if you'd like to come round and have tea," I added boldly (it must have been the sherry) "I'll prove it."

That was fifteen minutes ago and a car has just drawn up outside. And now I can hear the doorbell ringing...

Sold to HI, *1975*

The Big Dipper

It could have been a nice day, I thought.

We walked along the promenade, first Keith and Trish, holding hands, their heads bent close together, then me and Martin and Gina. Three's a crowd, I thought, and Gina shouldn't really have come at all. She hadn't been asked. She had only come because she was Trish's older sister and was at a loose end. I was nearest to the sea and I watched the waves as they approached and broke frothily on the shore, but I scarcely saw them. I was thinking about Martin.

Martin was the first real boyfriend I had had, apart from casual dates, partners to take me to school hops and things, but you couldn't really count those. They were generally stiff and spotty and all they talked about was football and their O-levels. But Martin was different, suave and good-looking with dark hair and brown eyes. I thought it pretty amazing that someone like him should even notice my existence, let alone want to take me out. He thought I was sweet and rather funny and he often laughed at the things I said, showing very white teeth. I loved to make him laugh and when, at the end of an evening, he'd suddenly take my hand in his or kiss me, I was on Cloud Nine.

But today with Gina here, it had all gone wrong. Everything I said seemed to fall flat like lumps of suet – but Gina, who had only met Martin today for the first time, kept up a flow of bright and easy chatter.

I watched a flock of seagulls sitting on the beach rise suddenly into the air and wheel, screeching, above our heads. "What a pity we didn't bring some bread," I remarked, "Then we could have fed the gulls."

Gina looked at Martin and they both crumpled up with laughter. And the difference was, now they were laughing *at* me.

"What's so funny about that?" I said crossly, but it was some hidden joke I couldn't share. I kicked at a stone and it went spinning crazily along the prom. I caught it up and kicked it again.

"You should have had a hoop," said Gina, and they laughed again.

I began to drop behind ever so slightly just to see if Martin would notice, willing him to notice. When he didn't I was mortified. Or perhaps he had and just didn't want to know – that was even more mortifying. Trish and Keith were now some distance ahead, then came Martin and Gina talking as though completely engrossed and last of all, me. I felt left out. It's not fair, I thought. Who could compete with the luscious Gina? Certainly not me with my naïve schoolgirl looks.

Tears like drops of salty spray stung my eyes and angrily I brushed them away. The sea was grey and so was the sky, grey and drab as the stone surface of the promenade. Presently we reached the fairground and Keith and Trish stopped and turned round.

"Well? How about it?" said Keith, "Still want to go?"

"You bet!" said Gina.

Oh no, I thought, not the Big Dipper, please not that!

"Wow, it's awfully high," said Trish.

We looked up and saw the giant structure towering way above the wall that surrounded the fairground, curving and looping like the tracks of a monstrous snake.

"We'll all go," said Gina. "It'll be great!"

"Aren't you scared?" asked Martin.

"Of course not!"

"There was that accident on the Big Dipper not so long ago," said Keith. "Five people were killed."

"Huh! That doesn't put me off," said Gina and her eyes flashed. "I thrive on thrills. The more risky a thing is the better I like it."

"You're not soft, are you?" said Martin admiringly.

I was silent. Ever since they had first talked of going to the fairground and having a ride on the Big Dipper I had said nothing, praying they might forget it. I was terrified of heights and had been ever since I was five years old and had nearly fallen off the parapet of a very high building. A balcony had broken loose and fallen away, twisting as it went, leaving me teetering on the edge. The thought, the very sight of the Big Dipper petrified me. I hated fairgrounds – the noise, the crowds filled me with panic – but I couldn't let the others know that. Gina would laugh and Martin would despise me and think I was soft. He didn't like a girl to be soft.

So we paid our money and went in and at once we were swallowed up in the throngs of people. Oh, the jostling crowds, the noise, the roar of the great machines! Everywhere I looked there were seething masses of people. They seemed to come down on me from all sides, pushing me, hemming me in. I was suddenly afraid. I longed to escape, to run away somewhere calm and quiet where I could be alone with Martin. But would he want to be alone with me? Right now it didn't look like it, he had eyes only for Gina, with her flushed cheeks and her cloud of blonde hair and her eyes sparkling with excitement. For him I didn't even exist. Just ahead Keith and Trish walked hand in hand. Oh, lucky, *lucky* Trish to have Keith! He'd never let her down. He was kind and steadfast. Behind came Martin and Gina, then me like the fraying edge of a piece of cloth. I was with them, yet not with them, unwanted and lonely.

There was so much to do and see at the fair, and we did it all. There were amusement halls where you lost a fortune on the money showers and the fruit machines. There were dodgem cars and roundabouts, the ghost train and the floating log, airguns and archery, popcorn and candy floss, hot dogs with mustard and dripping wet onions.

We did the lot, and at last we came to the Big Dipper. There was no escape. I stared with dread at the enormous switchback track round which the cars stampeded with a roar like some terrible pre-historic monster. Oh no, I thought, I can't, I can't... but the crowds seemed to lift me up and press me closer and closer.

"Come on, everyone," cried Gina, "There's hardly any queue."

"D'you want to go, Trish?" asked Keith.

"Well – I suppose so," giggled Trish nervously.

"Millie?"

I couldn't answer. My mouth was dry.

"You look quite white, Millie – are you all right?" asked Trish, concerned. But Gina said scornfully, "You're not *afraid*, are you?"

"No," I said, and my voice seemed to come from far away like the sea singing on the distant shingle. That's not *my* voice, I thought in panic. I mustn't faint. I mustn't let them know that I...

But Gina knew. Gina said, "You *are* afraid! I can see it in your eyes."

"You don't *have* to come," said Keith kindly.

Oh but I do, I thought. I have to come because of Martin, otherwise he'll think I'm soft and he'll despise me. I have to show him I can do it. I have to show myself.

Keith paid our money and we climbed into the little cars. When everyone was in there was a jerk and with a clang the great machine started. DOWN came the cars, and then up again – and then DOWN – like the undulating tail of a mighty dragon. Girls screamed with exhilaration and excitement, boys shouted and put up their hands in gestures of bravado. Up, up climbed the little cars, pausing very slightly as they reached the top of the incline in a terrifying, tremulous moment before their zooming descent and then whee-ee-ee they plunged down to the bottom and then on again, faster and ever faster. My heart felt as if it would burst against my ribs and I thought, I can't bear it, I can't, it's not real, it's not happening, just a dream, a bad dream... and the cars plunged down, down and then up, and from a great height I saw blobs of orange and red and blue and green that were the clothes of people in the crowd far below, and the colours danced and sprang before my eyes as the big dipper went madly racing on and on, and the roaring was in my ears and the orange spread like fire before my eyes and a great weight seemed to press the sides of my head like an iron clamp on an egg shell... and still we went on. But gradually, little by little we began to slow down – up again – down again... and finally we came to a shaky halt.

"Whew!" said Gina in front of me, "That was great!"

"Wasn't it just?" said Martin.

Everyone climbed out of the little cars, but I couldn't move. My legs felt like jelly and everything was spinning round and round.

"Don't tell me you want another go, Millie?" said Keith.

"You know what I could just do with now?" said Martin as if from a long way off, "Some fish and chips."

"Yes. Why don't we go and get some," said Gina.

"Millie?" said Trish, "Come on, we're waiting for you."

She put a hand on my shoulder, but just then a gulf of blackness swept over me and the ground seemed to rise up and hit me...

When I came to, Trish was bending over me anxiously. "Are you all right, Millie? Are you all right?" she was asking over and over.

"Yes," I murmured.

"Oh thank goodness! I was so worried. Keith's gone over to the First Aid van across there to see if they've any brandy."

I struggled to sit up. How kind Trish was! But where was Martin? I couldn't see him.

"Trish – where's Martin?"

"He's gone to get some fish and chips."

"Did he know I'd fainted?"

"Well – yes."

"And yet he went off to get fish and chips!"

"They felt there wasn't much point in all hanging round."

"They?"

"He and Gina."

"Oh I see."

So Martin had gone with Gina. It was final, I knew that now. What I had dreaded happening had happened. Well hadn't I always known that sooner or later it would happen, if not with Gina, with someone else? It had all been for nothing, that terrible, nightmarish ride, for Martin didn't really care what I did. I just hadn't faced facts. Yet deep down I had known that Martin wouldn't stick around for long.

Trish took my hand, seeming to sense my desolation.

"I'm so sorry, Millie."

"It doesn't really matter any more," I said, covering up to hide my hurt.

Keith returned with some brandy. "Here, drink this," he said, holding it to my lips. I gulped it and it ran down my throat like liquid fire and sent warmth spurting through every vein.

"Is that better?"

"Yes, thank you."

"Were you really so frightened, then?" he asked.

"Yes," I said, "You see I'm afraid of heights."

"Silly girl," said Keith gently. "You should never, never have gone on the Big Dipper. It's no disgrace to be afraid, you know. You don't have to prove yourself to your friends."

He was so wise, I thought. He might have been a thousand years old.

"Come on," he said, "When you're ready we'll go."

Slowly we all moved off, past the whirling roundabouts, the winking lights of giant puppets, the bright colours of huge balloons, the laughing faces of passing children, the cable cars wending their way slowly high above. There were pungent smells of sizzling waffles and frankfurters. There was the noise, the bustle, the hub of people. I walked through them as if in a dream and beside me were my friends, one on either side, their arms in mine.

Martin had gone. It was over between us, something that had never really begun, and strangely I didn't seem to mind any more. All of a sudden I was no longer afraid, no longer alone in the crowd.

Sold to Jackie, *1978*

The Girl Who Liked Cream Cakes

"I adore jewellery!" exclaimed Helen. "When I marry, it will be for money. Don't imagine I'm going to be a hotel receptionist for the rest of my life. Oh no! I've had my share of scrimping and saving. I shall marry a rich man – you'll see."

She looked around at her three companions, pitying them because they did not believe her: black-haired Miss Feather with the charming smile and flashing temper, making entries in the Cash Book in her thin, precise hand-writing; Janet sitting with pink cheeks, hunched over her cash box, trying to make her float balance; and mousey little Linda, watching with admiration in her thin face and looking as if she never had a square meal.

"I shall have lots of fabulous jewellery," Helen went on, "and a silver Rolls Royce with leopardskin seats, and I shall spend my winters in the south of France. There will be cream cakes every day, meringues and coffee eclairs and strawberry tarts, as many as I want. I'll dress every night for dinner, give extravagant parties and be the most fascinating hostess in Europe."

"And the fattest, I should think," said Miss Feather shortly.

"But Helen, what about love?" asked Linda. "Would you still marry him, even if you didn't love him?"

"Certainly," said Helen. "I don't believe in love anyway. It doesn't last. I've seen these 'true romances'. They start off all lovely and frothy but look at them a few years hence and you'll find they've gone flat, just like a tankard of beer with no head on it. So you might just as well pick someone rich in the first place. If you want to know something," she added confidentially, "I think I've met mine already – in Suite Five last night!"

Janet looked up from her cash box and Linda's eyes opened wide. She darted to the hotel register. "Lawrence Cunningham," she read out, "Baltimore, USA. Oh Helen, d'you really think…"

"Helen, will you stop filling up the girls' heads with your nonsense?" said Miss Feather. "You can take over my float. The Diary is up to date and there aren't many guests, so you should be in for a quiet evening."

"I knew it – I'm a pound down!" wailed Janet.

"Surely not! Have you checked it?" asked Miss Feather. "Here, you'd better let me look at it. Linda, don't forget to take those letters in for Mr Weston to sign, will you? You'd better go *now* dear, before he has his tea, or they won't catch the post."

"Go on Linda," said Helen, "see if you can get a smile out of old Fancy Pants."

"Not a chance," said Linda, picking up the letters, "especially now he's Acting Manager. He takes it all so seriously. When's Mr Harper back anyway?"

"Not till the end of the month," said Miss Feather.

"Meanwhile we're stuck with Fancy Pants," sighed Helen.

The girls laughed at Mr Weston, the Assistant Manager, because he was so formal and aloof. They had never seen him smile, although Miss

Feather said he did occasionally. He always wore a dark coat and immaculately-pressed pin-striped trousers, hence the nickname Helen had given him.

"There you are, Janet!" announced Miss Feather. "You forgot to deduct a pound for the petty cash in the bar. I didn't think you could be a whole pound down. Oh Linda, did you get the letters signed? Hurry up and seal them dear. Now Helen, don't let Suite Three for the time being will you, the decorators will be in tomorrow."

How she does fuss! thought Helen impatiently. *Come on you lot, on your way. My rich Mr Right will be coming through the doors of the lift a quarter of an hour from now and I must have the coast clear by then.*

She was a small girl inclined to be plump, for she had a weakness for food, especially cakes and puddings. But she had pretty blonde hair and blue eyes and a typical English pink and white complexion.

At last Miss Feather picked up her handbag. "Right!" she said briskly, "That's another day's work done. Good afternoon, girls!" and away she strode.

"Come on Linda," said Janet, "leave the post for Helen or we'll be here all night. I don't want to keep Humphrey waiting. And you needn't scoff about me and Humphrey, Helen. You wait, you'll find you can't get along without love either."

They picked up their belongings and left the little reception office and Helen was alone. It was very quiet in the hotel. Sounds of the orchestra could be heard from the restaurant, where the guests were drinking tea and eating stamp-sized sandwiches.

She sat and watched the doors of the lift a few feet away and presently, as if by magic, they opened and out stepped Mr Lawrence Cunningham. He was a handsome man of about fifty, with a lined, craggy face and penetrating grey eyes. There was no doubt at all that he was rich. His faultlessly-cut grey suit, his silk shirt, his gold watch and initialled cuff-links, even the large gold signet ring (which she personally thought vulgar), all proclaimed him as a person accustomed to having money.

"Hi there," he said. "Are you free now?"

"Well it's a little difficult at present because I've only just come on duty," she said. "But I think I could get away in about an hour. Shall I come up to your suite?"

"Sure, you do that," he replied.

He wanted a stenographer, and although a service was provided by the hotel Helen had had no intention of letting him use it when she could type very adequately herself. It would be a wonderful opportunity to be alone with this rich American.

Soon after 5 pm she left the reception desk and called the lift. "Fifth please, Page," she said. "And if any guests come in will you call me pronto – I'll be in Suite Five."

"Aye aye!" he grinned.

"Don't be cheeky, Page!" she retorted.

It was sumptuous in Suite Five. She had never been inside before. It was rarely used except for business conferences. It was panelled in white and gold, and a crystal chandelier hung from the ceiling. The carpets were thick and spongey and smelt new. A huge display of flowers stood in a corner.

"Have a seat," said Mr Cunningham, indicating a table where stood an electric typewriter and a pile of papers. "I'll get you to type this list in triplicate while I take a shower – OK?"

"Fine," she said.

But it wasn't quite as fine as she had expected. The list of items purchased from antique dealers in Europe seemed endless: Florence: bronze figure of dancer; 1 pair brass candlesticks; pair tall Florentine vases. Rome: portrait of woman by unknown artist; small silver casket @ 16th century; and so on. She wasn't getting to know him, she reflected, while she was typing the list and he was in the shower. More important, he wasn't getting to know her.

And worse, when she rose to leave the apartment some while later she was taken aback on being confronted by the tall, lean figure of Mr Weston, the Acting Manager.

"Just what does this mean?" he enquired coldly. "You'd better come down to my office and explain."

Ten minutes later, she knocked at his door. "Come!" he called. He sat languidly, his long legs protruding under the desk, and did not look at her for some moments while she stood forlorn as a schoolgirl. She had thought him attractive when she first met him, but that was before she had found out he had no sense of humour – or so it seemed. Besides which he was impossibly reserved. He couldn't unbend for a moment, or ever let it appear that he was in any way human. He constantly found fault with Helen, and it was not the first time she had been called to his office to be reprimanded.

"Sit down," he said at length. "There has to be a mighty good explanation for leaving the reception desk unattended for close on an hour. Well?"

She stared at him defiantly without speaking.

"Look," he said. "I'm not going to give you the usual lecture. I know what you're capable of. You know the job inside out. You can do the work of three receptionists when you want to. The trouble is, you hardly ever want to."

"That's not fair," she protested. "It was a quiet night, I instructed the Page to notify me if anyone wanted Reception. I was doing some work for a guest, actually. Some typing."

"You had no business to do that. You should have called in the hotel stenographer. That's her job. Yours is to sit behind that reception desk, whether it's busy or not. It doesn't include long chats to the housekeeper and the florist, or sneaking visits to the kitchens to eat up the cream cakes and other left-overs."

She blushed. "You're always picking on me. Whatever I do is wrong, and Miss Feather is always a paragon of virtue."

"Miss Feather is an extremely wise and experienced head receptionist," he replied shortly. "I can always count on her for loyalty and support. Let's leave her out of this."

"I'm sorry."

"Can I count on your loyalty and support?" he asked suddenly.

"Why, yes..." she was embarrassed.

"If I have picked on you it's only because I expect more of you than of the others. Let's start afresh, shall we? Take a pride in your job, you'll find it's worthwhile. And make it a rule never to fraternise with the guests. Now, don't let me down, will you Helen?"

The interview was at an end. She walked away thoughtfully. It was the first time he had ever called her Helen. She almost liked him. How angry he would be if he knew of her plans for the next day!

It was her day off: Mr Cunningham had asked if she would do some letters for him, after which he would give her lunch. That was a better proposition, she thought – very much better!

He dictated to her for about an hour and she transcribed direct on to the typewriter. Then he called the restaurant and gave his order. Within minutes a couple of waiters wheeled in a trolley-table laid for two with a white cloth, cutlery and glasses. There was smoked salmon, followed by roast pheasant with wine sauce and a bottle of champagne to accompany it. Helen tucked in with relish; it seemed hours since breakfast. Mr Cunningham looked at her in amusement.

"My, you sure do love your food," he remarked.

"Yes, well I don't have food like this every day," she replied between mouthfuls. "I do envy you, Mr Cunningham. It must be wonderful to travel around the world, seeing all the fabulous places, staying at all the most luxurious hotels, eating the most delicious food."

Then the most amazing thing happened.

"Listen Helen," he said, "That's given me an idea. How would you like it if I was to offer you a job as my stenographer? I've that much work on I could really do with someone with me all the while. I'll give you a good salary – what do you say?"

"Why," she said, "Mr Cunningham!"

"Larry," he said.

"Why, Larry!"

"Is it a deal?"

"It's a deal!"

She left the apartment feeling bubbly and slightly light-headed. The girls could scarcely believe their ears when she told them about it afterwards.

"I'll be leaving for Paris with Mr Cunningham next week," she announced triumphantly.

Linda's eyes boggled. "You're really going to marry him?" she gasped.

"Well – no," Helen admitted. "Actually I'm going as his secretary. But that's only one step away really."

"One step from something, I should imagine," said Miss Feather drily. "Quite what I shouldn't like to hazard a guess."

"Perhaps he's married already," said Linda.

"No, he isn't. He's separated from his second wife," said Helen. "He told me."

"That makes him a bit... shop-soiled," said Janet distastefully. "I must say I'm rather glad Humphrey is quite untarnished. He's keeping himself pure for me!"

"Whiter than white like washing powder!" said Helen.

"You needn't scoff at Humphrey," said Janet tartly. "He's respectable and honest, neither of which you'll be if you go to Paris with a man you hardly know who's old enough to be your father – speaking of whom, whatever your poor parents will say I can't imagine!"

"Oh don't be wet," said Helen. "Give them credit for being a little more broad-minded than yours!"

"Now, girls," said Miss Feather warningly, "You know how I feel about bickering."

"And you know how I feel about Janet," said Helen.

"Helen!"

"I'm sorry, I'm sorry, I didn't mean it. I love Janet – like I love a cold shower."

"That's enough!" said Miss Feather sharply.

"Anyway I'm going out now," said Helen. "I'm going into town to see about my passport and get my hair done and buy some new clothes. I'll probably stay overnight and break the news to the family. And tomorrow I'll see old Fancy Pants and give in my notice."

"Oh, it's so exciting," cried Linda. "And romantic. Don't you think it's romantic really, Janet? Don't you, Miss Feather?"

Yes, thought Helen on the train, it *was* exciting and romantic. Cashing sixty-six pounds, all that was in her post office savings account, was definitely exciting, and spending it all in one glorious spending spree was romantic. But – it was only doing it once in a blue moon that made it so. She didn't think she'd like to do it every day.

She got back to the hotel the next afternoon and was about to open the door when someone on his way out practically sent her flying. "I'm sorry," said Mr Weston, as they both bent down to pick up the scattered parcels.

"Oh Mr Weston, I wanted to see you."

"Will it wait? I'm just going out."

"It won't take a moment."

"All right. We'll go back into my office."

Still holding a pile of her parcels, he turned and went back up the stairs, she following. He unlocked his office door and motioned her to sit down.

"I want to give in my notice," she said straight out.

He looked thunderstruck. "I had no idea you were thinking of leaving!"

"I wasn't till yesterday. I'm going to Paris with Mr Cunningham. As his secretary," she added hastily.

"Mr Cunningham? Is that the American in Suite Five?"

"Yes."

"But he checked out this morning."

It was her turn to look thunderstruck. "He *can't* have!" she cried.

"I'm afraid he did."

"But I don't understand. He must have left a message for me or something. He wouldn't just leave without a word!"

"I'll check with Miss Feather." He picked up the phone and spoke for a moment, then replaced the receiver. "No, I'm sorry. There was no message."

"But he was taking me to Paris," she said forlornly. "He said so."

Mr Weston looked at her very kindly. "People don't always mean everything they say Helen," he said. "Perhaps he didn't think you'd take him seriously."

"Well, I did. I've got all my clothes and everything. I spent all my Post Office savings."

He looked at her for a moment without speaking. Then he said, "You need cheering up. Come on, leave your parcels here. I'll take you out to tea."

They went to Brown's, her favourite place, but so expensive she couldn't afford to go as a rule. They had a table in the corner, and there was a cheerful fire blazing, and the waitress brought them hot tea and crumpets dripping with butter and a plate of lovely, lovely cream cakes. Soon Helen forgot all about Paris and Mr Cunningham. It was suddenly so much nicer to be here at Brown's, with Mr Weston.

"I've got something to tell you, Helen," said Mr Weston presently. He was looking at her with such warmth in his brown eyes that she felt her heart leap. He was going to tell her something she wanted to hear but hadn't realised it until just now.

"Yes? Go on, tell me," she said.

"I like cream cakes too." His eyes twinkled with amusement.

"Oh," she said disappointed. "Is that all?"

"Not quite," he said. "You've got cream on your nose."

How could she have thought he had no sense of humour?

"Now tell me something I didn't know."

"All right," he said. "Finish your eclair, and then I will."

Sold to Hi! *magazine*

Who is Sylvia?

Sylvia is the girl I share a flat with. What is she? She's an angel. No, I don't think that's putting it too strongly. She is nice, kind and pretty. She's also clever and a super cook. And she has all the boys at her feet.

I expect you're wondering why anyone in their right mind would choose a girl like her to share a flat with. I rather wondered myself – but you see, she chose me. We were at school together and I was flattered that she would want me to share her flat.

It's a nice flat. Well, the furniture's nothing special, but we painted it white and Sylvia brought rugs and cushions from home and even made some curtains for the sitting room. I brought my books and pictures and Sylvia brought some beautiful china ornaments that she has in her bedroom at home, Wedgwood china figures. (I don't much like them actually, though I know they're beautiful and priceless and it's just that I haven't any taste.)

"And now we'll have a dinner party," said Sylvia when we'd made the flat nice. "I'll ask Tom and you can ask – well anyone you want."

"All right," I said, "I'll ask Bob."

"I'll do the cooking if you like," said Sylvia. "Let's make a list of what we'll want. Then you could go to the supermarket on your way home. And you'd better buy half a dozen wine glasses too as we haven't any."

"Couldn't we use tooth mugs?" I asked.

"Oh Alex, really!" said Sylvia, laughing – so I laughed too, as if I'd made a joke. You wouldn't think two girls in their first flat would have to bother that much over a meal for a couple of young men, would you? But Sylvia has very high standards. She's really sophisticated. Mum says she's always been more like a grown-up than a little girl, perhaps because she's an only child, I don't know. Anyhow Mum thought it would do me good to live with someone like her – might get me out of my sloppy ways.

When I staggered into the flat next day with the load of shopping, Sylvia was doing a lovely Constance Spryish arrangement with the flowers.

"How do they look?" she asked, stepping back to inspect.

"Gorgeous! You are clever, Sylvia!" I sighed enviously. She has that feminine knack of making the most ordinary place into a home.

"Well I'll get going with the food while you have your bath," she said. I didn't think it worth mentioning I hadn't been going to have a bath because I'd had one last night instead. Besides, all of a sudden I felt sweaty and dirty compared to her.

The men arrived and Tom had brought a bottle of wine which he opened and poured into the new wine glasses I had got from Tesco's. Sylvia's food was delicious. We had avocado with prawns to start with and then roast duck with a marvellous orange and brandy sauce. Her gravy was rich and meaty, not like the pale thick stuff I make. And then we had apricot soufflé with cream. Mm, scrumptious!

It was, you might say, a successful evening. Successful for Sylvia, that is. As we ate our way through the meal I began to notice Bob's eyes glaze over like the orange sauce, as he pretended to listen to the witty jokes I was making. I had to prompt him when to laugh. And whenever he decently could, he'd turn his head to look at Sylvia. I couldn't blame him. She was so attractive and talented, I'd have done the same in his shoes. We all watched fascinated as she talked, the feminine way she gestured with her slender, well-kept hands, the way she tossed back the cloud of fair hair that framed her face. We sat entranced, hanging onto every word she uttered.

"Bob, you're neglecting Alex. Her glass is empty," she chided him gently.

"Oh – sorry, Alex," said Bob absently.

Later Sylvia said, "Bob, why don't you and Alex go in the other room while Tom and I make the coffee?"

So we went and sat down in silence on the sofa and Bob watched the door all the time till Sylvia returned. Then I knew I'd lost him.

That was the first of many little dinners – and of boyfriends that I lost to Sylvia. There was Bob, then Ray, then Johnny, then Paul. She didn't steal them, they just fell at her feet. They had only to see her once to be blinded by the light and I was in the shadow, forgotten. After a while I began to anticipate it. Why should any normal bloke prefer me after they had seen her? Beside her I felt tall and gangling and clumsy and because I felt it, I was. She could cook like an angel, sew beautifully and arrange flowers. She could talk cleverly, but I was dumb and stupid. I just looked on, helplessly. I tried to think of ways in which I could shine, but there didn't seem to be anything I was half as good at as she was.

Whenever she cooked for a special dinner party I washed up in her wake and I thought, what a shame I never got complimented on my washing up. Nobody ever picks up a plate and says "What a well washed-up plate!" or looks admiringly at a spoon and says "There's a nicely-dried spoon!" And no one says when you do the shopping, "How delightfully you buy cornflakes and sugar, and what a well-chosen tin of baked beans!" But that's the way the cookie crumbles.

You might wonder why on earth I didn't keep my boyfriends to myself, why I always had to take them to the flat to be devoured and swallowed without trace, but when you share a flat with someone, sooner or later you're just bound to bump into their boyfriends and they into yours. When you've been out with a guy and he walks you back to your flat you more or less have to ask him up for a coffee, and sooner or later, wham bang, there she is all delectably done up in her negligée and wham bang goes another one. I should have hated Sylvia, but I didn't, she was so nice, so kind, she had no idea of what she was doing. And if she had, when they started ringing her instead of me, well what could she do about it? She couldn't help *being* there, could she?

But then one night I changed my mind about her. We were sitting around the flat, she and I, and Tom was there and someone new I'd met called Pete and we were chatting and watching the telly, you know how it is, and Sylvia said, "Pete, shall you and I go and make some coffee?"

"You bet," said Pete quick as a flash, so off they went and closed the door.

Well really! I thought. I was wild. She didn't have to do that, did she? Taking Pete and leaving me there with Tom? What kind of a friend was she anyway?

Tom came and sat on the arm of my chair. "Never mind, Alex."

"Why, does it show then?" I asked, almost spitting at him.

"No – I just meant there are plenty more fish in the sea."

"So what if there are," I said, "if they all get dredged up the same way? Oh I'm sorry, Tom!"

But he laughed. "I know just what you mean," he said. "I say Alex, I've got an idea – how'd you like to come out for a drink?"

"With you?"

"Yes."

"What about the coffee?"

"Blow the coffee."

"But what about them?"

"They'll be all right."

Well that was true, I knew *they'd* be all right. I thought it was so nice of Tom to do this, even if he was just being kind. He knew, without my saying, just how I felt. Perhaps he felt the same himself. After all, it couldn't be very nice for him seeing all the young men drool over his girlfriend.

So we went to the pub and had a drink and then another and we drowned our sorrows, and it was such fun and easy being with him and not having to worry. We didn't leave the pub till closing time.

"You've done me a lot of good, Tom," I said as we walked back.

"Come out with me tomorrow," he said.

"You don't have to feel *that* sorry for me," I said a little stiffly.

"You don't have to feel sorry for you, I just want to be with you," said Tom. "It's a funny thing, all this time you've been sharing with Sylvia and I've never really noticed you before. To me you were just like…"

"Part of the furniture?" I said. "I know. It's hard to notice anyone else when Sylvia's around. You're not the only one to find that out. It's like living with the sun, if you know what I mean. Golden and dazzling."

"You're funny and sweet and you make me laugh," said Tom, "and I think I'm beginning to fall in love with you."

He put his arm around me as we walked and pulled me close to him and I felt a wave of happiness go over me.

"But what about Sylvia?" I asked suddenly.

"We're just good friends," Tom said. "Coming round has been no more than a habit lately. Sylvia doesn't really want one special boyfriend, she likes a number. And d'you know what she told me the other day?"

"No?"

"She said she thought you and I would be right for each other."

"She said that?"

"Yes."

Ah. *Now* I understand about Pete and the coffee.

There, you see! Didn't I tell you Sylvia was an angel?

Sold to OK

The Summer Girl

When the summer season started he was back in his old place at the roundabout on the pier. It was an easy job really, nothing to it: all he had to do was take the money and work the starting handle. On sunny days, when the summer visitors poured down from London on cheap day return tickets, they filled up the town and overflowed onto the pier and then he was kept busy, but there were other days when the wind was wild and the sea stormy; the red flag kept bathers off the beach and slow-rising clouds of spray crashed over the promenade. Then the people stayed away and he had time to stand and stare and think about the girl who had come down last summer.

She was friendly and shy and naïve all at once, like a child. She had milky blonde hair like sand and plump, rosy cheeks and eyes green as the sea. A girl of summer.

"I like it here," she had said. "I feel free."

They had stood and leaned over the railings, and along the shore the long lines of white-painted Regency houses were a backcloth to the people, a swarm of multi-coloured, ant-like creatures that surged in all directions. Out here at the furthermost end of the pier it was like being at sea, adrift in the ocean.

"How do you mean, free?" the boy had asked.

"Free to be myself," she said.

"Aren't you always?" he asked.

"No," she replied. "People expect so much – don't you find? You can't do this and you can't do that. That's not the way to behave, they say. You always have to conform to their standards. But here I can forget all that. I can see for miles and miles, there's nothing ugly in the way."

He thought of the dark basement flat where he lived with its damp, peeling walls, of how glad he was to leave it each morning, shrugging it off like an ugly skin, escaping guiltily to the sea.

"I think I know what you mean," he said, "You've left home, yet you've come to your own place, and it's like a kind of haven. You can breathe, there's no soot or smoke, just the salty smell of the sea."

"Yes, that's it!" she cried, pleased because he seemed to understand. She smiled and he was entranced.

When would she come back? She had said she would.

"I'd like to work down here for the summer season, like you," she had said.

"What would you do?" he asked. He could not imagine her here amongst the rough and tumble of the pier people, selling cockles perhaps, or candyfloss.

She looked at him hesitantly. "I've got a friend who's a receptionist at the Grand Hotel," she said. "They take on extra staff in the summer. I might get a job there."

Had she come back? Was she there now? He kept watching for her to come along the pier, walking towards him with that carefree step, but she never came.

He looked down between the wooden slats and way below was the sea, green and frothy where it beat against the iron girders. Last summer he had dropped 50p and he and the girl had knelt quickly, but it had rolled away out of reach and fallen down, down, and disappeared from view.

She put a hand on his, soft as a butterfly, consoling him.

"Don't mind so much," she said, "It's only money. Money isn't important."

"Of course it's important," he said impatiently. He thought of his mother, her shoulders sagging with tiredness, stirring pans of stew on the stove in the dark basement kitchen, and of his father with his face creased with worry; the rows over money. "You'll just have to manage," his father said. "Other people manage. I don't know what you spend it on." But he did know, and so did the boy. It went, all went, on fees for his sister's ballet school. It was the mother's cherished dream to see her dance at Sadler's Wells – and they didn't really begrudge it, the scrimping, the making do, for everyone has to have dreams.

"Money makes all the difference," said the boy, thinking of these things.

"Oh, but you're so wrong," said the girl. "Why are people always overawed by money? It doesn't impress me. It's happiness that counts."

"But money makes you happy."

"No it doesn't. It makes you hard and selfish and mercenary."

"Well anyway," said the boy stubbornly, "You can't be happy without it."

"Can't you? Aren't you happy today? I am."

"Yes," he answered, "I am." And as he said it he made the most marvellous discovery. There was the sweet singing of the sea in his ears. "I'm happy," he said slowly, because *you're* here!"

"And I too," she said, "because I'm with *you!*"

They looked at one another in delight, with what they felt was something intangible that they could not express, but precious and lovely like the first fragile threads of a cobweb, glinting with gold in the early sunshine.

Far below them white-crested waves dashed against the iron girders of the pier and over their heads gulls wheeled, uttering harsh, plaintive cries.

"Look at the sea," she said, "It's so wild and beautiful. It's another world – and it's all ours!"

The boy laughed with sheer joy. Yes, it was all theirs – but only for the day. And the day passed so quickly.

"I wish it would never end," he said, feeling the minutes slipping away like grains of wet sand, sucked in by the tide.

"I'll come back," she promised, "Next year. My father will bring me."

"Just for another day?" he asked.

Again that odd hesitancy. "I mean, I'll get a job. Wait here, I want to give you something," she said suddenly, and ran off along the pier. When she came back she thrust a package into his hand, wrapped in a white paper bag. Inside he found a small plastic paperweight, one of countless souvenirs sold at the little shop further down the pier.

"It's a present," she said, "Look!" Inside the Perspex frame was a scene of deer and pine trees against a brilliant blue sky. She shook it and the deer stood in a snowstorm of glittering, tinselly flakes. "Isn't it beautiful?" she said with childlike pleasure. "Do you like it?"

He looked at the crude, plastic deer through the whirling silver paper flakes and saw the beauty that she saw. He had passed the souvenir shop a hundred times and seen these things displayed in rows without ever looking at them before.

"Yes – I like it a lot," he said.

He took to going past the Grand Hotel on his way home from work. The Grand Hotel was very grand. He could just about picture her there, neat and smiling behind a desk – but not himself. The Grand Hotel had its own double driveway and finely-rolled lawns sprinkled with palm trees and beds of scarlet geraniums. A great flight of steps led up to the door, flanked on either side by a glass-covered veranda where the rich sat with their elegant clothes and their cocktails; and barring the main entrance stood the Commissionaire, imposing and stately in a brass-buttoned uniform.

The boy from the roundabout ventured to the bottom of the steps and stood there in his shabby jeans and fisherman's sweater with a hole in the elbow. He fingered the hard, smooth shape of the paper-weight inside his pocket.

"What do you want, boy?" boomed the Commissionaire of the Grand Hotel.

"I was looking for someone," stammered the boy, "She might be working here."

"What is her name?"

But he didn't know her name. Defeated, he crept away.

And then he saw her. He stopped abruptly. She was sitting at a table on the terrace with a party of sophisticated older people. A distinguished man in a pale grey suit, her father probably, watching her fondly as she sipped her drink. Her gleaming milky-blonde hair was piled elegantly onto her head. She wore a mint-green suit and tiny pearls in her ears. She was ice-cool, serene and beautiful.

A young messenger-boy passed by, bearing a long cellophane-covered box of flowers. His uniform had the words 'Grand Hotel' embroidered on each sleeve.

"I say, who's that?" said the boy, stopping him, indicating the girl on the terrace.

"That girl? She's with the VIP party. Her father's an ambassador," said the messenger.

The boy from the pier stared at her and colour flamed into his cheeks. She had lied to him! She would take a job, she had said, in the hotel. Yet there she sat on the terrace like a princess. She had never had a job in her life, he could see that! She must have known all the time she would not be seeing him again. So that was why she had hesitated over what she would do and said her father would bring her here. She had patronised him; laughed behind his back probably, knowing she was above him, beautiful and rich and quite beyond his reach.

Well, he didn't want her. She was not the laughing pink-cheeked girl he remembered. He hated her with her high-piled hair and her expensive clothes, sitting there with her rich companions. He didn't want her, and he turned abruptly away.

How happy they were, the summer visitors! How they thronged everywhere in their open-necked shirts and kiss-me-quick hats. Smiles cracked their sun-reddened faces, lollipops dangled from the sticky hands of their children. They sauntered along the front and spilled over onto the pier and pressed themselves into deckchairs; they fell asleep to the strains of band music that blared from variously sited loudspeakers, and ice cream dribbled down their fronts.

The boy from the roundabout passed them swiftly, not looking at them. Bitter thoughts kept crowding into his mind and he tried to shut them out. He mustn't think, mustn't remember. But deep down he knew his dream of the girl was shattered. He slipped his hand into his pocket and drew out the paperweight. It was a cheap and tawdry thing! He tossed it over the iron railings and it spun through the air and fell like a stone, down into the sea below.

He threw himself into his work. The sun-filled days passed quickly and there was no time to stand and stare.

And then one day the weather changed. The sky was grey and stormy and a strong wind whipped up the sea into effervescent eddies like frothy pools of ginger beer. Mighty waves pounded the stones on the beach and in retreat, scooped up the sighing shingle from the shore. Not many people braved the pier that day, just a handful of fishermen casting from the jetty and the people on the stalls and the boy on the roundabout.

And all of a sudden he saw a girl coming along the pier, walking with an easy, swinging stride. She wore a blouse and gathered skirt, and her face was wet with spray. When she saw him looking at her she broke into a run. Her long hair rippled down her back like sand, her eyes were green as the sea and her smile like the sun.

Then gladness filled his heart. She had come back to him after all, his Summer Girl.

A Second Chance

"Guess who phoned today?" I said when Matthew got home from work.

He put his briefcase down in the hall. "I've no idea."

"Toby. Toby Miller."

"Oh? What did he want?"

"A bed for the night. He's coming up north on business."

"Oh." Matthew hung up his coat. "Does he want a meal too?"

"I imagine so, after driving all the way up from London. I got some rump steak and a bottle of wine and I've made a lemon cheesecake for afters."

"You're pushing the boat out a bit, aren't you Laura?"

"Well not really – I mean , I'm sure Toby's used to wine, he leads such a sophisticated life now. And it's not as if he comes up every day, is it? It must be ten years since we last saw him, at our wedding."

"I remember," said Matthew evenly.

"I do want to give him a good impression."

"Oh you will Laura, I've no doubt at all."

"Be nice to him, won't you Matt?"

"Of course – what d'you take me for?"

"You'll like him," I said. "I'm sure you'll get on really well when you get to know him."

But would he? I wasn't sure at all – or how *I* should get on with him either, come to that.

"What time are we going to eat then?" asked Matthew. "I'm ravenous."

"I've no idea, he didn't say what time he'd get here. I mean he couldn't really, could he, when he doesn't know how long it takes."

"Well – how about a cup of coffee then?"

"Yes of course, Matt, I'll make you one."

Yes. How would *I* find Toby – and how would he find me? Ten years older, that was for sure.

Toby had been in the Navy when I had known him. He used to ring me up whenever he had some leave.

"Laura?" he'd say. "Listen. I'm at Portsmouth. Can you come down and pick me up? I've only got forty-eight hours."

So I'd drop everything and rush off to wherever it was to meet him. Then I'd drive him back to spend the precious two days with his family or mine. My mother loved him, he was so tall and looked so handsome in his uniform. I loved him too and I thought he loved me – he acted as if he did – I was the only girl he wanted to spend his leaves with, but he was shy and reserved, he never said anything about love and I was much too unliberated to say it for him. We always had such a marvellous time and spent every possible moment together but we never seemed to get any further. And then the end of his leave would come and we'd say goodbye till the next one.

"Goodbye, Laura. It's been great."

"I thought so too, Toby."

"You're a super girl."

"Am I, Toby?"

"I think so. You're top of the pops!"

Oh, how he hated to get serious.

"Toby…"

"Yes?"

"Oh – nothing."

"Goodbye, then. I'll write to you."

It didn't make things any better to be cross-examined afterwards by my mother.

"Well? Has he gone?"

"Yes."

"Did he say anything?"

"No."

"What, nothing at all?"

"No."

"Oh dear. How disappointing for you, dear."

"I don't mind."

"How extraordinary you are, Laura. I wonder what it is about you that makes men so... undemanding. I must admit, I had received over twenty marriage proposals by the time I was nineteen."

"Good for you, Mother."

"You're so ineffectual somehow, dear. It's not as if you haven't had the opportunity, is it? I mean all those hours of tramping across moors and things. What on earth do you have to talk about?"

"Cows."

"Cows?" She snorted.

I laughed ruefully. "Everything, Mother, except the one subject you'd like us to talk about..."

As the years went by I lived for the brief times when I'd see Toby, and I wrote to him at addresses all over the world. I read and re-read his newsy, unromantic letters that always began "Darling Laura" and ended "Heaps of love, Toby." Does he mean it, I thought? Darling Laura, heaps of love? And if he did, was heaps of love enough? Not for a lifetime, I thought. But I was too proud to tell him what I felt.

Once he told me that he loved me, and I was ecstatic. I kissed him lingeringly. "I love you too, Toby."

"That's good."

"What are we going to do about it?" I asked next.

"Do about it?" He looked blank.

"Well I mean – don't you want to?"

"I'd never take advantage of you."

"I don't mean *that*. I mean – oh well never mind. If you don't know what I mean I'm not going to tell you."

Another time I said, "D'you realise? I'm four years older."

"Older than what?"

"Than when I first met you."

"Well so am I."

"But it's different for a girl. I seem to spend so much time looking forward to seeing you and so much time thinking about it when it's over. I hardly live at all between leaves."

"If you want to have other friends Laura, you go ahead. I won't stop you."

"You mean, you don't mind?"

"I can't expect you to hang around just for me," he said.

You could I thought, if we were engaged I would, oh gladly!

And then Matthew came along, Matthew – strong and capable and dominant. He left me in no doubt of *his* feelings – but even then I had to give Toby one last chance.

"How would you feel if I was to get engaged, Toby?"

He was certainly taken aback, I'll say that for him. But he soon recovered. "If that's what you want," he said.

I could have shaken him. "Don't you mind? Don't you *mind* if I marry someone else? I thought you loved me!"

"I do, Laura."

"Well you've a fine way of showing it."

"What have I to offer you?"

"*Are* you offering?"

"I've nothing. No money, no house, no security."

"So you're *not* offering."

But he wouldn't be pinned down.

"I've nothing to offer," he repeated.

So I married Matthew. I liked Matthew, even though I wasn't in love with him. Perhaps it will come, I thought. "It *will* come," Matthew said. But it hadn't. I'd never felt that same breath-taking excitement with Matthew that I'd felt with Toby. Not in ten years.

And now Toby was coming here, to our house, to stay with Matthew and me. And how did I feel? That same breath-taking excitement. There. I had admitted it.

"You've had your hair done," said Matthew.

"Yes." I felt myself blush. I turned away, not wanting Matthew to see, but he had.

"You look very pretty, Laura," he said gently, "and not a day older than on your wedding day."

Why did he say 'your' wedding day, I wondered? Why not 'ours'? I felt hurt in a funny way, hurt for him.

The doorbell rang.

"Will you go?" said Matthew.

"Yes. All right."

I ran through the hall, smoothing my hair as I went, glancing in the mirror as I passed. I flung back the door.

Toby was taller than I remembered and more handsome now, ten years older, more distinguished.

"Hello Laura," he said, taking my hands in both of his. We looked at one another for a moment.

"C-come in!" I stammered. "You found us all right then. How was the journey? I want you to meet Matthew. You haven't really met him before have you, I mean I know you met at the wedding but it isn't really the same thing..."

"Hello Toby," said Matthew heartily. "Here, give me your bag."

The heartiness was false. He's nervous, I thought in surprise, *nervous* – of Toby!

But Toby was no longer that shy, reserved young man I had known. He was confident and self-assured. "You look marvellous, Laura," he said. "You haven't changed a bit. You're a lucky man, Matthew."

"I know," said Matt a little grimly.

"I'm lucky too," I said.

"What's this – a mutual admiration society?" said Toby, laughing.

We sat down to dinner. I was glad we'd 'pushed the boat out' as Matthew put it. Matthew poured out the wine as if we had it every night, and Toby complimented me on my cooking. Afterwards we washed up, all three of us together in the little kitchen, making jokes and laughing, determined to be jolly; and we were too, carried along by the wine, but the atmosphere was as brittle as fine glass.

I stayed behind to make coffee and when I carried it into the lounge they were talking men's talk, in which I didn't join. I had been very keyed up all day but now I felt tired, exhausted even, and like an old balloon that deflates slowly, with wrinkles. Later I would go upstairs and remove my make-up with a chisel, chip off the smiling mask, and when I could safely hide my face in the dark I might dare to ask myself that terrifying question: did I still love Toby?

Next day I was the first up. Does he have early morning tea, I wondered? But we didn't, so I didn't offer it. Besides, he probably wanted to lie in a bit. Matthew and I had breakfast together, in silence much as usual, yet different. Is he really reading the paper, I thought, or is he wondering what I am thinking? Does he know that I feel like a caged bird, beating its wings against the wire door, wanting to be freed? Once he looked at me piercingly over the top of the paper and I couldn't meet his look. I had to turn away and felt unclean.

"What time is it? I must go," he said abruptly, pushing back the chair.

"Aren't you going to say goodbye to Toby?"

"Is he awake?"

"I don't know. How should I know?"

"All right, I'll just pop my head round the door."

He went upstairs. I carried our plates through and put them in the sink. I could hear their voices somewhere above me. Then Matthew came downstairs again. "Goodbye," he said and kissed me lightly on the cheek. "See you tonight."

"Yes." I began to wash the dishes slowly. I heard the front door slam and then the car start up. And now – I felt colour rise in my cheeks –

Toby and I were alone in the house. I was conscious of doing everything very meticulously, putting away the china in the cupboard, washing over the tops of the kitchen units, polishing them over and over so that I wouldn't have to look at Toby when he came down.

"Hello there, Laura."

"Hello. Did you sleep well?"

"Fine."

"What do you have for breakfast?"

"Grapefruit, and devilled kidneys from a silver dish."

I laughed uneasily. I felt shy and awkward with him.

"No I mean, what d'you have really?"

"Coffee and toast, no different from the old days. What about you?"

"I had mine with Matthew, but I'll have another cup of coffee with you."

We sat opposite each other at the breakfast table and I couldn't meet his look any more than I could meet Matthew's earlier.

"Here – wouldn't you like to see this?" I thrust the morning paper at him. He glanced through it while I sat fiddling with a teaspoon, or staring intently at the detail of pattern in small patches of carpet and wallpaper as if seeing them for the first time. I felt self-conscious with Toby, but soon he would be gone and perhaps that would be the best thing.

"What time is your appointment?" I asked.

"Three o'clock."

"This afternoon!"

"Yes. Do you mind? Had you made plans or will you spend the time with me? It's so long since I saw you, Laura. Shall we drive into the country and have lunch out somewhere?"

"Oh yes, do let's!"

I felt exhilarated. It was so different from the routine of housework and washing I had intended; besides, going out to lunch in the middle of the week was a treat, something I had come to accept as a thing of the past because it didn't fit into the frugal way of life I had with Matthew. I hurriedly grabbed my coat and bag and ran downstairs to join Toby. Outside in the fresh air I felt like that caged bird set free and warmed by the morning sun.

We drove through the flat built-up suburbs of the town until gradually the houses thinned out and the landscape changed. The countryside looked marvellous, rain-washed in the night and now sparkling, hung out to dry. Sun-dappled fields, thick with buttercups and meadowsweet, spread on either side of the road and fell away into rich, many-shaded folds of green. Small white-washed cottages hung like pendants in the hills beyond, and far off stretched the soft blue of distant mountain peaks.

"I'm glad we came," I said. I raised my arms luxuriously behind my head.

"So am I. Laura…"

"We've practically got it all to ourselves!"

"Are you happy today, Laura?"

"Yes!"

"Is it because you're with me?"

"I don't know," I said. I knew he wanted to talk but suddenly I wasn't sure I wanted to answer. I was so afraid we might spoil this beautiful, innocent day.

He stopped the car in a lay-by from where we could look down into the valley.

"Laura…" he began.

I turned away. "Tell me, when did you leave the Navy?" I asked lightly.

"Nine years ago."

"How do you like working in industry?"

"It's all right. I love you, Laura."

"It's too late," I said.

"And you love me, don't you? I know you do, I see it in your eyes."

"No you don't, you just imagine that you do. It's too late, Toby. You had your chance ten years ago."

"One more year. You only had to wait one more year. I'd have left the Navy then and we could have been married."

Did he mean it? Had I only one more year to wait for him? Oh it was so unfair!

"You didn't tell me that, did you?" I said. "You gave me no idea."

"And now…"

"Now I'm married to Matthew. We've got a good marriage, please don't spoil it."

"You don't love him, not as you loved me, not as we've loved one another all these years."

He reached out for me and held me and kissed me; and I felt as if I was standing on wet sand that was slipping from beneath my feet as it was drawn inexorably into the sea, and I was helpless against the tide.

"It's still there, just the same," said Toby.

"Yes," I said faintly.

"You'll have to tell Matthew. Tell him how it is with us. How it has always been."

"I don't think I can."

"You must, Laura."

"Don't let's talk about it any more, don't let's spoil this lovely day."

"Never mind," said Toby, "I can wait."

He released me and we lapsed into silence. I watched a far-off herd of cows wending their way like little wooden toys across the valley. We stayed there not speaking for what seemed an age.

"Would you like to look for somewhere to eat now?" said Toby.

"Yes. I'd like that."

Toby had a book, a guide to good restaurants, and he quickly found a smart, sophisticated place, architecturally unusual, built on several levels, where rich young men with sports cars brought beautiful girls. Its dining room jutted right out over the valley and a vast picture window like a wall of plate glass along one side opened up the whole landscape to the diners within. As for the food, there was a magnificent cold table with veal and ham pies and many kinds of meat including duck and venison and six sorts of pâté, and there was wholemeal bread and red wine. I was impressed.

"Do you often eat at places like this?" I asked.

"Fairly often," said Toby.

What different worlds, I thought. I looked around at the young men and beautiful girls who took it all for granted. They talked and laughed lightly because they came every day, but for us it was just once – the only time.

I thought about Matthew and wondered what he would think if he knew where I was, who I was with, and what we were planning to do. Were we planning anything? Toby perhaps but not me, not yet. Matthew was so strong, so unwavering – yet surprisingly afraid of Toby. Had he known what might happen? Was that why he was afraid? He was strangely vulnerable.

And Toby. He was something else. Not strong, not like Matthew but confident – yes. So confident I would go with him. He had only to crook his little finger and I would go, give everything up, give Matthew up... I had so nearly agreed! A life with Toby, sophisticated friends, eating often at places like this.

It was tempting, but it was not enough. For why should I imagine Toby had changed? He wouldn't commit himself to anything or anyone. He hadn't loved me enough ten years ago, so why should I think he loved me now? It was just an illusion.

I looked at him and wished suddenly it could be Matthew sitting across there. He was steady, dependable and very dear. He deserved better than he'd got. I'd cheated him, I'd never really given our marriage a chance. And I couldn't bear to hurt him any more.

"We must go," I said, "D'you realise what the time is? You're going to be late for your appointment."

"Yes," agreed Toby, "I'll have to step on it."

I offered to pay my share of the lunch, but he wouldn't let me. Just as well, it would have taken all my housekeeping, all Matthew's hard-earned money. And I was anxious to get home.

"You can drop me off at the end of my road," I said.

"You're a bit premature, aren't you? We'll see how the time is when we get nearer," he said.

We didn't talk much. Once he said, "You must tell Matthew. It's only fair. You must tell him."

Yes, I thought. I must tell Matthew. The countryside flashed by and now I didn't see it. Instead I saw Matthew's face as it had been that morning, strong and stern, a little sad. How would it be when I told him? How would it change?

"Here we are!" I cried, "Drop me off here."

"Are you sure? I could easily take you to the door."

"No thanks. I'd like the walk. Goodbye – I'm so glad I've seen you again."

"You make it sound like an ending."

"It is an ending."

"But I love you, Laura."

I said gently, "No more I think, than you ever did, Toby."

"But you love me!"

"No my dear, I love Matthew. It's taken your visit to make me see it, that's all."

He looked downcast, like a small boy who has dropped his chocolate biscuit in the gutter.

"I can't believe it, Laura," he said finally. "Write me a letter when you've really decided."

"All right then." At least I owed him that much.

I rushed home and made the house spick and span for Matthew. I tidied up and made the beds and hoovered and I did it all very quickly as if I was racing against the clock, against some unknown factor that would step in and cheat me as I had cheated Matthew, and I kept dashing to the window to see if his car was coming up the drive. Suppose he'd had an accident? Suppose he was lying dangerously ill in hospital and would never know what I had to tell him?

But at last I heard his key in the lock. I ran across the hall and flung myself at him. "Hello, Matt!"

"My goodness," he said gently detaching my hands from his jacket, "What's all this in aid of?"

"I've been on a long journey," I said, "With Toby."

His eyes clouded. "I thought you looked excited. Has he gone now – or it he still here?"

"No, he's gone – and I've come back to you, Matt. I love you. I love you so much. Things are going to be different from now on, you'll see."

"That's good," he said. "Well how about a cup of coffee for starters?"

"Coffee? Is that all you can think of?" I cried.

He smiled and took me in his arms.

"Welcome home, Laura," he said.

Don't Tell the Neighbours

Sophie knew the moment he came into the house that something was wrong. Normally he shouted "Hello Soph!" then closed the front door and began to take off his coat. Today there was no shout, just a long pause while she waited expectantly for him to come into the kitchen where she was grilling chops for dinner.

At last he came slowly in, holding two brimming glasses. When he looked at her his face was grey and drawn.

"Hello," he said with a faint smile. "I've mixed you a stiff whisky. You're going to need it when you hear my news."

"What is it, Paul?" Automatically she stretched out her hand for the glass. She could not imagine what it could possibly be. "I've lost my job," he said.

Visions of disaster had been flashing through her mind, but none seemed as dreadful as the one enshrined in that short sentence.

And that was how the nightmare started. At first she could only look at him blankly, unable to take it in. "It's not possible – not you!" she said. "You're one of the senior executives. You're a director. I know how much they rely on you, John Richards has often told me how highly he regards you." (John Richards was the Managing Director.) "They couldn't have fired you!"

Paul nodded. "The factory's closing down."

"I can't believe it," she said. "There's always been an Anderson Pratt here, it's one of the oldest and most secure firms in the north. Surely they can't just make everyone redundant?"

"Not everyone," said Paul. "Bill Kerr's got a transfer to Leeds and Jerry Dean's going to Bristol."

"And what about you? Does all your loyalty, all the extra work you've brought home, all the worry you've had count for nothing? You've given them twenty-five years of your life."

"Twenty-four."

"Well then, twenty-four. The best years. It's not fair!"

Angrily she dished up the food. One of the chops slid across the plate and landed on the floor.

"Watch what you're doing!"

"Who cares? The floor's clean enough. Anyway I'll have it if you're so worried."

"I'm not worried about that. It's the way we take this. We must be rational."

"I don't want to be rational!" cried Sophie, half sobbing. "Who wants to be rational? I can't help being angry at the way they've treated you, that's all, I'm only human!"

"I know, love."

"I don't know how they can do this to you after all you've done for them. Why you, of all people?"

"Why not me? It's happened to thousands of others." He picked up a large spoon and began dishing out the greens. They were overcooked and mushy, but they were not in the mood to notice.

"Of course you'll get another job," she said presently.

"Are you asking me or telling me?"

"I'm telling you. You'll have no trouble. Look at your friends, all the contacts you've built up over the last twenty-four years. They'll rally round, you'll see."

"Well – I expect so."

"Of course they will. Any firm would be lucky to have you, with all your experience."

"And all my age," Paul added wryly.

"You're only forty-two. That's not old!"

"It is in industry."

"But you'll be all right. I know you will."

"As long as you go on having faith in me." He reached out and took her hands in both of his and held them warmly. "I'm going to need your faith, Sophie. You must be brave and strong whatever happens."

They discussed it far into the night: the sort of job he would look for, the contacts he would renew. Meanwhile they would carry on as normal, no need to say too much to anyone; they would continue to live in their house and let the two girls remain at boarding school as long as possible. They could make their economies in other less obvious ways; no sense in letting the world see that you were down.

Next day Paul scanned the papers avidly, reading aloud the possibilities. Some of them sounded very attractive and he wrote several letters of application which he read aloud to Sophie. "Yes Paul, that's good!" she said. "That sounds very impressive." She sat back dreamily, imagining how it would be. Perhaps it was all for the best, perhaps it was fate stepping in to provide them with the chance of another life, a richer and more satisfying one than the old.

But the days passed, and with them the first negative replies to his letters arrived, and they realised it was not going to be as easy as that. Every day they watched for the postman, eagerly at first but later with dread. "Regret... unfortunately... wish you success," said the letters.

"It's bound to be hard at first," said Sophie. "Anyhow, I don't think you should rush into any old job."

"I'm not getting much of a chance, am I?" he replied bitterly. "Not even an interview."

As for all his valuable contacts, that was the biggest laugh of all. "Yes, my dear Paul," wrote a typical one, "I do remember you very well and have been deeply impressed with your work over the years. Unfortunately I am not now in a position to come up with anything useful as far as you are concerned, however I have passed on your letter to my colleague, and he will be writing to you in due course…" And of course the colleague always did write, with regrets and unfortunatelys and wishing-you-successes.

After a while, Paul stopped talking to Sophie about the jobs he was trying to get. He continued routinely scanning the ads and writing letters of application, but he did it silently, without much hope.

The worst part for Sophie, silly as it may seem, was having to keep up the pretence in front of the neighbours. At first, when things were still on a superficial level, it was what they thought that most upset her. She and Paul had kept pretty well ahead of the Joneses up till then and although she hadn't thought she was that sort of person, it had given her something she had always lacked: confidence. All her life she had been unsure of herself, and marriage to Paul with his money and position had given her a certain status. Deep down she could despise herself for thinking such things mattered, yet in the life she led, the people she mixed with, they *did* matter – why deny it? Now, with the position and the money gone, so was the confidence.

First of all she had to sell her car. "Not that I ever used it really," she explained, "except for running around the village. It will do me good to walk a bit. It will give me some exercise." Yet she walked dejectedly, slinking along and hoping no one would notice.

There were coffee mornings among her girlfriends at which the topics of conversation were shopping sprees, new clothes, trips to town, the theatre, dinners out in newly-discovered expensive little restaurants, holidays abroad, weekends in the country, fishing and golf and skiing and all the other leisure pursuits of the comfortably off. They also touched on education, mildly grumbling about increased school fees, the expense of school uniforms and all the other extras, those never-ending extras like music and ballet and elocution and fencing and riding and well, you name it.

Suddenly Sophie began to feel panic-stricken. She had nothing to say. There was no safe subject on which she could venture an opinion. They talked so innocently, those cheerful, rich, unthinking women, but did they know, had they guessed? Had there been something about Anderson Pratt in the papers which she had missed? Had they seen Paul lurking about the garden or taking the dog for a walk when he should have been at work? Had they noticed that her shoes were down at heel and her tights were sprouting ladders? Had they seen her furtively scrubbing the front doorstep when no one was about?

She would go home demoralised and depressed, and although she tried to hide it from Paul he always noticed and asked her what was the matter. She could not tell him of course, it would be like accusing him. So this was what redundancy meant: she had never thought about it much before. You never imagined it could happen to you. Gradually life at home became a strain for them both, simply because he should not have been there. He seemed increasingly irritated by her. Everything she did, every look, became to him an act of reproach, a silent accusation of failure. She knew that he felt guilty and therefore tried to avoid bumping into him as far as possible, so that she might spare him some of the guilt. And when they did meet, him mooching about, her up to her eyes in chores, she didn't know what to say to him. She didn't know what to say to anyone these days, she thought. Yet unspoken thoughts she had in shoals, like tiny fish milling about in a dark pool.

When it came out into the open it was a relief to everyone. Of course there had been a paragraph in the paper about the closure of Anderson Pratt and the redundancies of the directors, including Paul Rochester. They had known for some time but hadn't liked to say anything. Even then Sophie could not bring herself to really confide in anyone. What could she say without being disloyal to Paul? How could she tell anyone of his bad temper, his fits of depression or her growing fears for the future? She made light of it. She and Paul worried? Good gracious no! She kept up a falsely bright front which deceived no one. Of course none of her friends dropped her overnight and on the surface they were as warm as ever, but now a new note had crept in: embarrassment. They would say to her brightly, "Hello Sophie, how's Paul?"

"He's fine thanks." The ever-automatic reply.

"Has he got another job yet?"

"Not yet, well – he's in no hurry. He doesn't want to rush into anything."

"Of course not, I was only saying to Alan this morning, he should take his time and find something he really wants."

If only they knew, thought Sophie.

After a while she realized that they did, and were just being tactful. Their husbands had probably said forcefully over breakfast in that unkind, blunt way men have, "Another job? Paul Rochester? Not a hope, I shouldn't think. Yes, very sad." And they'd turned the page to look at the latest share prices, for men could quickly shrug off something that did not concern them directly. As for the wives, there was this new element in their association with Sophie – this embarrassment, this pretence that nothing was any different. They were not necessarily shallow women, but she was intelligent enough to see their embarrassment and recognize it as the first barrier.

"You and Paul must come round one evening."

"Thank you, we'd love to."

"I'm not quite sure what we're doing next week, Alan seems to have such a lot on…" They would break off quickly, further embarrassed at having made what they thought was a gaffe, and Sophie did not know how to convey to them she knew they had not meant to imply Alan – or Richard or Jeremy – had a lot of engagements while Paul had none… oh dear, it was all so complicated.

"Yes - well anyway, I'll ring you."

"That would be lovely."

Before, if they had not rung, she would have put it down to nothing more than forgetfulness, good intentions momentarily postponed, the pace of life, but now there was a more sinister reason: they did not want to. They were putting it off. Perhaps the wife had genuinely wanted to when she had made the suggestion, but to her husband it was all a bit of a bore. "What on earth shall we have to talk to them about, darling? It's all so damned awkward. After all we're not such close friends, are we?"

"I'm very fond of Sophie," the wife might have said. "Besides, I feel so sorry for them."

"Well there is that of course – but to be quite honest Liz, I've never had a lot in common with Paul. Besides, it's not a very good plan to – what I mean is, it doesn't really do one any good to…"

What he really meant to say and couldn't bring himself was that it wasn't going to do him any good to be seen hobnobbing with someone who was out of work. There was something contagious in mixing with people on the downward path. Just as in tennis playing with better people improved your game, while lesser players reduced your performance to their level, so it was important to keep up in the social world or be dragged down with the dregs. Cold-blooded it might be, but true nevertheless.

One day someone had a drinks party to which the Rochesters were invited and Paul got drunk. It wasn't noticeable at first, but presently from her corner Sophie could hear him laughing often and loudly, and then he began going on and on about some business trip he'd made to the States years ago. Then he had told a particularly dodgy joke to Marion Fuller's mother, who had looked quite disgusted. People began edging away. Sophie couldn't bear to look. She thought that if she kept very quiet and didn't move from her corner perhaps no one would realise she was there, she wouldn't have to own up to being his wife.

Out of the corner of her eye she saw he had grabbed hold of little Maggie McPhee and was dancing a polka with her in the middle of the room but *oh Paul,* she thought, agonized, *it isn't that sort of party*! Everyone was looking on in stony silence. She had gone up to him and said, "Paul, I think we ought to go," and he looked at her and said in a slurred voice, "Go? Why should we go, I'm jusht beginning to enjoy myshelf, firsh time in weeks, why d'you want to shpoil it? Nobody mindsh do they?" then he shouted loudly "DOESH ANYBODY MIND?" Oh God let me die, she thought, here, now, let me die! "Paul, *please* let's go!" she implored, and another guest, having pity on her, had taken him gently by the shoulders and led him out. "Come on old boy, let's get you home." Paul had allowed himself to be led out to his car, and Sophie, crimson-faced, turned the key in the ignition, started the engine and backed hastily out of the drive. Oh, to get away from those disdainful stares!

"I'm sorry," Paul said later, halfway through a silent meal. He was painfully sober.

"It's all right," she said gently.

"It's *not* all right Sophie, don't be so damn stupid, you know damn well it's not, why do you pretend, why do you have to be so glib?"

She was startled and horrified by this outburst. He was so prickly these days, anything she said… she had to be so careful.

"I didn't mean – that," she said, "just that I don't blame you for anything."

"Of course you do!" he snapped irritably, "why can't you be honest for a change?"

"But I am being honest. I really don't blame you, because I can understand what you're going through. It doesn't stop me being *sorry* it happened. You must see the difference."

"No one else'll understand, that's for sure."

"Probably not."

"How can you be so calm?"

"I'm not really. Underneath I'm all churned up."

Suddenly he pushed his plate away and sank his head into his hands. "What – else – can – I – do," he said between clenched teeth, "that I haven't done already? I've written a hundred and sixty-three letters applying for jobs, they just don't want to know, it's just a waste of paper and stamps."

"But you will go on, won't you?" she pleaded, "because one day someone's sure, sure to think you're just the person – "

"Why should they?" said Paul flatly.

"But you have to go on trying, don't you see, because it's our only hope! Otherwise you might as well give up."

"What makes you think I wouldn't rather do that? Hope? Hope isn't all it's cracked up to be you know. It's an evil, demeaning thing, keeping you clutching at straws. Without it you'd know where you were, what you had to face up to."

She had never seen him so despairing. Now her worries about what the neighbours thought seemed trivial in the extreme and she felt herself to be the most superficial of women. She went upstairs and wept in the lavatory, because it was the one place she could have privacy. She wept because she was trying so hard to be what he wanted her to be, strong and patient and having faith in him, yet every day he himself made it more difficult. He was changing before her eyes, and she did not think she liked this prickly, suspicious man. The house seemed oppressive to her and full of unspoken accusations. Was this how hatred began? She wanted to get away, yet when she found herself outside in the open air she was like a tortoise without its shell, exposed, blinking at the fierce light of curiosity bent upon her from all directions. She wanted to turn and run, but there was nowhere to run to. And was this going to go on and on, day after day, year after year until they were old and empty, played out and past caring?

But next day Paul told her he had come to a decision. "It's no use pretending any longer," he said. "I can no longer live in this way, in this place and among these people. I would rather shoot myself. Nothing we do from now on could be worse than trying to live this sham. I'm going to put the house up for sale and we must take the girls away from their school. You'd better write to them and explain everything. We'll move somewhere far away from here where we can make a fresh start. You can call it running away if you want, I don't care. I'm tired of living in this elegant little house on this elegant little town estate, having to hold my head up, trying not to see the pity in the eyes of my friends and the coldness in people I thought were my friends. I want to be accepted on my terms, not on theirs, and that means no more pretence."

This was the crunch, the point they had most dreaded, yet strangely now it had come she felt only relief. Nothing worse than this can happen, thought Sophie, that's one consolation for being right at the bottom.

A "For Sale" notice went up on the house and the two girls were brought home at the end of the first half. The school was very decent in refunding fees for the remainder of the term. The girls seemed bewildered but were not resentful. Maria was sensible enough at fourteen to realise what her father was up against, while Clare, aged eleven, hated boarding school and was glad to leave.

So they moved hundreds of miles away from their smart, money-conscious neighbourhood to a modest country cottage with a bit of land backing onto a farm where Paul was able to grow vegetables and soft fruit. Later on he planned to turn over a piece of waste ground to poultry so that they could produce and maybe sell their own eggs. Meantime he did jobs in people's gardens, mowing lawns, digging over flower beds and so on. Although the work was menial and the remuneration small, it afforded them a living and for Paul an inner peace he had not thought to find again. Sophie painted the inside of the cottage and made curtains, and presently found herself a part-time job behind the counter in the village post-office. It was a far cry from their top executive days, but they were content.

When Sophie woke up in the mornings she could lie in bed and look across the fields and watch a line of brown and white cows wending their way to the farm to be milked. "The views from here are perfect," she said dreamily, as she cooked breakfast later. "They knock Mavis and Geoffrey's weekend cottage into a cocked hat."

"Poor things," said Clare, "only having the weekends. I feel sorry for them. It's great here, isn't it Mum? Like being on holiday all the year round."

"Yes dear," said Sophie, "Really great."

Presently the girls went off to school on the local bus that turned round at the end of the road. They had settled into the new school very quickly, and already Maria had found a local riding stables that was prepared to let them exercise the ponies in exchange for some help in the holidays. It was all working out so much better than they could have hoped, Sophie thought.

She poured a cup of coffee for Paul. The cottage, though modest was quite sufficient for their needs. Surprisingly so, she thought. One really needs so very little to subsist: food, warmth and somewhere to sleep – everything else was superfluous. "I really believe I could live quite happily in a cave," she told Paul, "like the Ancient Britons did."

"That's a bit drastic isn't it?" Paul answered laughing.

Laughing? She looked at him again to make sure. Yes, he was laughing. It was the first time she had seen him really laugh for months. He looked carefree in his old corduroys and check shirt open at the neck. "I'll plant the potatoes and broad beans today," he told her. He liked working in the open air, it was relaxing, and for her there was a delightful charm about country life. She even took to baking her own bread, something she would not have thought possible a year ago.

The nightmare was ended. At last they had learnt to face up to life. She and Paul had looked disaster in the eye and had come through. For Sophie the cruelties and hurts she had suffered only served to make her a stronger person. She could look back on the days when what the neighbours thought had mattered so much and realise that was all superficial. Even the confidence which money and position had brought her had been a sham, but now her new-found strength gave her a confidence that would last. People could take them as they were, she no longer cared. She and Paul saw in each other a new tolerance, a new understanding of themselves and of others. They were suddenly aware that they had left the rat race behind them for ever, and that life was good again.

After the Honeymoon

My dear Sally

Can you ever forgive me for not answering your lovely long letter, written – five months ago! Yes, Sally, five months, I'm really ashamed, it's not as if I wasn't thrilled to get your letter. It really cheered me up – not that I needed cheering up exactly. Well, actually – maybe I did.

What is it like being married, you ask? Well I can't say what it would be like for you and Tim, but if he's anything like Gerald – my God, should I tell you? You've just no idea what you're in for, my poor, *poor* lamb! And I'm not talking about the honeymoon either, that was all right, that bit. Well, how could it have not been, that dreamy view, the balcony almost in the sea, the orange and lemon groves, that blue, blue ocean, dancing in the Greek tavernas, Moussaka and rough red wine. How could it not have been the most dreamy time of our lives?

No Sally, it was when we got back. The house looked so small somehow and so lacking in sunlight. Poky, I'd describe it. That's how

I described it to Gerald, anyway. Our furniture that we spent such hours and hours choosing looked cheap and ordinary. Our chair covers and cushions in their assorted sweet-pea colours looked like mix-n-not-match. And the garden looked small and overgrown and dreary. "What a let-down after Greece!" I said to Gerald, and he agreed. "Yes Cecile," he said, "but so's the cooking!"

He did grumble about my cooking. "If I have Angel Whip once more I shall turn into one," he said, "We've had it every night this week."

"Oh Gerald," I said reproachfully, "How could you say that? On Monday it was chocolate and on Tuesday, strawberry and on Wednesday, butterscotch…"

"And stew," interrupted Gerald as if I hadn't spoken. "Brown stew. Is that all you can make?"

"No, but I made a lot of it so's it would last."

"And by God it has. It's gone on and on and on," said Gerald.

"Never mind, one more day should finish it," I said cheerfully.

You know Sally, Gerald has this funny habit of not talking at breakfast. He likes to read the paper. Well as we only get one that leaves me with nothing but the back of the cornflakes packet, which is a bit limiting. And Gerald gets *livid,* absolutely *livid* if I so much as say "Will you pass the butter?" and I add "please" of course but it makes no odds. It's really extraordinary when you think of how he used to hang on my every word that I now have to eat dry toast and marmalade if I want to avoid a holocaust of abuse.

Being a wife is so much more difficult than you'd imagine, Sally. Take ironing, for instance. (Yes you *can* take it!) I had to iron this blessed evening shirt with a stiff collar one day, so I just sprayed a bit of instant spray starch over it from an aerosol tin and when I ironed it, it went brown. I mean, I didn't do a thing wrong, it just went brown all by itself. It was so unfair of Gerald to blow me up about that.

Then there was the day we decorated the landing and hall. The bit from the ceiling to the stairs is very long in places, so Gerald said would I stand at the bottom and he'd be on the ladder and he'd drop the roll and would I say if it was straight before he started sticking it down.

"OK?" he asked.

"OK fine," I said.

Well it looked as if it was straight. Well I'd hardly have said, "Yes Gerald, it's straight," if I hadn't genuinely thought it was, would I? But sure as eggs are eggs, when he stuck it all on and came down the ladder he literally went up the wall again. "It's crooked, it's crooked!" he yelled, and he went on in such a demented way I couldn't help looking at him more closely and wondering if there was something funny about his family.

"Well, don't just stand there!" he yelled.

"No, all right," I agreed placatingly, "What would you like me to do?"

"I'd just like you to stand there" (You see what I mean?) "and tell me if it's straight."

"I thought it was."

"You *thought* it was?"

That seemed to make him angrier than ever.

"You must be b… (you know what that stands for, don't you Sally? I won't write it in full) b… cross-eyed!"

So it all had to be peeled off and ten minutes later there we were again, him at the top of the ladder and me at the bottom waiting for the roll to fall.

"Now then Cecile – is it straight this time?"

"In my opinion," I said carefully, "it is, but that's just *my* opinion so don't blame me if you don't think it is when you come down the ladder."

"There's no need to be melodramatic," he said.

"I don't agree," I said. "I think there's every need. I need to insure myself against your quite unjustified wrath."

"Oh yes, well of course it's always my fault, isn't it? *You're* never to blame."

"No in all honesty I don't think I ever am. I wish I could believe you felt so too Gerald, but I have the sneaking suspicion you're being sarcastic. And incidentally Gerald, I didn't like to mention it before when you were ranting and raving so, but I think you've put the paper on upside down."

D'you know what he did then? He picked up a great big tin of citrus-yellow paint and threw it all over the wall. Yes, without a word of a lie, that's what he did. I couldn't believe anyone could be so childish. No one else I know would dream of doing such a thing – or would they? That's the funny thing about marriage, Sally – you never really know anyone till you're married to them.

I thought of walking out on him then, but I didn't, not that time, I helped clear up the mess instead, that came later. Should I tell you about it? Well you see it was when we were eating our lunch last Sunday and watching an old film on the box at the same time. It was such a silly argument we had. We couldn't agree about the main star and I said it was Joan Crawford and Gerald said it was Joan Fontaine.

"Don't be silly Gerald, it's not Joan Fontaine," I said, "Haven't you seen her in *Rebecca*?"

"Course I have and I'm telling you that's her," said Gerald.

"It's not, you're up the pole!"

"No I'm not, you are!"

"You always think you're right, don't you? You can never concede someone else might be right and you might be wrong."

"Not in this case, no."

"I'll go and look it up in the paper. That'll settle it."

"What does it matter anyway? For heaven's sake sit down and finish your lunch."

But I had to show him he was wrong. I got up, went into the other room, found the paper, looked at the back page and returned triumphantly to the living room. "A Season of Joan Crawford," I read out.

Gerald said nothing. He was watching the screen. He didn't have the grace to say he'd been wrong, so I said it for him.

"You see?" I said, "Why can't you admit it, Gerald? I was right and…"

"All right, all right."

"…and you were wrong."

"For God's sake sit down and shut up!" he said.

"I knew I was…"

"If you say one more word I'll throw my dinner at the wall."

"Right. But you…"

"One more!"

"Can't ever admit…"

Wham, Slam, Crash! He picked up his plate and hurled it, contents and all, at the wall. It was cottage pie and mushy peas. I'd progressed from brown stew, you see. It made an awful mess. We got up straight away, both of us and started clearing it up. Gerald was still angry and I was sobbing with bewilderment and frustration. "It took me ages to make that Cottage Pie," I sobbed. "By the time one's cooked all the mince and boiled and mashed all the potatoes –"

"Oh spare me the details," said Gerald.

"But it's such a waste!"

Our dog Whoopsie ate it in the end, our little black and tan Dachsie. But Gerald must be taught a lesson, I thought. Later on when he and Whoopsie had gone out for a walk on the heath, I packed all the dirty washing and a packet of soap powder into a suitcase and set off for the launderette – we don't have a washing machine, you see. And I left a note for Gerald on the hall table. It said, "I have gone away for a while. Please don't try to find me. Cecile." That'll teach him, I thought. That'll give him the shock of his life.

Off I went to the launderette with my new library book and I stayed there a good two hours, I should think. Long after the washing was finished anyway, because people kept nudging me and saying "Your machine's stopped, dearie" and I'd say, "Yes I know" and carry on reading. They looked at me very oddly, but I couldn't risk getting home before Gerald. I did want him to get his Awful Shock first. At last I thought he must be home by now, so I packed the damp washing into its plastic bag, crammed it back into the suitcase and walked home.

To my dismay the house was all in darkness though it was gone five.

I inserted my key into the lock and turned it. And there, the first thing I saw, was my note still on the hall table. Gerald had never even seen it. Feeling slightly stupid, I screwed it up into a ball and threw it into the waste paper basket.

I felt oddly flat. I sat on the edge of a chair and flicked over the pages of a magazine. I turned everything on and off, first the television, then the radio, then the kettle, then the oven. Why didn't he come home? He couldn't still be walking, surely? Perhaps *he* had decided to leave me!

Oh Sally, I went through such agony, you've no idea. You see, and I realised it then just how much, I really do love Gerald. Oh if only I could have one more chance, I said to the hideous vase on the windowsill Aunt Edith gave us, I'd show him just how much. But I couldn't help fearing I would never see Gerald again.

And then at ten minutes past seven the front door suddenly opened and in came Gerald and Whoopsie. "Oh Gerald, darling!" I cried, flinging myself all over him, and the dog flung himself all over me and we were in a terrible muddle on the sofa with everyone kissing or licking everyone else.

"Gerald, I've missed you so much – where have you been?"

"To the cinema."

"Oh – with Whoopsie?"

"It was *101 Dalmatians*," he explained.

"Oh, I'd love to have seen it."

"I'll take you one day, I promise. And when did you get back from the launderette?"

"Hours ago. At least two. But how did you know?"

"I found your note and then I found the dirty washing had gone, so I went to look for you and I saw you sitting in the launderette all on your own, reading a book."

"Oh!"

He hugged me and we both laughed.

"Gerald darling, I'm so terribly sorry it wasn't Joan Fontaine in that film."

"And I'm sorry about your lovely cottage pie and mushy peas."

"I'm so glad you only went to the cinema."

"And I'm so glad you only went to the launderette."

"You're never going to have Angel Whip again, I promise."

"No?"

"No. We can have the most delicious frozen apple pie or tinned rice pudding instead"

Gerald kissed me again. "I love you, Cecile," he said.

Well – I don't need to tell you the rest, do I? You see Sally, what I've learnt is this: you have to be a bit tactful when you're married, and you mustn't always be in the right. I mean you can be of course, and you probably are most of the time but you don't have to *rub it in*. You don't have to prove it to anyone else, after all as long as *you* know, you can wink at all the world over his shoulder.

All of that happened a week ago and life has been blissful ever since. Marriage is different but better far than you could have dreamed, so hurry up and take the plunge Sally, you and that Tim of yours, and we'll dance at your wedding.

Lots of love, Cecile.

Dear Aunt Gwyneth

In the morning Louise arrived suddenly at my office.

"Can I come in?" she said.

"You are in," I pointed out.

"I'm on the verge of divorce."

"You always are," I said. I looked at her, trying to assess how serious she was this time.

"I hope I'm not interrupting something – some great epic masterpiece," she said, but I knew she wouldn't care if she was. Nobody, least of all Louise, considered writing to be a proper job and everyone believed that writers were there to be interrupted.

She perched herself on my desk, on top of the morning post.

"I could do with a drink," she said. "Something strong from your secret booze cupboard."

"It is not at all secret," I said. "If it was secret you wouldn't know about it."

"Don't split hairs."

"Neat whisky I suppose?" I said. "Heaven know what it'll do to your liver." I poured some out for her from an already depleted bottle. "Well – what is it this time?"

"I want to consult you professionally, as Auntie Gwyneth. After all, if you can spend half your time answering problem page letters for a woman's magazine like *Truly Fair*, you can spend half an hour listening to my problem, surely?"

"Why not?" I said indifferently. Her sarcasm irritated me.

"Would you be able to give me a completely unprejudiced reply?"

"Of course. I'm a professional. What is your problem?"

"I really don't think I can go on any longer."

I had heard that before too.

"It's my husband," she said.

I had guessed it would be. It's always the husband – except of course, when it's the wife.

"What's the matter with him?"

"He's an absolute swine. A swine of the first water. Or is it order? Whatever it is, he's it."

"I see. Either would be correct. And what has he done, this absolute swine?"

"It's what he hasn't done I mind about. He hasn't talked to me, he hasn't listened to me, he hasn't even looked at me, not properly, for months. He's so completely wrapped up in his work. Sometimes," she said, and her eyes darkened, "Sometimes I think he doesn't love me any more."

"Surely people don't have to continually tell one another, not when they've been married as long as you've been married? How long is it – fifteen years?"

"Sixteen. Do you know he can't even remember our anniversary. It's today, but did he remember? Did he thump!"

I gasped at this. "That's very bad. That's inexcusable."

"That's what I think."

"He ought to be horse-whipped."

"Do you suggest that I…"

"Oh no – certainly not!"

"What *would* you suggest, then?"

But I couldn't think of a thing.

"Perhaps," I said slowly, "perhaps he's worried about something."

"Like what? He's got a good job. He gets a damn good salary. What's he got to worry about?"

"Maybe you're too extravagant. Maybe you're over-spending. Maybe you're always going off blueing his money on a new dress, or something."

"Why do you describe it as 'his' money? Surely it's *our* money. Didn't he promise to endow me with his worldly goods – such as they were? It should be share and share alike. I may not earn a salary but I work in the house. I house-keep, in my fashion. His goods should be my goods."

"Not if you don't know how to look after them."

"That's not relevant. We were married for better or worse. As far as I'm concerned, it's for worse. No really, I'm at the end of my tether. He is being quite Victorian in his attitude towards me. Grim and disapproving if I so much as spend 50p on a pair of tights. He either flies off the handle for nothing at all or else he's sunk in gloom all the time. The house is like a morgue. There's no fun in it any more. I long to escape."

"Then why don't you?" I said.

"That's what you advise, is it?"

"I didn't say that."

"You don't seem to be saying anything. Tell me, you should know, you're the one they all write to. Are all marriages miserable?"

"You're not miserable," I said.

"I am today," she insisted.

"What are you going to do about it, then?"

"I don't know. How can I leave him, really? Where could I go? If only we had a country cottage somewhere that I could escape to. Or if only I had money of my own, I could go to a hotel, or abroad for a while to think things over."

"You'd need a lot of money for that," I said.

"That's what I mean – if only I had money of my own!"

"D'you want me to give you some?"

"No," she said, "because I couldn't pay you back."

"I wouldn't anyway. I'm not going to provide the means for you to break up your marriage."

"So what am I going to do?"

"Stick it out, I suppose."

"And be unhappy?"

"Yes. That's life, isn't it? After all you're not unhappy all the time."

"But it's second-best. Why should I have to settle for that?"

"Because there's no alternative."

"It's so unfair. I don't know what went wrong. We used to be happy, or so I thought. I was, at least."

I said nothing. Why should I try to comfort her? She was not a little girl.

"I must say, I don't think much of your advice, 'Aunt Gwyneth.' You must have a lot of dissatisfied readers!"

"I guess that's what the Editor thinks," I said drily.

"I'm sorry. I don't mean it. I'm sure they all love you – but is it really the best you can do?"

"I'm not a miracle worker."

"I didn't think it would take a miracle," she said quietly.

There was a long pause. Then I said, "Have you ever thought what might be making him this way?"

"How should I know? He never confides in me about anything. He hasn't really talked to me for months."

"Perhaps he's worried."

"I doubt it. What's he got to be worried about?"

"What if his job were to pack up?" I said. "What then?"

"That's no problem," said Louise. "He'd get another job. He's good, he'd soon get something – and till he did I'd go out myself."

I looked at her in surprise. She could be so immature – usually was – but I felt she meant what she said.

She saw my scepticism. "You think I couldn't? I used to be a damn good secretary once – I could be a temp, or at least something in an office. Make the tea, perhaps. That's no problem," she said. "But what I'm wondering is, if he still loves me. If I thought he was bored or indifferent I'd walk out tomorrow."

"I'm sure he does love you," I said. "Deep down."

"Then he ought to show it."

"Like this?" I rose from my desk, took her in my arms and kissed her thoroughly. When I had finished she said, "Wow, that's quite something! Does Aunt Gwyneth do that for all her disgruntled readers?"

"To hell with Aunt Gwyneth," I said. "You're quite right, her advice is lousy. She'll be out on her ear before long, I'm afraid. I'm sorry I forgot our anniversary, but you know what my memory's like. What can I do to make it up to you? I tell you what, we'll go out to dinner tonight. I'll book a table at Alfredo's."

"Alfredo's!" she gasped, as well she might. "Oh Tom, can we afford it?"

"What the hell?" I said. "Aunt Gwyneth can pay. If the old girl's going to bite the dust anyhow she may just as well have one last fling."

Goodbye to Love

I was never in love till I met Greg. I didn't even know what it felt like. Graham and I had been married just five years then and I don't suppose I expected more from marriage than I'd got. I mean, every girl dreams of a white wedding and romance – but so many people I knew had been disappointed with the romance part. You can't go on being madly in love for ever, my older sister explained wisely. That's just for story books or old films that you watch on the box. No, I would settle for what I'd got, I thought. That was what life was all about, you grew up with your family and you went to school and when you left you got a job, nothing exciting, in an office most likely. You started going out with a local boy, twice a week you went out and on Friday nights you washed your hair. No one proposed or anything, it just became an accepted fact you'd get married in the end, so you had your June wedding with a marquee and champagne your Dad got cheap at the wholesale place near where he worked, and everyone had new outfits and your Mum cried. It was just the same when Jean got married last year, and would be the same for Trish in two years' time. After your stipulated fortnight in Majorca you came home and settled down in a little three-bedroomed house with all mod cons on a nice, desirable estate, with your sisters living round the corner. And in two years' time, you had a baby. That was how it had been for all of us, that was how we expected it to be.

I liked my little house with its mod cons. I washed my baby's nappies and hung them out to dry in our back garden, then I took her for a walk to the park in her pram. There were always lots of houses I could go to, my mother's or my sisters' or my girlfriends'. In the evening I'd cook a meal for Graham and then he'd go off to the pub for a drink and a game of snooker with his pals and my mum and my sisters or girlfriends would come in and sit with me and we'd dress-make or watch the telly. Last year Graham and I bought ourselves a colour telly on HP and next year it'd be a freezer. What more had life to offer?

But then Graham was moved to another area right up in the north-east of England, and our lives changed drastically. I had always known with Graham's job that he might be moved, but somehow I had never really thought that he would be. At first it was quite exciting, looking for a new house and everything. But then when the removal van had taken all our furniture and deposited it there, it was different. There was no going back now. No popping in to see Mum or the girls. We were miles and miles away in an alien setting.

Graham didn't mind. It was all right for him, a new job, promotion in a way and certainly a challenge. Besides he got out every day, not like me. I sat at home and felt lonely and homesick. I had no friends. There were days when I spoke to no one, not even the milkman. I waited eagerly for Graham to come home in the evening and was resentful of the time when he was too tired to talk to me, or even to listen. Didn't he realise that I was miserable and I depended on him for company? But he didn't seem to – or if he did, he wasn't very understanding. He treated me impatiently, like a second rather tiresome child. He made me feel I was a drag, and because he made me feel that way, I really began to be. I would sit and mope and feel sorry for myself and question where he'd been if he was late. And he'd be irritable and sarcastic.

I tell you all this because perhaps it'll make you understand better how things were with us when I first met Greg. It was at a party that we went to about six months after we'd moved, and it was given by a girl called Mavis West who had a little girl a few months older than Debbie. Mavis was an acquaintance rather than a friend, but she had been kind enough to baby-sit one night and she had promised to try and get Debbie into a local playgroup.

Greg was easily the most attractive man at the party. He was immensely tall and thin with a handsome, rather sensitive face and sad eyes. He was my idea of a poet.

"Mavis," I whispered. "Who's that man who looks like a poet?"

"Oh, you mean Greg Fraser," said Mavis. "He's a salesman actually. I'll introduce you, shall I?"

She led me through the throngs of people, chatting together in small groups. "Greg, I'd like you to meet a friend of mine, Rebecca Shaw. Rebecca doesn't know many people up here, she's come up from the south somewhere."

"Buckinghamshire," I murmured.

"Oh really?" Greg turned his soulful eyes on me with interest, as if Buckinghamshire was the moon. "I was down that way only last week."

"Were you? Whereabouts?" I asked eagerly.

"Beaconsfield."

"And how was it?"

"Green. Lazy. Dappled with sunlight. Another world."

"Yes, it would be," I said. A wave of nostalgia swept over me. We fell silent, and when I looked up I found Greg watching me. Someone had rolled back the carpet and there were couples dancing. "Would you like to?" asked Greg.

I looked around for Graham. He was standing near the door, deep in conversation with a bank manager. "All right," I said.

We danced and Greg bent over me protectively, treating me as a woman. It was the first time anyone had taken that much interest in me for years. When the dance finished he continued to hold my hand as if he had forgotten it was there, but I knew he hadn't. I was happy: it was such a little thing, but I felt wildly happy. I wanted the evening to last for ever.

On the way home I felt like a new person. "Did you enjoy it?" I asked Graham.

"Oh yes, it was all right," he said, "If you like that sort of thing."

I felt heady, as if I had drunk too much wine, which I hadn't. I suppose I was flattered, but suddenly I felt young and attractive and vital and alive instead of just rotting away in a place where nobody knew me and I knew no one. It was weeks before I saw Greg again, yet I treasured that evening, remembering over and over again the dark, smouldering looks he had given me and the way he had held tightly onto my hand when the dance was finished. I told myself it was the way he was with every girl – but somehow I knew it was just me.

About five weeks later I suppose, I was baby-sitting for Mavis and her husband Phil when the doorbell suddenly rang and there was Greg standing outside on the doorstep. "Is Phil here?" he asked, looking surprised to see me.

"No, he's out – they both are. I'm just baby-sitting," I explained.

"Oh well…" he seemed at a loss. "Perhaps I could come in and wait for them to get back?"

"That might not be for hours."

"But still, I'm not doing anything else. That is, if you don't mind."

"Oh *I* don't mind."

I wished I was wearing something more glamorous than my old skirt and sweater. We went into Mavis's sitting room and sat down gingerly on the edge of the sofa, and I felt shy –I think we both did.

"Would you like a drink?" said Greg presently.

"Do you think we should?"

"Oh yes, don't worry, Phil and Mavis won't mind. I've known them for years."

He went over to the drinks cupboard in the corner of the room.

"And your wife?" I ventured.

"We're separated," he said briefly.

"I'm sorry."

"Why should you be sorry?"

"It's always sad to hear of a broken marriage."

He gave me a penetrating look. "But yours is a happy one?"

"Yes," I said.

It was so easy to say, yet was it really? I had never thought much about it before.

We talked easily, Greg and I; there seemed so much to say.

"I've got a confession to make," he said once.

"What is it?"

"I knew you would be here tonight. I rang earlier and Mavis told me you were baby-sitting. She said she thought you wouldn't mind if I came."

I was astonished. That it had seemed so accidental yet had been planned beforehand – and with Mavis too. But now I knew he had wanted to see me again. I was warm inside and I felt my skin glowing, and Greg looked at me as if he could never take his eyes away, despite the old skirt and sweater.

"Are you really a salesman?" I asked him.

"Yes."

"What do you sell?"

"Nuts and bolts."

"Good heavens, and to think I thought you were a poet!"

We laughed. It was all so carefree, so easy, yet the knowledge that he should not really be here with me made it seem illicit and exciting.

And then came the moment when he reached across and covered my hand with his. "Let me see you again, Rebecca," he said.

"Oh, Greg…"

"Do you ever come into town? Let's meet for lunch."

"I don't know if I could do that."

"Say you will. Just for lunch. I'll give you my phone number."

Just lunch, he said. What could be the harm in that? Yet when I got home that night I didn't tell Graham I had seen him. And Mavis was surprising. She seemed to be aiding and abetting me in deceiving Graham. "If you wanted to meet Greg," she said meaningfully, "I'll always look after Debbie for you."

"Oh…" I didn't know what to say to her. "What on earth do you mean?" or "Why ever should I want to meet Greg?" didn't seem to ring true yet I wasn't sure I could trust her.

I thought about him constantly all the next week. It happened I needed something for Debbie that I couldn't get locally and I would have to go into town fairly soon. I kept wondering. Should I meet Greg? No I couldn't! Should I phone him? No, I wouldn't.

"Fairfield three double oh nine," said his voice on the end of the line.

"Hello," I said foolishly. "It's me," and I felt like a scarlet woman.

"Rebecca! You don't know how glad I am to hear your voice."

We arranged to meet for lunch the next day. Just lunch – but that was really how it began. It was wonderful at first. There was so much we had to find out about each other. There were so many questions to ask.

"Do you have coffee for breakfast? What sort of marmalade do you like? Do you listen to Radio Four when you wake up? I feel that all the years have been wasted that I haven't known you," said Greg.

I went around with my head in the clouds. "Somebody loves you, I wonder who…" I sang. I couldn't concentrate on anything, not even Debbie. I felt guilty but I couldn't help it. I didn't listen to her baby "scribble talk"; it went over my head, instead I was day-dreaming as I washed the dishes, re-living every moment I had spent with Greg, treasuring everything he had said to me, storing up the memories, hugging them to myself like a squirrel.

It was slow, our affair, slow and sweet, and we could savour it with lingering delight, bit by bit. There was the first time he kissed me and the first time he called me "darling" and the first time we made love. And I didn't care about anything else, not Graham or Debbie or my family down in Oxfordshire, just so long as we could be together for a few precious hours now and then. I didn't think about the past or the future and when I wasn't with him I was in another world, far away from Graham. Did he notice, I wondered? But I neither knew nor cared. No, that's not true, I did care, but it didn't stop me living on a knife edge like a dope addict that has to have his shot of dope. Now I knew what it meant to be in love and to be loved in return, and it gave me confidence and made me feel rich. No one, I thought, no one has more than I have with Greg.

Somebody once told me, or perhaps I read it in a book, that the best part of an affair is the beginning. They were right, whoever it was. It is the best part. It was the best part for Greg and me.

I can't tell you just when I realised the beginning had ended. It just dawned upon me gradually. At first I didn't really care if Graham found out about Greg and me, although I didn't want him to because I didn't want to hurt him, but if he did learn the truth then it must be fate. I would leave him. I would even give up Debbie to be with Greg and one day we would get married. But gradually, gradually I became afraid. Could I really give up Debbie? I wasn't sure that I could. And I wasn't *absolutely* sure that Greg would marry me either. Oh I was ninety-nine per cent sure, of course I was! I mean he loved me, he had often said so. Yet of the future we never ever spoke. He was living day to day too. I wanted to ask him, to be reassured – but I couldn't bring myself to do it. Perhaps I was afraid of his answer.

So the time passed and we went on living on a knife edge. And then came a bolt out of the blue.

"I don't know how to tell you this Rebecca," he said one day when we were at his flat. He had a drink in his hand and was twisting the stem around and around in his fingers.

I felt cold inside. I felt sure it was going to be something bad.

"What is it?"

"It's about Judy."

"Your wife?"

"Yes."

"What about her?"

"She wants a reconciliation."

"Oh," I said.

Oh... oh... oh... What an inadequate little word that is!

"I thought it was finished between you," I said in a small voice.

"We're separated, yes."

"I thought there was nothing left between you."

"You can't be married for ten years and have nothing left between you."

"I didn't know you still saw her."

"I met her about a month ago."

"Quelle chance!"

"Don't be bitter, Rebecca."

Me, bitter? I didn't want to seem bitter. "I just meant," I said carefully, "It was a coincidence that you should meet again when she lives in Scotland."

"She wrote to me," he explained. "Well what could I do? I had to meet her."

I didn't want to hear any more. My heart was breaking.

"She said she was ill," he added. "She asked me if we couldn't have a fresh start and try again."

"And could you?"

He was silent for a moment. "Well maybe," he said at last. "I mean we had a good marriage, once."

So did I, I thought silently, till I met you.

"I felt so sorry for her," he said.

Oh my God, Greg, don't say any more, I can't bear it!

But he went on and on. "She had been ill, she wasn't just saying it and you could see she'd had a rough time. She'd really suffered – and it was all my doing. I never realised how much I had made her suffer."

And what about me? I thought. Don't you care how I shall suffer?

But I said nothing.

Should you fight for love? I know some people do, but I didn't. Maybe I had too much pride. If he wanted to go, let him go. Or maybe

I didn't love him enough after all. That's what *he* thought, anyway. Or maybe he was just trying to salve his conscience.

"I've always felt it was just infatuation," he said.

"For you?" I said, disbelievingly.

"For us both. I've always thought that really, deep down, you loved Graham."

"Oh Greg, you hypocrite! You knew I loved you! You must have known. I'd have given everything up, everything, if you'd just said the word."

He was a little stiff, embarrassed, after that. It was the nearest we'd ever come to quarrelling. I had always sensed he wouldn't like quarrels and for that reason I had avoided them. And what man likes criticism?

After a moment I said, more calmly, "Is this to be our last evening, then?"

"Well…" he said and left it unfinished.

So he had come prepared never to see me again. I began to feel numb inside.

"Let's not quarrel, Rebecca," he said, "Let's make it a nice evening to remember."

For the first time I despised him, just a little. But I tried very hard to behave as though nothing had happened. I couldn't be happy, couldn't smile with my eyes but I managed to keep a stiff upper lip.

Yes, I didn't let my bitterness spill out. I wonder if it was a happy evening for him to remember? As far as I was concerned, I wanted to forget it.

Now I could see through Greg, but I still loved him, because you can't stop loving someone just like that. You go on loving them whatever their faults, however much they hurt you.

I went home to Graham and Debbie and somehow I managed to keep the ache, the pain inside me and to act as if nothing was wrong. I had to keep it to myself, for there was no one to tell. I acted like a robot. I did the housework and got the meals and washed them up afterwards. I dressed Debbie in the mornings and fed her and put her to bed at night. Everything was mechanical, except thinking. If only you could switch that off. If only you could stop thinking. Oh Greg, where are you now, what are you doing. Do you ever think of me? They'd play a tune on the radio, something we liked, we used to dance to, and I'd weep, profusely and without effort. Everything I saw through a blur of tears, a sea of misery.

I couldn't even drown in it. I had to wipe away the tears and wash my face. I had to put on this act for Graham and Debbie.

Hello Graham. Did you have a good day? Here's your supper.

Come on, Debbie, settle down, there's a good girl.

A clean white shirt? Yes, Graham, there's one in the airing cupboard.

How long can I go on with it?

But I must go on with it. One day it must end. One day the pain must grow less. After all nothing lasts for ever.

Somebody told me that once. Or maybe I read it in a book.

Suspicion

The funny thing was that I had always liked Lisa. She was my husband's secretary, and a quiet, shy little thing – mousey, I thought her. She called me Mrs Taylor and I didn't mind that because she was so very young, scarcely more than a schoolgirl when she first came to work for him. She would occasionally phone me with messages from Don such as "Oh Mrs Taylor, your husband asked me to ring and tell you he'll be catching the 6.18 tonight." Or she might say, "Mrs Taylor, your husband wanted to know if you were going out tonight because he's hoping to bring Mr Spears home for dinner." She sounded so quiet and deferential in her manner and, as Don scarcely ever mentioned her, I never gave her a second thought.

But then one day we were at a dinner dance with the Spencers – Bob works with Don – and when the two men were talking shop Val Spencer suddenly turned to me and said, "I see Don's got himself fixed up with a nice little dolly bird, Marian – aren't you madly jealous?"

I was so startled I nearly fell off my chair. "D'you mean his secretary, Lisa Jones?"

"Yes, I think that's her name."

"To be quite honest I've never really taken much notice of her. I certainly wouldn't describe her as a dolly bird!" I said.

"But Marian, she's gorgeous," said Val. "Everyone was talking about her at the last office do – of course you weren't there, were you?"

"I was in the nursing home, having Vicky," I said slowly.

"So you were!"

"I have met her. I thought she was rather nice. A thin little thing with mousey hair and specs."

"That's not how I'd describe her. You want to take a second look. She's probably in love with Don – that's the usual thing, isn't it, to have a crush on the boss? So flattering for a man, after being taken for granted by a wife in a dressing gown and rollers in her hair and a houseful of squalling kids."

I knew what Don thought of Val Spencer. She was catty and malicious, he had often said so. But I couldn't stop thinking of what she'd said. I didn't mention anything to Don but I thought about it all the weekend and all the next week, and at last I could stand it no longer. It was unreasonable of me, there was nothing I could do anyway, but I just had to go to the office and see for myself. So on the following Monday I left the children, Bobby, Mark and Vicky, with a kindly neighbour and caught the train into the city. I did some shopping and arrived at Don's office at about 12. It was so unusual for me to pop in on him unexpectedly like this that I hadn't even seen his new office, though he had been working there for at least two years.

"It's on the fourth floor," the Commissionaire told me. "At the end of the corridor, through the swing doors. Take the lift."

I did so, and on reaching the door at the end of the corridor, I knocked and entered. There facing me, sat Lisa at a big desk. She seemed glad to see me. "Why hello, Mrs Taylor! How are you? I suppose you want to see your husband, I'll just tell him you're here."

I didn't want to see Don, it was her I had come to see, and I watched her as she sprung up from the desk and crossed into the inner office. She was taller than I remembered and slim, certainly not too thin – she looked as good as I would love to look, dressed in a crisp pink check shirt and skirt with a wide belt that showed off her waist, and shoes with very high heels. I never wore heels like that when I was working because they didn't suit the life I led, and I wondered why office girls went to such trouble to look so smart. Who was it all for?

"I'm afraid he's still on the phone," Lisa apologised to me, "Would you mind waiting? I'd interrupt him but it's long distance..."

"Oh that's all right, Lisa – I'll wait," I said, sitting down in the chair she offered me.

"Will you excuse me if I..."

"Oh please carry on, don't mind me."

I studied her covertly. It must have been two years since I had last seen her and in that time she had certainly grown up and yes, she was lovely – but not in an obvious, screaming out way; she was lovely because she was natural and unspoilt. Her honey-brown hair hung about her shoulders, soft and shiny and well brushed, not the least bit mousey. Her large grey eyes were no longer hidden by spectacles – probably she wore contact lenses now. Her complexion was clear and pretty as a peach. Strange, she had worked alongside Don for two years and I had never noticed – but surely *he* must have? Not that he had ever given me the least cause to suspect anything, but you wouldn't be human to be unaffected by someone as young and lovely as Lisa.

"Your husband's free now, would you like to go in, Mrs Taylor?" she said, breaking into my thoughts.

"Thank you."

I went into the inner office. Don was very surprised to see me.

"You never mentioned you were coming into town today," he said.

"It was an impulse. I wanted something for Vicky."

"Where are the kids?"

"With Mrs Appleton."

"I hope she doesn't mind."

"She said not. She loves the children,"

"Yes, well – she'll need to."

"Excuse me, Mr Taylor," said Lisa, entering with a file and going over to the steel cabinet in the corner of the room.

"Of course," said Don absently, "Well Marian, what are your plans for the rest of the day? Or are you going home now?"

"I thought we might have had lunch," I said.

"Not today, I'm afraid, I'm meeting Tim Harris at one o'clock."

"Oh. Couldn't we go out for a drink, then? To that nice pub you took me to once, round the corner."

"You mean the Grapes."

"Yes, that's it."

He hesitated. "Look Marian, I'm sorry but I've got a load of work on and I don't really like drinking in the lunch hour…"

"Just one," I said quickly.

"I'm sorry, no."

I felt disappointed, like a child done out of a treat – which was silly because I hadn't really expected anything. It was unreasonable to assume he would be free at such short notice, yet I felt a fool in front of Lisa. I felt he had snubbed me, rejected me, in front of her. Why couldn't he drop everything at the chance of taking his gorgeous wife out to lunch when clearly Lisa had assumed that he would? But I'd got it wrong, hadn't I? It wasn't me, his wife, it was she, his secretary, who was gorgeous. And Don had got himself nicely fixed up with her. That was what Val Spencer thought, anyway.

Going home in the train I thought, Val Spencer's wrong because Don's not like that. Val Spencer doesn't know Don as I know him because he loves me, and anyway Lisa's too nice, she's not like that, and Val Spencer's wrong. That's what I thought on the train. But when Don got home that night I said something to him I hadn't meant to say at all. I knew it was silly to say it, I didn't want to say it but I said it. I said, "I hadn't realised Lisa had grown so pretty, Don. Do you think she's pretty?" and Don said, "Yes."

I suppose I had hoped he would say she wasn't his type or something, but that was asking for the moon, wasn't it? So why did I say of all things, of all the stupid things,

"D'you think she's prettier than me, Don?"

He said, hesitating, "She's very pretty, but so are you – in a different way."

"How do you mean, different?"

"Just – different."

"You mean, she's younger than I am?"

"Well partly, I suppose. She's pretty in the natural way of the very young."

"Meaning I'm not natural?"

"I didn't say that, Marian."

And there was a steely edge to his voice which stopped me probing any further.

It's a funny thing, but after that I could never turn on the television without seeing a play or a film in which there was a man having an affair with his secretary. There was a spate of them, they were on some channel or other every night of the week and it seemed a natural course of events in these plays that if a man was married he was tired of his wife but if he had a secretary they were in love – and not only that all the world was on their side and no one blamed him for being tired of his wife when she was such a bitchy, dreary old thing. I wondered what Don was thinking as he watched these plays with me. That he must be the only husband left in the world still faithful to his wife (if he was – because I was beginning, just beginning, to wonder) and why, when there was the lovely Lisa just waiting for him to pluck her off her peach tree, ripe and ready and madly in love with him, why be the odd one out? And apart from the television I couldn't pick up a newspaper without reading of men having a wonderful time with their secretary/mistress, living it up in all the wild, exciting night spots while their dreary, tight-lipped wives sat it out at home with the dirty kitchen sink and the washing.

I turned on the radio to be met with a blast of *Wives and Lovers*... "Watch out little girl, there are girls at the office and men will always be men..." I didn't know if all this brain-washing had worked with

Don or not, but I know one thing. It worked with me. I now firmly believed that all men were in love with their secretaries. They must be, because if they were human and not in their dotage it was the natural consequence of their working together. I started avidly reading the problems in newspapers and magazines, the ones that began "My husband has suddenly started working late at the office and has changed in his attitude towards me, do you think there is something wrong? "And yes," they said, "Yes, there's something very wrong here… As if we didn't know.

Gradually life became a torture for me. If Don was the slightest bit late home from the office I thought, it's started. Working late at the office. The first warning signals. But I won't say anything. I mustn't say anything. And as soon as he walked in the door I'd say, "You're very late, Don – what happened?" not sympathetically as I once used to say it but with a sharp, ugly edge to my voice; and he'd answer briefly, impatiently, leaving me no more satisfied with the answer than if I hadn't asked him in the first place. I pictured him and Lisa together, looking at one another across his desk, laughing at jokes I couldn't share. Perhaps they had lunch together, drinks at the Grapes. Perhaps he gave her lifts in his car and they sat talking when it was time for her to leave. Perhaps she asked him up to have coffee in her flat. Perhaps… it didn't bear thinking about.

I longed for the weekends when I had him all to myself. I'll make the weekends so wonderful, I thought, he'll remember them all the week. I won't be one of those wives in dressing gown and rollers like Val Spencer said. But sometimes I caught myself still in my dressing gown at ten o'clock because the baby had got me up early and I'd never got round to changing, never got round to doing my hair or even washing my face. There was cereal spattered down the lapel of my dressing gown where the baby had chucked her breakfast at me, there were toys littering the lounge and squalling kids. I sensed Don's impatience.

"I think I'll go round and see Harry Clarke," he said one morning.

"Again? You saw him last week."

"So what? Who's keeping count?"

"I just thought it would be nice if we had a quiet day, all the family together, for a change."

"I could say it wouldn't be nice, quiet, or a change!"

"That's a horrid thing to say!"

"I didn't say it." He laughed, but I didn't see the funny side.

"You did and you're cheating. Are you so bored with us? Would you rather be at the office?"

Oh fool, fool to let it get to this!

He didn't answer but said brusquely, "I'll take Bobby and Mark to the park for a bit. That'll get them out of your hair."

"They're not in my hair."

"You seem so irritated with them these days."

When they'd gone I wept, pushing the dishes along the breakfast table so that I had a space to rest my elbows, weeping with self-pity, wondering what had gone wrong with our lovely idyllic weekend. Then I went slowly upstairs because the baby was crying, and after I'd seen to her I dressed and washed my hair and put on some makeup. I caught a glimpse of my face and I looked discontented and older than my thirty years. There were lines now where there used to be none and the skin had sagged and grown coarse, not like the young dewy skin of Lisa. Lisa – always we were back to her.

That night when we were getting ready for bed I said to Don, and it was meant to be casual, one of those tossed-off remarks that mean nothing, "What does Lisa do with herself at weekends?"

"How should I know?" said Don.

Did he suddenly look watchful, on his guard?

"Where does she live? With her family?"

"In a flat, I believe."

"How funny. I wonder why she doesn't live with her family. Does she share this flat or live in it by herself, I wonder?"

"By herself."

"Oh, you do know then. Have you been there or what?"

"Of course I haven't been there. She told me once in the course of conversation."

"Do you think she's attractive, Don?"

"Who, Lisa?"

"Of course, Lisa. Who else are we talking about?"

"I don't know why we're talking about her at all. Can't you let it drop, Marian?"

I don't know why I didn't. I suppose I had reached the stage when I couldn't.

"Do you…" I said and hesitated at the enormity of what I was about to ask, "Do you – I mean, would you like to make love to her?"

"Oh for God's sake, Marian!" he exclaimed impatiently, "I'm married to you, aren't I? I love you and the children."

"But you haven't answered my question."

"And I'm not going to."

My heart sank to my boots. "Then you would," I said.

"Would what? What are you talking about, Marian? What do you *want* me to say?"

"I want you to say that you don't want to make love to her. Can you say that?"

"Marian, you're crazy."

"*Can* you, Don? Can you say it?"

"This is absurd. I don't know what's the matter with you, Marian. I think…"

"You can't, can you Don? You can't say it because it's not true. Why can't we be honest with one another?"

"Is that what you want? Honesty?"

"Yes."

"I think you've lost that lovely innocence you used to have when I first met you. You're getting narrow-minded and suspicious and imagining things that aren't true. I've not even thought of anyone else in all the time we've been married but now you're practically pushing me into it. After all, I am human you know. Men…"

"Will always be men?" I queried.

"Wouldn't be men if they didn't find girls attractive – but that doesn't mean they have to go to bed with them all."

"Only that they'd like to," I said drily.

"They are human," he repeated. "What's got into you, Marian? Why are you suddenly imagining these things about Lisa and me?"

"I suppose because of what Val Spencer said."

I told him what Val had said about him getting himself nicely fixed up with this dolly bird and how she was probably in love with him. He was very angry. "That wretched Val Spencer," he said. "She's just a malicious trouble-maker. Surely you can't accept her word in preference to mine? There must be trust between us or else there's nothing. Our marriage isn't all I believe it to be if we can't trust each other."

Oh, how I wanted to believe him – and I did, in a way, this time. I was comforted by what he had said – but there remained this little niggling doubt. Lisa was so attractive, I thought, how could Don help himself falling for her? How could any man help himself? If nothing had happened yet, it surely would, just give it time. I couldn't stop my fears and doubts came flooding back every time he was late home, or if he said, as once he'd said, he'd have to go into the office on the Saturday.

"But why, Don?" I tried not to ask but it just came out; and I was not consoled by his reply. "There's a file I've got to work on."

He could always say that, and how could I know if it was true or not?

"You should get paid overtime," I said tartly and he laughed.

"Not much chance of that!"

"Will Lisa have to go in, too?"

"Why should Lisa have to go in? It's her weekend." He gave me a hard look, almost hostile.

"Your weekend too, I should have thought."

"That's different. I'm one of the bosses."

I turned away, unable to face that look of accusation in his eyes. Accusing me of accusing him. I took a grip on myself and said lightly, "Will you be back for lunch?"

"Oh yes – no reason why not."

And so he was. I felt light-headed with relief when I heard his key in the lock, but though I tried to be extra nice to him, to cosset him, he wouldn't respond. There was that hard look still in his eyes when he looked at me. I made a joke, but I couldn't make him laugh. Someone had said on the radio that morning, if you can't laugh together any more, what is there left? Dear God, had we got to that stage? Could Lisa make him laugh, I wondered? But I must stop thinking about Lisa.

After that I began to notice that sometimes at the weekend Don was inclined to go out for some cigarettes or petrol and not come back for a couple of hours. My resentment would mount the longer he was gone. I couldn't settle to anything. The lunch would be drying up in the oven. I'd keep running to the window every time I heard a car – expecting to see the ice-blue Marina turn slowly into our gate. He'd come back at last, cheerful, affectionate, smelling slightly of whisky, and I'd try very hard to enter his mood but I could never hold back the inevitable "Wherever did you get to?" "I decided to pop into the Phillipses," he'd reply, or "Where've you *been*"

"I just fancied a pint so I called into the King's Head."

Questions, questions, and explanations.

"I wish you'd have mentioned you were going. I'd have liked to come too."

Silence. It was an impulse, I knew that, and besides, what about the children? I couldn't have left them. It was unfair of him to leave me behind knowing that I couldn't come, and unfair of them to stop me going. So unfair. Lisa had him all day and every day and in the very best of humour, but I only had what remained. What was left over.

His good spirits soon evaporated, leaving him quiet, morose. That evening, when the children were in bed, I went into the sitting-room to watch some television programme, and Don went into his study.

"There's something really good on at 8.30," I said.

"Uh huh," said Don, sorting out piles of unpaid accounts.

Later I made coffee. "Aren't you coming in, Don?" I said, taking him a cup.

"Can't you see I'm up to my eyes!" he snapped.

"You could do that in the sitting-room," I said, and added unwisely, "Are you so bored by my company you can't bear to sit with me these days?"

"For Christ's sake can't you stop it?" he shouted. "If you must know I came in here for a bit of peace. To get away from the never-ending questions. And that look you have."

I was horrified. "What look do you mean?"

"That tight little look you have every time I come home, when you think I've been up to something I shouldn't have been. I always know, if I'm the slightest bit late, that I'll see it – that tight little look of disapproval. I've done nothing, I keep telling you – but my God, one of these days I'll give you something to wonder about!"

I turned away feeling numb and sick. I had lost him. With my perpetual suspicion I had driven out all his feelings for me. He didn't love me any more. How could he love me, how could he love what I had become? For, and I recognised this fact, my jealousy had eaten me up, changed my whole personality. I was not the girl he had married. Was it too late, I thought, to change back, to be as I had been before these terrible suspicions had taken their hold?

For a while I managed to mask my feelings. I tried very hard. I didn't say a word to Don that would imply the slightest reproach. I didn't know what he meant by my tight little look, but I was determined not to let him see it again.

Suddenly things seemed to be going right for us again. He was sweet and loving just as he had been before, and I was reassured and happy.

Then one day came the bombshell. I phoned Don at the office to ask if he could get back in time for a parent teachers' meeting at Bobby's school and Don wasn't there. "Could I speak to his secretary?" I asked the switchboard operator.

"Lisa? She's not here either," said the girl.

"Oh…" It was three o'clock, or maybe five past. All the old doubts came flooding back.

"D'you have any idea…" I began.

"Of course," said the girl, "He'll be round at her flat."

I heard no more. I hung up, stunned and shocked. So it had happened at last. I had driven them together – and now Don was giving me something to worry about. What should I do? I must go up to London at once, here, now and confront them both.

I rushed upstairs and flung open the door of my wardrobe. Smart – I must look very smart. I put on my new suit, the one Don chose for my birthday, and brushed my hair till it shone. Then I picked up the baby and put her into her carry cot, grabbed Mark's coat and bundled them both into the car. I drove fast, mindlessly, to London. I knew exactly where to go. Lisa's flat was in Victoria Square, off the Pimlico Road. All I had to do was find Don's car. Then I would ring the bell and confront them both.

There wasn't a lot of traffic on the road and I did the journey in less than an hour. It was five to four as I reached Pimlico. I turned into the square and there, I could see at once, was Don's car. I had hoped that perhaps the girl might have been wrong – but how could I deny the certainty in her voice: "*Of course. He'll be round at her flat.*"

I don't know what I felt. In a funny sort of way it was relief that my suspicions were no longer groundless.

"Where are you going, Mummy?" cried Mark as I got out of the car.

"Just to see someone," I replied. "I shan't be many minutes. Now you be a good boy and don't waken the baby. You can crayon that picture with the butterflies, and try very hard not to go outside the lines."

It was quite difficult to find out which was Lisa's flat. I went to several big houses, each of which had at least ten doorbells, but I found it eventually. Miss Lisa Jones. I went up three flights of stairs, wondering what I was going to say. Should I be very angry, or pathetic and abject? *Please Lisa, leave him alone. He's got a wife and three young children to support – but you're young and pretty. You'll soon find someone else.* If it wasn't so dreadful I could have laughed, it was such a hackneyed situation, just like in some of the old Hollywood movies. Perhaps she'd deny he was there. Perhaps he'd appear from an inner room in a silk dressing gown and say, "Let me handle this, Lisa."

I rang the doorbell and waited.

Presently it opened and there was Lisa. She looked surprised to see me – and pleased. "Why hello – do come in, Mrs Taylor," she said.

"Is my husband here?" I faltered.

"Yes of course – we all are." She led me into her little sitting room and there were at least a dozen people. "We're playing truant from the office," she said with a giggle. "It's rather naughty, isn't it? But after all, one doesn't get engaged every day!"

"You're engaged?" I said.

"Yes – to Tim." She held out a hand and ushered forward an enormously tall, thin young man. "Tim, will you get a glass of champagne for Mrs Taylor? I'm sure she'll want to drink our health."

All this time Don was staring at me in embarrassed astonishment. "Marian!" he said, "Has something happened?"

I swallowed and said very quickly, "No, it's just that Bobby's form is having a parent teacher's meeting tonight and the headmaster asked specially if you could be there, he wants to talk to you. I rang your office and the girl on the switchboard said you were all round here so I thought maybe I could come and pick you up – when you're ready to come, that is."

Oh God, I thought, let him believe me. Let them all believe me. Let the switchboard girl forget exactly what she said. Just give me one last chance!

And from the way they were all looking at me so warmly, from the way Don stood up and held out his hand to draw me into their circle and from the way he looked at me with pride, I knew I'd got that one last chance.

From now on it was up to me to show that I deserved it.

Talking to John (1)

John, I've got something to tell you and I know you'll be annoyed, but I don't want you to say anything until I've finished. I hope you're in a good mood – you certainly should be, because you've had a jolly good meal and now that you're relaxing in front of the fire with your cup of coffee you should be nice and mellow.

Well anyway, there were lots of other times I might have told you, like when we were getting up this morning (and I certainly wanted to after lying awake worrying half the night) but you were cross because you said I'd used all the hot water and you hadn't enough to shave with. And all the books say you should only ask your husband for something when he's had a good meal and is in a generous mood like in the evening with soft music in the background – but I know soft music gets on your nerves, so I thought we'd make do with the crackle of the fire. Well anyway, here goes...

You know John, it isn't easy for me to tell you, in fact it's jolly hard and I'm as nervous as anything, but I don't want you to say a word until I've finished. It's like this: I can't manage on my housekeeping. I haven't been able to manage for months, actually. Now don't say anything John, I know you've always said that you don't want to know about the housekeeping and that it's my affair, but I think the time has come when it's your affair too. You don't realise how hard I've tried – how I budget right down to the last penny – but every week there's another price rise and you still go on wanting a cooked breakfast every day and cheese as well as pudding and I just can't do it any more. Yes, I know it's the same for other people. I *know* the Council Tax has gone up. And gas and electricity. And petrol, I *know* that. I can't help it.

What it really boils down to John is that £50 a week isn't enough. The food bills alone seem to come to £50 and then there's nothing left for the window cleaner and the children's lunch money and toothpaste and talc and stamps and writing paper. And every week some child or other seems to have a birthday party and I can't really get a decent present for less than £3 not to mention the wrapping paper and card on top. And these never-ending processions of people coming to the door, and it's all very well for you to tell me to say I never buy on the doorstep but you try saying that to a poor pathetic little man with chattering teeth in a soggy grey mac who tells you he's sold nothing all day.

So I go just a tiny little bit into the red each week and then I have to put it on my credit card and it soon begins to mount up and I've nothing to pay it off with and now, believe it or not, it's mounted up to £183.67p to be exact – and I simply haven't dared to tell you before. Besides I thought that instead of having a row every week we might just as well have one big row now and have done with it. So – if you could possibly see your way to letting me have a cheque for that amount - £183.67p – and give me a bit more, say £70 a week? I could start afresh. It would be such a relief, John. What do you say?

I know it must have come as a shock to you John, and it's not very nice for me either owing the milkman and the newsagent and the man who brings the vegetables and everyone, it makes me feel so immoral.

If you like though, I'd be prepared to put in that £50 Mummy gave me for Christmas although I'm sure Mummy didn't mean her Christmas present to be spent on groceries, but still I'd do it as a gesture. That would only leave £133.67p.......John? Oh dear I do wish you'd say something. I hate having to actually ask, it makes me feel so Uriah Heapish.

John! Why don't you say something? You're not asleep, are you John? Oh God. I suppose you've been asleep all the time. You haven't heard a word I've been saying. It's all been a waste of time.   Except   that you can't say I haven't told you and to be honest I am rather relieved you didn't hear, because I didn't feel much like a big row tonight. If we leave it another three months it'll be my birthday and then I'd be quite prepared to have the £133.67p as my birthday present from you and I know you don't usually give me as much as that but you could make it the next three birthday presents if you like and I can't say fairer than that, can I? Meanwhile in three months anything could happen, we might win the lottery or I might win that £1,000 in the Wholemeal Biscuit competition in the *Daily Mail* or we might get a legacy from an unknown uncle. You might even get a rise. I mean, these things do happen don't they? You read about them every day. Then I wouldn't have to tell you at all.

I must say I feel quite light-hearted now I've got it all off my chest, even if you didn't hear. I can't really think what I've been worrying about, I mean it can't be unusual not to be able to manage on one's housekeeping, there must be hundreds – thousands – of women like me. I should imagine it's more unusual if you *can* manage. There must be something distinctly odd, I should think suspicious, not to say abnormal about women who *can* manage. They are probably frightfully miserly. I don't suppose they give their families enough to eat. I can just imagine them, thin, tight-lipped, shrewish women who look affronted if you sit on a cushion. They must be awful to live with. You know John, you're jolly lucky I'm not like that, and I think it's so interesting to think how easily I could have been.

John, why is your mouth twitching in that funny way – and why are your shoulders shaking? You weren't asleep after all, were you John! I do believe you've heard every word I said – and you let me run on and get all worked up – and you don't even seem cross, not a bit!

I just can't believe it, I'm £183.67p in the red and you don't seem to mind! Shall we have the last of the Cyprus brandy to celebrate John? I mean I don't know about you but I certainly need a drink and otherwise it is rather a waste of having had that fillet steak and mushrooms for dinner isn't it and oh John I do wish you'd stop *laughing*!

This story was sold to She *magazine, 1975*

Talking to John (2)

John, have you got a minute? Well, you are only reading a book and you see there's something I feel we ought to discuss. (You know, discuss, John, talk about intelligently without getting annoyed.) I want you to put the book down and listen and possibly say something more than yes or no occasionally. (And could you move over a bit, I've got no pillows on my side?)

The thing is John, I feel you're not taking enough part in the children's lives. Time is slipping by and before you know it they'll be grown up and you'll be no more than a strange man they see at breakfast. Well, I know you earn their bread and butter but John, there's more to life than bread and butter.

Oh – don't do that, John, this is supposed to be a serious conversation. Well – later. I've hardly started yet. You see, I can't see why *I* always have to be the one to go to the school concerts and the church services and the plays. Well, someone has to go, John. Children need someone to cheer them on, to encourage them, clap and enthuse. OK, so you don't see the need. Perhaps you'll see the need to come to their twenty-firsts and their weddings when the time comes. I only hope you're invited. I only hope they've grasped you're "family" by then – but don't count on it.

Take that play Suzy was in last term, the one where she was the third buttercup – I didn't particularly enjoy sitting through the entire concert just to catch a glimpse of her through the legs of the children in front, but she was so excited about it I couldn't have forgiven myself if I hadn't gone. There were *lots* of Fathers there, too. Nearly all of them, I should think. If Mrs Parsons hadn't kindly invited me to sit with her and her husband I'd have had to sit by myself. I had to tell them you were working. Well I couldn't very well have said you don't like those sorts of things and were watching another James Bond instead, could I? It's not as if you haven't seen them all before anyway.

When there was an Italian Spaghetti Evening (oh do stop it John, I can't concentrate when you do that, later, I said) at the Church Hall in aid of the new church steeple I went because Robin got a note from school the week before saying they hoped all the parents would. So I did and it was all very jolly in a forced sort of way, but I was miserable. Nobody asked me to dance because it wasn't that sort of do, I mean it's all strictly husbands and wives. Not that I *wanted* them to, looking around my God no, but I could have done with a nice big hole in the ground to disappear into. Everyone asked me where you were and I said you were working and they said "Again?" and looked at me with pitying glances. I bet they think you've got another woman. I couldn't very well say you were watching the rugby, could I?

And as for fetes and bring-and-buy sales – for your information I do not adore them, John. I do not even like them, John. I go to them out of a sense of public duty and because I don't want Miss Peebles to think I'm a Bad Mother. I go because I can't think of a good enough excuse not to and because there's nothing I can do instead without feeling *terribly* guilty. But that's not to say I enjoy them. You see everything you want to see in the first five minutes and have to fill in the next hour and a half wandering round a couple of soggy, muggy tents admiring things you don't really like and fruitlessly seeking to buy back those things the family donated (like Tiny Tears and Paddington Bear) in a generous but since regretted impulse. You dread the arrival of more wretched little goldfish in their plastic bags that invariably die inside a week after you have gone to the expense of an alternative container to your mixing bowl, not to mention 55 varieties of fish food. They loathe them all and die to prove it.

Last week, when Robin was playing in the orchestra at the school concert, I think you should have been there even if they do sound like a lot of cats in the garden at 4 am. After all, it's jolly hard to play the violin and everyone has to start somewhere and you don't know for certain Yehudi Menuhin didn't sound like a cat in the garden once, do you?

And then today Suzy was in the swimming gala and I've been waiting all evening to see if you'd ask how she got on and you never did. You might show a little bit of interest. I know she was third out of three, I know she puts one foot on the bottom every fourth stroke but that isn't the point, is it? She tries. A bit of encouragement from Dad wouldn't come amiss, I feel.

Talking of encouragement – when I made that French Apricot Tart the other day it may not have seemed much to you but it did take me all morning and when I asked you for your opinion I didn't really want it if it wasn't going to be *complimentary*. There's a difference you see John, between being asked for your opinion and giving it. When Robin asked you what you thought of his composition on "What I Did In The Holidays" you weren't meant to say it was utter nonsense from start to finish. No, you see when he said he'd climbed Mount Everest and had lunch with the Queen well it was obviously not true, well I mean we don't have to be told do we, of *course* he hadn't climbed Mt Everest or had lunch with the Queen but you see, that's not the point of the composition. He was just using his little imagination, John, which is what compositions are all about. I mean, the teacher didn't really want to know what *he* had done in the holidays but what *a child* might have done. I know it's unlikely *any* child would have had lunch with the Queen but it's possible – oh John, don't side-track. When you're asked for your opinion next time just pick out the good bits and talk about those.

Did you say something? Yes I suppose I am going on a bit. I'm just having a moan, that's all. After all, we always said we'd be absolutely honest with each other. Yes, all right, goodnight, John. Goodnight? I didn't know you wanted to go to *sleep*. And they say *women* change their minds. Well, goodnight then.

There is just one more thing. Do you think you might for once manage a teeny weeny little garden fete on Saturday afternoon? You needn't stay more than half an hour… You *will?* You did hear what I said? You'll come to the fete? You really mean it?

Why John, that's wonderful, *thank* you darling! I take back everything I said. I didn't mean it about the children not asking you to their twenty-firsts and their weddings. I'm sure they'll remember who you are. They'll think you're an angelic daddy, just as I do. What would you like me to do in return? I'll prune the roses if you like, or I'll make you a sweater. I'll do anything you want.

Oh – all right then, I'll go to sleep. Goodnight, John.

If that's *really* what you want.

Sold to Story World, *1976*

The Babysitter

He said, "I'm not awfully happy about it. After all, we don't know her at all. What does she do? Have you actually met her?"

"No," she said, "I gather she's a student. She's very nice, according to Mrs Thornton. Very quiet and..."

"Well I don't give over-much for Mrs Thornton's opinions."

"Oh don't be so difficult Henry! What do you expect her to do, pinch the family jewels or something?"

"She wouldn't be the first babysitter to turn out to be a bit light-fingered."

Ruth and Henry were going to the cinema, and afterwards to the Hungarian restaurant in Everley, for a late supper. Quite a simple event really, yet event it was for they hardly ever went out. Henry did not mind much, he was getting so set in his ways these days, with his pipe and his bedroom slippers and his mug of cocoa. Really quite elderly, she thought. Yet Henry wasn't elderly, far from it, thirty-five, in the prime of life, and they should have been enjoying themselves. But they were not party-minded. He was not, and she – she liked to think she was but no, not really. She was not vivacious, perhaps not confident enough to be vivacious, and you did have to be vivacious to be a success at a party, otherwise you were just kidding yourself.

She was looking forward to going out more than she dared admit. What would she wear? Not that it mattered a damn really, I mean – she could hear her friends saying it – fancy dressing up to go to the cinema! And what a rush it was, when you had three children and you had to give them their supper and put them to bed and then have a bath yourself and dress and do your hair by quarter to seven at the latest so that you could be there for the last performance at seven-ten, well it took some doing. You needed to be organised. Ruth thought that she was very well organised.

She wriggled into the long-sleeved dinner dress and effortlessly zipped it up. Henry had thought it becoming when she had first bought it, and it fitted just as well now as it had then. She had not put on any weight, not an ounce, in spite of bearing three children. She could be justifiably proud of her figure.

"I wish we weren't going," said Henry. "I don't feel like going at all. I'd much rather stay at home by the fire."

Ruth felt irritated. She was sure he would enjoy it once the evening got going. It was just that he never made the effort, and the less he got out the less he wanted to. He was almost becoming a recluse.

Which nail varnish? It would have to be the scarlet because there wasn't much left of the pink, her favourite, just a little gluey bit in the bottom of the bottle. There – it was really rather vivid. Oh hurry up and dry! Her strap showed, she'd have to pin it, what was the time? The bell went. Damn!

"Ruth!" called Henry from the bathroom.

"Yes, I heard."

"Well, answer it!"

"Oh dear – can't you? I've just put varnish on."

"Ruth! For God's sake answer the door!"

"Oh – all right." He could not have heard. He often didn't when it suited him not to.

The girl stood outside on the doorstep. She looked young and modern in that odd sort of way. She wore tight trousers and an enormous man's sweater and no lipstick. Her fair hair was long and untidy, cut with a deep fringe that fell into her eyes. She made Ruth feel absurdly over-dressed.

She said, "I'm Marianne. You are expecting me aren't you?"

"Yes. Yes, of course," said Ruth. "Look – here's the lounge. Please make yourself at home. There are some magazines in the rack. Rather old I'm afraid, but perhaps you haven't seen them?"

"Oh I can't be bothered with magazines," said the girl. "Thank you all the same." She looked round her briefly. The sitting room. Their pride and joy, so warm and cosy – and suburban, thought Ruth, seeing it suddenly with the girl's eyes. They went into the kitchen and she pointed out a small piece of pie in the fridge, eggs, milk and cheese. "But just help yourself to whatever you want."

"Thank you," said the girl absently.

"The children are in bed of course. Well we must be off. You're sure you'll be all right?"

"Naturally," said the girl, "I love being alone."

Henry appeared at the door. "Oh… Good evening," he said. "Ruth, have you seen the car keys?"

"Aren't they in your pocket? No, wait, I think they're on the hall table."

At last they were ready. They stepped out of the front door, walked down the nice shiny path and climbed into the nice shiny car.

"What did you think of her?" asked Ruth.

"Who? Oh. She seemed all right. I didn't really notice to be quite honest," said Henry.

"She's certainly unconventional. Not exactly dirty but – well – untidy. And pretty too – in a sort of way."

"Pretty? Good Lord!"

"Didn't you think? Well, pretty eyes."

"Not my type. More to the point, will she be all right with the children?"

"Oh, I think so. Anyway, they never wake up. Henry," she asked coyly, "Am I your type?"

"Erm – of course!" he said, not exactly leaping for the bait.

It was a woman's film, and not very good at that. She could have enjoyed it if she had been with one of her girlfriends, but Henry kept shuffling and yawning and looking at his watch, as though it mattered what time it was when they had all evening. And the cinema was almost empty, which was not very cheerful. A cinema needs people, or it is vast and empty and pointless, like a school without children or a wood without birds.

When they got outside it was raining. With bent heads and upturned collars they crossed the car park, in which puddles had sprung up like weeds on the uneven, littered ground.

"What a shame," said Ruth, "just when you'd cleaned the car."

Henry merely shrugged before driving somewhat clumsily into Everley, while Ruth made bright little remarks as though they had just met, as she felt the occasion demanded conversation. But the Hungarian restaurant was closed. What an anti-climax! Not only just closed either; the blinds were down, the tables stacked together unlaid as if they had been like that all evening.

"But I thought…"

"Well, *I* thought…"

"But you couldn't have..."

"Well Mrs Thornton…"

"Mrs Thornton. God!"

They sat in the car undecided about what to do, the one irritated, the other on the defensive.

"Well anyway, there must be somewhere else," she said.

"At a quarter to eleven? You name it."

It was true. Everley's respectable citizens did not go in for night life. To be out at ten-thirty was daring, after eleven – daft.

"How about getting some fish and chips, then?"

"Heaven forbid. You know I can't stand those places. No, we'll just have to go home."

"Oh please, I'd much rather not. Besides there's nothing in."

"Look Ruth, I'm not going without supper. You can rustle up something, surely?"

She supposed she could. Not that she was very good at rustling things up, she liked to plan things in advance, not to have to improvise. But there were eggs – she might manage an omelette.

When they got home they found the babysitter reclining comfortably along the sofa, which gave Ruth a mild shock, as she and Henry always sat with their feet firmly on the floor.

"Well hello" they said, brightly. "Here we are! Everything all right?"

With a slight start she turned her head to look at them, then swung her legs gracefully to the floor.

"Hello? Why yes, not a murmur."

Henry unbuttoned his coat and went to stand with his back to the fire.

"Well I'd better go and do those omelettes," said Ruth reluctantly.

"Yes, you do that dear," said Henry. "I'm famished."

"Didn't you have a meal then?" asked the girl, surprised.

"No," she heard Henry reply as she went through into the kitchen. "My wife forgot to check if the restaurant would be open, and it wasn't." There was laughter.

Very funny, thought Ruth acidly. She dropped some butter into a pan and lit the gas. Back to the stove. What a way to end the evening. Of course it was her fault really, but Mrs Thornton had seemed so certain. When could you ever believe people, must you always check everything they said?

Henry seemed to be doing a good job entertaining the girl, judging by the laughter in the other room. Presently he came in.

"Darling," he said, "Make it three omelettes will you? Marianne hasn't eaten anything all evening."

"But why not? I showed her where everything was."

"Well – you know what kids are. I suppose she was shy of barging into a strange kitchen."

Ruth found this very irritating. "Huh!" she said, and chucked a couple more eggs into the bowl.

"I thought we might open a bottle of wine," said Henry.

"Good gracious, what for?"

"Well – it was your evening out and it did rather end up as a damp squib."

"*My* evening? Why *my* evening? As though I'm a child having a treat! It was our evening."

"Yes dear, our evening. Well a bottle of wine might be rather nice, mightn't it?"

She had to concede, tamely, that it might. She felt uneasy without knowing why. There was something different about Henry. She could sense an excitement in him, as if he had come alive for the first time in years.

She carried the tray carefully into the other room and laid the omelettes at each place, with bread and butter and cheese.

"Well this is very nice," said Henry, drawing up a chair, "Much better than the old Hungarian restaurant in Everley – and what is just as important, a darn sight cheaper!"

The girl sat down and looked expectantly at Ruth who picked up her knife and fork.

"Have some wine, Marianne," said Henry grandly, as though they had it every night, instead of just occasionally to save money.

"Oh thank you, I adore wine!" she replied with enthusiasm.

"Who doesn't?" said Ruth with a false little laugh that echoed disagreeably in her ears in the silence that followed. She was aware that she would dislike herself if she were someone else, and it was not a pleasant feeling.

"These are very nice – *pancakes!*" said Henry. "Darling, you're very good at pancakes. My wife," he said to the girl, "is an exceptional cook, as you can see."

They laughed heartily; the girl giggled till tears ran down her cheeks while Henry rocked to and fro in his chair. Ruth joined in at first, but presently, in the face of such excessive mirth, she gave up.

"You're really very cruel," said the girl at last. "They're not so bad!"

Ruth realised, and it came to her with a shock, that they were laughing at her. Not with her, *at* her. It made her unreasonably angry. *What is it that I expect?* She thought. *Loyalty? Yes, but I don't want loyalty as a right, part of the bargain you get when you marry. I want my husband to be loyal because he wants to be. But then again, surely I can bear to be teased – or have I lost my sense of humour? Or did I never have one?*

"My goodness, I'm hungry!" said the girl.

"You eat," said Henry. He plied her with bread and cheese. "I like to see an appetite. I hate people who pick at their food."

Ruth picked at her food. She had not thought about it before or even realised it consciously, but now she knew quite suddenly that she did.

"Did your evening go all right?" she enquired of the girl.

"Oh yes," said the girl, "Very pleasant thank you. I watched TV. I certainly didn't expect you back so soon. I must say your children are wonderful. I never heard a thing."

"No, you wouldn't with the TV on and the door shut," said Ruth.

"Ah, be fair Ruth," said Henry. "They never cry. Well, what did you see?"

"A very enlightening programme on the BBC about South America."

"Damn! Is it Tuesday today? I wanted to see that. I mentioned it to you, didn't I Ruth?"

"Did you?" she said.

"Surely you remember. I said I must watch that programme on Chile. Was it interesting?"

"Excellent. Superb photography. But very biased."

"Towards?"

"Exactly. Of course they always do. They always take the side of the underdog. I quite agree with them. I think it's essential to bring our attention to the under-privileged."

"You're so right," said Henry earnestly.

Oh Henry, thought Ruth, *what are you talking about? Have you any idea? And if you have, do you really give a twopenny damn about the underprivileged in Chile? And the girl,* thought Ruth, *talks pretentiously with the arrogance of the very young and Henry is fascinated. But if I were to talk this way he'd laugh, because he thinks he knows me inside out and he doesn't think I think at all.*

"Will you have some coffee?" she asked.

"No, thank you," they both replied.

"Well I'll get these things washed up then," she said.

"I must be off," said the girl.

"I'll run you home," said Henry.

"No – really?"

"Of course I will."

Of course. How inevitable it was!

When they had gone Ruth washed up and put the things away and laid the breakfast and heated the water for the bottles and filled them and took them upstairs. She did everything slowly and deliberately and without thinking very much. She would not think: it was a mistake to think.

She went and sat down in the lounge and picked up the paper, then tossed it aside and picked up a magazine instead. She looked at the clock. She picked up another magazine, but it did not hold her attention for a moment. At last she went upstairs again and undressed and washed and brushed her teeth.

Then Henry came home.

"You were ages," said Ruth.

"Yes – well – she made me a cup of coffee actually."

"Really? How sweet of her, especially as neither of you wanted any before you left."

"I could hardly refuse, could I?"

"You could have, if you didn't want any."

"Well maybe I did want some. Maybe I didn't before, but maybe I changed my mind. Do I have to ask your permission? Do I have to say, I'd like some coffee but I'd better not have any in case my wife doesn't like it?"

"Oh don't be silly, Henry. Why do you have to exaggerate? All I'm saying," she persisted (and how dreadfully petty she was being, she knew it but she couldn't stop), "all I'm saying is that it's funny you should suddenly want it when you didn't only five minutes before."

He did not reply.

"Henry..."

"Oh let it drop," he said.

She was silent, but not at ease. *What is it?* She wondered. *What is it that I dread?* But she could not explain, it was just some instinct that made her afraid. And because she was afraid, she continued to nag at him.

"Do you love me?"

"Of course I do." How impatient he sounded.

"You never say it."

"Well – people don't. We're not teenagers any more."

"We're not middle-aged either."

"We've been married twelve years."

"I wish, oh I just *wish* you'd tell me you loved me!"

"Ruth, I hope to God you're not turning into one of these neurotic women who are always..."

"So you won't say it. You won't say it because you don't think it."

"Ruth, I..."

"I think it's dreadfully sad."

"What's dreadfully sad?"

"When people stop being in love with each other."

He sighed. "I can't understand you," he said. "we go out, we have a pleasant evening and just because I run the baby-sitter home and stop to have a cup of coffee with her you turn like this. Jealous and narrow-minded and petty. It isn't like you at all. What's got into you? What is it you're afraid of?"

But she could not explain. You could not explain a premonition.

"You must pull yourself together old girl," he said. "You have been rather bitchy all evening you know. As though I were in love with her or something absurd."

Absurd, yes! She clutched at the word gratefully.

"Oh Henry, I *am* being absurd, aren't I?"

"Very," he said. "Silly old sausage!"

He put his arms round her and held her for a moment, and in that moment she felt a vast relief, a flood of warmth coursing through her, banishing all her fears.

Then he withdrew his arms and began to unknot his tie.

"We must do this again," he said. His voice seemed to come from a great distance. "Marianne is quite ready to come and babysit for us again. I thought we might go on Friday. I know how you love to go out."

She sat in front of her dressing table mirror and brushed her hair, looking at herself. The mirror was dark and shadowy and her face stared back at her, pale with enormous eyes. She knew now what would happen and that there was nothing she could do to prevent it. This was the beginning; or rather it was the end. She knew.

"Ruth?" he said.

"Yes."

"You'd like that, wouldn't you Ruthie? You ought to get out more often. It does you good. Well, what about Friday?"

"So soon?"

"Why not?"

Why not indeed? There seemed no possible reason she could think of.

"That would be lovely," she said bleakly. And she laid down her brush on the glass top of the dressing table.

The Cherry Stone

When I was fifteen I thought falling in love would be the most romantic thing in the world, but now I'm twenty I know better. It isn't romantic at all - it's just inconvenient.

It's a lovely hot summer afternoon and I am sprawling on the grass in our orchard, although 'orchard' is an over-glamorous term for the six weedy and undersized trees planted by my father in the optimistic notion that they would provide us with delicious fruit for years to come. Some hope! And grass is all very well, but it's so tickly and full of insects that seem to enjoy crawling over you and are enough to get anyone into a very bad temper. Besides, it is not as if it is a large orchard and we are overlooked by neighbours on three sides. It's almost too hot to write and certainly too sticky. But never mind – now I've made this discovery about love, I must get it off my chest while I'm still feeling irritated with Alastair.

Alastair is sitting in a deckchair not two yards away, asleep with his mouth open. At least I suppose he's asleep. He'd have a fit if he had the faintest idea what I was writing about. It's such a relief not to be in love with Alastair any more! You must forgive me if I keep mentioning this, but it only happened ten minutes ago and I'm so incredulous and excited about it. Now I can look dispassionately at him, and I keep having to do so, to make absolutely sure. It's quite true, his face – especially with the mouth open as it is at the moment – gives me no thrill whatsoever.

Alastair, I should explain, is staying with us for the weekend. He is, my family think, a very desirable young man. My father likes him because he calls him sir and his father owns a big engineering firm. My mother likes him because he gets up when she walks into the room. I met him five months ago and although he has never intimated to me that I am The One I can't help feeling – and my family can't help hoping – that I am.

If I wanted to be, of course.

Because suddenly I don't, not any more.

It makes me tired to think of the time I've wasted and the mental discomfort I've endured. I've lost touch with all my friends and I never seem to have the inclination to do any of the things I ought to be doing. I find myself on edge and snapping at people for no reason. One moment I'm up in the air and the next I'm down in the dumps.

I've disdained dozens of invitations just in case *the* one should turn up. More often than not it hasn't, and I have told everyone airily that I didn't feel like going out that night in any case. But there have been tears followed by sad, lonely nights and long periods of listlessness. I have had to sit for dreary evenings not too obviously near the telephone and to tell my family defensively that I really thoroughly enjoy sitting on a wooden stool doing nothing. I have managed to persuade everyone, including myself, that the best way to read a book is to turn the pages over rather quickly.

One of my greatest anxieties is the way I look. I have blue eyes and fair curly hair that's inclined to run wild if allowed. My figure's inclined to do the same, alas, because I'm hooked on bread and jam – nice white crusty bread and my mother's home-made strawberry – and I've had to give it up since I met Alastair because he likes his women racehorse-shaped. That takes some doing I can tell you, but I've done it for Alastair. Oh, but it's such a strain having to be beautiful all the time! I seem to be everlastingly washing my hair because everyone knows that girls In Love must wash their hair constantly even if it means starting the operations at four o'clock in the morning and having to go to the office with damp hair and sleepy eyes a few hours later. Once a week I go to Antoine's the hairdressers to get it professionally fly-blown. I mean blow-dried. And then you always have to be so clean. It's not that I'm usually dirty but I mean, you have to be *so* clean. At least two baths a day, and that upsets the family no end. My father says, "When can we have our bathroom back, if it's not asking too much?" (Ha ha, very funny.)

I never have any money, what with the hairdos and having to buy new clothes and shoes all the time. I've had all my family's birthday and Christmas presents for years to come. It's not as if it's appreciated either. Only three weeks ago I went to one of those sleazy mod shops where you need a torch to see anything and I bought a most spectacular, slinky dress that made me look really dishy. Hopefully I set out in it, prepared to dazzle everyone I met, most of all Alastair. Well, he noticed nothing! When we'd reached the coffee stage he did say casually, "Don't remember that dress. New?"

"Yes, I answered tremulously, "As a matter of fact it is."

"Hm," he said.

"Do you like it?" I said, fishing madly for a compliment, a small crumb of comfort from the superior male.

"To be quite honest," he said, "Not much. It seems a bit – well, tarty. I prefer your grey suit."

You know I do so dislike these honest people who insist on telling you the truth. *Tarty?* The cheek of it. Just because I get a few second glances. Besides, where's the romance in a grey suit? Still, I resolved that if that's what he liked, I would wear it. And wear it I have – and I bet he's sick to death of it by now.

You see, since meeting Alastair I've been so silly. I would do anything at all if I thought it would please him. I've really worked at it. I've studied Being In Love With Alastair like working for O-levels. I've read all those magazine articles by shiny, good-looking male stars on What Makes Me Fall For A Woman, and the list is always tough and depressing but I've got it all down to a fine art. I've learnt to perfection the art of telling white lies, like noticing a tie when I haven't, or saying I haven't read a book when I have. I've learnt not to win at tennis, to laugh convincingly at old, bad jokes and to drink sophisticated martinis as though I enjoy them. I've learned how to keep my mouth shut when I long to query a particularly smug or sweeping statement. I've learnt to be arch and coy in front of other women, to be scintillating and witty in front of other men, and to be small and soft and feminine when I'm alone with Alastair.

Well, now I'm not going to try any more. I'm seeing him with new eyes. I thought he was so incredibly wonderful, and then ten – well now it's twenty – minutes ago, I realised what he was really like.

I don't mean he's turned out a cad or anything, but suddenly he's as unglamorous as everybody else and just as ordinary. I used to think he was tall, dark and terribly good-looking, but now he is nothing to write home about, merely quite pleasant-looking (he's closed his mouth now). His conversation isn't brilliant (well of course mine isn't either, though I'm sure it could be. I always have visions of exchanging witty repartee with some distinguished man of letters at some exclusive dinner party).

His conceit is enormous, and although he professes to be quite fond of me he thinks mostly about himself. That of course doesn't matter since most men are the same – but what really maddens me is his pompous, conventional attitude. He can be so nice when he's on his own but as soon as he's somewhere formal, in a place where things are "done" or "not done" he becomes as stiff and conventional and shockable as the rest of them. He is so afraid of letting the side down or making a fool of himself that he becomes reserved, upright, humourless, the caricature of the Typical Englishman that foreigners find so amusing.

Perhaps I was always worried by Alastair's slavery to convention. I was tired of playing the part of the snobbish girlfriend who says and does the right thing, exhausted with keeping up the high standard I had set myself. And last night, for the first time, I broke down.

Alastair and I were sitting in one of the most fashionable restaurants in London, having a small cocktail before dinner, and at the next table was a pompous-looking man who was going on and on about how well his stocks and shares were doing or something, and I suddenly longed to do something to prick his self-important little bubble. My cherry had a stone in it, and a feeling of mischief and wickedness came over me. I leaned over and whispered to Alastair, "Do you know, I just feel like flicking this stone into that awful man's wine glass."

If he had laughed it would have been all right, because I would never really have done it of course. I would never have let him down in public like that and we could have laughed together at the idea of flicking the cherry stone. But instead he looked horrified and solemn. He said, "But my dear Mollie, you must be mad! What are you thinking of?"

That was when I saw red.

"I'm thinking," I said slowly and rather too distinctly, "that yes Alastair, I am mad. I must be totally up the creek to put up with you, Alastair. The trouble is you just don't appreciate me. You don't care that I've practically starved myself on your account, that I'll soon be bald with washing my hair so often, that I haven't a friend in the world because I never dare go anywhere in case you ring. You realise Women's Lib would disown me, Alastair? I'm a disgrace to my sex, I've let them down, you realise that, I suppose? All on account of trying to look like you want me to look and behave like you want me to behave. Well, I'll tell you this: it's about time someone shocked you to the core. You're just too pompous and self-satisfied for words and I'm hanged if I'll go on saying and doing all the conventional, proper things just because you expect me to. For the first time you're going to see me doing something I feel like doing."

Then, still staring furiously at Alastair, I flipped the cherry stone. It missed Mr Pompous's glass and landed squarely in the lap of the over-made-up, bejewelled lady who was sitting opposite him. She recoiled in horror and stared at it as if it was a poisonous snake.

I waited for Alastair to look scandalised, to leap to his feet and march out, but to my surprise he didn't. He just stared at me and said nothing. From then on we hardly said a word to each other and I thought he must be so angry that he couldn't bring himself even to speak.

At first I felt defiant and glad, and then I felt rather ashamed because really I've been a bit unfair about Alastair. He's been very kind to me on the whole and kindness, I suppose is not such a bad thing. He was supposed to be staying for the weekend and we were to travel up together in the morning. I told him that if after all he would rather not come, I would quite understand. He was very quiet, but he said he would come. I felt irritated and guilty and I have continued to feel irritated and guilty ever since – until just thirty minutes ago, when I made the big discovery that he no longer held any fascination for me.

Really, it's rather funny when you think that all the tears and all the toil have led up to this: I am going to give Alastair up and nobody knows about it except me. My family are on tenterhooks at the moment. Of course they would all love to be sitting out in the garden on this glorious afternoon, but they're trying to be tactful. If only they knew! I couldn't care less if they all came out – uncles, aunts, grandparents – the lot! If only they knew that Alastair and I have hardly exchanged a word all morning and that far from whispering sweet nothings in my ear he's been asleep all morning with his mouth open.

Another funny thing – I may have shattered his illusions about me, but I still get the impression he quite likes me. I'll have to break the news to him some time. He will be surprised – what a shock for his vanity!

Well it's about time I went back to a normal life again. I suppose if it hadn't been for the cherry stone I might have gone on for months or even years, biting people's heads off and being a complete bag of nerves and altogether rather horrible. What a dreadful thought. I must start seeing all my friends again. I'll phone them all tomorrow.

Oh dear, Alastair seems to be waking up. Whatever happens he mustn't see what I've been writing – where shall I hide it? Perhaps… yes. Underneath the rug.

I don't really know if I dare to add this part (another half hour has passed). After all I've been very definite in everything I've said so far. Of course women are supposed to be contrary, but not this contrary! I had planned on just letting you girls realise what I've realised – that falling in love is expensive and takes up a lot of time and energy; that it's nice and relaxing not to do it.

Then just now something very strange and unexpected happened. Alastair woke up and apologised. He said he had been stupid and unimaginative and stuffy last night and was terribly sorry and suddenly I forgot all about my big discovery. I forgot all the mean things I've written and all my irritation disappeared and I forgave him completely.

There's worse to come. It's going to look very absurd and illogical on paper, yet somehow it wasn't at all like that at the time.

Alastair asked me to marry him, and I said yes.

We're very grateful to the cherry stone; it's taught us both a lesson – Alastair is never again (I hope) going to allow snobbery and stupid conventions to swamp his sense of humour. As for me, I'm going to come down to earth and not behave like a silly little fool.

But still, I must have my last fling. Just for old time's sake I think I shall have to make an appointment with Antoine (the hairdresser) for Monday.

This story was my first acceptance. I sent it to Good Housekeeping, *who passed it to* Good Taste, *and it was published in 1955.*

Goodbye My Darling Daughter

I'm running away from school. Yes, Mother, I thought that would shake you. I'm running away from the routine and the petty senseless rules, the bells that tell you what to do and when to do it, the smells, that thick cloying polish on the floor and the disinfectant in Matron's room and the long-standing smell of cabbage wafting up the stairs. I'm running away because you're never free, even your spare time is scheduled for something on a timetable, and you can never be alone to think or walk or even breathe without a hundred pairs of staring eyes.

Don't pretend to be so surprised, so shocked. Did you really think I'd be happy here? Or didn't you think very much about what I'd feel one way or another? It was so easy, wasn't it, for you? To buy the uniform and pack it in a shiny new trunk, 2 tunics, 3 shirts, 3 knickers, navy-blue, 1 navy suit for Sundays… oh, if only you'd sent me away for the right reasons I think I could have borne it.

You came to Victoria: "Goodbye, my darling daughter!" But you didn't even stay to watch the train leave the station. I felt sick. My face was white and my hands were clammy, but your face looked much the same, smooth and brown with panstick make-up, imperturbable. "I don't like goodbyes," you said, "I might cry." Oh yes, you might. You might smudge your mascara.

I was thinking the other day how funny it was; I know all about you, yet you know nothing about me. You know nothing of how I feel. It's as if there's a great desert between us. When we're together I can't talk to you, can't ever find the words. There seems to be a choking tightness in my throat that stops the words from coming. It should be so simple for one person to talk to another, yet you are more at ease with the postman than you are with me. The trouble is, I'm always afraid you'll go away before I've finished, so I never really begin.

I first got the notion of running away during games-time. I was in deep cover. Imagine – girls playing cricket! But anyway, there I was miles from anyone with not a thing to do but study the daisies. I hoped the ball would not come my way, and it did not. I looked down over the wall and saw buses passing on the other side of the wire, and people, scarcely more than a few feet away. I had not seen people from outside since you sent me here – weeks ago? months? It seems so long ago.

Next day after games I dodged into the pavilion and hid there until everyone had gone in. Then I slid down the wall, scraping my knees all the way to the ground. There I was on the other side. It was four o'clock: I had three hours till supper when I would first be missed, four till bed-time when they'd know what had happened. By that time I would be far away.

And so it turned out. That I had no money was of no importance. There were plenty of long distance-lorries bound for the north. I like long-distance lorry drivers; they are open and honest and cheerful and what they say, they mean. There's no superficial gush. One driver bought me a meal at one of those cafés on the roadside lit by neon lights. It was warm and sweaty inside with all the lorry drivers eating. There were cakes in a dusty plastic container on the counter and bottles of red lemonade on the wall. Outside was the roar of great wheels pounding up the motorway. Far away in the school dormitory the girls were sleeping, but I sat shoulder to shoulder with the lorry drivers, eating sausages and egg and chips with vinegar, and I felt great waves of exhilaration – like that night my uncle took me into the West End and we walked down Piccadilly, jostling with the crowds. The feeling was the same that night – being alive and part of a vibrating world.

Oh Mother, don't you see we led such a sham life! Look at me now and then, don't just smother me with expensive kisses. Don't turn away, don't pretend I don't exist. Look at me, listen to me! I may be immature, but I think I can distinguish between what's genuine and what's false. I think I can see through the tinselly shop window of your artificial world. Oh Mother, only open your eyes a little wider and you'll see too!

I spent last night in a hedge, it was warm and smelt of stock and elderberry. When I woke it was dawn and the spiders' webs were glinting in the early light. I was only five miles away so I thought I'd walk – and now I'm nearly home. What will you be doing when I arrive? Will you be breakfasting on the veranda or arranging flowers in the conservatory or playing the piano in the drawing room? Which one of a thousand lady-like pursuits will you be following?

Or will you be in bed with your lover?

Do you think I don't know? Did you think I didn't know when I came into the room that day and you looked at me, you and him, that you didn't want me there? I saw the way you looked, the way he touched your neck, the way your face glowed afterwards. Your eyes were glazed, you were puffed up like those swollen, satiated ticks we used to pull off the dogs in Africa. I stamped on them and let the blood spurt over the ground, and I wanted to stamp on you and let the pleasure drain away into the thick pile of the carpet.

I'm not very far away now, only a few hundred yards from the garden gate. I'm beginning to think it was a mistake to have come. Yes, I'm sure it was. Already I can feel myself closing up inside. What will you do when I come in and disrupt your lives? It's such a beautiful morning and the garden looks almost perfect, the lawn is like velvet and the roses like wax with the dew still on their petals.

My feet crunch over the gravel as I walk up the drive. I stand for a moment at the door of the conservatory, where the sickly-sweet scent of the jasmine is almost oppressive. What will you do when I walk in?

Oh, but I know what you'll do: you'll send me back. This time you'll take me all the way there. It'll be a blessed nuisance to have to alter all your arrangements, but never mind. "I'll be back first thing tomorrow," you'll tell your lover. We'll sit in sorrowful silence on the train and in the taxi. And you'll knock on the door of the house-mistress's study and say, "I'm so sorry, Miss Brown, all the trouble we've caused you, I can't apologise enough… She's promised me faithfully it will never happen again."

I'll stand subdued, looking at Miss Brown's sensible shoes and that funny-shaped ink mark on the carpet. "Very well then," says Miss Brown, "Now run along to your dormitory."

And the autumn term will follow the summer, and the spring term will follow the autumn, and the summer will follow the spring – and what will become of me? Years and years hence I shall emerge transformed, one of a mould, polished and refined, a young lady with a public-school accent.

Then, I suppose, I'll be your darling daughter.

Never, Ever Tell

It was a shock to see her name in the newspaper after all those years. It must have been – what, some thirty years since that thing that happened when we were at school together, the one which had had so dramatic an effect on my life.

It was half-term and only three girls were left behind at our little preparatory school: Mary Snow, Charlotte Fox and me. Our relations all lived too far away, or for some reason they could not have us home then. It was the summer half-term and it looked as if there was going to be a heat wave. It was a desperate feeling to be left behind at school when everyone had gone, but Charlotte told us it would be fun. The few remaining staff would be extra nice to us, she said, and we would have special meals and go to bed when we liked. We might be taken somewhere for a treat, like a picnic in the grounds of a castle, or to the cinema if it was raining.

There were two members of staff on duty that weekend, Miss

Brown and Miss Rutherford, and they were nice enough, fairly harmless. But as luck would have it one of them went down with flu and had to be nursed by the other, so we were left pretty much to ourselves. There were no special treats and the food was no better than usual.

I felt apprehensive about being with Charlotte. Charlotte was a popular girl, at least I thought so at the time, but looking back I realise she was not liked so much as feared by the other girls. She had a forceful personality and could manipulate people into doing things that often they did not want to do. She was good at games and she had a quick, sarcastic tongue. She was someone to keep on the good side of, and woe betide you if you lost favour with her.

Mary Snow, on the other hand, was a timid creature. She had large, protruding eyes and a pale face and her hair was so fair it was almost white. Some people think white-blonde hair is attractive, but in Mary's case there was nothing attractive about it; it was just pale and lank, and her white eye-lashes matched it. She was a 'nothing person', Charlotte said: hopeless at games, hopeless at lessons and thoroughly wet. I agreed with her, because it was a good idea to agree with Charlotte. Charlotte always had to take sides with another against a weaker third and I was thankful to be with her against Mary, knowing that in other company *I* might well be the one to be left out, despised and bullied by the others.

That weekend, because it was hot and we were restless and bored with nothing to do, we turned our attention to teasing Mary. We were mean and unkind and I felt ashamed, but it was the law of the jungle: you had to catch or be caught, eat or be eaten. First of all we played Pig in the Middle with Mary as the pig. She ran, she leapt but she could not catch the ball. "Why do I always have to be Pig?" she asked.

"You don't," said Charlotte, "you just have to catch the ball." But Mary could never catch it, because we threw it miles too high above her head.

After a while it got boring, and we needed something else to do.

There was a part of the school grounds that was out of bounds. It included the kitchen garden, an orchard and a piece of wasteland containing an underground air-raid shelter, disused since the Second World War. We were greatly attracted by the kitchen garden and the orchard, especially now in the soft fruit season, so it did not take much for Charlotte to persuade us to go there.

"I mean, it's the obvious time to go, isn't it?" said Charlotte, "with everyone away and no one to notice where we are?"

So directly after lunch on the Saturday we crept out of the back door, through a small courtyard and into the kitchen garden. There we amused ourselves for a while picking the pea pods, splitting them open with a plop and scooping out the tender young peas. Then we turned our attention to the raspberry canes, where we consumed quantities of the fruit. It was very hot: the sun beat down upon us from out of a parched sky, scorching us, the earth, the glass in the greenhouses and the great domed cloches under which fat marrows reposed like sleeping whales. We ate and ate, stopping occasionally to wipe the juice from our sticky hands, and all around us the garden was alive with the humming and buzzing of insects, bees mostly, and wasps that hovered and dived at every turn.

When we had had enough we wandered on into the orchard. Presently Charlotte took hold of my arm and whispered something. I giggled. "Another thing," said Charlotte coldly, "have you noticed that she…" whispering again into my ear. We laughed unkindly whilst Mary shuffled along in silence, her eyes on the ground.

"Haven't you anything to say, Mary Snow?" called Charlotte.

"No," muttered Mary.

"Why not?"

"What is there to say?"

"What is there to say!" mimicked Charlotte. "You never do say anything, do you? I bet your head's absolutely empty inside. That does happen sometimes you know, Jess," she said to me. "You do get people with empty heads. You don't meet them often but if you were to split their heads open you'd find they're just like an empty coconut shell inside. That's what makes them a bit mental. Mary Snow is potty in the po!" she sang, "Mary Snow is potty in the po!"

I felt sorry for Mary, knowing how she must be feeling, but I did nothing to help her. Together Mary and I could have stopped Charlotte before it was too late. I might have tried it if I had been sure I could trust Mary, but I was afraid that she would side with Charlotte against me instead.

On we ploughed through the orchard and Charlotte made Mary climb a tree and see if there were any ripe plums, and while she was up the tree we ran away and left her. Presently we came upon the site of the old air-raid shelter. Out of breath and spluttering with laughter, Charlotte said, "Here's where we'll hide. Come on, she'll never find us here."

I hesitated. "I thought we were told not to…"

"Oh, come on," said Charlotte and thrust me down the overgrown steps ahead of her. At the bottom of the steps was a little door. We pulled away the undergrowth and pushed it open. Inside it was dark and musty, like a cave. There were some benches there and half a decayed bar of chocolate and a couple of mildewed cushions.

"It's not very nice," I said.

"Shh!" said Charlotte.

"She won't hear us down here!"

"She might."

"But we want her to find us, don't we?"

"I don't really care if she does or not."

We waited in silence, but nothing happened. After a while I said, "Well she doesn't seem to be coming, so we may as well go."

"No, I've got a better idea," said Charlotte. "You stay here and I'll find her and bring her back."

"She probably won't come."

"I'll say you've twisted your ankle and she'll have to come and help me lift you out." So saying, Charlotte went off up the stone steps, first shutting the little door behind her.

It was dark and there was this awful musty smell and I didn't like it at all. It seemed an age before I heard footsteps coming back again.

"Are you sure?" Mary was saying.

"Yes, go on – down those steps," I heard Charlotte answer.

I waited, holding my breath. The door opened slowly and Mary came in, followed by Charlotte, who closed the door quietly behind her.

"Are you all right, Jess?" asked Mary.

"Yes – that is – I'm not sure," I mumbled.

The three of us stood silently in the musty darkness.

"It's very dark," said Mary. "Charlotte, I thought you said Jess had hurt her ankle…"

"So she has," said Charlotte.

"It's so dark in here, I can't see," said Mary.

"Quick, Jess," said Charlotte suddenly opening the door. "Go on through!"

I had a momentary feeling of shock, then I ran through the door followed closely by Charlotte, who turned and slammed it shut again. "Quick," she said, "we need something to wedge it with."

From the other side of the door came a cry of terror.

"We're not going to leave her there?"

"Why not, it'll be a super joke. Pass me that big stone."

It was a great boulder that I could scarcely lift. "That'll do fine," said Charlotte pushing it against the door. "She won't get out of there in a hurry."

I could hear Mary beating her fists against the door.

"Let me out!" she cried, "Jess! Do you hear me? Jess! Jess! Let me out!"

She kept calling me, yet I did nothing to help her. Charlotte and I simply went up the steps and left her.

Tea had been laid for us in the dining room. It was a flexible meal consisting of milk and bread and jam with a cake or biscuit on Sundays. It was a meal you could take or leave as you wished, so that when Charlotte and I went in without Mary nobody noticed anything. Charlotte seemed to think it was a great joke.

"When are we going to let her out?" I asked several times.

"Not yet," Charlotte would reply firmly, "it would spoil everything," and weakly, if uneasily, I acquiesced.

Later on we saw Miss Brown, the Junior English Mistress. She looked harassed. "Oh there you are, Charlotte! Are you girls all right? I'm sorry I haven't been able to spend much time with you."

"That's all right," said Charlotte carelessly.

"Well, so long as you're enjoying yourselves," said Miss Brown. "If you don't mind I'll have my supper upstairs with Miss Rutherford tonight. She's not at all well, poor dear."

"That's all right Miss Brown," said Charlotte, "don't worry about us."

Thus another meal passed without Mary's absence being noticed. At supper Charlotte said, "I've got a good idea about tonight. I'll put a pillow in my bed so they think I'm asleep, then I'll go into the loo and pretend to be Mary, then when Miss Brown asks where Mary is you can say..."

"You don't mean you're going to leave her there all night!" I gasped.

"Why not?" said Charlotte coolly. "It would do her a world of good. Might toughen her up a bit – feeble creature."

But I was getting really worried by this time. It was nearly six hours since we had locked her in the air-raid shelter, and I resolved to let her out myself. Straight after supper I would go.

I said nothing to Charlotte and slipped away without her or anyone else noticing me. Through the kitchen garden I sped and thence through the orchard, until I came to the steps leading down to the shelter.

It looked different somehow. A couple of feet away from the entrance there was a crater of newly moved earth from which rose clouds of dust.

"Mary!" I called out in alarm, running down the stone steps. "Are you all right?"

There was no answer. I bent down and heaved the boulder away from the door and burst in. At first I saw nothing but a great wall of earth taking up all the space and the aluminium roof gaping and buckled where the walls beneath had caved in. Then I saw Mary. She was lying on the floor with a ton of rubble on her chest. Her eyes were open, but even in that dim light I knew she was dead.

I screamed, but no one heard me. I ran wildly back to the school building to find Charlotte.

"Mary's dead!" I cried hysterically, "We've killed her. She's dead."

"What on earth do you mean?" said Charlotte slowly.

I told her what I had found.

"We'd better go and tell Miss Brown," I sobbed.

"No!" said Charlotte. "We mustn't say a word. I'm not going to say a word and neither are you, Jess. If you say anything I shall tell them you did it and you'll be locked up in a dark cell for ever and ever and never let out until you go mad, because that's what they do to child murderers, Jess."

I stared at her aghast.

"And I'll tell them that *you* did it – so don't forget Jess, will you? Never, ever tell. Not a word. We haven't seen Mary all afternoon. She must have wandered off somewhere. We've no idea where she went. We never saw her."

And that was what we told them. First Miss Brown and then the police, and when they searched the grounds and found the air-raid shelter with the roof and walls collapsed and Mary's body lying half under the rubble they thought nothing but that a little girl had gone off to explore on her own when she thought no one would find her out. Nobody ever learnt the truth either from me or Charlotte.

I was ill later on that term and my parents took me away from school. I went to live in the country with my grandmother and two aunts and I had a governess to teach me, but I never seemed to learn anything very much. I could not concentrate for more than a minute or two at a time before my mind jumped elsewhere. I developed a stammer; they said it was nerves. I grew up without the company of other children and continued to live in my grandmother's house after she died. I never married, and I never saw Charlotte again.

And now, thirty years later, here I was reading that Charlotte Fox had been awarded the CBE for public services. Could it be the same Charlotte Fox? Surely there must be other people with that name? But no, it was the same. What irony!

I could not help wondering what services could possibly compensate for causing the death of a child and making another old before her time. For never a day passed without my thinking of Mary Snow and hearing her anguished cries, "Let me out Jess! Do you hear me, Jess? Let me out!"

This story won First Prize, Writers' Billboard, 2010

Matron Knows Best

"Run along to Matron" said Miss Frobisher, unaware of the dread her words caused. Matron waited like a fat spider in the doorway of Miss Frobisher's drawing room. Inside we were all safely gathered around the fire while Miss Frobisher read *David Copperfield* to us. Sometimes she opened a large tin of Petticoat Tail shortbread and passed it round, but that didn't happen often, for it was wartime and biscuits were rationed. Our school had been evacuated from the south coast all the way up to the Lake District, where there were no bombs.

"Lucky, lucky girls!" people said, but I saw only the rain-sodden hills and the loose stone walls that seemed to enclose us like the grey walls of a prison. Sitting on the thick-pile carpet in the firelight in Miss Frobisher's room while she read to us was the happiest hour of the day, but one we had to forego if we had mending to do, and tonight just as Miss Frobisher was about to start reading there was the inevitable knock on the door and Matron stood on the threshold with her list of names: "Natalie Moores… Julie-Anne Bellman… Rachel Turner…."

That was me again. I had missed more of *David Copperfield* than I had heard of it, for I was nearly always on the Mending List. My uniform was fifth or sixth-hand and wearing very thin. My grandmother, with whom I spent the holidays, had not sent it to the cleaners and my tunic was tatty and spotted with food stains. "Rachel Turner! You look as if you've been dragged through a hedge backwards," Matron was constantly saying.

"Run along to Matron," said Miss Frobisher now, and reluctantly the three of us got up and filed out of the room, following Matron up the winding stairs to the Sewing Room. She tossed our bundles of mending to each of us, socks for Julie-Anne and myself and a blouse requiring a button for Natalie. I looked with dismay at the hole in my sock: all of the heel had gone. I didn't know where it had gone, but it wasn't there. I would never be able to fill in the great space that remained. My darning mushroom went right through the hole and out the other side.

"Get a saucer out of the cupboard," said Matron.

"Yes, Matron. But a saucer isn't really the same shape as my heel, is it Matron?"

"Don't give me any of your cheek, Rachel Turner, just get on with it. I sometimes think you'll be late for your own funeral."

She sat in the corner of the room, her knitting needles clacking over a square of purple knitting. She was a large woman with black eyes and a fleshy nose, and her mouth was a great Cupid's bow of dark red lipstick. Her greasy hair was piled up on top of her head and secured with tortoiseshell combs. She wore a baggy hand-knitted jumper and a skirt made of puce-coloured wool, and from time to time she looked across at us over the top of her half-moon spectacles.

Presently Natalie finished sewing on the button. "Can I go now, please Matron?"

"Yes Natalie, you may go."

Julie-Anne Bellman held up her socks. "Can I go, Matron?"

"Let me see. Bring them to me. That's no good at all, you've just cobbled them." She took out a large pair of scissors and cut the stitches savagely. "There. Do it again."

Julie-Anne stood quivering before her, outraged and trying not to cry. Like me she was ten years old, and like me it was her first term at Cranley Chase.

"You did that deliberately!" she said.

"I *beg* your pardon, Julie-Anne Bellman?"

"You deliberately cut a hole in those socks and made it bigger so that I'd have to stay and miss the reading hour. You always pick on Rachel and me, don't you?"

I quaked in fear, but she went on, "You seem to enjoy having us in your power!"

"Go along to your dormitory," said Matron slowly. "Get undressed and go to the sick room. I'll be along shortly to take your temperature."

"Why? I'm not ill!"

"I think you must be. A hysterical outburst like that? I never heard anything like it!"

Julie-Anne picked up her things without a word and went out of the room. Her face was strained and white. She was homesick.

It wasn't so bad if you were one of Matron's favourites. The girls Matron liked were quick and confident, with neatly plaited hair, who kept their belongings tidy and whose uniforms stayed clean and well-pressed. Their clothes were new and smart and never needed mending.

Julie-Anne was in the sick-room for three days. On the fourth day we were in the middle of an Algebra lesson with Miss Frobisher when into the room marched Matron, dragging a wet and bedraggled figure in her wake. Julie-Anne wore pyjamas under her navy-blue raincoat and carried a stick over her shoulder to which was tied a pathetic bundle done up in a green spotted handkerchief.

"I found her on the hump-backed bridge near the five-mile cross-roads," said Matron triumphantly. "She was attempting to Run Away!"

We all gasped.

"Leave this to me, Matron," said Miss Frobisher. "Girls! Get on with the next problem by yourselves until I come back."

The three of them went out, leaving us to speculate what would happen next. In the event, Julie-Anne went back to the sick-room and we were told she had caught a heavy chill and was not to be disturbed.

All the same I did go in one day when no one was around. It was dark in there, for the curtains were drawn. I put on the light and was shocked to see how thin Julie-Anne looked and how white. She blinked – her eyes, puffed up and red with weeping, had grown accustomed to the dark. There was nothing for her to do, nothing to read but a Book of Common Prayer.

"I've prayed for her to die," said Julie-Anne, "but it didn't work."

I decided that I didn't like school. The only good thing about school was that you would go home at the end of the term. But you only had four or five weeks before you were back at school again and it started all over again. And this would go on for years, I thought. Years and years – they seemed to stretch ahead like the rest of my life.

Two weeks after Julie-Anne's first attempt at running away, she tried again, and this time she got all the way home. Someone said she'd gone on the Leeds train, disguised as an old woman in her school cloak. I hoped her parents wouldn't send her back and they did not. I never heard of her again.

Meanwhile we were preparing for Sports Day. Everyone said it was the best day of the year and I was excited, for I had the honour to run for our house.

"We'll win – we're bound to win with you in our team," said the others, "and then we'll win the House Cup!"

If only we could! My house had never won the Cup before and now we had a chance because I could beat all the competition, even the girls of thirteen. Running was the one thing I was good at. I don't know why really – I was a dud at everything else.

The day before Sports Day it was Mary Berry's birthday and her parents had driven up especially to deliver an iced chocolate cake for the birthday tea. Mary had invited nine girls, of whom I was one. What a treat! In those days we were often hungry enough to eat the toothpaste and we hardly ever saw a cake. Matron hovered nearby, smiling in anticipation and licking her lips.

"She's a greedy pig," I whispered to Mary. "Don't give her any."

I didn't think I could be heard, but Matron pounced on me.

"*What* did you say?"

"Nothing," I gulped.

"Oh yes you did. I heard you. What was it?"

"Nothing."

The others held their breath.

"You said, 'She's…' What was it?"

I stared at her speechless. I knew that if I confessed to what I had said she would be no less angry than she was in her ignorance of it.

"Don't you sit there and defy me, Rachel Turner. I distinctly heard you say, 'She's…' She's what?"

But I remained silent. Egged on by my friends' sympathy and admiration I could afford to be a heroine, brave and bold.

"You shall tell me, you shall!" cried Matron. "Leave the table!"

I slipped down from my chair and stood up. She grasped me by the arm and dragged me out of the dining room, up the narrow staircase and along the passage. When we turned right at the end I realised where we were going – she was taking me to her room! No one, to my knowledge, had ever been inside it before. It was a small dark room, smelling of TCP, with a dark red carpet and a bedspread made of hundreds of knitted squares – red and purple and green and orange. Beneath the bed I could glimpse a white chamber pot and over the bedhead was a large crucifix. The walls of the room were covered with religious pictures and texts with scarcely an inch of space between them. One of the texts said, "Prepare to Meet Thy Doom", and I was now prepared to meet mine.

"Now then," said Matron, still holding me by the arm, her nails biting painfully into my flesh. "*Now* we'll see – "

How right she was. It had been so easy to defy her downstairs in front of all the girls. Now I was alone with her in her claustrophobic little room and my courage ebbed away like sand giving way beneath the tide.

"What did you say?"

"Nothing, nothing!"

"What did you say?"

"I said — I said, she's a..."

"Yes? She's a what?"

"A greedy pig."

"So!" She stood back and her black eyes glittered with triumph.

"And why did you say that?"

"Why?" I asked nervously.

"Why?"

"Because — no reason."

"Ah! But there must have been a reason."

"No. I just said it."

She hit me hard across the face. Then she grasped me by the shoulders and shook me violently, finally thrusting me backwards onto the brightly coloured bed-cover. She bent over me, her face so near to mine that I could see little blackheads all around the soft white fleshy nose and where the scarlet bow of her lipstick was smudged onto her teeth and the heavy black hairs of her eyebrows that met in the middle of her forehead.

"*Why* did you say it? *Why?*"

"Because..."

"Yes?"

"When there's a birthday tea, you always..."

"What?"

"Hang around — until you get a piece of cake."

"At last we have it," she said. She stood up and folded her arms in triumph.

"Get into your night-clothes, go along to the sick-room and get into bed."

An icy chill went through me.

"But — I'm not ill..." I protested.

"I think you are."

"No I'm not! I'm quite well — I promise you, I feel fine!"

"It isn't a question of how you *feel*. You don't look at all well to me. You obviously have a temperature." She laid a hand on my forehead. "Yes. Quite definitely."

"But tomorrow is Sports Day!"

"So it is."

"There was a pause.

"I want to see Miss Frobisher!" I cried.

"Oh my dear, Miss Frobisher is far too busy with all she has to do for tomorrow, she couldn't possibly see you. Now run along and get undressed."

I shall write and tell my parents, I thought. But what could they do? They were far away in West Africa.

Slowly I took off my clothes and laid them on the chair by my bed. I put on my pyjamas, took my teddy bear and book and went along the passage to the sick-room. The bed was ready for me and the curtains drawn so that it was in darkness.

"I don't think we want that," said Matron, taking the teddy bear.

"Oh please let me have him, he's only small and he gets lonely by himself!"

"But if it turns out you have an infectious illness your little teddy would have to be burnt and you wouldn't want that, would you?"

Tears ran down my cheeks and splashed down the front of my pyjamas.

"Give me the book as well. You don't want to tire your eyes, do you? Better to sleep."

"But – I *can* get up tomorrow, can't I? Oh please, I earnestly beg of you!"

"It's far too early to say about that. We'll have to see if your temperature's down. Meanwhile you're better off in bed, believe me. You see – Matron knows best. Don't forget that, will you? Matron knows best."

The next day someone else ran in my place in the relay team, and my house didn't win the cup after all. When the war was over our school went back to the south coast again and Matron was dismissed.

Miss Frobisher told someone she had not been quite suitable, but it was difficult to find the right person for the job. In wartime, she said, you just had to take what you could get.

Sarah's Awakening

On Tuesday nights we had A-level English from six until nine at the Tech. "What a drag it is," said Audrey. "Don't you think, Sarah? Three whole hours – it seems to go so slowly."

I didn't agree. I hung onto every word our tutor said. His name was Mr Brown and he spoke with a Liverpool accent. He had a thin, whitish face and dark eyes that burned with enthusiasm. In his free time, he told us, he wrote poetry. He loved Shakespeare – yes, I really believe he loved him. He paced up and down the classroom telling us excitedly what a great chap Shakespeare was, waving his arms about and flinging back a lock of dark hair. I so much wanted him to notice me.

Sometimes in the coffee break he'd sit down at our table and he'd light a cigarette and smile with that heart-warming smile of his.

"Can I join you three?"

"Oh yes. Please do."

We were in a small group of mature students, all studying for our A-level English.

"Mr Brown," I said, "Would you say Hamlet was a Manic Depressive?"

"Not really," he replied. "Because I don't believe Hamlet was mad. But I think he was inclined to nervous instability. The Elizabethans would have called it Melancholia." He turned to look at me, his dark eyes seeming to burn into mine, and in that moment he seemed to have eyes for no one else. Did I imagine it, or did he look at me fractionally longer than necessary?

"We'll be discussing this more fully next week," he said.

He seemed uncared for, I thought compassionately. His threadbare tweed jacket hung on his thin frame and there were buttons missing from his cuffs. When he got carried away, he'd throw off his jacket and roll up his sleeves. I noticed his shirt was coming undone at the seam where the machining had worked loose, but I thought then that with his sensitive yet noble face, he was the very personification of Hamlet.

I spent hours on the essays he set and waited eagerly for him to mark them. We'd hand them in at the end of one lesson and he'd bring them back for the next. I pictured him sitting up into the small hours in his lonely garret room, reading them. He sometimes talked of his lonely garret room, but we didn't know if perhaps it was meant to be a joke.

"Not a bad effort, Miss Cooper," he told Rosemary, and she beamed with gratification. "But you mustn't be content with merely noticing the imagery. Go on to comment on its effectiveness."

"Yes, Mr Brown," she said.

"I'm afraid you missed the point, Miss Benson," he said, and Audrey blushed. I felt for her, being shown up in front of the whole class, but he added as compensation, "You'd better see me in the break."

I stared at him longingly. Surely he must feel something of what I was feeling? Perhaps he would catch it from me, like measles. I willed him to look at me and at last he did.

"Yours was an interesting one, Miss Leigh," he said. "You'd worked very hard on it and you've come up with a new angle. Was it your own idea?"

"Yes, Mr Brown."

"You have an unusual and original mind," he said, smiling at me across the room. I thought I'd faint with happiness.

I wondered what he did at nine when our class was finished. He might stop off for a drink in the pub with his friends. They'd all be poets and artists, wearing threadbare tweed jackets and jeans. Then he'd go back to his lonely garret room.

"Do you really live in a lonely garret, Mr Brown?"

"Well…" he laughed. "Not really, Sarah. I have a studio flat."

"He called you Sarah," said the others.

So he did!

A studio flat. There would be loose woven rugs on the floor, I thought, and Habitat furniture. There would be surrealistic paintings on the blue-washed walls and a bleak couch in one corner where he'd sleep at night. There he'd write his poems, missing meals and burning the midnight oil.

I lived in a compact, comfortable semi-detached house in the suburbs and I was ashamed of the cosiness of it, for I felt he would despise that sort of living. Wall-to-wall carpets were not in his scheme of things. Better to have high moulded ceilings, shabby but noble, and not enough to eat. An unhappy childhood, parents who had neglected me and gone out drinking, that would have done for a start. Perhaps beatings. I wanted to arouse his sympathy, to make him see why I had this unusual and original mind.

The months went by and we went on to other things. We read Richard II and then Ibsen, novels by Hardy and Jane Austen, short stories by Saki and D H Lawrence, Blake's *Songs of Experience* and Chaucer's *Canterbury Tales*. He took so much trouble with us, wanting us to understand what he understood, to see what he saw.

"Look at me, Sarah," he said. "It's important that I make you *see.*"

And suddenly I did see. I understood the strange language of Chaucer, I warmed to his characters, to the irony and humour of Jane

Austen, the stark simplicity and sadness of Blake.

I read and re-read Hamlet until I knew it backwards. When Audrey and I tested each other I, unlike her, always knew who had said what to whom. She could never catch me out.

"Oh, this boring stuff!" said Audrey.

I looked at her, shocked.

"Well, it is," she said defiantly. "It's boring and pointless."

"How can you say that?" I cried. "It's tremendous. It's great literature. It makes me proud to be British. Shakespeare was the greatest of all the playwrights in the world, ever. Doesn't it make you proud too?"

"Not particularly," said Audrey. "After the exam I shall get all my notes and text books in a heap in the garden and make a bonfire of them. It will give me a lot of pleasure."

"You have no soul," I said.

"You really love Hamlet, don't you?" she said curiously.

"Yes. I love him and I love all the characters. I feel as if I've made the most enormous discovery. I see now why Shakespeare's great. I used to pretend, but now I understand."

"So speaks the star pupil," said Audrey, laughing.

"What d'you mean?"

"You were always Mr Brown's favourite," she said. "Rosie and I saw it, right from the start."

The exam loomed nearer and we were into the last stretch. Now all anyone talked about was revision.

"I'm sure I won't remember all my quotations," sighed Rosemary.

"Don't try to learn too many," said Mr Brown. "When you come to write your essay, jot down the points you want to make and use a quotation to prove your point, but make sure it's apt."

On the last night of the course he invited us back to his flat for coffee. He lived quite near the college right in the city and it only took a short while to walk the distance. It had been raining and we walked in little groups through the wet streets, skirting the puddles.

The flat was large and airy and it wasn't bleak, as I'd imagined. There was a copper urn with a beautiful arrangement of flowers, and no surrealistic paintings, but soft blurry watercolours around the walls.

"It's a bit chilly in here, I'll stick on the electric fire," he said. "Sit down, if you can find anywhere to sit. Here – catch, Sarah." he tossed me a fat scarlet cushion. "Are there nine of us?" he asked, going into the small kitchen to make coffee.

We sat around and talked about the exam.

"The main thing is not to spend too long on one question," said one of the mature students, a balding man with horn-rimmed spectacles.

"My sister says the most important thing is to read the paper," said Rosemary. "A good ten minutes, she says, before you even pick up your pen."

I sat on my cushion on the floor and felt completely happy. I could feel the warmth of the electric fire on my legs.

"It will take a while to filter," he said, coming into the studio and setting cups and saucers on the coffee table. He brought in a lemon cake on a plate and some shortbread. "All home-made," he said proudly.

"It's a delicious cake. Did you make it, Mr Brown?"

"Not me, I'm afraid. Jennie did."

"Jennie?" we said, not understanding.

"My wife. She should be in any minute. She takes a sketching class on Tuesdays."

I stared at him blankly.

"I didn't know your wife was a painter, Mr Brown," said the bald man with spectacles.

"Yes, she did all these," he replied, indicating the framed watercolours that hung around the walls.

I followed his gaze automatically, seeing the blurry soft-coloured paintings with unseeing eyes. I felt as if my heart was breaking.

"Talk of the devil," he said, "here she comes now."

A girl came in, a pretty girl with fresh pink cheeks and untidy fair hair. She bounced up the steps into the studio.

"Hello darling," she said, stooping to kiss him lightly on the back of his neck.

"Hello Jennie," he answered, and he reached up to put an arm around her waist and draw her to him. "These are my students," he said, and she smiled round at us, a warm friendly open smile.

"I've heard all about you," she said, "and what a clever lot you are."

I did well in the exam. I got an A. I sent a card to Mr Brown, telling him. I thought it was the least I could do to let him know and thank him, for I knew I wouldn't ever see him again.

The Wicked Stepmother

I first met Daniel when he was nine years old. He had black hair and huge brown eyes set in a sad, thin face. He was just the sort of little boy I longed to have for my own. I wanted to read to him at bedtime and cuddle him a little when I said goodnight. I wanted to take him for walks and picnics and swimming in the river. I wanted to make him smile and see the sadness disappear from his big brown eyes.

But it was not to be. My presence reminded him of his mother's tragic death two years before. It might have been all right if I had been a sort of nursemaid or housekeeper, then he might have been able to accept me – but not as I was, his father's new young wife. That was enough for Daniel to cast me, almost pleasurably, I think, in the role of the wicked stepmother.

It was my idea to meet him alone; I thought it would help to introduce myself, to meet him somewhere unconnected with the home he still associated with his mother. I went to the railway station to meet his train at the end of the school term. There weren't more than a dozen or so passengers getting off at our small country station and I picked him out at once, a small pathetic figure struggling with a huge suitcase. I was struck at once by the pity of it, that this very vulnerable small boy should have lost his mother and been sent away to an impersonal boarding school from the age of seven years. It seemed cruel and senseless; but now I was here to comfort him and make up to him for his loss.

"Hello, you must be Daniel," I said warmly, going up to him and holding out my hand. "I'm Christy."

He shook hands stiffly. "How do you do?"

"Let me take your suitcase."

"No, it's quite all right thank you."

"Oh come on, it's nearly as big as you are!"

"No really, I can manage it myself, thank you."

It was my first rebuff, but I thought it was only politeness on his part, or a wish to be independent.

"I thought you might like to go and have tea somewhere."

"You mean – with you?"

"Yes." I was not put off. "I think there's a farm near here that serves cream teas, that might be rather nice don't you think?"

"You mean Broad Oaks. It's quite near."

"You've been there before then?"

"Yes, I've been there with my… I've been there often."

There was a slight pause.

"Perhaps you'd rather go straight home?" I ventured.

He nodded. "If you don't mind going without your tea."

"No," I said slowly, "I don't mind."

On the journey home I tried to draw him out a little.

"And how do you like school?"

"Not at all."

"I'm sure there must be some things that you like?"

He concentrated, his brows drawn together in a frown.

"Only at night when I'm in my cubicle. I look up at the walls and pretend I'm all alone in a world without any people in it."

"Don't you – like people?"

"No. Only my father. He's the only person I like – or want."

And at last I had an idea of what I was up against.

When we got home I watched the reunion between father and son with a pang. Their obvious joy at seeing one another again was so great that I felt like an intruder.

"Let's go for a walk, Daddy," pleaded Daniel, tugging at his father's hand and off they went, so that Daniel could make sure everything was just the same. Everything was, except for my being there. That was the trouble, I think, that everything should be just as it had been when Daniel's mother – Miles's first wife – was alive. It was bad for me, bad for us all. It was like living in a house of ghosts. I tackled Miles about it soon after Daniel's arrival, asking if we couldn't move somewhere quite different. He was very sweet but quite adamant.

"But I think it might make things easier between Daniel and me," I pleaded.

"But Daniel is happy here, it's his home. The one stable thing in his whole life. He belongs here."

"Well Daniel doesn't think I belong here, and I don't believe I do either."

"I know it's very difficult for you darling, but give it a chance," said Miles. "I want you to grow to love the house too. It was built by my great-grandfather. It would be a tragedy to leave it."

"It might be more of a tragedy not to!" I burst out.

"Come now Christy, you're being melodramatic! It may take a little time but you'll see, all these memories will fade and you'll feel as happy here as I am."

After the first weekend Miles went back to work as usual, and Daniel and I were on our own. I couldn't help feeling nervous, although I told myself it was ridiculous, I mean fancy feeling nervous of a nine-year old boy! For his part Daniel didn't seem to care in the least. He seemed quite indifferent towards me. I tried very hard to think of things to do which would be fun for both of us, but I always got a rebuff.

"How about a game of Racing Demon?" I'd ask.

"No thanks."

"Oh come on Daniel," I'd coax him, "as a favour to me. I'm just in the mood for a game of cards. It'll be fun, you'll see."

"I'd rather not."

"Well – shall we play pelmanism? Or perhaps there's one you could teach me?"

"I don't like card games."

It was the same if I suggested a walk or a bathe in the river or a visit to the cinema. He was polite – just about – but cold and unyielding, as though we were enemies in a cold war. There seemed no way by which I could reach him and by trying I only earned his contempt. He had a bicycle and this was always the preferred alternative to any plans I might have. He would never say he was going out or where, and while he was away I felt vaguely uneasy, wondering if he were quite safe. Sometimes I imagined that he had had an accident or been kidnapped and I was always very relieved to see him come home again, even though he'd slip up to his room without a word.

There was a woman in the village, a Mrs Foster, who had come to the house to look after him when his mother died, and one day I went to see her. I wanted some advice, to know where I was going wrong with Daniel, but she didn't know what to suggest. She had always found him a quiet, good little boy and probably she thought I imagined things. "Poor little mite," she kept saying over and over, "How he misses his poor mother!" She did tell me all the things he liked to eat, so that I could go home and cook some of his favourites – spaghetti with tomato sauce, chocolate cake, meringues, jam roly-poly pudding – yet when I did so he never failed to hurt me as much as he could by accepting an ample portion then leaving most of it uneaten, or even saying point-blank, "Did you make it?"

"Yes."

"Oh well, no thanks."

And he played the old, old trick of playing me off against his father whenever he could, twisting things I'd said, taking advantage of the rare occasions I laid down the law to get round his father to let him off.

"Do I have to go to bed now, Daddy?"

"It's not your usual time, is it?"

"No, but *she* said…"

"You mean Christy?"

"Yes. Christy said I'd to go, even though it's that special Western on tonight and you and I were going to watch it together, Daddy."

"Oh yes." An exchange of rueful glances. "But if Christy said you'd got to go to bed early, you'll just have to miss it. What did you do?"

"I only pulled a face when she asked me to do something. She thought I was being rude."

"No more than that?"

"No Daddy, honestly."

"Well – it must have been rude, that's all. Christy wouldn't send you to bed early without a reason."

Or would she? I could almost read the doubt in his mind.

"But it's my best programme, Daddy!"

"I know – sorry, Danny! Just be more careful next time."

The old harridan! I could feel them thinking it. I even felt it myself. And that's the way it always happened.

One day I arranged for us to go for a picnic. I had a friend with a little girl of eight whom I thought might be company for Daniel. I packed a picnic lunch of cold chicken, apple pie, a thermos of coffee and a bottle of ginger beer for the children. Then I called up the stairs to Daniel, who was in his room. "Are you ready, Daniel? We ought to leave in about ten minutes."

"I'm not coming," said Daniel.

"Don't be silly, Daniel, of course you're coming!" I said brightly.

"No I'm not. I'm staying here."

"Please Danny – I want you to come!"

"Well I don't want to. And don't call me Danny. That's what Daddy calls me."

I felt angry and helpless. "I think we've had enough jokes for one day," I said sharply. "I'm going now, are you coming with me?" I hoped to call his bluff, but he called mine instead. "No. I told you."

"But you can't stay here," I said, now a little frightened.

"Why not?"

"There's nothing for your lunch and – well you can't stay by yourself, it's just out of the question."

This started a new, more ridiculous track than ever.

"Well I'll go and see Daddy."

"You couldn't get there by yourself!"

"Yes I could! I'll hitch a lift."

"But he's in his office."

"Well I'll wait outside until the office closes."

"Oh this is silly!" I cried. "Look Daniel, let me come in and talk to you for a moment."

"I'm listening," he said, but he wouldn't open the door.

"Why do you hate me so much?" I asked. "I'm not trying to take your mother's place, you know, I wouldn't do that, but I do want to be your friend. I'm not the wicked stepmother you seem to think me. Please don't fight me."

"Fight you?" he cried. "That's just what I'll do, as long as you stay here."

I began to weep, but he took no notice.

"Of course you're trying to take my mother's place, in my father's heart, but you can't because he still loves her, he's told me so, and he always thinks about her and when you're with him he wishes it was her instead of you. I do hate you, you're not my friend, you're my enemy and I want to nail you in a house of sticks and burn you down."

By now I was weeping quite hysterically, and I ran to my room and flung myself onto the bed. I did not see how I could go on. How could our marriage survive this wall of hatred? It seemed Daniel had won.

When Miles came home that night he found me packing.

"I'm sorry Miles," I said, "but I can't go on as things are with Daniel and me. I must get away, must have a break."

"Christy, what is it, what's happened?" he demanded. "If Daniel's upset you I'll thrash the living daylights out of him!"

"I don't suppose it would help if you did," I said. I felt weary and helpless. "Don't ask me about it, ask Daniel. I don't want to talk about it any more, I don't even want to think about it. I'll go to my sister's for the time being. Then – well, we'll see." I picked up my sponge bag, brush and comb and laid them at the top of the suitcase. Then I closed the lid.

"All right, darling. Perhaps it's a good thing for you to have a break. You've been letting things get on top of you just lately. I'm sure Mrs Foster will be prepared to live in for a week or so and housekeep and I'll take some leave so you've no need to worry about us. You enjoy yourself with Sheila and Mac."

I think he had no idea to what a pitch we had come and how serious I was. Far from being worried as to how they'd cope, I couldn't have cared less at that moment. Oh, but that's unfair – I did care about Miles, he was a dear even if he was blind to everything that had been going on.

"I'll take you to the station."

"Thank you."

"I'll call you every day. We can lunch together sometimes."

"No Miles. I don't want you to contact me at all – not until I've sorted things out a bit."

He looked puzzled and hurt. "All right then – if that's what you want. I don't know what all this is going to achieve, do you? I know one thing, I'll miss you. I'll miss you a lot."

"I'll miss you too."

Then he drove me to the station and put me onto the London train.

I stayed nearly a month with my sister and brother-in-law. It was lovely at first to be amongst people who wanted me, to have none of the strain of wondering what to say, what to do, no one to talk to. One couldn't tell one's husband his son was a fiend but one could tell one's sister. Both she and Mac were very sympathetic, and it did me good to get everything off my chest. And there was time to think. But kind as they were, I knew this was only a temporary refuge; it wasn't my home and I didn't belong here. Where did I belong, I wondered?

There was no word from Miles and although this was what I had wanted, I felt injured somehow. I don't know what I expected, I half thought he might come rushing up to London to collect me, but he kept strictly to his side of the bargain to leave me alone. I pictured him and Daniel having a marvellous time, just the two of them, doing all the things a father and son would want to do without a wicked stepmother to get in the way and spoil everything. But it wasn't fair – I wasn't like that at all! I had never wanted to take Miles away from Daniel. I only wanted the three of us to be happy together. I would have done anything to make Daniel happy. Now it seemed that because of him my marriage was wrecked and my life ruined.

I saw my life stretching ahead and myself swept like a piece of driftwood here and there but nowhere for long, and worst of all, separated from Miles.

Suddenly I thought I wouldn't let it happen. I would fight. If Daniel thought of me as the wicked stepmother, all right I would *be* the wicked stepmother! The more I thought about it the more it seemed like a good idea. I would be wicked – not so much physically as mentally. I would not beat him or put him to bed and give him crusts and water – but I would play him at his own game. I would set out to damn him in his father's eyes. I would trick him in every way I could. I would tell lies about him and be deceitful, just as he had been about me. I would lead my own life as far as I could without letting him in any way interfere with my enjoyment. I would not try any more to win his friendship. Instead of continually trying to please him, I would make my own plans without worrying whether he approved or not. I would not forget that I was married to Miles for better or worse, and there were our lives to consider. It was our home, just as much as it was Daniel's, and I would not allow him to drive me away a second time. This would be a battle of wits to save my marriage. There was nothing to lose, since Daniel already hated me and had driven his father and me apart.

I sent a wire to Miles to tell him I was returning, and he met my train at the station. He seemed overjoyed to see me, though he looked a little strained I thought, and thinner.

"Where's Daniel?" I asked casually.

"Gone out on his bike. Mrs. Foster's there so he can go home any time he wants."

Huh! I couldn't imagine him wanting to if he knew I was returning. He would be out all day, more likely. Ah well! I set my teeth. Master Daniel was in for a shock.

"D'you know, I think he's missed you," said Miles.

"I can imagine," I said, but my sarcasm was lost on him. "Did he tell you so?"

"No – just a feeling I have."

I suppose some people would miss having a fly around to pull its wings off, if it managed to escape.

"Well," said Miles. "Tell me about your visit. Did you enjoy yourself?"

"Yes, thank you."

All afternoon we sat in the garden and talked of this and that, but although I had him to myself there was a wall of reserve between us. I suppose it was rather hard really; he knew neither why I had gone away – not the real reason – nor why I had returned. He certainly knew nothing of my plan of campaign, and I could tell him nothing. Even when he wasn't there Daniel was like a barrier between us.

He returned in time for supper – cooked by Mrs Foster so no reason for him not to eat it. He was quiet as usual and polite. Oh yes, I knew that deadly politeness. It might last as long as Miles stayed at home, then it would give way to the usual vitriolic beastliness. Well, let it start. I would give him as good as he got.

The next morning I got up and went downstairs to get the

breakfast. Miles was having a lie-in and I decided to spoil him and take him his breakfast in bed, a thing I had never dared do while Daniel was around in case he might be jealous. Daniel came down while I was preparing the tray and helped himself to cornflakes. He ate them, then he got up and went into the garden. He didn't say a word all this time. I picked up the tray, fetched the paper and carried them both up to Miles. When I came back I sat down at the table to have my breakfast, and presently Daniel came in. He was holding a rose that he must have picked in the garden for its petals were still wet with dew, and he gave it to me.

I looked at him for a long moment and neither of us spoke. I was in turn astonished and suspicious, and then suddenly I understood. Miles had been right, Daniel had missed me. I suppose all along he had longed for someone to take his mother's place, and had been glad when his father told him he was going to have a new mother. But I think he expected the new mother to be an exact replica of his first mother, and when he saw me, how different I was, he couldn't accept me. I was the Wicked Stepmother because I wasn't his own mother. Yet although he tried to be as difficult as he could, there was a battle going on inside him which he had hardly realised until I went away. This was the second time someone who wanted to make him happy, to mother him, someone who needed his confidence had gone away, and although he wouldn't admit it even to himself, he wanted that someone back. Mrs Foster was not a substitute.

This realisation came to me in a flash, and I was filled with compassion for Daniel. But I had to hide it because he didn't know it himself, yet. I had to go very gently and to assume nothing. It was like trying to win the trust of a small wild animal: one false step and it would scurry back into its burrow. We stood for a long moment and I waited, almost holding my breath.

Then he looked at me, straight in the eye, not smiling but not all tensed up either and said casually, "If you're having a cup of coffee I'll have one with you."

Nothing world-shattering, but it's a start. A sort of breakthrough. I'm not pretending he'll welcome me now with open arms, but somehow I think the Wicked Stepmother has gone, for good.

Sold to Red Star Weekly, *1971*

Beth

I was very close to my mother, and when she died a year ago I was shattered. Life would never be the same without her. I thought my father felt the same way – but I was wrong. I must have been wrong, or he wouldn't have come into my room one night and told me he was going to marry Beth.

"Beth?" I was hurt and angry. "You don't mean the barmaid at the Feathers?"

"Yes."

I felt sick. "So that's where you kept going," I said bitterly. "I did wonder!"

Beth was nineteen, only four years older than me. She was pretty, I suppose, if you like the gipsy look. She had a mass of unruly black hair and rather a sallow complexion and big dark eyes. But to me there was something slightly unwholesome about her. She didn't seem to be too fussy about bathing, and I could imagine her coming down to breakfast without brushing her hair first or washing.

"You can't mean it," I said.

"My dear," said my father very gently, "I love her."

It was like a nightmare.

"But she's much too young for you. You're nearly fifty!"

"She doesn't mind that."

"You're old enough to be her father," I said. "She could be my sister. I think it's disgusting."

"I hoped you wouldn't think like that," he said quietly.

"Well I do! What does a young girl like that want with an old man like you?" I wanted – oh how I wanted – to hurt him as much as he was hurting me. "And what about Mum?" I said, "I thought you loved Mum!"

"Of course I did," he said, "This doesn't alter anything about what I felt for her."

"I think it does," I insisted. "You're being disloyal to Mum."

"Your mother wouldn't have wanted us to go through life without love," he said.

"Oh, *love*!" I sneered. "You and that barmaid. You call that *love*?"

"I call it…"

"Stop it, Vicky!" he said angrily. "Don't say anything you may regret. You hardly know Beth."

"Neither do you, come to that. Oh Dad, don't, don't do it! Please! We're happy here aren't we, you and I, just the two of us? I'll hate her, I know I will. I'll run away. I'll…"

But my father just looked at me rather sadly and patted me on the shoulder. "It'll be better than you think," he said, and went out of the room.

I sobbed into my pillow far into the night. It would be *worse* than I thought, not better. I felt sure it would be much worse.

That weekend he brought Beth to our house. She swaggered in in a quite brazen way, and you could see her rounded breasts and even the nipples showing through the thin material of her Hungarian blouse. There was something earthy about her. She wore a bracelet round her ankle and high-heeled wedge sandals which revealed dirty jagged toenails. The blouse was a grubby white and where it slipped off one brown shoulder you could see the tattoo of a fish. How my mother, herself so meticulously clean and neat, would have disapproved, she so hated tattoos! But then she was different from Beth in every way. How could my father not see that?

I have to admit that Beth was very nice to me, very friendly. I don't know whether she set out to be or whether it just came naturally, but I wished she wouldn't be. I didn't want her friendship. I wished she would be horrible and cruel instead, so that I could hate her with a clear conscience. I had always thought, as a small child, that people were either all good or all bad, that there were no shades of grey, and I wanted her to be all bad, because anything else made me feel disloyal to my mother. It hurt me deeply that my father should even look at someone else, and choosing someone so young and blatantly attractive as Beth was an insult to Mum. I suppose I was a romantic – I believed that people like Mum and Dad should fall in love and be happy ever after. It was unthinkable that the Prince should look elsewhere. If Cinderella had to die, then the Prince should pine for her forever and break his heart. That was what I believed.

Beth often came to the house after that first time. I kept away from her as much as I could and tried to be as disagreeable as possible, but she didn't seem to notice and just carried on being friendly to me. I don't know if she was thick-skinned or just thick, but I began to feel I was wasting my time. After she had gone I would grumble about her to my father, taking a sadistic delight when I was able to find fault.

"D'you know Dad, she's left the electric fire on *all night!* I'm surprised it didn't start a fire."

"Did she tell you she'd broken one of Mum's best glasses? Well I found the bits in the dustbin wrapped in the *Daily Mail*."

"She's very deceitful, Dad. She tells lies. You know she told us she'd got two A levels? Well I met a girl who was at school with her and she says she didn't even get any GCSEs, let alone A levels. I wonder what other lies she's told you, Dad. I bet there's lots of things. I shouldn't think she'll be faithful. She doesn't look the faithful sort, somehow. This girl I met who was at school with her says she was always flirting with boys, even with the teachers, she said. Fancy that, Dad! I expect that's why she didn't get any GCSEs, don't you? I expect she's only marrying you for the money, I bet she'll go through all your money and be annoyed when she finds out there isn't as much as she thought."

But no matter what I said it didn't make any difference. I couldn't put my father off. If anything, I made him more determined than ever. A few weeks later he and Beth went off to the registry office and got married, so that was that. I didn't go, of course. I could *not* have gone.

Beth didn't want to live in our little house. She wanted Dad and her to have a new house with new things in it, so that she could make what she called 'a clean start'. She gave up her job at the Feathers and Dad took some leave and they went house-hunting every day, while I went to school. They found a lovely house in the country, with a nice garden, and my Dad bought it for her. He spoiled her rotten and would deny her nothing. My mother would have loved it, as she had always hankered after living in the country. It was detached and brand new and full of labour-saving devices, including my Dad. He was very labour-saving – he hardly ever let her wash a cup. She had all new carpets and curtains and was thrilled to bits with everything. I was surprised there was enough money. I had always thought we were fairly hard up, yet here was Dad giving in to Beth's every whim and watching her delight like an indulgent parent.

I hated the way they carried on together, as if I wasn't there sometimes. They'd go running up and down the stairs giggling like children, and hold hands at breakfast, and Dad would keep running his fingers along her bare arm or the back of her neck. I pretended not to see. I wished I hadn't seen. I wanted to wipe out all those mental pictures of them kissing and canoodling together, but it kept coming back before my eyes.

Gradually things became more normal. I began to accept Beth's house as my home, which I had never thought I could do. And though I tried, I couldn't go on hating her forever. She was too light-hearted, too easy-going, too happy. She was always singing, and she'd tell us jokes and make us laugh. I tried not to laugh because it seemed disloyal to Mum, but sometimes I couldn't help myself.

So we continued to live, rubbing along together, in Beth's house, and I found myself torn between liking her and not liking her. I liked her spontaneous fits of generosity when she'd suddenly give me something, a sweater or a pair of shoes, and if they weren't what I'd have chosen myself at least it was a kind thought. But I disliked her untidiness, her slovenly ways and the fact that she wouldn't keep the house as clean for my father as she should have done – nor herself, for that matter. I found it distasteful the way she'd wander around in her underclothes with a safety pin fastening a broken strap and her hair unbrushed, just as you'd expect from a gipsy – or a slut. But I had to admit, she seemed to make Dad happy. He was content like I'd never seen him before. He had a sort of joyous, contented glow about him, like an electric fire at dusk.

One day I had a bad headache and got sent home from school. "You've been working too hard, Vicky," said my teacher kindly. "I've noticed you looked pale and strained for some time now. Take the rest of the week off and have a good rest."

"Yes," I agreed, "I'll do that."

It took me an hour to get home on the winding country bus. I wondered if Beth would be pleased to see me. I had got the feeling she was quite glad to say goodbye to Dad and me each morning, to have the day to herself.

I unlocked the front door with my latch key and called out, "Beth!" but there was no reply. She must be out. Slowly I walked upstairs to my room.

Then I heard the low gurgle of her laughter and the sound of a man's voice from behind the closed door that led to hers and Dad's bedroom.

Except that it wasn't Dad's voice.

I forgot my headache. Sometimes a headache is a luxury you haven't time to indulge. Without a second thought I ran noiselessly downstairs and into the little lobby where the phone was kept. Then I picked up the receiver and dialled my father's office.

"Hello, Dad?"

"Vicky! Is that you?"

"Yes, it's me, Dad."

"What is it?"

"You'd better come home straight away."

"What's the matter?"

"It's Beth."

"Beth? Is she all right? Is she ill?"

"I don't know Dad, but she wants you to come home straight away."

Then I hung up.

I've often wondered since why I did it. Was it a sort of revenge? I suppose it was. Revenge on my father for marrying Beth. Revenge on Beth for daring to think for a single moment she could take the place of my dearest mother.

When I had put the phone down, I went out of the house. I wandered down the country lane beyond the garden gate, then climbed over a stile and into a cornfield. There I sat on the little grassy path by the side of the corn, watching a skylark winging its way far, far above in the thick blueness of the sky. Up and up it went and its song was so lovely, but it didn't make me feel any better. The grassy path wasn't that comfortable, there were little stones on it and I could feel one, quite a sharp one, biting into my bottom, but I stayed in the cornfield because I didn't want to be in the house when my father came back. I felt sort of frightened inside. I kept telling myself that the man I'd heard with Beth would have gone by the time my father got home and nothing would come of it. Perhaps it wasn't too late to phone my father and tell him not to come after all, it was a mistake. But I didn't, I just kept on sitting in the cornfield, till the sun began to sink in the sky and a cool breeze started to ripple through the corn.

It was tea time before I went back to the house. I found my father there alone. One look at his face told me everything.

"Where's Beth?" I ventured nervously.

"She's gone," said my father. "She won't be back. You were right about her, Vicky, all along the line. She was no good."

Once, not long before, I'd have been glad to say 'I told you so', but now I wished so much I had been wrong. And why, *why* had I done such a thing? I had betrayed Beth, who had never done me any harm. Perhaps if I had said nothing my father would never have found out. He could have gone on with that enjoyment of life he had found with her – that innocent, childlike happiness she had brought us.

"She was no good," said my father heavily.

"Oh but she was – there was a lot of goodness in her," I said.

He looked so sad.

"I'll find her. I'll bring her back for you!" I cried.

"No," said my father, his shoulders slumped. "I couldn't take her back, nor would she come. It's over."

I knew then he was right. I felt such pity and sadness for him – but for myself, I felt only disgust.

So now we're alone, Dad and me, in Beth's house. He has to live with his memories. And me? I have to live with myself.

The Winning Streak

I've done the most awful thing, and soon they're all going to find out. I wish I was dead – oh why did I do it? I must have been mad! If only I could turn the clock back. Just half an hour, that's all I need, half an hour. Half an hour between me and disgrace – but that's the trouble, isn't it? You can never turn the clock back.

It all started about three weeks ago when I went home one day and announced I was going to the Grand National with Fiona Campbell.

"Fiona's father has a box in the County Stand, so we'll have a marvellous view," I said, "and there'll be a really super lunch first with caviar and smoked salmon and champagne."

They were all green with envy. "What a lucky girl you are, Merry," said my mother.

"But you don't like caviar," said my sister Janice.

"I've only ever had it once," I said, "and I daresay it grows on you."

"Oh, I do hope not!" said my brother Billy. We laughed.

"They must be very rich, these Campbells," he added.

"They're not short of a penny or two," I said. "Mum, d'you think Anne would lend me her new fur and leather jacket? Fiona says it can be very cold at Aintree but I do want to look good. D'you think she'd let me have it?"

"I don't know," said my mother. "You'll have to ask her when she gets home. She probably will."

"Oh, it's not fair, I've always wanted to go to the Grand National!" cried Janice.

"Never mind – I'll tell you all about it," I promised. "I'll make you feel as if you'd been with me, every minute."

The day arrived – a breezy March day with plenty of sun. "A good day for the races," I said with satisfaction. I wore my new tweed slacks and Anne's jacket with my County Stand badge on it and a silk Jacqmar scarf.

"You look really County," said my sister Anne approvingly. "Now don't forget my bet for the National. Have you written it down? A pound each way on Blue Bunny."

"And I want a pound each way on Silly Billy," said my brother.

"You said it." I grinned and ducked to avoid a cushion. "What did you want, Mum?"

"Esperanto - £1 each way."

"That's what I'm having – a pound on Esperanto and a pound on Latin Lover," said Janice. "How much are you taking, Merry?"

"Four pounds, altogether."

"Will that be enough?" said my mother.

"It'll have to be, it's all I've got," I replied, stuffing all their pounds into my purse. "It's not as if I'll have to pay for anything."

At half-past eleven the Campbells arrived in their grey Mercedes. There were already queues of cars waiting to get into the Aintree car parks and stacks of people milling down the road towards the main entrance. Once inside the gates there was a mass of bright colour and a hotch-potch of people of all sorts and sizes, some scruffy, some smart, but all cheerful and optimistic with the day's prospects before them.

Fiona's Uncle Robbie queued up to get us all race cards and we went up the staircase leading to the terraces and found our box. A little disappointing – somehow I'd imagined plushy red velvet seats instead of wooden tip-up ones. Still, the lunch was superb, champagne flowed and there were strawberries flown over from Jersey or somewhere. Everyone was very nice to me in a vague sort of way: "So this is Fiona's little friend Merry – and very charming too, if I may say so, we'll have to have a get-together later on my dear." Then they'd drift away.

"Come on," said Fiona, "we don't want to hang around here all the time. Let's get down below amongst the crowds and see what's going on. It'll soon be the first race and we want to get our bets on."

"Oh – do we bet on other races besides the National?" I asked.

"Of course, silly! That's part of it," said she tossing her head. "We'll go to the saddling enclosure first and then the paddock. Now stick close to me Merry, or you'll get lost."

I stood with her and watched the horses for the two o'clock race walk round the paddock with their trainers. They all looked nice to me, but all much the same.

"What do you look for, Fiona?" I asked.

"Oh, various points – bone structure, weight and so on," said Fiona. I don't think she really knew in spite of being a farmer's daughter. "I fancy Number Three," she announced.

I looked at my race card and out of the blur of names one seemed to rise up and float before my eyes. No. 11 – Sproggatt's Newt.

"That's the one I'll have," I said.

"Honestly, Sproggatt's Newt! Whatever made you choose that?"

"Oh – just a feeling I've got."

"Come on then, we'll go over to the tote and put our money on."

There were little queues of people at each selling booth. I gave £1 to Fiona and she put £1 each way on No. 3 and £1 for a win on No. 11.

"We haven't time to go upstairs now, we'll go and watch this one from the rails," she said. "Stay close to me."

We ran through the crowds, round Tattersalls Stand, past the bookies and out onto the rails.

"Look – they're lining up for the start," said Fiona. "Mine's emerald green with white sash. What colour's yours?"

I looked at my race card. "Scarlet with royal blue hoops."

Everyone was pushing forward, pressing us onto the rails. Then the cry went up "They're off!" It was very exciting.

"And it's No. 3, Jemima, in the lead," said the voice from the loudspeaker.

"Yours, Fiona," I said but she looked glum. "Too early," she said, "They have to go round twice you know."

Twice we watched the horses till they grew small, like little toys far off on the horizon, and then a few minutes later they were racing up the home straight with Prince Regent in the lead. "Come on, Prince Regent!" bawled a voice nearby.

"And now Sproggatt's Newt is coming up strongly on the inside," said the Commentator.

"That's mine, that's mine," I cried, "Come on Sproggatt's Newt, come *on!*"

"And at the post it's Sproggatt's Newt from Prince Regent and Bystander..." boomed the loud speaker.

"You've won!" said Fiona.

"Yes, I've won, I've won!" I cried, hugging her with excitement.

"Let's go and get your winnings," she said, "And start thinking about what to have in the 2.35. Have you any more brilliant hunches? You're probably one of those lucky people who can see into the future."

"Oh well I don't know about that," I said modestly.

I collected £5.46. It seemed too good to be true. It was so easy.

"Quick, hurry!" said Fiona, "What are we having for the next one? Here, these are the runners."

I took her card and looked at the list through half-closed lids. This time it was 'Friday's Child' that seemed to isolate itself from the rest and stand out before me. "That's what I'll have," I said to Fiona. "Two pounds each way on Number Six, that's Friday's Child." I gave her £4.

"I say, you are lashing out," she said, taking the money. She looked at me with a new sort of respect. Larger bets gave one an elevated status somehow.

We went up on the roof to watch the 2.35. It was windy up there but exciting. You could see the whole racecourse. People were friendlier and, ourselves included, less inhibited. "Come on, Friday's Child!" we shouted and jumped up and down on the steps as it thundered past.

You'll never guess – I won again! And Fiona won too, because she'd copied me. We were over the moon. This time I collected more than £15. It was so incredibly easy. We went back to the box.

"Well, and how are you two getting on?" asked Uncle Robbie, genially.

"Fantastic! Merry's doing frightfully well – she got the winners of both the last two races."

"I say, I say! What a lucky little lady you are!" said a fat man with spectacles. Suddenly they were all looking at me with respect and admiration, as if I'd done something really clever.

"What are your tips for the National?" they asked.

I felt shy. I looked at my race card and there were lots of names and they all came up at me, one after the other – Esmeralda, Phineas Phinn, Donkey Boy...

"I don't really know," I said feebly.

"We'll go and watch them walk round the paddock," said Fiona, "and see if you get a sudden hunch."

"Tell you what Merry, will you put a bet on for me?" asked Mrs Campbell, "I'll have £10 each way on Esperanto."

"That's what my mother picked," I said. But I didn't tell her she'd only put £1 on it. I took the money and went with Fiona to the paddock. There was a terrific scrum there with everyone wanting to see Blue Bunny, the favourite. We watched as No. 43, Donkey Boy, passed in front of us.

"What d'you think of that one, Fiona?"

"It's grey. I don't like greys," said Fiona.

"Except when they come in at a hundred to one," said a hefty young Irishman at my elbow, turning to grin at us.

"That one won't," said Fiona.

"Wanta bet?" said the Irishman. "Listen girls, I'll give you a tip. Put your money on Donkey Boy. He's an outsider but he'll do it, see if I'm not right."

It seemed like fate somehow.

"I had thought of Donkey Boy myself," I said doubtfully.

"Go on, put it on, I'd like to do you a good turn. Put a tenner on and win yerself a thousand quid."

"If it wins and I don't back it I'll kill myself," I said,

"And if you do and it doesn't you'll kill *me*!" He laughed. I laughed too.

"Oh come on, Merry," said Fiona. "Look, I want to go to the loo. You put the bets on and I'll meet you by the hamburger stall in ten minutes."

She gave me her money and I made my way over to the tote. First I put on the pounds for Fiona and the family, then to the ten pound booths with Fiona's mother's money. I still hadn't decided what to have myself. If I put £1 on Donkey Boy and it won I stood to get £100 back – but what if I put £10 on like the Irishman said? I'd get £1000! What couldn't I do with £1000? After all I *was* on a winning streak…

My purse was still crammed with notes from my first two winnings and on a sudden impulse I crammed them all down on the counter and pushed them under the glass. "£10 each way on Donkey Boy please," I said. I felt great.

I met Fiona and we went back to the box to watch the National. It was exciting and spectacular and there was a wonderful atmosphere amongst the crowd. It was just as I'd dreamt it'd be. Except for one thing. Donkey Boy fell at Bechers on the second time round. Twenty quid down the drain, just like that. Twenty quid – it was terrible. The favourite, Blue Bunny, won. The crowd went wild. Esperanto was third.

Mrs Campbell seemed quite pleased. "I should get something,

anyway!" she remarked. Mr Campbell opened some more champagne and poured us each a glass. No one else in our box had won anything, but no one else seemed to mind except me, and I couldn't show it. I had to pretend to be as cheerful as the rest of them, for if you sat with the Campbells you couldn't be a bad loser.

"Merry darling," said Mrs Campbell expansively, "You'll be an angel and collect my winnings, won't you?"

I said I would.

"And I've had a tip for the 4.30. Rumpelstiltskin. Would you put this on for me for a win?" She gave me a crisp ten-pound note.

"Are you coming, Fiona?" I asked.

"No, I feel a bit sick. It must be the champagne. I'll sit this one out. You don't mind going on your own, do you?"

"No, all right."

I waited in the long queue on the pay-out side of the tote, but it didn't move at all and I began to get worried I would miss the 4.30 race. I decided to put Mrs Campbell's bet on first and come back for the National winnings later when the crowds had lessoned.

It was a pity I had no more money to have a bet myself. I stood in the Sell £10 queue and as I looked at the runners for the 4.30 I got the most persistent hunch. Pal O Mine was going to win. I just knew it. I've still got a winning streak, I told myself, where I made the mistake was in taking the tip from that Irishman. I should have relied on my own judgment.

As if to confirm my thoughts, I overheard two men talking behind me.

"Number nine'll do it," said one.

"You reckon?"

"It's a dead cert."

I looked at my card. No. 9 was Pal O Mine. Oh, if only I'd got some money left I could back it!

"What about Rumpelstiltskin?"

The first man laughed. "Not a chance, mate. Might as well put your money down the drain."

It seemed to be fate that they should mention that horse at that moment. Mrs Campbell, you're going to lose, I thought in anguish.

"Yes?" said the clerk behind the grill.

I swallowed. "£10 for a win on No. 9," I said.

The die was cast.

Well, I thought, it makes no difference if Mrs Campbell's going to lose her money anyway – I've just borrowed what she's going to lose. But I'll win with it and then I'll buy her a bunch of flowers. It seemed so very logical.

I only just had time to get to the rails as the race was starting. I had to look out for a jockey in black with a scarlet cap that were the colours for No. 9. There was the usual crush of people pressing forward, the usual excited cry, "They're off!"

"And as they get away it's Cooch Behar in the lead," said the commentator. Too early, I thought. I shook my head like any seasoned race-goer.

"And it's Cooch Behar, then Anteater, then Pal O Mine, then Hunter's Walk, then Sundial…"

I watched the little group of horses rounding a bend, but I couldn't make out the individual colours and had to rely on the commentary. They were all pretty much in a bunch, but now Anteater was in the lead and Cooch Behar had dropped behind, while Pal O Mine stayed at third place till the second time around, when he moved up into second. It was just exactly right. And as they came up to the final straight he'd know just how much sprint to put on to take the lead and win.

And then suddenly from nowhere another horse came up from behind, a grey with green and white colours, No. 14 – it was Rumpelstiltskin! And as Pal O Mine strained to pass the leader, up came the grey on the rails and outstripped them both at the winning post.

I had lost – but what was far, far worse, Mrs Campbell had won. And so now you see why I wish I was dead. Mrs Campbell would have won about two hundred pounds and I couldn't even give her back her stake money! How could I face her or the others ever again?

At last I turned away in despair and went to join the Late-Pay queue at the tote to collect the National winnings. Anne had won nearly £6 and for their place bets on Esperanza Mrs Campbell got £15 and my mother £1.50. I pocketed the winnings and moved away.

Now I'd have to go back to the box and face them, all the Campbells. They'd be so shocked. I could already see the pained expression on Mrs Campbell's face as she looked at me. What a friend for Fiona! "Fiona, my dear, I don't really think Merry is quite the person for you to associate with."

"Too right, Mother, you don't have to tell me! Why she's nothing but a thief!"

Thief! Thief! rang in my ears. I couldn't go back! Not yet. What could I do now?

"Hello, there," said the hefty young Irishman at my elbow, "You look down in the dumps."

"Is it any wonder?" I said, "Because of you I'm on the road to ruin."

"Is that so?" he said, "I'm sorry to hear it."

"You don't look very sorry. My life is at an end, I might as well kill myself and you stand smirking as if it's a joke."

"Glory be, is it that bad?" he said. "Tell you what. I'll take you for a jar and you shall tell me all about it."

"I can't," I said, "Not if it's a public bar. I'm under age."

"A cup o' tea then."

"All right."

We sat in a dark, crowded tearoom and over a thick white china cup of strong tea I told him the whole story. He shook his head.

"Aren't you the foolish one?"

"You don't have to tell me that," I said indignantly. "I want some sympathy with my tea."

"I'll tell you what," he said, "How much have you got now?"

"Nothing at all, I told you."

"What about your family winnings?"

"Oh that – £7.45 altogether."

"Tell you what I'll do. Give me the £7.45 and I'll give you a £10 note. You can give it to the woman and say you didn't have time to put it on for her what with having to collect her winnings and all, there wasn't time before the race started."

I brightened. "I could do that," I agreed.

"I'll make you a loan of the £2.55 and you can mail it to me at your leisure." He scribbled his address on the back of the race card. "There, Tim O'Riley's the name. After all," he grinned, "It's the least I can do for setting you on the road to ruin."

"Oh thank you! I'll repay you just as soon as I can."

"And have you learnt your lesson?"

"I certainly have. I'll never gamble again – at least not with other people's money."

"And they won't even know you did. You've a water-tight story to tell 'em."

But as I left him and mounted the steps to the private boxes I knew I couldn't tell it after all. It was just adding one more lie onto everything else. I might as well be hanged for a sheep, I thought. Slowly but now calmly I went back into the box.

I was greeted rapturously.

"Merry my dear, here you are!" cried Mrs Campbell. "We wondered where you were."

"Wherever did you *get* to?" said Fiona. "You missed the 4.30 and the 4.55."

"She probably saw them both downstairs," said Mr Campbell. "Or from the roof. Did you go up to the roof, lass?"

"Er – no, I was down at the rails," I said.

"What d'you think about my win on Rumpelstiltskin?" said Mrs Campbell proudly.

"Yes, did you see Mummy's horse winning the 4.30?" said Fiona, "Wasn't it exciting?"

"We reckon she should have got about two hundred pounds," said Uncle Robbie.

"Did you collect all the winnings?" asked Fiona.

"For the National, yes, but not the 4.30," I said.

"Oh well…" Mrs Campbell looked slightly surprised, "Never mind. James will go for me, won't you James? I'm sure you must be tired of standing in queues. Give him the ticket dear, and he'll go."

"I didn't put it on," I said.

"You didn't put it ON?"

"I heard a man say it would be throwing the money down the drain so I put it on another horse instead."

There was a stunned silence.

Then Mr Campbell burst out laughing. "And you thinking you'd won a couple of hundred quid, Joan!" he said.

"Why, you naughty girl, Merry!" said Fiona, shocked.

"Oh I don't know," said Mrs Campbell, "I'm rather touched that she should have tried to make me some money on another horse when she thought mine was a dud."

But I couldn't let that pass, could I? Not really.

"I wasn't trying to make the money for you, Mrs Campbell," I said. "It was for myself." And in case she still hadn't grasped it I said, "I took your money and gambled with it."

"I say, she certainly likes to turn the knife," said Fiona's uncle, laughing.

"I was going to buy you some flowers," I said, "Out of my winnings."

"Well, that was nice," said Mrs Campbell. She was determined to look on the good side. I had really underestimated her.

"I'm very sorry," I said, "I'll never, ever do it again."

She smiled. "I'll say one thing, Merry, you're honest – I do like honesty in a girl," she said. "And after all, what's a couple of hundred pounds between friends?"

Crossed Lines

He had noticed her waiting on the station platform at Birmingham New Street, but not because she was pretty; it was because of her clothes. They were really funny, he thought (funny peculiar, not ha-ha). She looked like a rag bag. Nothing matched. The skirt was too long and too narrow, the jacket too big and too baggy, and the shoes were too flat and too pointed. They looked like old granny shoes. She had a funny little face too, like a robin's. *Oh God,* he thought. *I must make darn sure I don't sit near her, or I won't get any work done. She'll chirrup all the way to Cambridge.*

She had noticed him too, standing on the platform, and had thought he looked boring. His hair was too neat, his mac was too clean and his jeans were too new. She didn't like the goody-goody sort, they had no character. Still, she thought, he would be a good travelling companion. He wouldn't lunge at her in a tunnel or steal her purse while she slept. Nor would he whine all the way like the small boy also waiting for the train with his mother, who had already started an incessant chime of "Can I have…?"

So she chose a seat opposite his and sat down with a plonk.

Oh God, he thought, *just my luck. Does she expect me to put her suitcase up on the rack?*

"Shall I put your case up on the rack?" he asked.

"Oh, thanks."

Now he's going to try and get off with me, she thought. Not so safe after all.

The train started with a jerk. She turned and looked fixedly out of the window. She looked at the backs of lots of little houses with untidy gardens, filled with junk. *And maybe bodies,* she thought with a thrill of horror, *buried under the rubble of broken glass, cardboard boxes and old dolls' prams. I mean they've got to be buried somewhere, haven't they? These people you read about in the papers, that get murdered and disappear?*

I wonder if he expects me to talk to him, she thought, *I suppose I ought to make a gesture, seeing as he put my case up on the rack.*

"What a lot of rubbish!" she said.

"Yes," he said with an inward groan. What was she talking about? She had a copy of *The Sun* on her lap.

"Do you think there are bodies buried amongst that rubbish?" she asked.

"I've no idea," he said shortly.

Oh God, she was one of those. A loony. Just his luck to sit opposite a loony, and a three-hour journey ahead, too. Well not quite three hours. Two and three quarters. Quite long enough.

"I mean, they've got to bury them somewhere," she added.

"Who?"

"The people who murder them."

"Murder who?"

"The bodies that are dug up – like you read about in the papers."

Did she expect an answer to that? Did he honestly expect an answer to that? He sighed and opened his briefcase, the attaché sort, extracting a pad of A4 lined paper and a B pencil with a very sharp point.

"I should think that would break," she said, "If you pressed on it."

"Should you?" he said. "Should you really? Well it may interest you to know that if it does, it won't matter because I have a pencil sharpener in my pocket."

"I see you're the sort that likes to take care of every emergency," she said. "I expect you have a roll of Elastoplast in your pocket in case you cut yourself, and a bottle of aspirins in case you get a headache."

"No, I don't actually," he said coldly.

What an irritating girl she was! He took a textbook out of the briefcase and opened it at page eighty-three. He started to jot down some figures on the pad. Suddenly the pencil snapped and the point of lead rolled onto the floor.

"Oh dear," said the girl. She didn't say "I told you so" – surprisingly. They watched it wobble to and fro.

"I suppose you will want to sharpen it out of the window," she said, "so as not to make a mess on the floor."

"Yes," he said, although he hadn't thought of that. He considered the floor was messy anyway and a bit of pencil sharpening wouldn't make much difference.

He stood up and heaved the window open.

"Be careful," she said. "You wouldn't want your head knocked off by a train going the other way."

"No I wouldn't," he said, "but that couldn't happen. The lines don't run that close."

"They always look as if they do to me," she said.

"But they don't," he said.

He sharpened the pencil. A gust of wind, or maybe it was just the air, blew the sharpenings back into the compartment, where they landed on the girl's lap.

"Oh – sorry!" he said.

"That's all right," she said, shaking her skirt. "I'm afraid the floor will just have to get messed up after all."

He tried to close the window, but it seemed to be stuck.

"Shall we have the window open for a bit?" he suggested.

"I'd rather not," she said.

"Don't you like fresh air?" he asked, irritated again.

"No I do not," she replied. "It's cold and draughty. I like it stale and muggy. It's much more comfortable."

"Well I'm afraid I can't close it now," he said after another attempt. "Shall I try?"

"You won't be able to budge it, it's stuck."

"But it wasn't stuck before you opened it," she said logically.

He shrugged. "Please yourself," he said.

She stood up and managed to close it quite easily. He didn't say anything. He wanted to yell and shout with irritation. He picked up his notebook again. He began to jot down some figures.

"What are you doing?" she asked.

"Economics."

"Oh how boring!"

"That depends on your point of view."

"I bet it's boring from any point of view," she said, "If you're honest."

He made no reply. He was covering a page with calculations. He was not sure they were correct. "If you're honest," said her voice insistently inside him, "If you're honest…"

"I think I'll go and get a coffee," she remarked.

Again he didn't answer.

"Would you like me to get you one?" she continued, "As you're so busy?"

"No thanks," he said.

"Oh, go on," she said disarmingly.

"All right. Thank you."

She was away ages and he was able to get quite a lot done. He found the calculations he'd made when she had been there were not correct after all. She had put him off. Nor was he able to make the most of her absence. He found himself unable to concentrate. Where the hell was she? He could just do with that cup of coffee. She was taking ages. Perhaps she had gone to the loo. Perhaps she had fallen down the loo.

Perhaps she had found him so boring she had got herself another seat in a different part of the train. But she had to come back for her suitcase, he thought with some relief. Then he thought that she could leave it till they got to Cambridge, if that was where she was going, and come for it then. He felt quite dejected.

Suddenly there she was like a bit of flotsam, drifting jerkily down the central aisle.

"Sorry!" she said. "Did you think you were never going to get your coffee?"

"Oh no!" he said, "Not at all."

"There was an awfully long queue," she said, "And only one man on."

"Oh." He felt extraordinarily glad to see her.

"I bought you a Kit Kat," she said.

"Thank you. How much do I owe you?"

"Three pounds twenty pee," she said at once.

"There you are," he said, thinking it was quite a lot and she must have made a bit on the deal. He felt disappointed. He hadn't expected her to be a cheat. Nutty as a fruit cake, but not a cheat.

"No," she said presently, "That can't be right. "Two pounds eighty."

She gave him two 20p pieces and he felt a great relief, not because of the money.

"Where are you going?" she asked chattily.

"Back to university," he said.

"Oh I see. Bristol or Exeter?"

"Neither. Cambridge."

"You're going back to Cambridge – now?" she said surprised.

"Yes," he said. "What's so strange about that?"

"Because this train is going to Bristol," she said.

"You're going to *Bristol*?" he said, "But I'm going to Cambridge."

They looked at one another and she shook her head. She might have known it.

"You're on the wrong train," she said.

"Or *you* are," he said.

"I don't think so," she said, "I do not make stupid mistakes like that."

And then the announcement came thundering over the Tannoy: "All passengers are advised that this train will shortly be arriving into Cambridge. All passengers for Cambridge please, ladies and gentlemen."

"Oh well," said the girl brightly, "I've never been to Cambridge – perhaps you could give me a guided tour?"

Fateful Turning

If Sandra had not turned that particular corner, all that followed would not have happened. She had just seen Roger off at Victoria Station and was deep in thought. There was so much to sort out in her mind – why did some people lead such complicated lives? She didn't really know that part of London too well but had a vague idea that if she went up Grosvenor Place and turned right into Piccadilly she would reach Green Park. How wonderful to see flowers and trees and green grass after the drab grey streets of the city. She would go into the park and sit on a bench in the sun and kick off her high-heeled shoes and have a cigarette and maybe she would be able to decide what to do. It was her decision, Roger had told her that.

But coming round that corner into Piccadilly – how was it people always met in Piccadilly? – she ran straight into Nan Rigby. She hadn't seen her since they had worked together after college, but she looked exactly the same.

"Why, Sandra!" she shrieked, "How extraordinary, I was only thinking about you today. How are you, it's been ages! We *must* have a chat. What are you doing now, could we have lunch?"

"Well... all right then," said Sandra.

"I know a marvellous place in Jermyn Street, not too terribly expensive either." She laughed. "I still haven't landed my millionaire – not yet anyway – so I still have to watch the pennies."

"Who doesn't?" said Sandra, somewhat bitterly. Nan didn't look as if she'd had too hard a time of it, not compared to some – herself for instance.

They went to a little Italian place and ordered thick onion soup and Spaghetti Bolognese. It tasted good, better than the corned beef and lettuce Sandra was used to having in Paddington with the Higginses.

"Well now, Sandra, tell me all about yourself," said Nan eagerly, tucking a paper napkin under her chin. "I remember you were engaged to a builder. Did you marry him in the end? Are you still working as a children's nanny? That was where we met, you and me, and I've been nannying ever since. But perhaps you have children of your own?"

So many questions – now it will all come out, thought Sandra, reluctantly. She resigned herself to telling Nan all about it.

"No, I didn't marry John in the end. I got myself up the duff and had a baby, a boy. My parents are bringing him up now and I see him quite a bit at their house in Croydon. Anyway the next year I met Roger. He was in the Royal Navy. We got married and were happy enough to start with. But it was difficult with him being away at sea so much and I got lonely. I was silly enough to have an affair, and then I found I was pregnant again..."

"Oh, Sandra!" said Nan.

"I know. It was stupid, the man was married so it wasn't going anywhere. This time my parents didn't want to know so we had him adopted. Roger wasn't impressed - but he did forgive me in the end."

"So what now? Did you go back to being a children's nanny?"

"No. I wanted to but there wasn't anything available at the time.

Right now I've just finished a job I had in Paddington, with an old couple. They were sweet but it was all a bit depressing. He died and she went into hospital, so it came to an end."

"But what about your marriage?"

"That ended too – a year ago. Funnily enough I met up with him today. Roger. He wants us to get back together."

"And are you going to?"

"I don't know. I can't decide. He thinks we could make it work this time but I'm not sure…"

"Sandra," said Nan, "I've got an idea – I could help you and… well, you could help me too." She seemed full of suppressed excitement.

"What do you mean?" asked Sandra.

"You see I've got an interview this afternoon for a really marvellous job as a children's nanny with this Lady Someone or other. I believe they're very rich and the pay's fantastic and it's in a super part of London too, Belgravia – very posh. Much more exciting than an old couple in Paddington!"

"Yes, but how does that help me? It's your interview, not mine."

"But don't you see, it could be yours," said Nan, "You could go instead of me."

"But why wouldn't you want to go yourself?"

"Because I just happen to have met this incredibly rich and fascinating man who wants to take me on his yacht to the Bahamas."

"But Nan, how could I go when this Lady – whoever she is – expects *you?*"

"You've only got to tell her I'm not available after all, but that you're a children's nanny yourself, between jobs, and you've got references – you have, I suppose?"

"Yes of course."

"She'll snap you up!"

"But what about this man with the yacht? Do you really know him? It sounds a typically hair-brained scheme to me – what are you going to do on the yacht? You might get yourself murdered or something!"

"Oh no, he's not like that at all – he's dishy!" sighed Nan, her eyes all sparkling and shiny.

Sandra thought about it. The question was, should she give Roger another chance? Could they really make a go of it? It might be a great mistake to go back to him. If only you could see into the future. Perhaps if she hadn't run into Nan again – but she had, and perhaps it was fate. Perhaps it was the fresh start that she needed.

"All right, Nan," she said. "Give me the address of your interview."

It was a very elegant house in Lower Belgrave Street, one of those tall houses with steps leading up to a white front door and black railings. She went up the steps and rang the bell. She felt slightly apprehensive, but she needn't have worried. A maid of some sort answered the bell.

"Have you come about the Nanny's job?" she said. "You are expected. I'll tell her ladyship you're here."

She took Sandra upstairs and showed her into a long, high-ceilinged room with sash windows draped with yellow velvet curtains. There was a beautiful Persian rug on the floor and some nice antique furniture. Sandra didn't know much about antiques, but they looked good. She sat down gingerly on a yellow brocade-covered chair. The next moment in came a slight red-haired woman – very much the same sort of build as herself really, in fact she couldn't help thinking that they looked rather alike, although she would have described herself as slim, while this lady was definitely thin.

"You must be Miss Rigby," said the woman, extending a hand.

"Well no, actually," said Sandra, and quailed as the woman's thin eyebrows arched in surprise.

"The thing is, Miss Rigby couldn't come – she's going abroad – and I'm a friend of hers and she thought that perhaps as – I am between jobs – you might take me on instead."

The woman didn't say anything for a moment; she just looked at Sandra very hard. Then she said, "Are you a children's nanny?"

"Yes, I am."

"The last nanny I had was a teacher. But it doesn't really matter, as long as you're responsible with children. I must say, I like your face."

She went on to tell Sandra about the children, what ages they were and what her duties would be. She seemed pleasant enough but quiet, very reserved. She never seemed to smile. And then she said she was separated from her husband, and that created an instant bond between them.

"No doubt you will meet my husband, he has access to the children and comes here from time to time. Have you any children?"

"No." It was easier to lie, not to go into all the details.

"Are you married?"

"Yes, but we're separated."

"If it's not an impertinent question, is there any chance of your being reconciled?"

And in that moment Sandra made up her mind about Roger. "No chance," she said.

"Because I don't want someone who's only going to stay a few weeks. I've had too much of that in the past. The children must have a bit of continuity."

"I do understand – and I'd stay as long as... well, as long as you wanted me."

"I can't ask for more than that," said the other and smiled. She was nice when she smiled, rare though it was.

They talked a bit more and it was decided that Sandra should start the following Monday, subject to her references being satisfactory. Then she left. There was no sign of the maid, so she let herself out.

As she descended the steps and turned to go down the street she nearly collided with a very tall, dark and handsome man, smartly dressed in an expensive overcoat. He had black eyebrows that almost met across his forehead and a black, military-style moustache. He stared at her for a moment, then abruptly said, "I beg your pardon," and went up the steps to the house.

A black taxi cab was standing at the kerb, its engine running; evidently the smartly-dressed man had just got out of it. "Need a cab, madam?" called the driver.

"No thank you," said Sandra. She might have just landed a job, but she didn't have the cash to pay for a taxi.

"OK madam, no problem," said the driver cheerily. "Only I just dropped Lord Lucan off and I thought you might be one of his staff needing a lift somewhere."

The Cabin Boy

They arrived in Egypt in January, she and her friend. They were to stay for two weeks – two weeks of sunshine after the snow and ice and cold of England.

Every morning they had breakfast on a terrace under a palm tree. They had yogurt with honey and bananas and croissants with apricot jam. "We shall put on lots of weight," they said ruefully, "We shall have to go on a diet when we go home." But right now they would enjoy the sunshine and the blue sky and just being away, which was delightful in itself.

It was illuminating to watch the other guests and wonder at the enormous amounts they piled onto their plates, and amusing to watch the little birds, sparrows mainly, that flew down to eat anything left on the tables. Little did the other guests realise that the birds were eating the food they had collected for themselves while they went back to the buffet for more.

The hotel was quite nice, she and her friend decided. The gardens were a painter's palette filled with colour, scarlet and yellow and pink hibiscus, crimson and orange and purple bougainvillea, basil with bluey-mauve flowers and other shrubs whose names they did not know. There were many gardeners constantly weeding and watering, for the earth was bone dry: the gardens had been created out of the desert. They had to walk past the flowers and shrubs and palm trees every time they went to their rooms, and they enjoyed the walk, for it was the only exercise they would have. Though warm enough to lie on the sun-beds, it was too cold to swim. They each had very good rooms on the third floor at the top of the building, large double rooms for which they had paid a supplement, each with a big double bed, a table and two chairs, a bathroom with shower and a balcony.

There were no chambermaids, they noticed. All the work in the hotel was done by men. They had a cabin boy – she called him a 'cabin boy' rather than a 'chamber man' – who welcomed them and told them they should let him know if there was anything they needed.

For a few days all was well. But one night quite early on, there was a terrible storm. It started when they were having dinner on the terrace, and they watched lightning light up the sky followed by loud thunder. Then came the rain, more and more rain, opening up great puddles that spread over the dry earth.

The rain continued and then later, when she was in bed, she saw that the water was coming into her room, under the doors leading to the balcony. She watched with horror as it came further and further until it was all around her bed.

She rang Reception, but they seemed unconcerned. "It is the rain, quite normal," they said. "Do not worry."

That was all very well, but she did worry. She watched the water rising. She needed to go to the bathroom and had to lift up her nightgown and paddle through the water. It was now in the bathroom as well. She waded back, taking a towel and drying her feet with it before getting back into bed, and she made an island of things she could do, a pile of books and crosswords, for there was no question of sleeping.

Outside in the corridor she could hear a lot of noise; a loud crash, and then another. There were Russians outside talking excitedly, some of them screaming. She sat back in bed watching the water rise and soon it was ankle deep all over the room. She was afraid.

She began to wonder if there was a tsunami coming and if so, what she should hold onto. You had to hold onto something or be swept away. She wondered how long she could hold her nose above the level of the water – but that was stupid.

It did not come to that. Many hours passed and morning came and she was still there. She had not had to hold onto the bedhead or keep her nose above the level of the water. How stupid she was to be as scared as that! What a wimp. She *would* see her family again! Yet it wasn't very nice to be in a bed surrounded by water. It was not what she had expected from this holiday.

She had a shower and dressed with difficulty, having to put on trousers and sandals that became soaked with water below the knee. She met her friend, whose bedroom had also been flooded, but only a little. They went down the spiral staircase and through the gardens to the restaurant, where they had their breakfast. Everyone was talking about the flood. There had been a lot of damage in the hotel and several ceilings had come down – that must have been the crash she had heard - but the hotel was high up and there were no deaths, as in the lower part of the resort. The airport was closed, more ceilings were down, cars were submerged and people had died; about eleven, someone said. One person on a boat had drowned. Everyone was shocked and amazed, as there had been no rain in this area for sixteen years.

After breakfast the cabin boy came to her room. He seemed particularly glad to see her, to be looking after her, but she was still upset about the flood and the amount of water in her room.

"No worry," he said. "I make good. I make good very quick."

"I will go out," she said, but he said, "No – you stay."

He took her hand and led her to the bed and bade her sit down. Then he set to work to clear all the water, sweeping it into a sort of dustpan and emptying it into a bucket. As each one filled up he carried the buckets through to the bathroom and emptied the water away. There were five buckets full before it was finished. Then he mopped the whole floor with a wide mop until finally all the water was gone and he stood back, smiling at her.

"Is good?" he asked.

"Very good," she agreed. "Thank you."

"Are you…" – he hesitated – "marry-ed?" He made three syllables of the word.

"I was," she said, "but my husband died."

She brought out her snapshot of her husband and showed him.

"Your husband very lucky man," he said, and repeated, "Your husband very lucky man. I go there?" He indicated the other side of the bed, and she laughed. It was not to be taken seriously.

The next day he came to her room and brought her three extra bottles of body lotion. "Is very good," he said. He took her hand and bade her sit on the bed, then he tipped some of the lotion onto her hands and arms and very gently rubbed it in. "Is very good," he said, "you must put this on to stop too much sun." He looked at her with such warmth, making her feel special.

Later she told her friend, who occupied a room further down the passage,

"I've been propositioned," she said, and related what had occurred.

"Hmm," said the friend. "I think someone's looking towards his tip."

"Of course." Yes, that must be it. How could she have thought anything else? She was, after all, years older than him, and although people told her she looked young for her age and had a lovely smile, it could not mean that the cabin boy liked her in any special way.

And yet the special treatment continued. Next he brought a kettle, together with a basket of tea bags. Then he fetched a mug and a teaspoon. He boiled some water and poured it onto a tea bag. She did not like to say that she disliked Indian tea and drank only herbal. He wanted to put sugar into it, but she shook her head at that. He gave her the mug of tea, black with no milk, not as she would drink it, but she did not like to hurt his feelings. He stayed to watch her drink, and surprisingly, it was good, better than she expected.

And then one night when it was very cold he brought a thick towelling bath robe. "Very cold tonight," he said. "You wear this and you not be cold. Lift arms," he commanded. She did so and he put her arms into the sleeves of the robe.

"Thank you very much, you are very kind," she said. "What is your name?"

He said something she did not understand. It sounded like Mohammed. Was everyone here called Mohammed?

"Write it down," she said. She gave him an envelope and a pencil, but he didn't take it, or maybe he could not write. She took the pencil and wrote 'Mohammed' on the envelope and said, "Like that?" He looked at what she had written and smiled, but without really comprehending.

Then one day he knocked on the door of her room. She was sitting on her balcony and got up at once when she saw he seemed upset. "I shall miss you," he said, "For tomorrow I go away. I go to Cairo on holidays. I shall miss you very greatly."

If he was going away tomorrow she must give him his tip – this was what he had been waiting for, probably. She gave him the equivalent of £10. He took it without comment and repeated, "I shall miss you very greatly. I have present for you." He gave her a bottle of Ambre Solaire sun tan lotion. "Is very good," he said, "Factor 10. To remind you of me."

"Oh," she said thoughtlessly, "But I have some already." She showed him her bottle. "Factor 30."

He looked disappointed. "Is no good?" he said, indicating his bottle.
"Oh yes," she said. "It is very good."

He kissed her on both cheeks and gave her a great hug.

Then she felt his erection and sprang away. He looked mortified.

"I very sorry," he said. "I very, very sorry." He paused. "Are you angry?"

"No," she said, "I am not angry."

He took her hand and very gently kissed it.

"I never felt like this before," he said. "Not in all my life." He repeated it. "I never felt like this before in all my life."

"Oh," she said. It was inadequate, but she did not know what else to say, except, "Goodbye. Thank you. You were very good to me and very kind."

Later she told her friend what had happened and about the bottle of sun tan lotion. "I expect someone left it behind," said her friend.

"Yes, probably that was what happened," she said. But he had had nothing else to give.

Afterwards she thought again about the last words he had said to her: "I never felt like this before – not in all my life."

And she was glad.

This story won Dark Tales On-line, *2010.*

Cousin Tessa

We were so bored that summer, Lionel and I. It seemed to rain all the time. We stood at the window and watched the slanting lines of rain beat against the glass and drip onto the wet roofs outside, and saw the gleaming wet cars pass down our road, shooting water from the puddles and making clouds of dirty spray.

As usual I was spending the holidays with my cousins, for my father was abroad. Aunt Rachel was out a lot during the day – she worked part-time in a dress shop – so we children were left pretty much to ourselves.

"What shall we do now?" said Cousin Lionel for the fourth time.

"Monopoly again?" I suggested half-heartedly.

"It's not much fun with two and Tessa won't play."

"She might. I'll ask her. Tessa? Will you play Monopoly?"

"Sorry – I'm just going to wash my hair."

"Well after you've washed it, couldn't you just play a frightfully quick game of Racing Demon? It wouldn't take long."

"Sorry, Lizzie. I'm expecting a call from Jonathan."

Cousin Tessa was in love. She was just sixteen and suddenly she had grown up. She always used to play with us or take us out, and we'd have such fun, she, Lionel and I. Then she went to a dance and met Jonathan and he brought her home afterwards, and next day I teased her about it. I said, not really believing it, "You like Jonathan, don't you Tess?" and she blushed, so then I knew she really did.

Later that day Jonathan phoned and asked her out and after that it sort of spread like a forest fire and it took over everything else. Tessa mooned about all day and had these interminable sessions on the phone. Lionel and I listened in on the extension in Aunt Rachel's bedroom and giggled to ourselves at the inanity of their conversations:

"Darling Tessa, I had to phone you."

"I'm so glad you did, Jonathan."

"Were you thinking about me, Tessa?"

"I'm always thinking about you. I think of nothing else."

("That's true enough," muttered Lionel glumly.)

"What are you doing now, Tessa, right this minute?"

"I'm sitting on the window seat in the dining room. The telephone's green. I'm looking through the window at the rain dripping from the trees. They're green too. Is it raining where you are?"

"Yes, here too. What are you wearing, Tessa? I just want to be able to picture you."

"Oh Jonathan you are funny, and I do love you! Well, if you really want to know I'm wearing a pink cotton shirt and denim jeans and my hair is wet because I've just washed it."

("Huh! She didn't tell him she's got her rollers in," growled Lionel.)

("Shh Lionel! They'll hear.")

"What are you going to do this afternoon, Tessa?"

"Well – I don't know really. My dear young brother and cousin keep pestering me to play Monopoly with them. I might have a game, I suppose."

("The cheek of it!" we whispered indignantly).

"I'm going to have to go now, sweetheart. I have a train to catch at one o'clock. It won't be long till tomorrow night, will it?"

"No... darling," said Tessa softly. I guessed she was hesitating over that word because she wasn't used to saying it.

"Goodbye, my love."

"Goodbye... goodbye..."

We thought it was awfully funny, Lionel and I. We giggled about it and wondered if they really kissed when they were alone, those long, long kisses like you see on television. Sometimes they seem to half-eat each other. I couldn't imagine my lovely cousin Tessa doing that, half-eating someone. We teased Tessa endlessly and she laughed and blushed and her eyes were bright and sparkly. We listened in to all the phone calls to begin with. Then after a while it got boring. I mean really, when you've heard one you've heard them all.

June - July – August. Soon the holidays would be over.

And then the phone calls stopped. Several days passed and there wasn't a single call for Tessa.

When we asked about Jonathan, she was quiet and withdrawn and didn't blush at all. She was really more white than pink. We thought she might have played Monopoly with us or something, but she just mooched about in her room. We thought she was a dead loss.

One day Lionel said, "I've thought of such a funny joke, Maggie."

"What?"

"Well why don't I go out to a public call box and phone here and you answer and tell Tessa it's Jonathan?"

"D'you think so?" I said cautiously.

"Well it would be funny, wouldn't it? She'd rush to the phone and have one of those stupid 'Hello darling' conversations and all the time it'd be me!"

"I see what you mean," I said. A wave of excitement ran through me. "Do we dare?"

"Why not? Should be good for a giggle."

After all, it was raining and we had nothing else to do.

So Lionel popped out to the phone box on the corner and I stayed in, hovering near the dining room door.

Suddenly the phone began to ring. I ran and snatched up the receiver.

"Hello," said Lionel. "This is me. Is that you?"

"Yes, this is me too," I said.

"Well, go and get her then."

"All right. I'll listen on the extension."

"Hurry, before I start to laugh. And don't you laugh either, or she'll guess. Go on, then!"

"Tessa!" I cried, "Telephone! I think it's Jonathan."

She came running into the dining room. I caught a glimpse of her face as she passed and I'll never forget it. She was radiant. Her cheeks were pink and her eyes were shining. I was suddenly afraid – but it was too late.

I went into Aunt Rachel's bedroom and picked up the extension.

"Oh darling," she was saying, "Oh darling. I thought you were never going to call me again. I've been so miserable and now – oh I'm so happy! Darling, where have you been, where are you? When am I going to see you again?"

There was an awful pause, and a sort of choking sound at the other end of the line.

"Jonathan?" said Tessa.

Oh no, I thought.

"*Hello,* how *are* you, my darling?" said Lionel in a deep, strangled sort of voice. He didn't sound a bit like Jonathan.

Another pause – then a terrible sort of half moan, half scream.

"Lionel, it's you! Oh, how could you, how *could* you!" cried Tessa, and flung the phone down. She must have run out of the house then, because I heard the front door slam.

A few minutes later in came Lionel. He was excited and pleased with himself. "Where is she?" he asked.

"She's gone out."

"Oh. Did you hear me? Wasn't I good? '*Hello, hello,* how *are* you, my darling?" he mimicked.

"You were awful. Awful. It was a nightmare. Oh Lionel, I wish we'd never done it. You didn't see her face."

Lionel looked slightly uneasy.

"Where did she go, anyway?"

"I don't know."

"Maybe I'd better go after her."

"Yes. And I'll stay here in case she comes back."

But she didn't come back, and Lionel returned alone. We waited for her all afternoon but she still didn't come.

Later on, when Aunt Rachel got home, a police car came and they told us there'd been an accident. Tessa had been knocked down by a car. The driver never saw her, he said. She must have walked under his front wheels. She seemed in a daze.

"She couldn't have felt anything," the policeman said comfortingly, "it was too quick for that."

"What a terrible accident," they all said.

Accident? Well perhaps it was – but Lionel and I will never be sure.

The rest of the day and the days that followed we stood by the window and stared out at the rain. The trees were wet and the grass was wet and the cars splashed through the dirty puddles as they passed our house.

And every day, every day, it keeps on raining.

This story won Dark Tales On-line, 2010.

The Do-Gooder

I suppose there must be one in every community, someone others can turn to when they're in trouble. Someone well-balanced and sensible and not at all neurotic. Someone, in fact, like myself.

Our community is a fairly large estate with houses and bungalows of every size and shape to suit every pocket. It is pleasantly situated in a semi-rural position with lovely open-plan gardens in which roses abound and trees line the road on either side – not very large trees, but they will grow bigger. There are fields about, but not too many, and shops on one side of a crescent where you can easily park your car. It is, in other words, an eminently desirable place in which to live.

Our house was one of the very first to be built. It is one of the 'Cotswold' type (the most expensive, I may add, just in passing) which means that it has 4 beds, 2 baths, 1 en suite, large through lounge with woodblock floor and downstairs cloakroom with low level WC, so you see I was in a position to get to know all the new people as they moved into the estate. What a blessing it was for them to have someone to welcome them with a pot-plant and a warm friendly note inviting them in for a cup of tea and advice on where to get their meat or have their hair done.

"Now then," I would tell these families as they moved into the houses all around me, "You mustn't hesitate to call on me if there's anything at all I can do for you. Do you have young children? Yes, well you can count on me any time to baby-sit, I mean you don't want to pay some exorbitant amount to a stranger when I'll willingly do it for nothing. Or if you're feeling under the weather and there's something you want from the shops, just let me know. Or if you'd like me to put something in my freezer I'd be only too delighted. I prefer to buy fresh myself so there's always plenty of room in my freezer. Don't hesitate, just pop in any time."

And of course they always do. My husband laughingly says I ought to put up a board saying 'Opening Hours 9-5', but naturally he's only joking. You can't be sure people won't want advice in the middle of the night and quite frequently they do. My husband says he doesn't know what it is about me but I seem to attract all the lame ducks in the neighbourhood. Or should it be dogs? No ducks, I think. Well of course, I know what it is. I just love people. I simply *love* people. It doesn't matter if they're old or young, I just love the whole human race. And I suppose instinctively they know it, because I'm always the one they come to with their problems. You see I have a down-to-earth, level-headed way of looking at life and they think me shrewd and worldly wise. Well, it's easy to give advice to other people isn't it? You can see so clearly what they ought to do.

First of all there was Katie Reade. She lived with her father and mother at No. 56, the dormer bungalow with the mustard-coloured front door. I was really worried about Katie. "That girl," I told my husband when we were getting ready for bed one night, "Is going to end up on the shelf if she doesn't watch it. She should forget Frank Swift and settle down with John instead."

"John?" said my husband.

"Nice John Evans from No. 64. The one with the glasses and the Sealyham dog called Nancy."

"Oh him. Isn't he rather dull?"

"Better a dull husband than none at all," I replied. "And she can't expect to keep him dangling for ever."

"I hadn't realised he was dangling."

"He's only round there every night and all weekends, whether she's in or not."

Honestly, men! They can live right opposite a house and not see who comes and goes. Blind as bats.

"You'd better have a word with her," said my husband climbing into his half of the bed and reaching out for his paperback.

"I certainly intend to," I replied tartly.

I caught Katie one evening when she was nipping out to the pillar box.

"Now then Katie," I said catching sight of the name on the envelope, "You've been writing to Frank Swift again."

She looked surprised and oh, my heart went out to her, so pale with great dark rings under her eyes. "Now Katie," I said, "There's something I've been wanting to say to you for a long time. Come into my lounge and we'll have a nice chat."

"Oh, but Mrs Rimmer…"

"No buts. I won't take no for an answer. Someone has to talk sense to you and if your mother won't do it, I must."

I installed her in my lounge and gave her a stiff whisky and ginger. I think she drinks it. Anyway I thought it would do her good.

"You must see," I said kindly, "Frank Swift is no good. He's just a womaniser. Out and out. Or should it be through and through? *Why* don't you give him up?" I said. "You must see it for yourself, Katie. Frank Swift spells nothing but trouble and unhappiness. You must know that, if you're honest."

"Oh Mrs Rimmer," she said and her poor blue eyes filled with tears.

"Sometimes one has to be cruel to be kind," I said. "I've so hated watching him trample all over you. Now have a good cry, don't mind me. Get it all off your chest."

I gave her a handkerchief, rumpled but clean, and she wept buckets into it and sobbed uncontrollably against my chest. I just held her without speaking until there were no more tears and she handed the handkerchief back wordlessly. Well, not quite wordlessly.

"You're so kind, Mrs Rimmer," she whispered.

"I know, I know," I soothed her gently.

"I've been so wanting to tell someone about it."

"Well you should have come over before. I'd have listened to you any time of the day or night."

"What ought I to do, Mrs Rimmer?"

"I think you know that for yourself," I said softly.

"Give him up and marry John?"

"Yes, Katie."

"But John is so dull," she breathed.

"My dear Katie, *all* husbands are dull eventually," I said, with the accumulated wisdom of years. "With some it's just sooner than others. And John is a decent young man who'd never let you down."

"You know so much about life, Mrs. Rimmer."

"I've been around," I said with a light laugh.

Before you knew it they were engaged, and then shortly afterwards, married. Well I didn't really expect to be asked to the wedding. Although I did think, if it hadn't been for me – but, well – there you go.

The next person I was able to help was Lorna Lewis. I'd noticed for quite a while that she often wore dark glasses, even when it was winter and there was no sun. I know one doesn't expect such things to go on in such a nice neighbourhood as ours but one ought to use one's imagination. One shouldn't go around with one's eyes shut. One must put two and two together.

"If you ask me," I said to my husband darkly, "her husband's beating her up."

"Well my dear," he said wearily (the poor dear works so hard) "you'll know what to do."

I was pleased he had such confidence in me, but I don't mind admitting that Lorna posed me quite a problem. That poor wretched woman, how could I help her?

The opportunity came one day when we were at the newsagents, waiting to pay our respective bills. I like to pay mine weekly, myself, but I noticed Lorna had let hers run on for more than three months. And she was wearing the dark glasses, although it was a foggy November day.

"Lorna, my dear, how are you?" I said. "Now listen, I wonder if I could possibly ask you a favour…"

(I've noticed that when you want to help someone it's very often a good ploy to ask them to help you first. Makes them less suspicious, you know. It's just a little ploy I've employed successfully over the years. And it worked with Lorna, too.)

"Oh Mrs Rimmer," she said, "Well I am rather involved just now, what with…."

"Lorna, I won't hear of your refusing," I said. "It won't take much of your time, I promise. It's about the Jumble Sale in aid of the new church steeple – could you possibly manage to come to my house at four this afternoon?"

"Well I would, Mrs Rimmer, but…"

"Oh super, I'm eternally grateful – and do call me Prue, everyone does!"

(Well not Katie Reade perhaps, but then she is only very young and would naturally feel it disrespectful not to call me Mrs. Rimmer.)

Anyway, Lorna came round at four and I ushered her into my lounge and insisted on her taking off her dark glasses.

"No really, Mrs Ri… I mean Prue," she said, "I have conjunc…"

But her words trailed away as I removed the glasses gently to reveal a beauty of a black eye at the purple and yellow stage.

"Oh my dear," I said, "Was it Desmond?"

"Actually you won't believe it, but I walked into a door."

"I know, I know," I said with great compassion. "You can relax now, you're with friends here. Not a word will be breathed outside these four walls. I have so often wondered and worried about you, Lorna."

(She lives at No. 17, you know, the house with the white chimney stack and the jonquil yellow door.)

"You can tell me, my dear," I said, "It is Desmond, isn't it?"

She hesitated for a moment. Then, as if suddenly reaching a decision she nodded.

"I knew it," I said. Now you sit down by the fire. I'm going to make you a nice strong cup of tea. You need a bit of spoiling."

I knew she would have really preferred something stronger, but I thought it would be unwise to encourage that. I happen to have noticed that there have been rather a lot of bottles amongst her rubbish lately.

"I've got a confession to make to you Mrs Rim... I mean Prue," she said. "I simply loathe tea. Could I possibly ask you for a small gin?"

"I'll have to refuse you, Lorna," I said sternly, "And you and I both know why. Now you sit and relax there while I make the tea."

Presently I came back with the tray and poured out the tea, and she poured out all her problems. The poor wretched woman, how my heart bled for her! Desmond, as I'd suspected, was an absolute demon. He had a terrible temper and when he was in his cups as they say (I don't actually, but some people do) he became very violent. Many was the time he'd beaten her up. Her body was black and blue from bruises.

"My dear, you must leave him," I said.

"I can't, I can't," she moaned, wringing her hands in despair. "I'm so afraid of what he'll do."

"But don't you see, Lorna, you're going to lead a most wretched life, and how will it end?"

"I have my own solace," she said secretively.

"Drinking is no answer – oh how can I make you see it?"

"It may not be the answer, but it stops me caring. I don't give a damn when I've had a few."

I felt extremely sad. I couldn't see how I was going to get through to her.

"You *must* leave him, Lorna," I said. "Things will never get better for you. They will only get worse. A leopard can never change his spots. What is it that binds you to this evil man? You have no children."

"No," she said sadly.

"You must take the bull by the horns and go. It's no use shutting the stable door after the horse has bolted."

"But that's the problem – the horse has no intention of bolting."

"I was really thinking of him as the bull."

"And the leopard?"

"Well – the leopard too, yes."

"So I'm the horse?"

"Yes."

"Yes. I see."

She left shortly after that. I felt sure some of my advice would stick. "It's really so kind of you to have listened to my problems," she said, "And I'll think about everything you've said. I promise you Prue, I'll really try very hard to leave my husband. But it'll take a lot of doing."

"Better to be safe than sorry," I called as she went down the path.

"I can't thank you enough," she called back. Then, surprisingly, she laughed. I couldn't see that there was anything to laugh about. I suppose she was putting on a brave face. (Or do I mean front?)

It's funny the way everyone turns to me when they're in trouble. They find me so understanding, you see, and ever ready to lend a helping ear. I mean a sympathetic hand. Well you know what I mean.

Only a little while ago there was Alice Falconer. Poor Alice. Her husband has got a bit of a roving eye, you know. He's what you might call one for the ladies. Not that there's any harm in him. And it must be quite hard for him coping with an exhausted wife and a new baby. She probably feeds him on microwaved meals instead of a good solid steak and kidney pie or a nice Sunday roast, so you can't be surprised if his eye wanders a bit. That's what I said to Alice. I told her she should turn a blind eye to her husband's little affairs, if she wanted to keep him, that is. Which she does of course, because she loves him – but I couldn't help feeling she was being rather unreasonable. I myself am frightfully broad-minded about that sort of thing and I felt if I could overlook her husband's affairs with other women, why couldn't she?

"What you don't seem to realise Alice," I said, "Is just because you marry someone you don't own them, body and soul. You're just two individual people living in the same house, that's all."

"But surely he should be faithful?" said Alice. "Is that so much to expect?"

I paused for a moment's thought. "Well, I think it *is* Alice," I told her gently with my worldly-wise wisdom. "I mean why *should* he be faithful, when it comes down to it? In this day and age?" (I always like using that phrase). "I mean in this day and age, why should two people have to be faithful to one another all through their lives? It's so dull. Wasn't it Stevenson who said" – I warmed to my theme, which actually had only just occurred to me – "that when a man marries, the road lies long and straight and dusty to the end. Or it might be the grave. Yes, I'm almost sure it's the grave. Well anyway, you see my point. There's no reason why, in this day and age, it should be like that. And it works both ways, you know, you can have affairs too."

"But I don't want to," said poor Alice. "I love Mike and I just don't want anyone else, and he loves me, I'm certain he does, so why does he need anyone else? Why can't he just be happy with me and our baby?"

"What you don't understand, Alice, I told her, "Is that to a man, hopping into bed with someone doesn't mean a thing. Not a thing. It's no different from going to a football match."

"Oh, I would have thought it was, a bit," said Alice.

"Not in as much as you forget all about them when they're over."

"Mike doesn't. He remembers every detail. He even remembers ones he went to years ago, in the eighties."

"Let me try to make you understand a bit better," I said. "Would you describe yourself as sylph-like?"

"Not exactly."

"Quite so," I said, "And what would you say is your particular weakness?"

"I don't know – anything sweet, I suppose. Chocolates."

"There you see," I said, "When you have a box of chocolates in the house you feel this terrible temptation to have one, but you know you oughtn't. Still, you know it will be delightful if you do, so in the end – as they're there – you succumb and it *is* delicious (or perhaps disappointing if it's nougat) and either way you feel terribly guilty. And you forget the taste almost at once. And that," I ended triumphantly," is exactly how a man feels when he succumbs to the odd temptation of popping into bed with someone. No more, no less." I felt very pleased with my analogy, and Alice seemed comforted.

"Yes – well – perhaps it is a bit like that," she agreed, frowning, "although I should have thought when he knows how much it hurts me…"

"Now Alice!"

"If he really loved me he could be a bit stronger-willed…"

"Alice! I want you to promise me that you won't go thinking on those lines any more. It's just self-defeating. What you must do is something constructive – like getting dressed up in a black negligée when he comes home from the office."

"Oh no," she said, "I couldn't possibly do that. "Why, quite apart from the fact that I haven't got one, I'd feel so dreadfully self-conscious and the baby would probably be sick down the front of it or the dog would leave its hairs all over it or I'd spill gravy on it or something."

"Well anyway you know the sort of thing I mean. You'll just have to use your imagination to think of something constructive you could do."

It's so easy to give people advice. The trouble is you can't always be sure that they'll take it. The very same day, after talking to Alice Falconer, I heard that Katie Evans had left that nice John Evans and gone off with Frank Swift. After all I told her about him too. I'm afraid she's going to be very unhappy. And you know I told Alice Falconer to use her imagination and think of something constructive to do? Well she did. I heard from my daily that she'd banged Mike on the head with a frying pan.

And this morning I heard the strangest thing of all – about Lorna Lewis from No. 17, the one whose husband knocks her about? Well it seems she's going to have a baby – *his* baby. And it appears he doesn't knock her about at all, she was just winding me up. Having me on. What an extraordinary thing to do. Some people are so extraordinary.

Apparently she's suffered from conjunctivitis for years, *that's* why she wears dark glasses. And rumour has it she and her husband Desmond are one of the most happily married couples on the estate. Would you believe it? Well I couldn't be more pleased. That's one of the things I love about life – you never know what's around the corner.

One of the most surprising things I find is the number of people who keep moving from this estate. I can't think why – you'd think having found such a highly desirable place to live they'd want to stay put – but no. They're fixing a For Sale notice on the house opposite right this minute. That's the third one in the road this week. It's sad to say goodbye to old friends, but never mind, there's always a silver lining around every corner, and anyway we could do with a bit of fresh blood in the place.

The Girls in the Office

"Are you the temp?" said Doreen.

"Yes."

"Right, you can hang your coat up over there."

She was what you might call mature, Doreen, with blonde-tipped hair that might otherwise have been pepper and salt, i.e. brown and grey. She wore elegantly-shaped spectacles with blue tinted lenses and a suitably dark skirt and blouse, just right for the office.

"You must be Janice's replacement. I hope you've got a sense of humour. You'll need it here." She laughed, indicating what an excellent sense of humour she herself had.

The door opened and Esme entered. "Got the Ashleigh file, Doreen?"

"No, it's still with Mr Elliot. Why, do you want it?"

"Yes. Need to check some figures for the eighth of Jan o-seven."

"You can have it as soon as I get it back from Mr. Elliot. By the by

Esme – this is the new Temp. Phyllis, isn't it?"

"Philippa, actually…"

"S'pose you're Janice's replacement," said Esme, not particularly interested. She was short and plump, of an uncertain age, with hair of an extraordinarily unnatural shade of red. She wore very high heels and dark stockings with little things on, diamonds or beetles or something.

"One thing you'll have noticed, Phyllis," said Doreen, "it's a very friendly office, this. Some offices, everyone talks about everyone else. I couldn't stand working in an office like that, could you Esme?"

"Not likely," said Esme. "You sure you haven't got that file, Doreen?"

"Of course not – if I say I haven't, I haven't. She doesn't trust me I'm afraid, Phyllis!"

"Philippa actually. Not that it matters."

"Fiona in yet?" asked Esme belligerently.

"You must be joking"" said Doreen. "*Not* Miss High and Mighty."

"Don't know how she gets away with it," said Esme. "It's never before ten, and does anyone say anything, do they fiddle! Mr. Davenport never says a dickie bird. Just 'cause she lives further away than the rest of us she gets away with bloody murder. She and her lah-di-da bloody accent."

"I say, excuse our French!" said Doreen with an embarrassed little laugh, "I'm afraid some of us are inclined to get a little carried away at times!"

"Anyway, can't stand around talking – got to get on," said Esme. "Don't forget the file, Doreen!"

"Just one tip, Phyllis," said Doreen after she had gone. She leaned forward in her chair and lowered her voice. "Between you and me, Phyllis…"

"Philippa, actually. Not that it really matters…"

"Between you and me, Philippa, you've got to watch Esme. She's very deep. She can say one thing and mean another. She never tells you her private thoughts. Two-faced, that's what she is, so don't say I didn't warn you. Oh and by the way, Phyllis, I'm sorry to have to mention this – but it's your job to make the tea. Mr Davenport didn't mention it to you, did he? No, well I might have known he'd forget – well anyway, we always have the first brew about now. Janice is supposed to make the tea when she's here, though I must admit she's not very good about it. You always have to remind her. She seems to resent it somehow, though I can't think why – after all, she *is* the Junior so it's part of her duties, but for some reason she seems to think it's beneath her. Between you and me, Janice is a spoilt brat. Daddy's darling – know the sort? Anyway, keep that under your hat. There'll be nine of us for tea, Phyllis, including the men and we've each got our own cup, you'll find the list in the kitchen, up the corridor next to the gents' toilet. And by the by, Mr Rees-Williams likes his very weak and milky."

Fiona was in the kitchen already. "My dear, are you the new temp? What *fun*! I'm Fiona. I'm just defrosting my sandwiches under the grill," she explained, "or they'll still be iced up at dinner time. It's absolutely throwing it down outside. I got simply soaked." She began to take off her tights. "D'you mind if I just hang them up near the spout of the kettle while it boils to try and dry them a little, they're absolutely soaking and one doesn't want to catch pneumonia. My dear, what *fun*, I can see we're going to see eye to eye…"

Her eyes were large and round, with brown rings round them like a tabby cat. She wore a loose, sack-like garment and dangling art nouveau earrings. "I wish you'd replace Janice altogether," she said, "She's a terribly sneaky little thing, causes the most ghastly trouble when she's here, always talking about everyone behind their backs and one can't stand people who do that, can one?"

"So *there* you are, Fiona," said Doreen. "We did wonder where you'd got to – well not me, but Esme did happen to mention it in passing."

"Good Lord! The wretched female," said Fiona.

"*If* you can call her that," said Doreen with a significant laugh.

"Good Lord. You don't think she's one of *those*, do you Doreen?"

"Well, between you and me, Fiona, I've had my suspicions for some time."

"But she's married."

"What difference does that make?"

"How ghastly. She makes me want to absolutely throw *up*," said Fiona.

"By the by, you've met Phyllis, have you?" said Doreen. "She's the new temp, Janice's replacement."

"Philippa actually, not that it really matters…"

"Between you and me, Fiona, I can't help finding it a relief not having Janice around. She was rather getting on my nerves."

"Oh, absolutely! I know exactly what you mean!"

"Have you noticed the way she's been sucking up to Mr Rees-Williams lately? The trouble is, *he* seems to lap it up. I must admit, between you and me, I can't help finding it rather irritating."

"The thing is, my dear, she's got S.A. and we haven't. There's just no denying it."

"I can't imagine why. Just because she's got big boobs, I suppose. *And* knows how to flaunt them."

"Absolutely! And of course she's not backward about coming forward, is she? If you know what I mean."

"Some of her tops have such plunging necklines you can practically see her navel," declared Doreen. "Disgusting, I call it. And embarrassing. You don't know where to look."

"Mr Rees-Williams knows all right!" said Fiona with a dirty little laugh.

"By the by, Phyllis," said Doreen, "I need hardly tell you, need I, not to pass on anything you may hear between these four walls. But then, it's not as if you know Janice, is it? Or are ever likely to meet her, because when she comes back you'll be somewhere else."

"It must be funny being a temp," said Fiona. "Rather fun, I should think."

"I don't think I should like it," said Doreen, "Always having to leave one's friends. Not belonging anywhere. Always having to move on.

Oh, *SUGAR!* Here's that b… file Esme wanted. Listen Phyllis, would you mind very much taking it to her? Her office is across the hall."

Esme looked up from her desk, annoyed at the interruption.

"Oh, the Ashleigh file. Put it down there. I knew she'd have it all the time, the silly cow."

"Yes, well…"

"It's all right, you needn't try and cover up for her, she's a prize bitch, is our Doreen. Drinks too. Smelt it on her breath many a time when she's bent over me first thing in the morning. Wouldn't surprise me if she wasn't a lizzie."

"A lizzie?"

"Lesbian, dear. Where were you brought up? Bit green for a temp aren't you Phyllis? Philippa? Whatever your name is."

"It's Philippa, not that it matters."

"No, I don't suppose it does, seeing you're only here for the week. Well, you'd better be going back now or she'll be wondering where you've got to, the silly bitch."

"So *there* you are, Phyllis. Where *have* you been? Did you give that file to Esme? What did she say? Did she say anything about me?"

"Oh no! Nothing at all."

"Anyway, it's twelve o'clock. Dinner time. We always eat our sandwiches in this office, all together. It's so much more friendly. Esme! Fiona! It's twelve o'clock girls, come on draw up your chairs and let's have a nice chat. What shall we talk about today? I want to hear all about your new Autumn Outfit, Fiona."

"Did you see the programme 'bout drug addicts on the box last night?" said Esme.

"Such *fun!*" said Fiona, "Although actually one was watching the play on BBC 1. One finds those reality programmes so depressing."

"I thought the play sounded depressing. Wasn't it about someone who murders someone and then eats them?"

"Yes, but it was only made up. Not like real life. Anyway, Doreen, have you decided where you're going for your hols next year?"

"Yes – I'll tell you all about it, and then we can talk about Janice," said Doreen happily. "That's what I like about this office, it's so friendly. I'd hate not to work in a friendly office!"

The New Girl

0855 *Well here I am – first day in my very first job. It' s strange but exciting. I wonder where I should put my coat? I do hope I'm going to like it here and that they'll like me.*

"Hello. Who are you?"

"Oh – I'm sorry, I didn't see you. I'm Mary Jones."

"Well Mary Jones, don't look so startled. I'm not going to eat you. I'm Rosabelle, by the way. I'm the MD's PA."

She's gorgeous. I wish I could look like her. She seems very busy doing whatever MDs' PAs do. I wish my nails were long and red.

0905 "What ought I to do, do you think, Rosabelle?"

"Do? In what way? Look I'm sorry love, but I've got mountains of work, I really can't stop to chat."

"Well I mean, oughtn't I to take my coat off? And where should I sit?"

"Oh God, do whatever you like, don't ask me. On second thoughts you'd better wait till Miss Beazley gets in. She'll tell you what to do."

That's the one who interviewed me. She was old and stern but quite kind. I wish she'd hurry up and get in. I feel so silly not knowing what to do.

0910 *There's the phone ringing – two phones – I wonder if I ought… but I wouldn't know what to say.*

"Mary Jones? Telephone!"

"Yes, I wasn't sure if you'd want me to answer."

"I certainly do. And you'd better start pretty darn quick, it's part of your job."

"Which one should I answer first?"

"The one nearest, for God's sake!"

0912 "Hello?"

"Is that Smith, Papoose and Murgatroyd?"

"I think so."

"Well either it is or it isn't."

"I'm sorry but you see I'm new here and I've forgotten the name of the…"

"Yes, yes, all right. Is Mr Smith in?"

"No, he's not."

I don't know what Mr Smith looks like but I'm certain he's not in because nobody is in except Rosabelle and me – unless he's hiding behind the filing cabinet of course and that's hardly likely.

"All right, tell him to phone me back, would you?"

"I certainly will. Goodbye."

Now for the other phone.

0915 "Hello? This is – this is – Smith…"

"Papoose and Murgatroyd."

"Yes it is, how clever of you!"

"I'm interested in the Barrymore account."

"Are you?"

"Is it ready?"

"Well it might be. I'm not sure."

"Oh Lord, it was supposed to be ready yesterday."

"Well I expect it is, then. I mean if it was expected yesterday and it wasn't then I certainly expect it's ready today."

"Well, have it sent to my office, will you?"

"I certainly will. The – what account, did you say?"

"Barrymore."

"The Barry Moore Account. I see. Could you just hold on a moment and I'll ask."

0917 "Rosabelle. There's a man on the phone and he wants to know if the, er… Barry Moore account can be sent to his office and I said it could. Can it?"

"I don't know. I don't have anything to do with that side. Who is it?"

"He didn't say."

"Well for God's sake ask!"

"Yes, Rosabelle."

0918 "I'm sorry but could you tell me your name, please?"

"Poppycock."

"I'm sorry, I didn't quite catch. Poppy what?"

"Poppycock, Poppycock!"

"Thank you. I'll certainly see to it."

"Rosabelle?"

"What is it now?"

"He said his name was Poppy Cock."

"Rubbish, it couldn't have been that."

"Well that's what he said and he sounded awfully cross."

"Better tell Miss Beazley when she comes in. What about the other one?"

"What other one?"

"The other phone call."

"Oh yes. He wanted Mr Smith to call him back."

"Who did?"

"Oh dear. I'm so sorry, Rosabelle – I didn't ask his name…"

0925 "Now Miss Jones, are you experienced in typing accounts?"

"I guess not, Miss Beazley."

"Well here's your chance to start. It's the Barrymore account. I want six copies on the large paper, that is one top plus five, carbons in the drawer. Underline in red on the top copy, last year's figures in red on the left-hand column but no red figures on the fourth copy, that's for next year's draft…"

10.30 "Could you make some tea, Miss Jones? Well you'll have to go back to that later. You'll find the cups in the cupboard behind the filing cabinet: tea and sugar on the shelf above, spoons in the drawer, kettle in the Ladies' cloakroom on the floor below…"

10.35 "Who the hell's that, Rosabelle?"

"It's only the new girl."

"Oh. What's she like?"

"Unremarkable, Tishy. Quite unremarkable."

Were they talking about me? No of course not, I'm just imagining it. I wonder how many spoonfuls I should put in? There only seem to be eight cups – but nine of us, Miss Beazley said. Why does that girl Tishy have to giggle like that? Oh I'd DIE if I thought they were talking about me!

1040 "Hello! You must be the new girl. I'll help you take the tea round. I'm Sue."

1050 "You can take this in to Mr Papoose, Mary. He doesn't take sugar."

"Yes, Sue. Oh Sue, who was that guy? Going out of the office as we came in?"

"That's Harry. He's in our other office."

"He looked nice."

"He's all right."

1105 "Miss Beazley?"

"Yes, Mr Murgatroyd?"

"Is that the new girl?"

"Yes, Mr Murgatroyd."

"Tell her to come into my office, will you? I want to give her some letters."

1155 "Well you'll just have to leave that for now, Miss Jones. In any case you'll have to start it again. You don't put double lines under totals in the middle columns, and only in grand totals, not sub-totals, in the left-hand column, that's the one in red, and in the right-hand column which is black but not in the middle columns, whether they're red or not. Oh dear, Miss Jones, I do hope you're going to catch on a little quicker than this."

1205 "Right, I'm off to lunch now, Miss Beazely."

"Very well, Mr Papoose."

"I doubt if I'll be back this afternoon. Tell Mr Fogg will you, if he rings?"

1215 "Miss Jones, I'm going to lunch now, so could you hold the fort till 1.15? And don't forget to tell Mr Fogg about Mr Papoose not being in till tomorrow if he rings."

1235 "Well, how do you like it here?"

"Fine thank you, Sue." *I hate it, and I'm not coming in tomorrow.*

"Oh good."

"Don't you go out for lunch?"

"No, I bring sandwiches to the office."

"Where do most people go for lunch?"

"Joe's if they're feeling flush, or Macdonalds. That's your phone ringing."

"Oh, excuse me. Hello? Hello?"

"Poppycock here."

"Oh, Mr Poppycock, I'm so pleased you've rung."

"God – not you again!"

"I know what you're going to say, Mr Poppycock, and I'm working on it."

"You are?"

"The thing is I've never done one before but I assure you, you'll get it as soon as – hello? Are you there?"

How funny, he's hung up. He can't have been feeling very well.

1440 "Miss Jones!"

"Yes, Miss Beazley?"

"Have you finished that letter yet?"

"Not quite yet, Miss Beazley."

"I see."

(Mustn't panic – mustn't make another mistake – should that be insurance

or insurgency?

1505 "Answer the phone, Mary Jones, for goodness sake!"

"Yes, Rosabelle. Hello? Oh Mr Fogg! We were expecting you to ring. Now what was it? Oh yes. Mr Baboon – won't be back today…"

1510 "Have you finished that letter yet, Miss Jones?"

"Not quite yet, Miss Beazley."

"I see."

(No, she doesn't see. She doesn't see at all that I absolutely hate it here and I'm miserable. I'm not coming in tomorrow and that's flat. I'll go on the dole. I'll go on the streets. But I won't come back to this awful place.

"Well you'd better leave that anyway and finish the Barrymore account. Mr Colloquot wants it urgently. He's furious."

Mr Collycot? She must mean Poppycock. Where's that blessed red carbon? Well he would be, wouldn't he? For your information Miss B, he wanted it yesterday and you can't blame me for that because I wasn't here yesterday. Why wasn't it ready anyway? Grossly inefficient I call it.

1525 "Mary Jones! How about making some tea? We're all parched in here."

That's good. How parched do you have to be to actually die of thirst?

"All right, Rosabelle."

"And make sure the cups are clean, there was lipstick on mine."

"Yes, all right." *I hate you all, especially you, Tishy, or whatever your name is. Tishy, I ask you – sounds more like flu.*

"Shall I help you with the tea? I'll wash the cups if you like."

"Thank you, Sue. That's nice of you."

I take it back. I don't hate you, Sue. Quite the reverse.

1550 *Now for those accounts. What was it she said? Red columns on the left. No red figures on the fourth page. No double underlining in the middle columns – I'll never remember!*

1655 I'll just check through those two sheets if you've finished with them, Miss Jones.

"Yes, Miss Beazley."

Don't you dare tell me to do them again, don't you dare!

1705 "They seem to be all right, dear."

Snakes alive — she called me dear!

"I'll take them down to Mr Colloquot right away."

1725 "It's gone twenty-five past. Are you ready, Rosabelle?"

"Hang on a moment, Tishy."

"What about you, Mary Jones?"

"I'm still doing these letters. Should it be instants or instance?"

"Whichever makes most sense, I suppose."

"Neither makes sense."

"Well, that's old Murgatroyd for you."

1735 "Now you get your coat on and forget the letters, Miss Jones."

"Yes, Miss Beazley."

"And could you call in at Mr Colloquot's office on your way out? He wants a word with you. Second floor, third office on the right-hand side. Take the lift."

1740 "Can I help you?"

"Yes, I'm looking for Mr Poppycock. I mean, Copyquok."

"Oh no! Don't tell me! So *you're* the new girl!"

"Yes. And you're…"

"Harry Colloquot."

"You mean - Mr Poppycock?"

"None other!"

"But you can't be! You're not a bit as I imagined!"

"Why?"

"You sound so cross and crabby on the phone!"

"Come to that, you sound half-witted — and I know you're not because I've seen your typing. It's really very good, you know — just a couple of small mistakes, but we won't talk about those now. Tell you what — let me buy you a drink to celebrate your first day, and then I can show you how very uncross and uncrabby I really am!"

The Lift

"Hello, Geraldine!" said Dr McCarthy, touching his hat. Nobody else I knew wore a hat, but Dr McCarthy did. And he always, always got my name wrong. I found it boring, but he thought it was funny.

"You mean Georgie," I said.

He laughed, a great bellow of laughter that made the flesh shake under his chin like jelly. "Georgie – Geraldine, these new-fangled names," he said. "Why can't you call yourself something plain and simple like Joan or Mary?"

Our two dogs strained in an effort to get at one another's bottoms and I jerked Sam's lead, anxious to get away.

"Broken up for the summer hols, have you? Whatever will you find to do with yourself all day?"

"I expect I'll think of something," I muttered, unwilling to stay and explain that I could never be bored living by the sea. We lived in a tall white Regency crescent with gardens in the middle where you could play and where people walked their dogs. The McCarthys lived in the flat above us. He was a great friend of my parents, a fat jolly man, popular with everyone. My mother said he was Kindness Itself. He was always helping people, lending them stuff they needed, working out ways they could save money on their gas bills, starting their cars when their batteries were flat. He gave all the children sweets and little syringe things that they could use for water pistols. He was always telling jokes, but he told them with a straight face, so you never knew if he was being serious or not and you never knew when to laugh.

Mrs Mac was rather strange. I only ever saw her in the mornings out with her dog Polly, which she loved more than anything else. Polly was a Miniature Dachshund with long silky hair and a dear little face. Mrs Mac would talk aloud to it in a silly way and everyone thought her odd, but I liked her.

"Hello Georgie, you're getting so grown up I hardly recognise you, how old are you now, eight it it? Oh ten, I hadn't realised, how time flies, it's frightening, don't you think it's frightening? But I suppose you don't even think about it, do you? That's one thing young people never realise until it's too late."

"Too late for what, Mrs Mac?"

"Oh – just too late," she said vaguely, having probably forgotten, her grasshopper mind skipping ahead onto something else. "May the Good Lord preserve us all."

I suppose she must have been quite religious, for she often called upon the Good Lord. And often when she spoke to you her eyes would brim with tears, I didn't know why.

"Why do Mrs Mac's eyes fill with tears when she talks, Mum?" I asked. My mother was making a pie, and she flung the pastry roughly across the pastry board before answering.

"I think Mrs Mac feels everything very deeply," she said. "She's a very sincere person, you know." She took up the rolling pin and sprinkled it with flour.

"But why does she forget what she's saying halfway through saying it?"

"She's got a very quick mind, Georgie, but so full of thoughts and so quick it's always leaping ahead. And then she forgets what she was thinking."

"She must be very clever – having such a quick mind," I said.

My mother hesitated. "I wouldn't have said *clever* exactly," she said.

One day when I met her in the gardens Mrs Mac beckoned to me, putting her face very close to mine and staring into my eyes with her watery ones. "You and I, Georgie, are two of a kind," she said.

"How do you mean, Mrs Mac?"

"We're solitary people. We don't need anyone else. As long as we have our little dogs we'll be all right."

I hadn't thought of that – and I didn't think Sam would like being called a little dog. He was a Bassett Hound and very long.

"Will you come to tea with me, Georgie? I'd like you to come to tea. Come tomorrow at four o'clock."

"All right Mrs Mac, I'd like to."

"Goodbye dear child, may the Good Lord bless you and keep you."

The next day at four o'clock I got into the lift. It was very old and moved slowly with a terrible clanking noise till it reached the top flat. I pushed back the heavy iron gates and there was Mrs Mac at her front door, waiting for me.

"Come in, dear child," she said.

It was the strangest place I had ever seen, dark and full of furniture like an antique shop. They had been somewhere in the East and there were lots of carvings and black wood and beads and an elephant's foot and a stuffed alligator stool. There were china lamps shaped like figures and silk shades with long fringes and carpets hanging on the wall.

We had a good tea, hot buttery crumpets and a chocolate cake that we shared with the little dog. After tea we pushed the trolley back and got down on the floor and played Old Maid.

All of a sudden we heard the sound of the lift clanking its way up to the top floor.

"Oh my goodness, it's the Doctor!" cried Mrs Mac. She leapt to her feet, and the next moment he entered the flat.

"Lawrence – I didn't expect you so early!" she said.

He said nothing. I could see him through a mirror, hanging up his hat on a stuffed elk's head in the hall and his neck was all red and bulging. Mrs Mac was hurriedly piling the tea-things onto the trolley and one of the cups fell through her fingers and broke on the floor. Tea spilled over the rug. The little dog shrank shivering behind a chair.

"You clumsy oaf!" said Dr McCarthy.

I stared at him in surprise.

"I'm – I'm sorry, Lawrence," she said.

"I dare say tea will enhance it," he said. "I dare say the Iranians should have stained it with tea before they sold it."

"I'm sure it will come out, I'll sponge it with Borax."

"It might have been worth ten times as much with tea on it, what do you think, Jemima?"

"I don't know," I said.

He looked at me. "Oh well," he said. "It's no use crying over spilt – tea, is it? Get the joke? Spilt milk? Spilt tea! Ha ha!"

I laughed politely. I wanted to get away into the sunlight. Mrs Mac ran to get a cloth from the kitchen.

"I think I'd better go now," I said.

After that I didn't see the McCarthys for a while. The weather was suddenly very warm and I spent all the time on the beach, in and out of the sea. My hair grew frizzy, bleached by the sun and matted with sea water.

One day I came back trailing wet bathing things and sand from my shoes and found a group of people in the hall, their backs to me, looking down at something on the floor. "What's the matter?" I said, "What's happened?"

A woman from next door turned round. There's been an accident, it's the little dog," she said.

"Oh *no!*" I cried pushing through the people - my mother kneeling on the floor, my father standing nearby, and Dr Mac.

"Not – Polly?"

But I could see that it was Polly lying there. I touched her. Her fur was silky and warm but there was a stiffness like those awful velvety-covered dogs people hang in their cars, with great gaping red mouths and lolling tongues.

"Must have had a heart attack," said Dr Mac. "Of course she was too highly bred, you know. Too nervous."

"What a shame. She wasn't very old, was she?" said my mother.

"Four."

"Shame. Mrs Mac will miss her."

Miss her? I didn't know what she would do without the little dog. I ran upstairs to see her and tell her I was sorry, but she wouldn't come to the door. After that she got very depressed and stayed in her room all the time, and Dr McCarthy had to leave his other patients and look after her. My mother offered to help, but Dr Mac said it was all right, he could manage.

"Poor Dr Mac," said my mother, "He is so good to her."

"Poor Mrs Mac, you mean," I said, "She was the one who loved Polly."

One day about a week later, I took Sam up to the top flat. I had seen Dr Mac going out so I knew he wouldn't be there. I had to ring the bell for ages before she came to the door. She was in her dressing gown, even though it was afternoon, and the flat was darker than usual because the curtains were drawn.

"I thought perhaps you might like to see Sam," I said, "now you haven't got Polly any more."

She didn't answer. Her face was very white and there was a red spot of colour on each cheek. She looked like a Dutch doll someone gave me once, made of wood with round spots of red on its cheeks just like hers, but its hair was neat and black while hers was wild and grey, like the stuff my mother used for cleaning saucepans.

"If you like," I said, "I'll leave Sam with you when I go to the beach. He doesn't really like it, so he can keep you company."

She looked at me strangely and I couldn't tell what she was thinking. We are two of a kind, I thought, both solitary people.

"Don't you think you're being a bit *too* solitary?" I said timidly. "It can't be good for you to be as solitary as you're being."

There was a long pause. At last I said, "Well, it was just an idea I had. I'm sorry to have bothered you." I turned to go. "At least you must be glad that Polly is being kept by the Good Lord."

Tears filled her eyes and brimmed over, running down her cheeks. She made no attempt to dry them.

"Would you like a tissue?" I said. "I've got one in my pocket. It's a bit screwed up but not really dirty." I put it in her hand and after a moment she wiped the tears away. Then she took hold of my free hand in both of hers and drew me into the flat.

"I'll tell you something," she said, "but you mustn't tell a soul, do you hear? Polly didn't die like everyone thought, it wasn't a natural death or an accident, it was…"

She stopped abruptly and stood listening and then I heard the sound she had heard. It was the dreaded sound of the lift, the heavy clanking noise as it came nearer and nearer. I felt goose flesh prickling my skin and the tiny hairs stood out at the back of my neck.

"Quick!" she said, "You must go. Go down by the stairs!"

But it was too late. The lift had arrived. Mrs Mac shrank back against the wall. I stood as if frozen, unable to move. We held our breath and heard the great iron gates pushed back, steps outside and then the sound of a key turning in the lock. The next moment Dr McCarthy entered the flat.

He looked surprised to see me. "Why, if it isn't Geraldine!" he said. "What are you doing here?"

"Nothing," I said.

"Nothing? How can you be doing nothing? You are talking to my wife, are you not?"

"Yes."

"Then you are doing something, not nothing. You must be more positive, my dear. And when someone asks you what you are thinking, don't say you don't know either, because you must know."

"Yes."

"So what *are* you thinking?"

"I don't know," I stammered. "I mean – I – I do know – but I can't tell you!"

He looked at me curiously. "Am I such an ogre, then?" he said. He turned to his wife. "You look tired, my dear. You had better go to bed."

She went slowly, one hand clutching the wrap of her dressing gown, the other holding onto the banister.

"My wife is ill," said Dr Mac. "She imagines things. She has been ill for a long time, but now she is worse. It is since the dog died."

"How *did* the dog die?" I asked.

"It was a heart attack," he said. His eyes held mine. "Let me see if I can find you a sweet." He dug deep into his pocket and brought out a toffee wrapped in cellophane. "Yes. Here you are."

I hesitated, then took it from his outstretched palm. I thanked him, turned and fled through the open door and ran down the stairs, not stopping till I reached our flat. It was flooded with sunlight that half blinded me after the darkness upstairs.

"Mum!" I burst out, "do you think Dr Mac is ever unkind to Mrs Mac?"

My mother looked startled. "Of course not! What has she been saying to you?"

"Nothing. Nothing at all."

"She's not well, you know. I think she invents things, makes things up. It's very sad. Dear old Mac is a saint, the way he looks after her."

I said nothing. I picked up a piece of parsley and shredded it into tiny pieces.

"What's the matter now?"

"I don't know."

"Must you fidget like that? I wish you'd take the dog for a walk or something. You're getting on my nerves."

"All right." I went slowly, dragging my feet on her polished floor.

"Here's five pounds. You can get me a loaf of bread and some mushrooms on your way home. And an ice cream if you want one," she added more gently.

We were going away to Brittany the last two weeks in August, leaving Sam with the McCarthys. I didn't like the idea, but I was helpless to prevent it, for you can't make parents not do things if they are determined to do them. My father strapped our luggage onto the roof-rack and we were ready to go.

Dr Mac came to see us off.

"Are you quite sure you don't mind having the dog?" said my father. "It's very good of you, Mac."

"We feel so much better than if we were leaving him in kennels," said my mother.

"*I* don't feel better. Not at all better," I said.

"Don't be so silly and embarrassing, Georgie," said my father sharply.

"But there's something I want to tell you, Dad, something you ought to know," I began. Dr Mac was watching me and suddenly he said, "Don't forget our secret, Jemima."

"What secret?" I asked.

"Surely you remember? Oh I can see I'll have to remind you." He bent inside the back window and whispered into my ear. "I do hope Sam doesn't have an accident in the lift like poor Polly," he said.

"Goodbye, Mac, goodbye," said my parents. "Thanks so much for everything. Dear old Mac!"

And he stood there by the side of the road, smiling and waving till he was lost to sight.

This story won first prize, Dark Tales

The Fir Tree

Afterwards Mrs Layton often wondered what had made her choose to spend that Christmas at Fir Tree House. Something had happened to Christopher there; what it was she couldn't tell, but he was different. Somehow he had lost that gentle childlike innocence, almost from one day to the next. Besides that, someone had died. One of the guests, an elderly chap, had been found dead on Boxing Day and that had naturally thrown a dampener over things. It was not something that any of them liked to remember, yet somehow she couldn't get it out of her mind. She felt uneasy, and she couldn't help wondering...

Fir Tree House was a tall, rambling old building, so thickly enclosed by the fir trees to which it owed its name that it had become dark and gloomy. The estate on which it was built was wild and bleak and the gardens had not been well looked after. It was some twenty years since the owners had sold out and the place had been turned into a hotel. It had not been a great success, but did sufficiently well to be worth while keeping on. Mrs Brown, the manageress, was an unambitious woman, quite satisfied with the steady income it brought her. Once a week she put an advertisement in the local paper. Most of her guests were elderly, retired people who liked the plain food and appreciated the peace and quiet.

It was late evening when Mrs Layton arrived with her three children, and apart from one or two lights the house was in darkness. Mrs Brown came to the door to greet them.

"Come in," she said. "How very nice it is to see some young people here. Christmas is never a festive season without young people, is it? Will you want something to eat, perhaps?"

The three Layton children shook their heads politely. "We stopped for dinner on the journey," said their mother, going to sign the register. "We're all tired, so I think we'll just go straight up and have an early night."

"Come along then, let me show you your rooms," said Mrs Brown. "Take the cases, will you Mildred?" She turned to Mrs Layton. "I've put your two daughters in the twin room next to yours, in the front of the house. You've got a lovely view overlooking the rose garden. And the young gentleman is on the third floor. I'm sure his young legs will think nothing of the extra flight of stairs!" She waggled her finger at Christopher, who shrank away.

Mildred left the girls' suitcases inside their room and then led Christopher up the third flight of stairs. She turned a short way down the passage and opened a door on the left. It was a small room, clean, plain and impersonal. Most of it was taken up by a large bed; Christopher bounced on the edge of it to test the springs and heard a dull, clanging sound. The furniture was sparse, heavy mahogany. There was an old-fashioned marble-topped wash stand and a table covered with a white crocheted cloth.

He went over to the window and drew back the thin curtains but outside was only darkness and he could see nothing but the outline of the fir trees. Presently he unpacked and got ready for bed.

Christopher had been asleep for several hours when something woke him. Someone was walking quietly along the passage outside his room. The footsteps reached his door – and then they stopped. There was silence.

He threw aside his bedclothes and went over to the door and opened it. There was nobody there. Whoever it was had vanished, and there was not even a light to show where they had gone. It was draughty in the passage. Christopher shivered, thinking he must have imagined it, then went back to bed and was soon asleep.

The next day was Christmas Eve. Outside it was dark and cold; the fir trees seemed intent on shutting out all the light. But inside the house was cheerful, the hall and other downstairs rooms had large log fires burning, and when Mrs Brown suggested that the children could help put up some decorations they agreed eagerly. They gathered armfuls of holly from the hedges and strewed it lavishly on the tops of the pictures and the windowsills. Some of the guests brought down Christmas cards and these were put up on the mantelshelves. The atmosphere was quite different from that of the evening before. The children ran in and out of the rooms and the guests were infected with their high spirits.

At lunch time the dining room was full. The Laytons shared a table with two other guests, Miss Pew and Mr Hargreaves. Miss Pew was a tall woman with red cheeks and an Eton crop who talked incessantly. Mr Hargreaves, on the other hand, spoke little. He was an elderly man with a military style moustache and a sad face, and Christopher could not help noticing that he kept staring at him. All through the meal he would look up to find Mr Hargreaves' eyes upon him, almost as if he was afraid of something.

"This place is very full this year, never known it so full," remarked Miss Pugh. "I suppose it's good for business, but personally I prefer it when there are just a few of us. More select y'know. Present company excepted, of course!" She laughed and blushed in discomfiture. "D'you play Bridge, Mrs Layton?"

"I used to when my husband was alive, but now I play seldom."

"Have to get you going again," said Miss Pugh heartily. She turned to the children. "Just begun your school holidays, have you?"

"Yes," said Rosemary. "It's great – Christmas Day tomorrow and then four clear weeks."

"Will you be staying at Fir Tree House all that time?" asked Mr Hargreaves.

"No, just for a week or so I imagine," said Mrs Layton. "We're in the process of moving but we aren't able to take possession of the new house just yet."

"Meanwhile we're just going to enjoy being here," said Jane "Do you know the countryside round about?"

"I know there are some fine walks in the district," said Mr Hargreaves, "and one or two historic buildings you should certainly visit, if you get the chance."

"Speaking of which, this is a very old house you know," said Miss Pugh. "It used to belong to a family by the name of Hardy. Had it for generations. There's an interesting story of how the family died out, you might like to hear it? Seems that one Christmas about fifty years ago, two brothers, Matthew and Christopher Hardy – the last of the line – had a violent quarrel which resulted in an accident. Christopher Hardy fell from a tall fir tree and was killed. Matthew disappeared that night and was never seen again."

"What an extraordinary thing," said Mrs Layton.

"Yes," said Miss Pugh, "Wasn't it?"

"Mother," said Rosemary, "We've finished our lunch. Can we go now?"

"All right dear," said her mother. "What are you going to do with yourselves?"

"We've got some Christmas parcels to wrap up," said Jane.

"I shall climb that tall tree, outside my bedroom window," said Christopher.

"I shouldn't do that if I were you," said Mr Hargreaves quietly.

"Oh, why not?"

"It's not safe. None of those trees are safe. You can hear them creaking in the wind."

"Mrs Layton," said Miss Pugh, "Can't I persuade you into a game of bridge after lunch? There's nothing else to do here."

"Oh, very well then."

They rose from the table and went into the library.

It began to snow. "How lucky," said Jane, staring out of the window in the lounge. "If it had waited till tomorrow it would have been too late. This will be our first white Christmas for ages."

All afternoon it snowed silently, and by tea-time everything was white. The tangled garden was transformed into a fairyland of ethereal beauty. At half-past four the long curtains were drawn and there was tea and toasted crumpets with butter round the fire.

That night Christopher heard the footsteps again. As before, they seemed to pass along the passage and stop at the door of his room. He leapt out of bed and hurried over to open the door, but once again all was quiet. He waited; there was nothing.

He lay in bed and thought about it, puzzling as to what it could have been. It was an old, creepy sort of house, perhaps it was haunted? But of course that was absurd. He did not believe in ghosts, just as he did not believe in fairies or Father Christmas. Presently he fell asleep again and dreamed.

He dreamed of a boy of about his own age whom he found lying face downwards in the garden beneath the fir trees. The boy was dead; Christopher had never seen a dead person, but he knew it from the way the body lay with arms and legs splayed out on the grass. He bent down and turned the face of the boy towards him – and then he got a dreadful shock. It was like seeing his own reflection in the mirror! It was not his face, but it resembled it closely enough for him to feel he was looking down at his own dead body.

He felt a helpless anger. "It should never have happened," he said aloud, "not like that, he was too young to die!"

Then he awoke trembling, but the dream, as dreams so often do, stayed with him vividly. He felt he was there still and the anger and the helplessness were with him, looking at the boy in the garden.

The wind was getting up and the window rattled. He got up and closed it, and drew back the curtains and looked out at the night, but all he could see were the shapes of the fir trees. Like sentinels, they watched him from the darkness. He shivered and went back to bed, and after a while he fell into a troubled sleep.

It was Christmas morning, and downstairs everyone was cheerful and hearty. At their table Mrs Layton had heaped parcels around each plate and they wasted no time in opening them. Rosemary and Jane were delighted with everything and Christopher tried to enthuse as they did, but somehow he could not raise much genuine excitement. His heart felt heavy. To him the guest house was dreary and this Christmas lacked the genial, happy atmosphere which generally surrounded it.

At lunch time all the tables were placed together in a block and decorated with red crepe paper and holly, candles and crackers. Mrs Brown presided at the centre of the table and smiled benignly at the assembled company as they set about the turkey and cranberry sauce.

"It may be conceit on my part," she confided to her next-door neighbour, "but I rather pride myself on Christmas at Fir Tree House. We're like one big, happy family, don't you think?"

"Certainly," replied the neighbour, who was wondering if there might be second helpings of turkey.

"You do things *so* well here, *dear* Mrs Brown," said her other neighbour more generously.

There was an air of festivity as the day progressed, but somehow Christopher could not share in it. He had the strangest feeling of foreboding.

That night when everyone had gone to bed and all was quiet he lay awake and listened. It was nearly half-past twelve when he heard the footsteps. He got up and put on his dressing-gown and slippers. Quietly, apprehensively he opened the door. The landing was cold and draughty and the house was quite dark. He groped his way to the stairs and peered over the banisters. All was quiet.

Then suddenly he heard the footsteps again, coming slowly up the stairs. For some seconds he stood quite still, incredulous, unable to move. There could be no logical explanation of that eerie sound. Now the steps had reached the landing on which he stood and if he made a dash for his room – as he felt a great desire to do – he would unavoidably meet whoever it was on the way round. There was nothing he could do but climb the last flight of stairs to the attic.

How dark it was up there! How cold, how quiet – except for the footsteps, which were coming steadily nearer. They had reached the staircase, and now they began to climb the stairs, following him. Christopher was almost at the top. The third step as he came to it creaked, then he was on the landing, uncertain which way to turn.

He heard the stair creak again, right behind him, and stood riveted to the spot, his back against the wall. The footsteps paused, then came to the very spot where he stood holding his breath. Here they stopped abruptly.

What could he do? He couldn't stay on the attic landing in the intolerable silence with whoever it was. He dared not go back down the stairs in case the owner of the footsteps had preceded him and was waiting for him at the bottom. Then he remembered that one of the guests slept up in the attic – if he could only find the room – wait….. There was a door right behind him. He slid his hand behind his back, felt for the door handle, turned it and went in.

Mr Hargreaves was sitting in an armchair with a small reading lamp beside him, engrossed in a book.

"Well, well!" he said, "Come in."

Christopher glanced back at the dark landing and closed the door firmly.

"I'm sorry to disturb you," he said, "but would you mind if I stay here for a while? I've just had rather an unpleasant experience – I'm still wondering if it's not a dream."

Falteringly he began to describe what he had heard. There was a silence after he had finished speaking. "I suppose you don't believe me," he said.

"Oh yes, I believe you," said Mr Hargreaves. "The footsteps you heard," he added slowly, "were the footsteps of my brother."

"Oh I see," said Christopher. "Your brother. But where is he now?"

"He's here in this room."

"But I don't understand!"

"No? But he's here, just the same."

"You mean, he's a ghost? I don't believe in ghosts. At least I never did before I – came here."

"I had better tell you about it," said the other at length, "after all you have quite a lot to do with it."

"Me?"

"Yes, you. You look so much like him, you see. You even have the same name. You must be about the same age as he was when he…"

"Who? I don't understand. Who are you talking about?"

"My brother Christopher. You see my name is not Hargreaves at all, but Hardy, Matthew Hardy. It was my family who owned this house many years ago, and I who lived here when I was a boy with my mother and father and my brother Christopher. He was younger than I was – a good-looking boy with fair hair and blue eyes, like yours. He was always happy and laughing and full of mischief and everyone loved him, everyone but me, for you see I knew him as he really was. He wasn't so nice underneath, it was just a thin veneer of charm the others saw. Besides, I was jealous of him. We were both talented boys but he always outshone me in everything, in work and games and drawing and acting and singing. I thought how unfair it was, because I was good too, I knew I was, but no one ever commented on my achievements because his were that much better. If he wasn't there, I thought, they'd notice me.

"One Boxing Day, the day after Christmas - it must have been exactly fifty years ago – we were playing with our Christmas presents in front of the drawing room fire. My father had given me a gold watch and I was immensely proud of it, and suddenly Christopher snatched the watch and ran off with it. I told you he was full of mischief. I was furious. I chased him into the garden, shouting at him to give it back, but he shinned up one of the fir trees and when I reached the bottom of the tree he laughed at me and dangled the watch from his little finger. "'Come down!' I shouted, 'You'll drop it, I know you will!' But he only climbed all the higher.

"I swung myself up into the lowest branch and began to follow him up the tree. I saw that he had put my watch loosely over his wrist and now he taunted me, waving his arm about so that the watch slid to and fro, now up to his elbow, now down to his little finger. I had almost reached the branch on which he stood when suddenly the watch slipped right over his hand and fell all the way down through the branches of the tree to the ground.

"He said, 'I'm sorry Matt, I didn't really mean to let it go!' But he was grinning, and I knew that he had. He had broken my watch, my most treasured possession, and I hated him. How I hated him. The intensity of my hatred shook me, and for a moment I couldn't see him at all, he was just a red blur before my eyes. The next moment I saw him again quite clearly. I looked at him very steadily, and then I reached across the trunk of the tree and pushed him with all my might.

"He overbalanced and clung onto my hand and screamed out, "Matt, hold me Matt, I'm falling!" but I wrenched my hand away and thrust him from me. He fell, slithering between the branches to the ground.

"I climbed down and looked at him, and he was very still, lying in an awkward, almost grotesque position, face down with his arms and legs splayed out. I turned him over and he looked at me and said, 'You shouldn't have pushed me Matt, and you'll wish you hadn't for you can't cheat me out of my life. I'll come back. Some day, somehow, I'll come back.'

"And then he died. I got up and ran away from that place and I've never been back all these years, until now."

He finished speaking and Christopher was silent. He was not surprised, nor shocked. He almost felt he had known what was coming, had known it all along.

"The footsteps…" he said.

"They were yours, weren't they? You heard yourself. He is here in this room, for he is you and you are he. You came back, Christopher, just as you said you would."

"Yes I did," said Christopher Hardy. And he smiled.

The Laughter of
Agnes Mallory

Agnes Mallory was a strange woman. I was afraid of her. She was small with white hair and bright, penetrating eyes which missed nothing. Her smile was repellent but fascinating, so that one could not help staring at her. But it was her laugh that I feared: it was like the harsh cackle of a witch.

She was my mother's friend – who knows why or how, so different were they, but perhaps it was because my father and her husband, Henry Mallory, were close associates. I only know that she greatly valued my mother's friendship and was possessive about it, and my mother, for her part, was flattered by her constant attention. She was sharp, witty and intelligent. It was said she had strange capabilities: that she had learnt many skills from her African grandfather who had been a witch doctor, and that she had certain powers that were unaccountable. Latterly, since her marriage, she had turned her skills to such diversions as reading her friends' palms and telling their fortunes. For this reason, and also because she was an intelligent conversationalist, she was a very popular member of the European community when her husband was stationed in a town. She was much in demand at dinner parties, and because everyone is everlastingly curious to know more about themselves, there was always a fresh cluster of people wanting their palms read or their fortunes told. She was very thorough in her pronouncements; she took it all very seriously and would not read everyone's palms. If she read yours, you felt honoured and you were excited and apprehensive at the same time – and when you saw the verdict you were shocked. So truthfully did she portray your good and bad qualities that it was like a slap in the face. All these things about Agnes Mallory I learnt from my mother, afterwards.

That summer it happened that my father had some business matters to discuss with Henry Mallory, who was at that time stationed at a small outpost in the Nigerian bush, and we stayed for ten days in their district. Whilst we were there we often went to her house during the morning for coffee. My mother would take her sewing, whilst she smoked endless cigarettes, and they talked about people and places I did not know. But I scarcely heard their conversation. I would sit on the edge of my chair dreaming, and uneasy because I was so conscious, every now and then, of her frequent sharp glances in my direction. The cigarette smoke created a haze around her, and idly I imagined her crouched in black over a large cauldron, stirring its steaming contents.

She spoke to me the first morning we were there. "Well, and so you're Catherine," she said. "And how old are you?"

"Nearly fifteen," I answered.

"And what do you want to do when you grow up?"

"I want to be a writer," I answered. I knew my mother was blushing because she thought I was conceited to say so. But that was what I wanted to do, and I could see no harm in saying so, just as my friends said they wanted to be nurses or school teachers.

"Catherine has a vivid imagination, but I'm afraid her English is not good," my mother said to excuse me.

"Ah," said Agnes Mallory, "I have no doubt that if she wants to be a writer, a writer she will be."

She stared at me with her piercing eyes and I stared back at her curiously. I had never seen eyes like that before. They bored into me, seeming to read my thoughts, and when I looked into them I seemed to lose myself in their depths, in a world that was blurred and hazy one moment and harsh and jagged the next.

Suddenly she laughed, and I started and came back to earth.

"Boy!" she called, and rang a bell at her elbow several times in short succession. A young black steward in an immaculate white uniform appeared with a tray of cups and a silver jug of steaming hot coffee.

"Put it down there," she commanded, pointing to a table at her side. He did so and stood back, waiting while she poured the coffee. His eyes never left her face, as though he were afraid of missing something. He handed me a cup and offered me the sugar in a silver bowl, but when I picked up the tongs I found that my hand was shaking and I could not use them. I struggled to grasp a lump of sugar, but each time it slipped out and at last, fearful that she would notice my clumsiness, I laid the tongs down without taking any. I did not like my coffee; it was black and very, very bitter.

Eventually my mother said it was time we went. She collected her sewing things and rose from her chair.

"Thank you, Agnes," she said, "That was a most enjoyable morning. Now don't forget, this evening, half-past nine. Come along, Catherine!"

But I needed no telling. I was longing to be away, out of the darkness of the Mallorys' house. "Goodbye!" I called almost cheerily as I leapt down the stone steps. Soon I should be back in the sunshine, I should be able to relax, breathe again. The sunlight in the garden was just ahead, and beyond it the road leading back to our house.

I found myself thinking about Agnes Mallory the rest of the day. There was something about her that I did not like, but I did not know what it was.

That evening after dinner, she and Henry came over to play bridge with my parents. For a time I sat in a nearby chair with a book, but I could not concentrate on reading. Hundreds of the flies that appear at night time in Africa kept falling against the flickering oil lamp at my side; at last I moved away from the lamp and sat near the bridge table watching.

Agnes Mallory was winning. I had known, even before they started, that she would win. She would win all evening. She was that sort of person – shrewd, efficient, watchful, confident – not the losing kind. That afternoon I had wondered what it was about her that I did not like. Now I thought I liked nothing about her – not her bright, piercing eyes, nor her frizzy white hair, nor her bony face, nor her thick lips.

Nor her laugh.

But it is a strange fact that one can get used to almost anything over a period of time; after a week of seeing her constantly, I grew used to Agnes Mallory. She was someone I did not like, feared even, yet I accepted her as one accepts eating and sleeping and all the everyday things in life.

I enjoyed staying in that small, isolated district. I went for a good many long walks with our two dogs; I sat for hours, reading or just thinking, in a funny little summer house at the bottom of our garden, taking a good many over-exposed snapshots with my Brownie box camera, and Henry Mallory kindly developed them for me in his dark room.

I made a friend of an old Ibo boatman down by the river, and he allowed me to go out in his canoe. It was only a rough, heavy thing made from the trunk of a tree; half way up one side there was a round hole about five inches in diameter which he explained was to let the water out, but in my case it let the water in and I was always sinking. Then I would have to wade through the thick yellow mud up the bank, where scores of Africans would collect to howl with laughter at me, and scream "Crocodile! Crocodile!" and double up again. The only one who was not amused was the old boatman, who had to get the boat up from the river before it touched the bottom, yet although he looked severe and scolded me at the time he was always magnanimous enough to lend it to me again the next day.

One evening near the end of our stay I went for a different walk with the two dogs, Jess and Jupiter. We went by the ravine along the road overlooking one of the most primitive villages in the Eastern Provinces. I had heard stories of their cruelties to people and animals, their ferocity, their strange beliefs and customs, and I was eager to learn more. That evening I could hear the sounds of warlike drums, weird chanting and every now and then a scream, which to my mind sounded full of fear and pain.

Yet it was a beautiful evening. The sky was torn across and across with streaks of flame-coloured light, and oddly shaped gold and black clouds like heavy sea-vessels moved steadily past. It was an evening full of mystery, and I felt unaccountably excited.

Foolishly perhaps, I determined to discover more of the sinister happenings down in the village. The dogs were delighted to have the chance to find a new walk and ran ahead, leaping from side to side, sniffing the ground and chasing elusive moths. We left the open road at the edge of the ravine and plunged down the steep, dark lane which led to the village. After the beauty of the fading sunlight the gloom of the downward road was strongly intensified. The trees grew thickly, projecting their dripping foliage from either side, covering the way and shutting out all sunlight. The further down we went, the darker and denser it became. The atmosphere was uncanny. I wondered whether to turn back. But my own curiosity and the dogs kept me going on – I had rarely seen them so excited.

Before us, to one side, was the village. The beating of drums and the chanting seemed very close, but we could see nothing. There was only one narrow path from the right, twisting down through the jungle, which led, I supposed, to the village. The dogs halted and looked round uncertainly, then back towards the path where the glistening trees beckoned, inviting us to investigate. But whether I approved mattered not at all. Soon they were on the path, running ahead as usual, and I followed, excitement rising in me.

The ground was soft and the mud warm after a recent shower of rain. Blurred prints of bare toes told of the many who passed there daily. Presently the path curved sharply, and there below us lay the cluster of little round huts, closely huddled together like beehives.

We struck away from the path, fumbling and groping our way to a ledge round to the side, about half way down. From here we had a view of the strange festivities proceeding in the clearing below. Inside a large, thick circle of squatting figures was a fire around which men danced to the rhythmic sound of drums. The dancers were half-naked, decorated with beads and shiny paint. Some wore skins and most wore masks. Their slowly-swaying bodies were patterned by the flickering firelight and in the shadows the sullen faces of the drummers brooded. A tall man standing near the fire replenished it often with narrow logs and sticks; the fire curled itself over them and folded them in, and thrust its long tongues upwards. Outside the circle groups of villagers stood about, watching and singing, drinking palm wine from deep, earthenware pots.

I looked down on them from my retreat and saw the dark night and the glow of the fire. Its light illuminated the curving, heaving bodies of the dancers, the sweat shining on their backs and the grotesque outlines of their masks. I heard the waving, wailing chant and the beating of drums. I felt like an intruder. I kept fearing my presence must soon be discovered if I stayed, yet I could not drag myself away.

All of a sudden I noticed that the two dogs were no longer with me. They had not gone ahead of me, so I turned back and climbed up through the trees to the path where I had last seen them, and called them softly. But they were nowhere to be seen. I set off round the sharp corner. Then to one side I saw a flickering light, and at the same time heard the short, excited barks of the dogs. Apprehensively I sped between the trees in the direction of the light. There was a solitary hut in its own compound, away and hidden from the rest of the village. An oil lamp on the floor near the opening lighted up a strange and gruesome assortment of objects around which the dogs were circling, sniffing and barking. There in the dust was a collection of whitened bones, the tusks of an elephant, the skin of a crocodile, and with them a human skull.

Jess passed close by where I stood in the shadows, and I reached down to grab her collar. As I did so I heard a sound: it was a laugh, a harsh chuckle, grating the twilight air. It was strangely familiar. I turned.

She stood, an old woman wearing a brightly coloured native garment, with a long curved scythe in her hand. In front of her I could make out the crouching form of Jupiter, holding some shapeless object in his jaws. The woman, gliding forward, swooped with the scythe, and Jupiter, startled, dropped the object and jumped away. She ran on him, lunging from side to side with her cruel weapon, uttering low, harsh cries. He dodged in circles and she beat the ground and hacked the undergrowth around her. I was aghast at the rage and passionate enjoyment behind the vicious blows. She looked mad.

At last Jupiter slunk out of her range with his tail down and both dogs crept swiftly away, back towards the path. Running and stumbling over the undergrowth I followed them. In my haste to get away from that horrible place I was pursued by the nightmarish memory of the flashing blade cutting the air, and the rasping laugh. Surely there could be only one laugh like that – and yet it was impossible.

Back we fled up the winding path. I was terrified at the thought of pursuit and still so dazed that I did not notice the sudden silence. The strange chanting had faded, the beating drums had ceased. We reached the point where the path met the road. The dogs ran straight on up, undeterred in their headlong flight, and I followed, gradually slowing down to a walk. Eventually I left the dark road behind and came on to the open top of the precipice. The black terror of the night had spread up from the lower road like a plague. I had not before noticed how deep and vast was the gorge, how swollen the rocks. Dipped in moonlight, they jutted out formidably into the chasm.

We were now passing the Mallory house; the lamps were lit and I could see the flies clustering thickly around. The white-uniformed figure of a steward was laying the table on the veranda. I continued past thankfully, and at length reached the refuge of our own house. It felt good, so good to be back.

That night after dinner, the Mallorys came round for drinks. I watched and listened carefully, but everything was as usual. Henry Mallory and my father enthusiastically discussed plans for the future of the station, while Agnes Mallory recounted some of her experiences from previous tours. She talked well and with interest; and I had to admit, as I sipped my orange squash, that she could be charming. I watched the colourful lizards wriggle across the ceiling and thought what an imaginative fool I was. Of course, I told myself, she could not possibly be the same person as the mad old woman in the village – there, I had admitted this absurd thought to myself. How ridiculous it sounded. What would my parents have thought if they had known my shocking suspicions of an old friend of theirs? Why, I would be ashamed to tell them.

The evening wore on and at last she rose to go. My father sighed with irritation, for he was having an interesting chat with old Henry.

"It's a lovely night," he said, "what about a short stroll around the station?"

"What a good idea!" said Agnes Mallory, "I haven't been out all day and I would like some fresh air." She looked straight at me. Her eyes were fathomless: I could not tell what she was thinking. Then she smiled round the room at everyone.

"Well – shall we go?" she said.

As they went out into the garden an unaccountable shudder passed right through me, leaving goose pimples on my bare arms.

I went upstairs to bed.

The following two days passed uneventfully. I tried hard to forget my experience with the dogs. I kept admonishing myself for my childish suspicions. Why, she even said she had not been out all day. That proved it. Curiously, their laughs were perhaps similar, but no one could think anything more.

In the evening two days later we began to pack, for we were leaving early the next day. I was glad to go, although it had not been an unpleasant visit. It was a beautiful place and our house had been more comfortable than the houses on many larger stations than this. Two more days had passed, reading in the summerhouse, playing half-hearted tennis with my mother, boating on the river, or just sitting drinking squash in the evenings. Two more days, and it was all very peaceful, very pleasant, very real. By the time we were ready to go I had almost convinced myself that I had imagined everything I had experienced on that strange walk.

Finally, there we were, sitting in the car with all our luggage strapped on, my mother and father in front, myself and the dogs in the back. The Mallorys had come out to see us off, and the usual pleasantries were exchanged. Then Agnes Mallory poked her head in the window at the back of the car and stared at me strangely.

"You'll have to look after those dogs of yours," she said. "They made me very angry the other evening."

I stared at her aghast, and two thoughts came swiftly into my mind: could it be that she was so psychic that she knew of my encounter with the old African woman in the village? That she knew I thought she was that woman, and was having a cruel joke? Or more sinister still, could it be that in fact she really was that old woman, that the village was *her* village – and was the blood in her veins so strong that every now and again she felt compelled to return to that other life, to live once more in her own primitive mud hut, and to practice again her remarkable powers of witchcraft?

"Why, listen to that lovely bird!" cried my mother. But my ears were filled only with the harsh cackle of the laughter of Agnes Mallory as the car moved slowly off and rounded the bend in the road.